Growing up near the beach, **Annie West** spent lots of time observing tall, burnished lifeguards—early research! Now she spends her days fantasising about gorgeous men and their love lives. Annie has been a reader all her life. She also loves travel, long walks, good company and great food. You can contact her at annie@annie-west.com or via PO Box 1041, Warners Bay, NSW 2282, Australia.

Julia James lives in England and adores the peaceful verdant countryside and the wild shores of Cornwall. She also loves the Mediterranean—so rich in myth and history, with its sunbaked landscapes and olive groves, ancient ruins and azure seas. 'The perfect setting for romance!' she says. 'Rivalled only by the lush tropical heat of the Caribbean—palms swaying by a silver sand beach lapped by turquoise water… What more could lovers want?'

D1458921

Also by Annie West

Inherited for the Royal Bed
Her Forgotten Lover's Heir
The Greek's Forbidden Innocent

The Princess Seductions miniseries

His Majesty's Temporary Bride
The Greek's Forbidden Princess

Also by Julia James

The Greek's Secret Son
Tycoon's Ring of Convenience
Heiress's Pregnancy Scandal

Mistress to Wife miniseries

Claiming His Scandalous Love-Child
Carrying His Scandalous Heir

Discover more at millsandboon.co.uk.

WEDDING NIGHT REUNION IN GREECE

ANNIE WEST

BILLIONAIRE'S MEDITERRANEAN PROPOSAL

JULIA JAMES

MILLS & BOON

All rights reserved including the right of reproduction
in whole or in part in any form. This edition is published
by arrangement with Harlequin Books S.A.

This is a work of fiction. Names, characters, places, locations
and incidents are purely fictional and bear no relationship to
any real life individuals, living or dead, or to any actual places,
business establishments, locations, events or incidents.
Any resemblance is entirely coincidental.

This book is sold subject to the condition that it shall not,
by way of trade or otherwise, be lent, resold, hired out
or otherwise circulated without the prior consent of the publisher
in any form of binding or cover other than that in which it is published
and without a similar condition including this condition
being imposed on the subsequent purchaser.

® and TM are trademarks owned and used by the trademark owner
and/or its licensee. Trademarks marked with ® are registered with the
United Kingdom Patent Office and/or the Office for Harmonisation
in the Internal Market and in other countries.

First Published in Great Britain 2019
by Mills & Boon, an imprint of HarperCollins*Publishers*
1 London Bridge Street, London, SE1 9GF

Wedding Night Reunion in Greece © 2019 by Annie West

Billionaire's Mediterranean Proposal © 2019 by Julia James

ISBN: 978-0-263-27342-7

MIX
Paper from
responsible sources
FSC www.fsc.org   FSC® C007454

This book is produced from independently certified FSC™ paper
to ensure responsible forest management.
For more information visit www.harpercollins.co.uk/green.

Printed and bound in Spain
by CPI, Barcelona

WEDDING NIGHT REUNION IN GREECE

ANNIE WEST

Dedicated with thanks and affection to the people of Corfu, whose warmth made my first visit to that beautiful island so memorable.

CHAPTER ONE

'CONGRATULATIONS, CHRISTO.' DAMEN grinned and gripped his friend's arm in a hard clasp. 'I didn't think I'd ever see the day.'

'You didn't think I'd invite you to my wedding?' Christo smiled. Who else would he ask to stand up as his best man but Damen, his friend since childhood?

'You know what I mean. I never expected to see you married till you'd played the field for another decade and decided it was time to breed some heirs.'

The look that passed between them revealed their shared understanding of what it meant to be the sole male heir to a family dynasty—Damen's in shipping and Christo's in property. There were expectations and responsibilities, always, even if they came with the cushion of wealth and privilege.

At the thought of his newest responsibility, Christo rolled his shoulders. The stiffness pinching the back of his neck was familiar. But now he could relax. With the wedding over, his plans fell into place. He'd had a problem and he'd fixed it, simple as that. Life could resume its even course. The glow of satisfaction he'd felt as he'd slid the ring onto Emma's small hand burned brighter.

Everything had worked out perfectly.

'I'm glad you could get here at short notice.' Despite Christo's lack of sentimentality, it felt good to have his old friend with him.

Besides, it would have looked strange if there'd been no one from the groom's side, even at such a small wedding. Damen had arrived in Melbourne just in time for the private ceremony. Now, in the gardens of the bride's home, this was their first opportunity to talk.

'She's not what I expected, your little bride.'

Christo raised an enquiring eyebrow.

'She's besotted with you for a start. What she sees in you...' Damen shook his head in mock puzzlement, as if women didn't swarm around Christo like bees around blossom. It was another thing they had in common.

'Of course Emma's besotted. She's marrying *me*.'

Christo had no false modesty about his appeal to the opposite sex. Besides, he'd wooed old Katsoyiannis's granddaughter carefully, taking his time in a way that wasn't usually necessary to win a woman. Having his proposal rejected hadn't figured in Christo's plans.

He'd done an excellent job. A spark of heat ignited at the memory of Emma's wide-eyed gaze and the eager way she'd returned his perfunctory end-of-ceremony kiss, tempting him to prolong it into something more passionate. Christo's hands had tightened on her slender waist and he'd found himself looking forward to tonight when he'd take her to his bed for the first time.

Damen huffed out a laugh. 'There speaks the mighty Christo Karides, ego as big as the Mediterranean.' He frowned and glanced back at the house, as if confirming they were alone. Everyone was at the wedding breakfast on the far side of the building. 'But, seriously, I was surprised. Emma's lovely. Very sweet.' Another pause. 'But not your usual type.' His look turned piercing. 'I'd have thought her cousin more your speed. The vivacious redhead.'

Christo nodded, picturing Maia's pin-up-perfect curves in the tight clothes she favoured. Her confidence, her sexy banter as she'd tried to hook his attention. She would have succeeded, too, if things had been different.

A twinge of pain seared from Christo's skull to his shoulders and he rubbed a hand around his neck.

'You're right, she's gorgeous. In other circumstances we'd have had fun together.' He shook his head. His situation was immutable. Regrets were useless. 'But this is marriage we're talking about, not pleasure.'

A muffled sound made Christo turn to scrutinise the back of the large house. But there was no movement at the windows, no one on the flagstone patio or sweeping lawn. No sound except the distant strains of music.

He'd have to return to the celebration soon before his bride wondered what was taking him so long.

A beat of satisfaction quickened Christo's pulse. 'Emma's not sexy and sophisticated like her cousin, or as beautiful, but her grandfather left her the Athens property I came to buy. Marriage was the price of acquiring it.'

Damen's smile faded. 'You married for *that*? I knew the deal was important but surely you didn't need to—?'

'You're right. Normally I wouldn't consider it, but circumstances changed.' Christo shrugged and adopted a nonchalant expression to camouflage the tension he still felt at the profound changes in his life. 'I find myself in the bizarre situation of inheriting responsibility for a child.' Saying it aloud didn't make it sound any more palatable, or lessen his lingering shock. 'Can you imagine *me* as a father?'

He nodded as his friend's eyes bulged. 'You see why marriage suddenly became necessary, if not appealing. It isn't a sexy siren I need. Instead I've acquired a gentle, sensible homebody who wants only to please me. She'll make the perfect caring mother.'

Emma's hands gripped the edge of the basin so tight, she couldn't feel her fingers. That was one small mercy because the rest of her felt like one huge, raw wound throbbing in acute agony.

She blinked and stared at the mirror in the downstairs rear bathroom. The one to which she and her bridesmaid had retired for a quick make-up fix as the bathroom at the front of the house was engaged. The one with an open window, obscured by ivy, that gave onto the sprawling back garden.

In the mirror, dazed hazel eyes stared back at her. Her mouth in that new lipstick she'd thought so sophisticated was a crumpled line of colour too bright for parchment-pale cheeks.

Around her white face she still wore the antique lace of her grandmother's veil.

Emma shuddered and shut her eyes, suddenly hating the weight of the lace against her cheeks and the long wedding dress around her shaky legs. The fitted gown, so perfect before, now clasped her too tightly, making her skin clammy, nipping at her waist and breasts and squeezing her lungs till she thought they might burst.

'Did you know?'

Emma's eyes popped open to meet Steph's in the mirror. Instead of turning into a wax doll like Emma, shock made Steph look vibrant. Her eyes sparked and a flush climbed her cheeks.

'Stupid question. Of course you didn't know.' Her friend's generous mouth twisted into a snarl. 'I'll kill him with my bare hands. No, killing's too good. Slow torture. That's what he deserves.' She scowled ferociously. 'How could he treat you that way? He must know how you feel about him.'

The pain in Emma's chest intensified from terrible to excruciating. It felt as though she was being torn apart. Which made sense, as she'd been foolish enough to hand her heart to Christo Karides and he'd just ripped it out.

Without warning.

Without anaesthetic.

Without apology.

'Because he doesn't care.' The words slipped through numb lips. 'He never really cared about me.'

As soon as she said the words aloud Emma felt their truth, despite the romantic spell Christo had woven around her. He'd been kind and understanding, tender and supportive, as she'd grappled with her grandfather's death. She'd taken his old-fashioned courtesy as proof of his respect for her, his willingness to wait. Now she realised his patience and restraint had been because he didn't fancy her at all.

Nausea surged as the blindfold ripped from her eyes.

Why hadn't she seen it before? Why hadn't she listened to Steph when she'd spoken of taking things slowly? Of not making important decisions while she was emotionally vulnerable?

Emma had been lost in a fairy tale this last month, a fairy tale where, as grief struck yet again, her Prince Charming was with her, not to rescue her but to be there for her, making her feel she wasn't alone.

Everyone she'd loved in this life had died. Her parents when she was eleven, abruptly wiped out of her life when the small plane they'd been in went down in a storm. Then her grandmother four years ago when Emma was eighteen. And now her opinionated, hopelessly old-fashioned yet wonderful Papou. The sense of loss had been unbearable, except when Christo had been beside her.

She drew a sharp breath that lanced tight lungs, then let it out on a bitter laugh. 'He doesn't even know who I am. He has no idea.'

Wants only to please him, indeed!

A homebody!

Obviously Christo had believed Papou, who'd insisted on thinking she studied to fill in time before she found the right man to marry!

Maybe Christo thought she lived in her grandparents' house because she was meek and obedient. The truth was that, despite his bluster, Papou had been lost when her grandmother had died and Emma had decided to stay till he recovered. But then his health had failed and there'd been no good time to leave.

The tragedy of it was that Emma had thought Christo truly understood her. She'd believed he spent time with her because he found her interesting and attractive.

But not as attractive as her *vivacious, gorgeous* cousin Maia.

Pain cramped Emma's belly and her breath sawed from constricted lungs.

Bad enough that Christo viewed her as a plain Jane compared with her *sexy siren* cousin. But the fact he hadn't noticed that Maia was warm-hearted, intelligent and funny, as well as sexy, somehow made it worse.

Christo was a clever man. According to Papou, his insightfulness had made him phenomenally successful, transforming the family business he'd inherited. Clearly Christo didn't waste time applying that insight to the women he met.

Because we're not important enough?

Because he thinks we're simply available for him to use as he sees fit?

What that said about his attitude to women made Emma's skin shrink against her bones.

He had a reputation as a playboy in Europe, always dating impossibly glamorous, gorgeous women. But in her naivety Emma had dismissed the media gossip. She'd believed him when he'd assured her his reputation was exaggerated. Then he'd stroked her cheek, his hand dropping to her collarbone, tracing the decorous neckline of her dress, and Emma had forgotten her doubts and her train of thought.

She'd been so easy to manipulate! Ready to fall for his practised charm. For his attentiveness.

Because he was the first man who'd really noticed her.

Was she really so easily conned?

Emma lurched forward over the basin as nausea rocketed up from her stomach. Bile burnt the back of her throat and she retched again and again.

When it was over, and she'd rinsed her mouth and face, she looked up at her friend. 'I *believed* in him, Steph. I actually thought the fact he didn't respond to Maia was proof he was genuinely attracted to *me*.' Her voice rose to something like a wail and Emma bit her lip.

She'd been gullible. She'd brushed aside her friend's tentative questions about the speed of Christo's courtship. At the time it had made sense to marry quickly so her Papou could be with them. And when he'd died, well, the last thing he'd said to her was how happy he was knowing she had Christo and that he didn't want her to delay the wedding.

She should have waited.

She should have known romantic fantasies were too good to be true.

'I've been a complete idiot, haven't I?' She'd always been careful—cautious rather than adventurous, sensible rather than impulsive—yet she'd let a handsome face and a lying, cheating, silver tongue distract her from her career plans and her innate caution.

'Of course not, sweetie.' Steph put her arm around her shoulders, squeezing tight. 'You're warm and generous and honest and you always look for the good in people.'

Emma shook her head, dredging up a tight smile at her friend's loyalty. 'You mean I usually have my head in the sand.' Or in books. Papou had regularly complained that she spent too much time with her nose in a book. 'Well, not any more.' She shuddered as ice frosted her spine. 'Imagine if we hadn't heard…'

'But we did.' Steph squeezed her shoulder again. 'The question is, what are you going to do about it?'

The question jolted her out of self-pity.

Emma looked in the mirror, taking in the ashen-faced waif dressed in wedding lace. Suddenly, in a burst of glorious heat, anger swamped her. Scorching, fiery anger that ran along her veins, licking warmth back into her cold flesh and burning away the vulnerability she'd felt at Christo's casual contempt. The flush of it rose from her belly to her breasts and up to her cheeks as she swung round to face her friend.

'Walk away, of course. Christo can find another *sensible* woman to care for his child and please him.'

Silly that, of all the assumptions he'd made about her and the games he'd played, what rankled most was that he'd recognised her longing for physical pleasure. For *him*.

A shudder ran through her at the thought of how she'd looked forward to pleasing him and having him reciprocate with those big, supple hands and that hard, masculine body.

Now the idea of him touching her made her feel sick.

Especially as the reason he'd abstained from sex clearly hadn't been out of respect for her and for her dying grandfather. It had been because sex with the dowdy mouse of the family hadn't appealed to him. If Christo had been engaged to the beautiful Maia, there'd have been no holding back. They'd have been scorching the sheets well before the wedding.

A curl of flame branded deep inside Emma's feminine core. In the place where, one day, a man she loved and who loved her back would possess her. She'd thought she'd found him in Christo Karides. Now all she felt was loathing for him and disappointment at herself for believing his lies.

'I'm so relieved.' Steph's words tugged her into the present. 'I was afraid you might think of staying with him and hoping he'd eventually fall in love with you.'

Emma shook her head, the old lace swishing around her shoulders. Papou had been proud that she'd wear the same veil his bride had worn to her wedding. This marriage had meant so much to him. But it was a sham. Christo hadn't only made a fool of her but of her grandfather too. She'd never forgive him that.

'I might be the quiet one in the family but I'm not a doormat. As Christo Karides is about to find out.' She met her friend's eyes in the mirror. 'Will you help me?'

'You have to ask?' Steph rolled her eyes. 'What do you have in mind?'

Emma hesitated, realising she had nothing in mind. But only for a second.

'Can you go up to my room and grab my passport and bag? And my suitcase?' The case she'd packed for her honeymoon. The thought was a jab to her heart. She sucked in a fortifying breath. 'You'll have to come down the back stairs.'

'Then what?'

'I'll book a flight out of here. If I can borrow your car and leave it at the airport—'

'And leave Christo Karides to face the music when his bride disappears? I love it.' Steph's grin almost hid the fury glittering in her eyes. 'But I've got a better idea. Forget the airport. That's the first place he'll look. With his resources, he'll be on your trail within hours. Head to my place and wait for a call.' She reached into her purse and pulled out her key ring, pressing it into Emma's hand. 'I'll get you out of Melbourne but so he can't trace your movements. I'm not the best travel agent in the city for nothing. It's going to be a real pleasure watching him stew when he can't find you.'

For the first time since overhearing Christo's conversation, Emma smiled. It didn't matter that her cheeks felt so taut they might crack, or that the pain in her heart was as deep as ever. What mattered was that she had a way out and a true friend.

Suddenly she didn't feel so appallingly alone and vulnerable.

'Thank you, Steph. I can't tell you what it means to have your help.' Emma blinked against the self-pitying tears prickling the back of her eyes.

She'd cried when she'd lost Papou. She refused to shed tears over a man who wasn't fit to speak her grandfather's name. A schemer who'd played upon the old man's love and fear for his granddaughter's future.

'But you'll have to be careful not to give me away.' Emma frowned at her friend. 'One look at your face and Christo will know you're hiding something. He may be a louse but he's smart.'

Silly how speaking of him like that sent a fillip of pleasure through her. It was a tiny thing compared with the wrong he'd done her, but it was a start.

Steph shook her head and put on the butter-wouldn't-melt-in-her-mouth expression that had fooled their teachers for years. 'Don't worry. He won't suspect a thing. I'll tell him you need a short rest. He'll accept that. He knows this has been a whirlwind, plus you're missing your grandfather.'

Steph's words sent a shaft of longing through Emma for the old man who'd been bossy and difficult but always loving beneath his gruff exterior. She blinked, refusing to give in to grief now.

'Great. You go upstairs while I get this veil off.' There was no time to get out of the dress, but she couldn't make her escape in trailing lace. 'I'll hide it in the cupboard here, if you can collect it later and look after it for me?'

'Of course. I know it's precious.' Steph put her hand on Emma's arm, squeezing gently. 'Just one more thing. Where are you travelling to?'

Emma turned to the mirror and started searching for the multitude of pins that secured the veil. 'The only place that's still home.' Her aunt and uncle, Maia's parents, had inherited this house and Papou's Australian assets. She'd got the commercial property in Athens that had then been signed over to her husband to manage. She'd have to do something about that, she realised. Plus, she'd inherited her grandparents' old villa in Greece. The one where she'd gone each year on holiday with her parents till they'd died. 'I'm going to Corfu.'

It was the perfect bolthole. She'd never mentioned it to Christo and, anyway, he would never look for her on his home turf of Greece.

She could take her time there, deciding what she planned to do. And how she'd end this farce of a marriage.

CHAPTER TWO

EMMA STEPPED THROUGH the wrought-iron gates and felt the past wash over her. She hadn't been to Corfu for years, not since she was fifteen, when her grandmother had grown too frail for long-distance travel.

Seven years, yet it felt more like seven days as she took in the shaded avenue ahead curling towards the villa just out of sight. Ancient olive trees, their bodies twisted but their boughs healthy with new growth, drifted down the slope to the sea like a silvery green blanket. Nearby glossy citrus leaves clustered around creamy buds in the orchard.

Emma inhaled the rich scent of blossom from lemon, kumquat and orange trees. Her lips tightened. Orange blossom was traditional for brides. It had been in short supply in Melbourne during autumn, unlike Greece in spring.

She shivered as something dark and chilly skipped down her spine.

What a close shave she'd had. Imagine if she hadn't learned of Christo's real agenda! She cringed to think how much further under his spell she'd have fallen. Given his reputation, she had no doubt his skills at seduction were as excellent as his ability to feign attraction.

Swallowing down the writhing knot of hurt in her throat, she grabbed the handle of her suitcase, hitched her shoulder bag higher and set off towards the house.

She was sticky and tired and longing for a cold drink. Silly of her, perhaps, to have the taxi drop her further down the road, near a cluster of new luxury villas that had sprung up in the last few years. But she didn't want to take the chance of anyone knowing she was staying here, in case word somehow got back to Christo.

She'd confront him in her own time, not his. For now she needed to regroup and lick her wounds.

Emma trudged down the drive, the crunch of her feet and her suitcase wheels on the gravel loud in the quiet. Yet, as she walked, her steps grew lighter as memories crowded close. Happy memories, for it was here her family had gathered year after year for a month's vacation.

Drops of bright colour in the olive grove caught her eye and she remembered picking wildflowers there, plonking them in her grandmother's priceless crystal vases, where they'd be displayed as proudly as if they were professional floral arrangements. Swimming with her parents down in the clear green waters of their private cove. Sitting under the shade of the colonnade that ran around three sides of the courtyard while Papou had taught her to play *tavli*, clicking the counters around the board so quickly his hand seemed to blur before her eyes.

They were gone now, all of them.

Emma stumbled to a halt, pain shearing through her middle, transfixing her.

She took a deep breath and forced herself to walk on. Yes, they'd died, but they'd taught her the value of living life to the full, and of love. Even now she felt that love as if the old estate that had been in Papou's family for years wrapped her in its embrace.

Rounding the curve in the long drive, she caught sight of the villa. It showed its age, like a gracious old lady, still elegant despite the years. Its walls were a muted tone between blush-pink and palest orange that glowed softly in the afternoon light. The tall wooden window shutters gleamed with new forest-green paint but the ancient roof tiles had weathered to a grey that looked as ancient as the stone walls edging the olive grove. Despite being a couple of hundred years old, the place was well-maintained. Papou wouldn't have had it any other way.

Nor would Emma. She was its owner now. She stood, looking at the fine old house and feeling a swell of pride and belonging she'd never felt for her grandparents' Melbourne place. This was the home of her heart, she realised. With precious memories of her parents.

A tickle of an idea began to form in her tired brain. Maybe, just maybe, this could be more than a temporary refuge before she returned to Australia. Perhaps…

Her thoughts trailed off as the front door opened and a woman appeared, lifting her hand to shade her face.

'Miss Emma?'

The familiar sound of Dora Panayiotis's heavy accent peeled the years right back. Suddenly Emma was a scrawny kid again. She left her bag and hurried forward into sturdy, welcoming arms.

'Dora!' She hugged the housekeeper back, her exhaustion forgotten. 'It's so good to see you.'

'And you, Miss Emma. Welcome home.'

Emma flicked her sodden hair off her face as she reached for the towel, rubbing briskly till her skin tingled. Early rain had cleared to a sparkling bright afternoon and she hadn't been able to resist the lure of the white sand cove at the bottom of the garden. Turquoise shallows gave way to teal-green depths that enticed far more than the pool up beside the house.

Since arriving she'd sunk into the embrace of the villa's familiarity, feeling that, after all, part of her old life remained. How precious that was.

For four days she'd let Dora feed her delicious food and done nothing more taxing than swim, sleep and eat.

Until today, when she'd woken to discover her brain teeming with ideas for her future. A future where, for a change, she did what *she* wanted, not what others expected.

A future here, at the villa that was her birthright.

For the first time since the funeral and her disastrous wedding day, Emma felt a flicker of her natural optimism.

Her training was in business and event management. She was good it and had recently won a coveted job at an upmarket vineyard and resort that she'd turned down when she married because she planned to move to Athens with Christo.

Emma suppressed a shiver and yanked her thoughts back to her new future.

She'd work for herself. The gracious old villa with its private grounds and guest accommodation was perfect, not only for holidays but as an exclusive, upmarket venue for private celebrations. That would be where she'd pitch her efforts.

Corfu was the destination of choice for many holiday makers. With hard work and good marketing, she could create a niche business that would offer a taste of old-world charm with modern luxury and panache.

It would be hard work, a real challenge, but she needed that, she realised.

Wasn't that what she'd always done? Kept herself busy whenever she faced another loss so that she had no choice but to keep going? It was her way of coping, of not sinking under the weight of grief. She'd adapted to a new life in a new state with her grandparents after her parents had died. She'd taken on the challenge of supporting Papou after her grandmother's death.

It was easier to focus on the ideas tumbling in her brain than the searing pain deep inside. To pretend Christo hadn't broken her heart and undermined her self-confidence with his casual dismissal.

Emma's mouth set in a tight line. She was still angry and hurt but now she had a plan, something tangible to work towards. That would be her lifeline. Today for the first time she no longer felt she'd shatter at the slightest touch.

Today she'd contact a lawyer about a divorce and getting back her property and—

'Miss Emma!'

She turned to see Dora hurrying around the rocks at the end of the private beach. Her face was flushed and her hands twisted.

Emma's heart slammed against her ribs. She knew distress when she saw it, had been on the receiving end of bad news enough to recognise it instantly. Foreboding swamped her. She started forward, hand outstretched, her beach towel falling to the ground. Was it her aunt or uncle? Not Maia, surely?

'I came to warn you,' Dora gasped. 'Your—'

'There's no need for that, Mrs Panayiotis.' The deep voice with its bite of ice came from behind the housekeeper. 'I'm perfectly capable of speaking for myself.'

Then he appeared—tall, broad-shouldered and steely-eyed. Christo Karides.

Emma's husband.

Her heart slammed to a stop, her feet taking root in the sand. The atmosphere darkened as if storm clouds had covered the sun. Was it the effect of his inimical stare? For a second she couldn't breathe, an invisible band constricting her lungs as she stared into that face, so familiar and yet so different.

Then, abruptly, her heart started pumping harder than before. She sucked in a faltering breath.

He was still the most handsome man she'd ever seen with his coal-black hair and olive-gold skin contrasting with clear, slate-blue eyes. Eyes that right now seared her right down to the soles of her feet.

Desperately Emma tried for dispassionate as she surveyed those proud features that looked like they'd been etched by a master's hand. Strong nose, square jaw, the tiniest hint of a cleft in that determined chin. Only the small silvered scar beside his mouth, barely visible, marred all that masculine perfection. Perversely, it accentuated how good-looking Christo really was.

Handsome is as handsome does. She could almost hear her grandmother's voice in her ears.

This man had proved himself anything but handsome. Or trustworthy. Or in any way worth her notice.

Wrangling her lungs into action again, Emma took a deep breath and conjured a reassuring smile for Dora. 'It's okay. Perhaps you'd like to organise some tea for us in the main salon? We'll be up shortly.'

As acts of hostility went, it was a tiny one, ordering tea when she knew Christo liked coffee, strong and sweet, but it was a start. Emma preferred conciliation to confrontation yet she had no intention of making him feel welcome.

Silence enveloped them as Dora hurried away. A silence Emma wasn't eager to break.

She told herself she was over the worst. The shock, the disillusionment, the shattered heart. But it was easier to believe it when the man she'd once loved with all her foolish, naïve hopes wasn't standing before her like an echo of her dreams.

Yet Emma wasn't the innocent she'd been a week ago. Christo Karides had seen to that. He'd stripped her illusions away, brutally but effectively. She was another woman now.

Pushing her shoulders back, Emma lifted her chin and looked straight into those glittering eyes. 'I can't say it's good to see you, but I suppose it's time we sorted this out.'

Christo stared at the woman before him, momentarily bereft of words for the first time in his adult life.

He told himself it was the shock of seeing her safe and healthy, after almost a week of worry. It had been uncharacteristic of gentle, considerate Emma to vanish like that, as all her friends and relatives kept telling him. He'd worried she'd been injured or even kidnapped.

Till she'd called her aunt and left a cryptic message saying she was okay but needed time alone.

Time alone!

His blood sizzled at her sheer effrontery.

What sort of behaviour was that for a bride? Especially for the bride of Christo Karides, one of the most sought-after bachelors in Europe, pursued wherever he went.

That had been another first—finding himself frantic with anxiety. Christo recalled the scouring, metallic taste of fear on his tongue and the icy grip of worry clutching his vitals. He never wanted to experience that again.

Nor did he appreciate being made a laughing stock.

Or enduring the questioning looks her relatives had given him, as if her vanishing act was *his* doing! As if he hadn't spent weeks carefully courting Katsoyiannis's delicate granddaughter. Treating her with all the respect due to his future wife.

Christo clamped his jaw, tension radiating across his shoulders and down into bunching fists.

It wasn't just discovering Emma hale and hearty that transfixed him. It was the change in her.

The woman he'd married had been demure and sweet-tempered. She'd deferred to her grandfather and been patiently eager to please Christo, with her ardent if slightly clumsy responses to his kisses.

The woman before him was different. She sparked with unfamiliar energy. Her stance, legs apart and hands planted on hips, was defiant rather than placating.

The Emma Piper he knew was a slight figure, slender and appealing in a muted sort of way. This Emma even looked different. She wore a skimpy bikini of bright aqua. It clung to a figure far more sexy than he'd anticipated, though admittedly he'd never seen her anything but fully dressed. Her damp skin glowed like a gold-tinted pearl and those plump breasts rising and falling with her quick breaths looked as if they'd fill his palms to perfection.

A feral rush of heat jagged at his groin, an instant, unstoppable reaction that did *not* fit his mood or his expectations.

Christo dragged his gaze up to her face and saw her eyebrows arch in query, challenging him as if he had no right to stare.

As if she wasn't his runaway wife!

'You've got some explaining to do,' he murmured in the soft, lethal voice that stopped meandering board meetings in a second.

But, instead of backing down and losing the attitude, Emma jutted her rounded chin, lifted her cute, not quite retroussé nose in the air and planted her feet wider, drawing his attention to her shapely legs.

The heat in his groin flared hotter.

Slowly she shook her head, making her tangled, wet hair slide around her shoulders. Sunlight caught it, highlighting the dark honey with strands of gold he'd never seen before. But then they'd spent most of their time indoors, in her grandfather's house or at nearby restaurants. The bright Greek sunshine revealed details he simply hadn't noticed.

'You've got that the wrong way around.'

'Sorry?' Christo drew himself up to his full height, looking down on the slim woman before him. But, extraordinarily, she simply stared back, her mouth set in a mulish line. Her stare was bold rather than apologetic.

For a second he was so surprised he even wondered if the impossible had happened. If this wasn't Emma but some lookalike imposter.

But Christo Karides had never been one for fantasy. He'd been a pragmatist since childhood, with no time for fiction.

'Have you any idea how worried everyone was?' His

voice was gruff, hitting a gravelly note that betrayed the gut-deep worry he'd rather not remember. 'I even called the police! I thought you'd been abducted.'

He'd mobilised the best people to scour Melbourne and the surrounds, praying something terrible hadn't happened to his quiet little spouse.

There were ruthless people out there, including some ready to take advantage of a defenceless woman. His brain had kept circling back to the possibility that when he found her it would be too late. He'd never felt so helpless. The memory fed his fury.

'I rang my aunt to explain that I was safe.'

'You didn't ring *me*!' Christo heard his voice rise and drew a frustrated breath.

Was she wilfully misunderstanding? The woman he'd wooed had seemed reasonably intelligent and eminently sensible. Not the sort to disappear on her wedding day. He leaned into her space, determined to get through to her. 'I half-expected to find your abused body abandoned somewhere.'

He saw shock work its way through her, making her eyes round and her shoulders stiffen. Then she shook her head again as if dismissing his concern as nothing. 'Well, as you can see, I'm fine.'

'Not good enough, Emma. Not nearly good enough. You owe me.' An explanation to start with but far more after that.

'Oh, that's rich coming from you.' Her mouth curled up at one corner.

Was she *sneering* at him?

Christo covered the space between them in one long stride, bringing him close enough to inhale the scent of sea and feminine warmth that made something in his belly skitter into life.

Shackling her wrist with his, he tugged her close enough to feel the heat of her body.

'Stop it, Emma. You're my wife!'

Her voice when it came was so low he had to crane forward to hear it. Yet it throbbed with a passion he'd never heard from her. 'And how I wish I wasn't.'

Christo stared down at her. Never, in his whole life, had he met a woman who wasn't pleased to be with him. He'd lost count of the number who'd vied to catch his attention. Yet this one, the one he'd honoured with his name and his hand in marriage, regarded him as she would a venomous snake.

Had the world gone mad?

Where was his sweet Emma? The woman who revelled in his smiles, the gentle, generous woman he'd selected from all the contenders?

Her mouth twisted into a tight line as she stared down at his hand on her wrist. 'Let me go now. Marriage doesn't give you the right to assault me.'

'Assault? You have to be kidding.' His brow knotted in disbelief. As if he'd ever assault a woman!

'It is if I don't want to be touched and believe me, Christo, the last person on this earth I want touching me is you.'

Her voice was sharp with disdain and her nostrils flared as she met his stare. Something thumped deep in his chest at the unexpected, unbelievable insult.

Deliberately he dropped her hand and spread his empty fingers before her face. Anger throbbed through him. No, fury at being treated with such unprovoked contempt.

'Okay, no touching. Now explain.'

At last Emma seemed to realise the depth of his ire. The combative light faded from her eyes and her mouth compressed into a flat line. Abruptly she looked less fiery and more…hurt.

Christo resisted the ridiculous impulse to pull her close. He'd met enough manipulative women not to fall for a play on his sympathy.

'I know, Christo.' Her voice was flat, devoid of vigour. 'I know why you married me. There, is that enough explanation?'

'It's no explanation at all.' Yet the nape of his neck prickled.

It wasn't possible. He'd spoken of it to no one except Damen and then he'd ensured they were out of earshot. He'd left his blushing bride with her beaming family on the other side of the sprawling house.

He wasn't ashamed of what he'd done. On the contrary, his actions had been sensible, laudable and honourable. He'd offered marriage and the promise of his protection and loyalty to this woman. What more could she want? His actions had been spurred by the best of motives.

Except, looking into those wide, wounded eyes, Christo recalled her untutored ardour. Emma's shy delight at his wooing.

He'd told himself she didn't expect his *love*.

The old man had made it clear his granddaughter would marry to please him. Christo assumed she understood that behind the niceties of their courtship lay a world of practicality. That he'd wed for convenience.

But you never spelled it out to her, did you?

Christo silenced the carping voice.

No one who knew him would believe he'd been bowled over by little Emma Piper.

But Emma didn't know him. Not really.

For a second he wavered, surprised to feel guilt razor his gullet.

Till logic asserted itself. She'd chosen to marry him. He'd never spoken of love. Never promised more than he was willing to give.

Emma had flounced off in a huff and made him look like a fool. It was a part he'd never played before and never intended to play again.

Indignation easily eclipsed any hint of culpability. 'Nothing excuses what you did, Emma.'

'Don't try to put this on me, Christo. You don't even *want* me. You'd prefer someone beautiful and vivacious, like my cousin.'

Was that what this was about? He shook his head. He should have known this would boil down to feminine pique.

Emma was such an innocent that she didn't understand a man could be attracted to a woman and not act on that attraction. That a man of sense chose a woman who'd meet his needs.

Emma was that woman, with all the qualities he required of a mother for his ward. Even her defiance now just proved she had backbone, something he admired.

Plus she was more, he acknowledged. He met soft hazel eyes that now sparked with gold and green fire, feeling his blood heat as he took in her delectable figure and militant air. Christo acknowledged with a fillip of surprise that he wanted his wife more than he'd thought possible. Far more than he recalled from their restrained courtship.

There was a vibrancy about her, a challenge, a feminine mystique that called to him at the most primitive level. Gone was the delicate, compliant girl so perfect for his plans. This was a *woman*. Obstinate, angry and brimming with attitude. Sexier than he'd realised.

Lust exploded low in his body, a dark, tight hunger so powerful it actually equalled his fury.

'I married *you*, Emma. Not your cousin. I gave you my name and my promise.' How could she not understand what those things meant to him? 'That's far more important than any fleeting attraction.'

But Emma refused to be convinced. She shook her head,

wet hair slipping over her shoulders. Trails of sea water ran down from it to the miniscule triangles of her bikini top. Christo followed those wet tracks to the proud points of her nipples. Another wave of lust hit him and his flesh tightened across his bones as he fought the impulse to reach out and claim her.

'You're mine.' The words emerged as a roughened growl.

She stiffened, her chin jerking higher. 'Not for long. I'm filing for divorce.'

Like hell she would!

He'd carefully chosen Emma after considering all the options. Every reason he'd had for making her his wife still stood.

He needed her to make a real home instead of the bachelor flat he'd lived in for years. He needed her to be a mother to Anthea, providing a stable, caring environment for the little girl who was a stranger to him and with whom he had no hope of building a rapport.

Besides, Emma was *his*, and what Christo possessed he kept. It was in his nature.

Then there was today's revelation. That he wanted his wife with a hunger more powerful than he'd thought possible. That just standing here, fully dressed while she wore nothing but a bright bikini and a frown, brought him closer to the edge of his control than he'd been in years.

He intended to have her.

On his terms.

'File away, *wife*.'

He saw her flinch at the word and vowed that one day soon she'd purr at the sound of his voice. The thought of his runaway wife, eager for his touch, offering her delicious body for his pleasure, made the blood sing in his veins.

'But, before you do, I'd advise you to investigate the consequences. Divorce isn't an option.'

CHAPTER THREE

EMMA GROUND HER TEETH.

She was tired of men trying to rule her life. At least Papou had acted from love, not self-interest, wanting to see her 'safe' with a 'good' man before he died. Christo Karides had no such excuse. Her battered heart dipped on the thought but she refused to crumble as the familiar hurt intensified.

Instead she watched the tall figure of her husband turn and saunter back along the beach without a glance in her direction.

He should have looked out of place, ridiculously over-dressed, wearing a tailored dark business suit on a sandy beach. Instead, as she watched his easy stride, the latent strength in those broad shoulders and long legs, a thrill of appreciation coursed through her.

What a terrible thing desire was.

Her love, still fresh and new, had been battered away, swamped by pain and outrage. Yet standing in the sunlight, shivering not with cold but with a heat that she tried to label fury, Emma realised in horror that things weren't so simple.

She despised Christo Karides.

She loathed the cold-hearted way he'd set out to use her.

She vowed never to trust a word he said.

Yet as she watched him disappear around the end of the beach honesty forced her to admit she still desired him. That hadn't disappeared with her trust and her fool-ish dreams.

In Melbourne she'd thought the slow pace of his wooing sweet, proof he was considerate to her grief. At the same time she'd hungered for more than gentle caresses.

Now that hunger coalesced with the white-hot ire in her belly, producing an overwhelming mix of emotion and carnal need. She wanted to hurt him for the hurt he'd inflicted on her, yet at the same time she wanted...

Emma gritted her teeth and forced herself to breathe slowly.

She did *not* want Christo. She refused to allow herself to want him.

What she wanted, what she *needed*, was to free herself of him and this appalling marriage. She had plans, didn't she? An exciting scheme that would require all her energy and skill and which promised the reward of self-sufficiency in this place she loved.

Who did he think he was to decree divorce wasn't an option?

He might be the expert negotiator, the consummate sleazy liar who thought her easy pickings, but he was about to discover Emma Piper couldn't be steamrollered into compliance!

Forty-five minutes later Emma made her way from her bedroom to the salon with its expansive views of the sea.

Instead of hurrying to shower and dress, she'd taken her time, after having checked with Dora that Christo was, in fact, still on the premises. With that knowledge she'd locked her door and set about deciding what to wear.

Ideally she'd have worn a tailored suit, severe and businesslike. But Steph had persuaded her to splash out on new clothes for her honeymoon, reminding her that Papou would have wanted her to enjoy herself.

There was nothing businesslike in her wardrobe here. In the end, Emma gave up worrying about what impression her clothes might give Christo. She'd dress for herself.

The swish of her lightweight sea-green skirt around her bare legs reminded her of the holiday she was supposed to be enjoying. That she intended to enjoy as soon as *he'd* left. Her flat sandals were beach-comfortable rather than dressy and she wore a simple top that was an old favourite.

But she pulled her hair up into a tight knot at the back of her head and put on make-up, feeling that armour was necessary for the upcoming confrontation.

Ignoring the way the door knob slipped in her clammy palm, Emma opened the door and walked in.

To her surprise, Christo wasn't on his phone, absorbed in business, or pacing the vast room in obvious impatience.

Instead he stood at one end of the room, perusing the family photos her grandmother had collected. Generations of photos, mainly taken here on the Corfu estate to where Papou had brought his Australian bride before they'd decided to live full-time in her home country.

Christo swung around. His pinioning stare brought all the feelings she tried to suppress roaring into life.

After a moment Emma gathered herself. *She* had nothing to answer for.

She opened her mouth to ask if he needed another drink, then shut it again, annoyed that innate politeness made her even consider making the offer. Instead she crossed to a comfortable chair and sat.

'We need to talk.' Good. She sounded calm yet cool.

Silently one black eyebrow rose with arrogant query. The effect might have made her squirm if she hadn't been prepared.

'Or, if you prefer, I'm happy to finalise this via our lawyers.'

To Emma's chagrin that didn't dent his composure in the least. He strolled the length of the room, stopping to tower over her long enough to make her wonder if she'd made a mistake, taking a seat. Then, just before she shot to her feet, he settled into a chair, not opposite her but slightly to one side.

Emma silently cursed his game-playing and shuffled round to face him. Her skirt rode up at one side and she tugged it down, wishing she'd worn jeans instead.

Annoyingly, Christo looked utterly unruffled.

Until she saw the fire in his eyes and the determined set of his jaw.

Clearly he wasn't used to being crossed.

Good. It was time someone punctured his self-absorption.

'I'll file for divorce in Australia. I assume that's easiest.' Her tight chest eased a fraction as she spoke. It would be a relief to take action after days of doing nothing but grapple with disappointment and hurt. It was time to stop the self-pity.

'That's not a good idea, Emma.'

She frowned. 'I can't stay married to a man I despise.'

For an instant she thought she read something new flare in those heavy-lidded eyes. Something that sent a shiver tumbling down her backbone.

Emma sat straighter. What did she care if he wasn't used to hearing the truth about himself? He'd behaved appallingly and she refused to pretend otherwise.

'I know you're upset by your recent loss, so I'm willing to forgo the apology for your behaviour. But—'

'Apology for *my* behaviour?' She barely got the words out, she was so indignant.

Annoyingly, Christo simply nodded. 'Disappearing from your own wedding breakfast is hardly good form.'

She goggled at him.

'But your aunt and I convinced everyone you were completely overwrought. That the wedding had come too soon after the loss of your grandfather.' He spread his hands. 'I took the blame for wanting an early wedding, but your family understood and were very sympathetic.'

Emma opened her mouth then closed it again, feeling pressure build inside like steam in a kettle.

This was unbelievable!

'You made it sound like I had a breakdown? And they *believed* you?'

He shrugged, the movement emphasising the powerful outline of his shoulders and chest. 'What else could they believe? Your suitcase was gone, with your purse and passport.' His eyes narrowed to glowing slits that belied his relaxed pose. As if he were even now calculating how she'd managed to get away. Did he suspect Steph of helping? Had he bullied her into confessing? Steph hadn't mentioned it, but then she wouldn't.

'Once your aunt got that nonsensical message from you, of course she wondered.'

Emma shot to her feet. 'It wasn't nonsensical. I explained I needed time alone to think things through.'

Christo merely lifted those sleek black eyebrows and leaned back. 'Exactly. What sane woman would do that when she had a caring family and a brand-new husband to share her problems with?'

'Except *you* were the problem!' Emma heard her voice rise on a querulous note and swung away, pacing across to the window.

The view across the terrace to the private cove and bright sea did nothing to calm her fury. No one, not even her *papou* at his most obstinate, had got under Emma's skin the way this man had. Had she ever been so furious, her thoughts skittering so wildly?

How straightforward her world had been, how easy to be calm, before Christo Karides had slithered into her life.

Emma's heart hammered high in her chest at his gall, implying she was an emotional wreck who'd had a breakdown.

With a huge effort she pushed that aside. 'You said you'd worried I'd been abducted. But you knew I'd taken my luggage.'

Another nonchalant shrug. 'That wasn't clear at first. Your friend Steph didn't seem quite sure. And, even if you *had* left of your own free will, you could still have got into trouble. You're not used to being by yourself.'

Emma blinked. Christo made her sound like a child. Clearly he had no concept of the fact that she'd run Papou's house and some of his local investments for years. She'd chosen to live there for Papou's sake, not because she lacked independence.

Pride demanded she set the record straight.

She swung round and met that complacent, slate-blue stare, feeling the instant buzz of reaction as their gazes clashed. Immediately she changed her mind. Why explain to a man who'd soon be out of her life?

The notion eased the tightness cramping her chest and shoulders.

'We're wasting time. What's done is done.' It was time they moved on.

'I agree.' Yet the way Christo surveyed her, like a cat poised outside a mouse hole, warned her the next step wouldn't be so simple.

It was on the tip of her tongue to demand an apology but the way he sprawled there, ankles crossed nonchalantly, arms spread across the upholstery as he surveyed her, Emma knew she had no hope of getting satisfaction on that front.

The only satisfaction she'd get from this man was knowing she'd never have to see or hear from him again.

'It's in both our interests to end this quickly,' she began. 'Would an annulment be faster, do you know?'

'You think I'm an expert on unconsummated marriages?' For the first time Emma saw more than a flicker of annoyance in Christo's preternaturally still expression. Did he think she impugned his manhood by mentioning an annulment? She wouldn't be surprised. 'But I can tell you it would be a mistake.'

'How so?' Maybe annulments weren't simple after all.

'Because I refuse to consider it. Can you imagine the press furore if it became public?' He shook his head with grim disapproval.

'Frankly, I don't care. All I want is to be shot of you.'

His eyes narrowed to steely slits and his stare turned laser-sharp, scraping her throat and face. Emma crossed her arms and refused to look away.

'You've led a sheltered life. You have no idea how disruptive media attention can be till you've lived in the public eye.'

He was right. Emma had seen the articles about his business prowess, defying the odds when Greece's economy had faltered and his global investments had continued to return so spectacularly. And more, about his private life, all those assignations with beautiful women.

She shrugged one tense shoulder, her lips twisting in distaste. 'I'll cope, if it means ending this marriage quickly.'

'You really think you'd be able to deal with paparazzi camped at your door? Following you wherever you go? Digging up dirt—'

'There's no dirt to dig up!' At least not about her. Who knew what secrets Christo guarded?

'They'd invent something. The press are good at that.' He paused. 'Unless you have the power to keep them in check. As I have.'

Emma shuddered at the picture he painted of her hounded by photographers, of scurrilous stories in the tabloids, of friends and family pestered for interviews.

'If not an annulment, then a divorce.'

Christo spread his hands in mock sympathy. 'You'd still be hounded relentlessly.'

Emma lifted her chin. 'Maybe I'll sell my story to them

instead. Have you thought of that? I could make big bucks and then they'd leave me alone.'

For a second Emma thought he'd surge to his feet. She read the quickened pulse throbbing at his temple and the severe line of his mouth and knew Christo Karides wasn't used to such defiance.

Did people always do as he demanded? It was time someone broke the trend. Satisfaction filled Emma at the thought of being the one to disrupt his plans. She wasn't a pawn to be played to suit his schemes.

'Good try, Emma, but you won't do it.'

'You think you know me so well?' She sucked in a rough breath, trying to control the wobble in her voice. It didn't matter that fury, not hurt, made it unsteady. She hated the idea of seeming weak before this man. 'You have no idea who I really am. You never did.'

For what seemed an age, her surveyed her. 'I know you're a private person. You don't wear your heart on your sleeve.' He paused and she wondered, choking down hurt, whether he realised he was rubbing salt on her wounds.

For she *had* worn her heart on her sleeve. She'd been gullible, believing the unbelievable—that handsome, charming Christo Karides, with the world at his feet, actually cared for mousy little Emma Piper.

She spun on her heel and hurried across to the window, feigning interest in the view she knew as well as the back of her hand. It gave her time to deal with the honed blade of pain slicing through her.

Silence swallowed the room. When Christo spoke again his voice had lost that easy, almost amused cadence. 'What I mean is, you have more pride and integrity than to share anything so personal with the gutter press.'

Was he complimenting her? Emma blinked out at the sunlight glittering on the Ionian Sea and told herself it was too little and far, far too late.

'Coping with the press is a problem I'll deal with when I have to. My priority now is getting a divorce as quickly as possible.'

'That's not going to happen, Emma.'

Was that *pity* in his voice?

Her hackles rose. She swung round and was relieved to find she'd been wrong. That tight jaw spoke of impatience, nothing softer.

'You can prolong the process but you can't stop it.' That much she knew.

'You're my wife. We made vows—'

'Vows that meant nothing whatsoever to you!' Hearing her voice grow strident, she paused, hefting a shallow breath. Emma needed to stay calm, not fall apart. She'd run from him once, overwhelmed by the disillusionment that had rocked her to the core. She refused to give in to emotion now.

'I vowed to honour you, to cherish and look after you.' He'd never looked more proud or more determined. 'I have every intention of doing just that. This misunderstanding—'

'There's no misunderstanding. You cold-heartedly set about marrying me for a property deal.' As if she were a chunk of real estate! 'And to get a carer for your child.' Emma dragged in another breath but couldn't fill her lungs. 'Your baby is your responsibility. Yours and your lover's.'

An image filled her mind of Christo as she'd imagined him so often, sprawled naked in bed. But this time he wasn't smiling invitingly at her, he was kissing another woman. Their limbs were entwined and…

Emma banished the image and ignored the sour tang on her tongue that might, if she thought about it, be jealousy.

When she spoke again her voice was ragged. 'Together you need to look after the baby, not foist it on someone else.'

Her heart pumped an unfamiliar beat as adrenalin surged. Emma wasn't used to confrontation. She was a negotiator, a people pleaser, not a fighter. But something inside her had snapped the day she discovered Christo's motives and she still rode that wave of indignation.

She didn't know which was worse—that he'd played on her emotions and callously made her fall for him, or that he'd tried to palm his baby off on someone else. An innocent child deserved its parents' love.

What sort of world did the man inhabit? Surely one far removed from hers, where family and friends were everything.

Suddenly she realised he was on his feet, prowling towards her. Emma swallowed but stood her ground.

Fortunately he stopped a couple of paces away, so the illusion of distance held, though she caught a hint of the aftershave he used—cedar, spice and leather mingling with warm male skin. To her dismay, a little shimmy of appreciation shot through her.

'*Not* my child.' His voice was silky and soft but she heard the edge of anger. 'I would never be so careless.'

No, she realised, Christo was careful and calculating. Everything planned. Even down to choosing a suitable bride without a trace of sentiment or true feeling.

'And not a baby but a little three-year-old girl. The child is my stepsister's. She died recently.'

'I'm sorry.' Emma felt herself soften. She knew about loss, knew the struggle to keep going when everything seemed bleak.

Was it possible grief had made Christo act out of character? Could that explain…?

No. One look into those severely set features disabused her of that notion. She'd been right the first time. Christo didn't act in passion. He was a schemer who plotted every move.

'I barely knew her. Only met her once, years ago.'

'Yet you're now responsible for her child?' It made no sense.

He shrugged. 'There's no one else.'

It was on the tip of Emma's tongue to say that must be the case because no sane person would entrust an innocent child to such a man. But she bit the words back. She processed his words—*no one else*. But that was right: he was an only child and his parents were dead.

'The father?'

'If she knew who he was, she never said.' He paused. 'No one is going to come along and claim the girl.'

The girl.

He didn't even call the poor kid by her name.

Sympathy flashed through Emma. She understood what it meant to lose your family young. One day her parents had been there, seeing her off to school. The next, they'd been gone.

But she had her own battle to fight. She couldn't be swayed by emotion. That had been her downfall before.

'You both have my sympathy. But that's no reason to prolong this marriage.'

'Can you think of a better reason than to nurture a motherless child?'

How dared he talk of nurturing when his plan was to palm the child off on her?

'Of course I can. What about—?'

'Yes?' He leaned closer.

'Love', she'd been about to say. Marrying for true love.

But it hadn't been true and it hadn't been love, at least on his side. It had been a marriage of convenience.

As for her own feelings, Emma was ashamed of them. Especially since, despite everything he'd done, she wasn't as immune to this man as she wanted to be. Just as well there was no chance of him turning around and trying to persuade her he loved her. Even now she dreaded to think how effective he might be, given how he'd conned her the first time.

'I'm not getting into an academic discussion about marriage. I'm sorry for your niece...' *in more ways than one* '...but she's your responsibility. Take care of her yourself.'

Again, Emma felt that pang of sympathy for the little girl with no one but Christo to care for her. But he had money with which to bring in the best nannies. Once they were divorced, he'd find another wife. He'd proved how easy that was.

'Either agree to a divorce or leave. I have business to attend to.'

'Business?' His eyebrows shot up and for the first time she felt she'd truly surprised him.

'I have arrangements to make. A future to plan. A future without you.'

Stormy eyes surveyed her and she felt the force of his disapproval. No, more than disapproval. Sheer fury, if she read the thickening atmosphere correctly.

Once she would have hurried to placate, or at least redirect, that anger. Years living with Papou had made her adept at averting storms, finding ways of making him change his mind over time.

Today Emma stood her ground and rode the wave of displeasure crashing around her. If anything it buoyed her higher, knowing Christo could fume to no avail.

'These arrangements, do they require capital?' he asked finally.

'That's none of your concern.' He was stringing this out, hoping to undermine her confidence. Clearly he'd swallowed Papou's line about her needing to be looked after and guided.

As if part of her degree hadn't been in business management! Clearly Christo had missed that part of their conversation, probably distracted by planning how to tie her to his niece's nursery.

'On the contrary, it is my concern, if you're hoping to use your grandfather's property as capital.'

Something dropped hard through Emma's middle, like a stone plunging into a pool of arctic water. Chill splinters pricked her body.

She didn't like the triumph in Christo's eyes. As if he knew something she didn't.

But that was impossible. She already knew control of the valuable real estate in Athens had been handed to Christo on her behalf. Emma intended to change that, along with her married status.

'It's not my grandfather's property now. It's mine.' Her gaze swept the gracious room. This place, so full of precious memories, was her solace now, her home.

And more. It was her future. Her one asset, given her savings after years studying and looking after Papou were negligible. She'd get a loan using the property as collateral and invest it in the business she'd establish.

'If only that were true.' A deep voice cut through her thoughts.

She swung her head round to face him.

Either Christo had the best poker face in the world or he really did have bad news for her. Emma had a horrible feeling he was about to pull the rug out from under her feet…again.

She hiked her chin up, ignoring her stomach's uneasy roiling. 'If you have something to say, say it. I've had enough games.'

That sharp gaze held hers an instant longer then he shrugged. 'It seems your grandfather didn't tell you everything.'

That did it. Emma's stomach was now in freefall. She shifted her feet wider, bracing herself for the axe she sensed was about to drop, curling her hands into each other behind her back where Christo couldn't see.

'Go on.'

'He believed you needed a guiding hand. Which is why he left me in charge of the Athens property.'

'And?' Was he dragging this out to torment her?

'And your other inheritance, the estate here, is yours with the proviso that for the next five years any decision to sell or develop it, or take a loan against it, is subject to my approval. I have the right to veto any change of use if I don't believe it's in your long-term best interests.'

He smiled, a baring of white teeth that looked carnivorous rather than reassuring. 'Look on me as your business partner.'

Emma had been prepared for something but not this.

The blow struck at her knees, making them shake and threaten to collapse. Frantically she redistributed her weight, standing taller and hauling her shoulders back to glare at the man surveying her with that smug hint of a smile on his too-handsome face.

'I'll fight it. I'll challenge it in court.'

'Of course you will.' If she didn't know better, she'd almost have believed that soothing tone. 'But do you know how long that will take, or how much it will cost? How it will eat into your inheritance?' He paused, letting her digest that. 'You could lose everything.'

Main force alone kept Emma where she was. If she thought she had a hope of doing it, she'd have slammed a fist straight into Christo's smirking mouth.

She was still reeling, her brain whirring fruitlessly because, outrageous as it sounded, it was just the sort of thing her old-fashioned Papou might have done. Especially as he'd known his grandson-in-law-to-be was a commercial *wunderkind*.

He'd wanted to protect Emma. Instead he'd tied her to a man who wasn't fit to enter this house.

Belatedly she realised she should have insisted on reading every line of every legal document herself. More fool her!

'I'll still fight it.' Her voice was strained, her vocal cords pulled too tight.

'That's your prerogative.' Christo paused, that searing gaze stripping her bare. 'But there's an alternative.'

'What is it?' She didn't dare hope but she had to know.

'Simple. Meet my terms and you can do as you like with this place.' His mouth lifted at one corner in a hint of a smile but Emma knew in her very bones this would be anything but simple. 'I'll sign your inheritance into your control. All you have to do is fulfil your vows and live as my wife for a year.'

CHAPTER FOUR

'LIVE AS YOUR WIFE? You've got to be kidding.'

A flush climbed Emma's pale cheeks and her greenish brown eyes glittered more brightly than he'd ever seen.

She was a pretty woman but indignation made her arresting.

Christo surveyed her curiously. She vibrated with energy, her breasts heaving and her mouth working. She looked...full of passion. That hadn't been on his checklist.

The news he'd become responsible for his stepsister's child had come just before his visit to Australia. He'd picked Emma as a suitable bride because she'd make a good mother and a compliant wife.

But Emma was far more than either of those things, he realised. Instinct had drawn him to her with good reason. Her allure was more subtle and intriguing than surface glamour. His body tightened in anticipation.

He wanted his wife.

Wanted her more by the minute.

And he intended to have her. To salvage his pride after being dumped like an unwanted parcel at his own wedding. Because he had a score to settle. But above all because he'd desired her ever since their first gentle kiss. Her breathless ardour had unlocked something deep inside that had grown and morphed into something very like need.

'There are two things I never joke about. Business and family.' The first because it was his lifeblood, the second because he never made light of anything with such power to destroy.

'I *know* why you married me, remember? I *heard* what

you told your best man.' Emma's lips thinned as she pulled her mouth tight and the colour faded from her cheeks.

Christo didn't like her pallor. That drawn look made her seem fragile. Vulnerable. Reminding him that she looked that way because of him. He was responsible.

'I never lied to you.'

'Not specifically, but you made me believe—' She bit her tongue and looked away.

Christo could finish her sentence. He'd made her think he was falling for her. That he was a man capable of love.

Something dark slithered through his belly, drawing nausea in its wake. Without a second thought Christo stifled it. He didn't have the time or inclination for feelings. Nor for pointless self-recrimination.

'It's done now. And my offer is on the table.' An offer she *would* accept.

Her face swung round and the impact of all that barely contained emotion slammed into him. To his surprise, Christo welcomed it.

Because he'd rather have his wife angry than sad and defeated. It was a new concept. He filed it away for later consideration. Along with the dark shadow edging his conscience.

'You can't want me to live with you. I despise you.'

If Emma expected that to derail his plans, she really was an innocent. But then she hadn't come from his world but from what appeared to be a close, loving family. For a second Christo pondered what that would be like.

'You might be surprised at what I want and what I can live with. Besides, you owe me.'

'*I* owe *you*?' There it was again, that shimmer of defiance, that surge of energy that made his wife the most interesting woman he'd met in years. Even the fact that her vibrancy was due to inconvenient *feelings* didn't deter him.

'You gave your word. You made promises to me, Emma.'
He even enjoyed the taste of her name on his tongue.

How would that pale golden skin of hers taste?

'You really expect me to share a house with you?'

'And a bed.'

She goggled up at him as if he spoke Swahili instead
of English.

'You're not serious.' For the first time since he'd arrived
he saw her falter, grabbing the back of a nearby chair.

That hint of vulnerability ignited a trail of gunpowder
right through his considerable self-control. Was the idea of
sex with him really so appalling? He refused to believe it.

Christo enjoyed women, within strict parameters, and
he knew sexual attraction when he saw it. A week ago his
demure bride had been counting the hours till they were
naked together. Soon she would be again.

'But I am. You're mine, Emma, and I intend to have you.
At the very least you owe me a wedding night.'

Emma gripped the carved back of the antique chair and
willed the room to stop spinning.

This was crazy. Impossible.

Yet Christo Karides stood there looking as implacable
as ever. More so. Before the wedding she'd seen a gen-
tler, more restrained man. Now she saw the real Christo,
haughty and demanding. Over the top with his outlandish demands.

'You'd force me into sex?'

For the first time since he'd stalked along the beach—
sexy, brooding and starkly dangerous—she saw him recoil.

'I'd never force a woman. What sort of man do you think
I am?' He even had the temerity to look outraged!

'I know exactly what sort of man you are and the question stands.' Stronger now, Emma let go of the chair back

and slid her hands to her hips, adopting a combative attitude to hide her nerves.

'The answer is no. Sex with an unwilling woman… Never.' He shook his head, grimacing with distaste, and Emma felt the knot of tension in her chest loosen.

Then his gaze zeroed in on hers and suddenly she was short of breath.

'But you want me, Emma.' His certainty was infuriating and devastating, because it tapped into a weakness that shouldn't exist any more. She despised herself for feeling a tiny tug of response to his words. 'And I'll make sure you enjoy every single minute of it.'

His searing look clogged the protest in her throat. Or maybe it was her body's reaction to the images his words evoked. Heat blasted her. She reminded herself she hated him.

'If nothing else, I expect to share the wedding night we missed.' Something shifted in his eyes, something that spoke of calculation and determination. Emma shivered and rubbed her hands up her arms.

'You're demanding a year living with you and one night of sex? That's totally bizarre.'

He spread his arms, palm up. 'I need a wife to help my niece settle in. I have no skills with children.' His mouth twisted and for a second Emma thought she read something else in those slate-dark blue eyes. But it was gone before she could identify it. 'Even I know she needs more than a nanny. She needs a kind, caring parent figure to help her through the worst of the change. Don't forget, she's been through the trauma of losing her mother. *You* know how important it is that she has someone there for her.'

Damn the man. He was right. Emma didn't want to get involved. Yet she couldn't prevent a pang of sympathy for the little girl who'd lost her mother. And who apparently only had Christo to rely on! Poor kid.

Emma's bruised heart squeezed on the girl's behalf. At least when she was orphaned she'd had her grandparents, aunt and uncle. They'd closed ranks around her, a tight circle of love and support.

But she couldn't afford to be swayed, no matter how sorry she was for the child.

'As for us enjoying each other sexually...' Christo's deep voice cut through her thoughts. 'Once we begin, I'm sure we'll both want far more than one night. I'm confident we're well-matched physically.' His voice lingered on the last word, drawing unwanted heat from Emma's midsection down to the aching hollow between her legs. The sensation was new and unnerving. 'But I demand at least one night. Those are my terms.'

Despite her intention not to show weakness, Emma shuffled back half a step. 'It's preposterous!'

Christo said nothing, merely folded his arms over his chest and lifted one eyebrow.

Emma cast a look around the dear, familiar room. It would break her heart all over again to leave the family villa. But better that than what Christo proposed.

'I'll see you in court.' Her voice was crisp and decisive, despite the jittery whirl of emotions. 'Even if I have to walk out of here with only the clothes on my back. I'll go back to Australia, to my family and friends, and begin legal action to divorce and get back what's mine.'

Even if justice took years. Even if her inheritance was depleted in the meantime. She'd work and support herself.

She couldn't contemplate the alternative.

'That would be unfortunate.' Christo's arms fell to his sides, fingers flexing, and Emma wondered if he was restraining the impulse to reach for her. She pushed her shoulders back, meeting him eye to eye, knowing she had no alternative than to face him head on.

'I understand your uncle's business is dangerously over-extended. Even with the recent inheritance from your grandfather. If one of the investors were to withdraw it would be disastrous. The repercussions would impact not only him but your aunt and cousins. They could lose everything.'

Words choked in Emma's throat as her larynx tightened. She stared, wide-eyed, absorbing the threat in those softly spoken words.

Papou had said Christo was clever and daring. That he had a nose for business and a ruthless edge. Would he really be so ruthless as to destroy her family out of pique because she'd turned him down?

Emma wanted to doubt it but she couldn't take the risk.

'Are you *threatening* my family?'

She couldn't read anything in those arrogant features but determination.

'Do I need to?' He shook his head. 'There'd be no threat to them if you simply abided by your vows. With you as my wife I'd feel obliged to support your uncle if his company was in danger of floundering.'

Emma sucked in a breath. It was true her uncle's construction company had been through rough times. Now she thought about it, there'd been talk of Christo investing in it. But her head had been so full of other things that she hadn't paid much attention.

Now she was paying attention, far too late!

The walls pressed in on her. Or maybe it was the net this man had cast around her drawing tight.

Had Christo really invested in her uncle's company to ensure she complied? Or was it an empty threat?

Emma stared into eyes the colour of a stormy sky and felt something inside shrink. He was implacable, as merciless as a winter storm that wrought destruction on everything in its path.

Whether Christo had put money into the business for

purely financial reasons or as shrewd emotional blackmail didn't matter. Emma couldn't let him destroy her family.

'My grandfather was right about you. You really are utterly ruthless.' She grimaced, remembering Papou's enthusiasm for this man. 'To think he actually *respected* that. I'm glad he never had to find out what sort of man you truly are. You're a bully, Christo Karides.'

He didn't even blink, just stared back, eyebrows slightly raised, as if waiting for her to capitulate.

Emma swallowed hard, tasting a coppery tang. She realised she'd bitten down on her lip so hard she'd drawn blood and hadn't even felt the pain.

Frantically she ransacked her brain for an out. Something that would free her from this nightmare. But her luck had run out the day she'd fallen for this wolf in a tailored suit.

Why, oh, why had she broken the habit of a lifetime and acted rashly, marrying so quickly?

Because you fell for him. Hook, line and sinker.

The knowledge was acid, eating at her insides.

'I want to live here, in Corfu. Not in Athens.' Emma refused to let herself stop and think about the implications of what she was agreeing to.

'That works. My Athens apartment isn't designed for a child. This is much more suitable.'

If she needed anything to remind her of Christo's priorities, this was it. His first thought, his only thought, was for the child he expected her to mother. Everything else, even the sex he said he wanted, was secondary. But then he'd never really been attracted to Emma. The demand to share a bed was just male pique, because she'd escaped becoming another conquest.

She crossed her arms, clamping her fingers hard into bare flesh.

'Don't tell me you're willing to leave Athens?' Was

there, perhaps, hope that the threats had been a ploy? That he had no intention actually of living with her?

'It's only an hour by plane. I'll spend week nights on the mainland and the weekends here. That way Anthea will have a chance to get used to me.'

For the first time he'd called his niece by her name.

And for the first time that Emma could recall, Christo looked uneasy. His voice lacked its usual confident tone.

At the thought of spending time with Anthea? It didn't seem possible. Christo was the most assured man she knew.

Emma didn't understand this cold-hearted stranger. He showed no compunction or remorse about threatening her in the most outrageous way, yet one little girl unsettled him?

But Emma had enough to deal with. Firmly she pushed aside curiosity about the girl and her relationship with Christo.

'I need time to consider.'

He shot his cuff and sliced a glance at his designer watch. 'You have ten minutes.'

'Ten—'

'I have business to attend to. I need this wrapped up.'

As if she were an item on a meeting agenda, to be crossed off before he moved onto the next matter.

Once, Emma would have murmured something placatory and avoided further direct confrontation. But that had been with her darling Papou, whose quick flares of impatience had masked genuine worry for her future and fear that his failing heart would give out before he saw her settled.

Settled! With this arrogant...

'Of course making money is far more important than dealing with real people.'

Her words brought that laser-sharp gaze back to hers. Emma swallowed hard at the impact of that silent scrutiny.

Did he see past her bravado to the woman grappling with hurt and shock?

'Talk to your uncle, Emma. He and your aunt are real people, aren't they? Ask him how strong his business is.'

In the past Christo's deep voice had sent a thread of molten heat trailing through her insides. This time it created crackling frost along her bones.

Of course she'd talk to her uncle, but she knew he'd confirm what Christo said—that his company was vulnerable. One thing she'd learned, when Christo Karides wanted something, he didn't leave anything to chance.

'If I agreed to stay with you for a year...' Emma forced down bile '...how do I know I can trust you to keep your word?'

His eyebrows shot high, as if no one had ever questioned his integrity. She found that hard to believe.

'I'll have a contract drawn up.'

A contract setting out such a...personal deal? Her mind boggled. Yet she couldn't trust his word. Look at how he'd fooled her with his suave, persuasive ways.

'I won't sleep with you.'

He merely smiled. The man was so full of himself.

'It's not sleep I have in mind.' This time, despite every shred of indignation, despite his insufferable arrogance, Emma felt a tell-tale flutter in her belly. As if the woman who'd loved and longed for this man was still here, eroding the foundations of her anger.

'The contract will arrive tomorrow.' He looked as if he was going to say more then shook his head. 'Anthea and I will be here on the weekend.' Then, before Emma could find any words, he strode from the room.

Sure enough the next afternoon a courier arrived.

Emma was dishevelled after hours trying to quell her fury and fear by exploring the estate from top to bottom.

She'd checked out every inch of the villa, its outbuildings and the neglected villa next door which Papou had bought and hadn't got around to renovating. If Emma was to turn this into an exclusive small function centre, that second villa would be a wonderful asset.

If she was still here in Corfu.

If she didn't cut her losses and go home.

Except she'd called her uncle and knew she had no choice. He'd confirmed that Christo had invested heavily in the family construction company. He'd even added that things would be tight without Christo's support.

Support!

Emma shivered and looked down at the sealed envelope in her hands. It felt like a ticking time bomb. Her hands were clammy and, despite the cool breeze through the open front door, she was overheated.

The sound of the courier's car accelerating onto the main road broke her stasis. She tore open the envelope.

There it was, in excruciating detail. Christo had signed over control of the Corfu property, and a sizeable share of the expected profits of the Athens redevelopment. In return she'd live as his wife for a year. She'd take no lovers. She'd appear with him as necessary in public and behave with expected decorum. She'd accommodate his niece. She'd grant no media interviews about their relationship, ever.

And she'd have marital relations with Christo Karides at least once.

He'd actually had the gall to include that in the contract! His signature slashed the page just below it.

All Emma had to do was sign and she'd have the property that should already be hers.

For long moments she stared at the document. Then something snapped. Emma shoved the contract back into the envelope, breathing hard.

Dared she?

But what alternative did she have?

She'd keep this safe as proof of her husband's intentions and manipulations in case she needed it in a future court case. She'd delay filing for divorce till the twelve months was up. She'd give his niece a home, poor little kid. She'd even put up with Christo staying every weekend.

But as for the rest... She might be cornered but she had her self-respect. Emma refused to sign. She and Christo Karides would be married in name only.

If that wasn't good enough, she'd swallow her pride and go to the press. It was a distasteful last resort. Emma valued her privacy and shuddered at the thought of laying herself bare for the world to read about. But selling her story might provide enough money to tide her family and her over till she won back what was hers.

For the first time since Christo had sauntered back into her life, all arrogance and outrageous demands, hope stirred.

She could do this. She *would* do it.

She'd throw herself into creating her business and at the end of the year she'd get her property back. Christo was bluffing about them having sex. He had to be. It was just bruised masculine pride talking.

He'd only drawn up the contract to satisfy her concerns that he'd renege on the deal. Now she had his signature proving he intended to hand over the property, she was safe. She had to believe that.

All she had to do was endure fifty-two weekends without trying to kill her infuriating, selfish, diabolically annoying husband.

CHAPTER FIVE

THE FOLLOWING SATURDAY morning Emma and Dora stood in the villa's entry, watching a driver open the back door of a long, black limousine.

Emma's breath snagged in the back of her throat and her pulse pounded, waiting for Christo to emerge. But it wasn't he who appeared. Or a little girl.

It was a woman, and what a woman.

Emma had told herself nothing Christo did now could surprise or hurt her.

She'd been wrong.

Watching long, toned legs appear, narrow feet in high-heeled sandals and a tall, sinuous figure in a tightly fitted dress, everything inside Emma stilled. Then the woman turned to look about her and the sun danced on glossy sable waves that cascaded around slim shoulders and framed a face so beautiful it belonged on a magazine cover.

Emma felt as though she'd been slapped in the face.

He'd brought his lover with him. To her home.

Her home!

Abruptly the nerves making her anxious melted away, replaced by incandescent fury.

Emma's gaze locked on the woman, so she didn't even notice Christo emerge from the car, or the little girl who stood awkwardly between the two adults, until Dora started forward with words of welcome.

Emma blinked and looked again, taking in the tableau before her in freeze frames.

The beauty was looking tentatively at Christo, who frowned mightily. But he ignored the woman, his attention fixed on the child who must be Anthea. A little girl with tight brown plaits and pale, skinny hands clasped before her. She didn't look at either of the adults beside her, but stared warily at Dora, who smiled and welcomed them.

Finally Christo turned, his eyes locking on Emma's. Even braced for it, she was stunned by that sudden sizzle of connection. No, not connection, she told herself. Fury.

She stalked forward, intending to confront him, only to falter when Anthea shrank back, not towards Christo or his girlfriend, but towards the solidly built driver.

Emma's anger ebbed as other emotions rose. Guilt for scaring the kid with her sudden surge of movement. Sympathy and remembered heartbreak. Memories of grief and insecurity. Of feeling alone in a world that didn't make sense after her parents had died.

Emma dropped to a crouch before the little girl, discovering soft brown eyes, a smattering of freckles and a mouth that hooked up at one side as she bit her cheek.

'Hello,' she said quietly. 'I'm Emma. You must be Anthea. Is that right?'

Silently the girl nodded, her eyes wary and huge. Emma's chest tightened as if her ribcage shrank around her heart. She watched Anthea's hands tighten convulsively on each other and repressed a frown. At the very least the poor kid should have a teddy or something to cuddle given none of the adults with her could be bothered offering comfort.

'Do you like rabbits?' Emma asked impulsively, thinking of the toy rabbit she'd rediscovered in the room she'd used as a girl. Washable and soft, it had survived years of snuggling almost intact.

Anthea didn't answer, just lifted her shoulders in a tiny shrug and bit her lip harder. Emma waited for one of her companions to step in and reassure her. But a quick glance showed Christo standing back as if the girl had come with a health warning. The woman was no better, busy surveying Christo through her lashes.

'Would you like to come inside and see one?' Emma smiled. 'He can't hop or eat grass but he likes spending time with little girls and he loves being cuddled.' She paused. 'Do you like giving cuddles?'

'I don't know.'

The whisper stilled the last buzz of Emma's dying temper. She forgot about her unwanted adult guests and focused totally on the too-serious face of the girl before her. The girl she hadn't wanted to build a close relationship with, because she knew it could only lead to pain when they went their separate ways after twelve months. Emma had told herself it was up to Christo to forge a bond with his niece, not her.

Now that notion died an abrupt death. Emma couldn't ignore this little girl whose reserve and tension told its own sorry tale. She wanted to wrap her close and tell her everything was going to be okay. Instead she kept her tone light.

'Then let's find out, shall we? I'll take you to him if you like.' She rose and reached out her hand.

Anthea stared at it as if she'd never held an adult's hand in her life. She shot a swift, upward glance at the others, almost as if expecting reproach, then reached out and touched Emma's fingers.

Anthea's tiny hand was cool in hers but Emma was careful not to betray surprise at that or the tremor she felt pass through the little girl. Instead she smiled and turned towards the door, catching Dora's eye. The housekeeper would see to the adults. Right now the priority was this little waif and making her feel comfortable.

The enormity of the situation hit Emma again, making her falter for a second. She was about to take on responsibility for a child, a child who, obviously, needed love and lots of it.

But Emma couldn't turn her back on the girl. This had nothing to do with Christo's threats. It was about recognising the blank shock on Anthea's face, the feeling of loss and fear, the dreadful uncertainty.

Emma had been there. She couldn't treat the girl as a pawn in some power play.

She stepped into the house, Anthea tentatively returning her grasp. 'He's a very special rabbit, you know. He's lived here for a long time. I hope you like him.'

Christo surveyed the spacious bedroom suite he'd been given and tried to turn his mind to practicalities, like Wi-Fi access. Instead he found himself staring at the perfect curve of blue-green sea in the cove, his thoughts in turmoil.

Not only his thoughts. His gut roiled with unfamiliar emotion.

It wasn't the Ionian Sea he saw. It was Emma crouching before his niece, cajoling her into a response after hours of the kid being silent and withdrawn.

He'd known all along that Emma would make a great carer. She was warm-hearted and generous. Her body language around the girl had been fiercely protective, yet her expression had been soft, something that he was sure would turn into love one day.

His gut clenched.

Christo couldn't remember ever being so close to such naked maternal tenderness. Any sort of tenderness, come to that. Except the fleeting sense of intimacy he got from sex. The short afterglow that made the mirage of emotional intimacy seem almost as tangible as physical closeness. Until logic kicked in, reminding him it was a fantasy.

Impatient, Christo marshalled his thoughts, ignoring the unfamiliar pang as he recalled Emma's expression and his unwarranted reaction.

He opened the French doors and stepped onto the wide terrace.

Emma's reaction might have been all he could wish for but Anthea's nanny was another matter.

He gritted his teeth at the thought of the woman who'd been recruited so carefully to provide the best care for his step-niece. He'd left the recruitment to experts. After all, what did he know about selecting a child minder?

Now he saw he should have taken a hand, vetting the applicants himself. The woman with such excellent experience and references—the woman who had been soberly dressed and devoted to her charge, the time they'd met previously—had transformed utterly. He'd been confronted at the airport by a siren more interested in batting her eyelashes at him than caring for Anthea.

He sighed and shrugged out of his jacket, dropping it over the back of a chair. He'd sometimes had the same problem with temporary office staff. Women who were all business till the day they found themselves alone with the boss. A boss who regularly featured on those 'hottest, richest bachelor' lists.

The question was, did he fire her effective immediately or give her notice? It would take time to replace her. And even he, used to others doing his bidding, didn't expect his wife to take sole charge of Anthea.

Anthea. Who looked so like her mother.

Christo shoved his hands in his pockets and stepped out onto the grass. He'd deal with the nanny later. With everything later. For now he needed fresh air.

Ever since he'd boarded the plane and seen Anthea with her big brown eyes, Christo had felt claustrophobic to the point of nausea.

It was pathetic. It was all in his head. Yet he felt the tension notch higher with each breath.

Being with the child brought back memories he hadn't revisited in years.

Turning his back on the house, he lengthened his stride.

* * *

'Where have you been?'

Christo stopped in the shade of a wide, twisted olive tree, locating the source of the question.

Emma. His wife.

Heat ignited low in his abdomen. Satisfaction. And more besides.

Instead of being pinned up, her hair was around her shoulders in a drift the colour of wild honey. Was it the sunshine that made it glow? In wintry Melbourne the colour had been more subdued. Like the woman.

Maybe the difference was her bright, summery clothes. In a sleeveless wrap-around dress the colour of apricots, she looked good enough to eat. Especially as the light fabric skimmed breasts and hips and that narrow waist which had so fascinated him when he'd held her close.

Christo's groin grew heavy. She stood with arms folded and hip jutting in a confrontational stance that triggered a reaction deep in his psyche. Something he could only describe as very primitive and utterly masculine.

'Walking,' he murmured, watching her eyes flare brighter. As if she struggled to contain her emotions.

Was that what she'd done before? Kept her emotions under wraps?

The woman he'd courted in Australia had been reserved and eager to please. Christo had thought he wanted the quiet, compliant Emma. But there was a lot to be said for vivacity. For passion.

'You don't think it would have been helpful if you'd stayed with Anthea? Helped her settle in?'

Christo settled his shoulders back against the rough bark of the tree and slowly crossed his arms. 'You were doing a fine job. Better than I could have done. My skills don't lie in that direction.' Give him business any day. Wrangling a profit in a difficult commercial environment was far easier than dealing with family or feelings.

Emma shook her head gain, dark blonde waves slipping around her shoulders. 'That's no excuse. You should have been there. You're her uncle.'

Step-uncle. But Christo didn't correct her.

'It's not me she needs. It's someone like you, with a knack for dealing with children.'

'Don't think you can get out of your responsibilities so easily.' Her voice was low and even but determined. 'You need to build a relationship with her. When we divorce, I won't be around to take care of her.'

There'd be no divorce.

Christo planned to keep Emma as his wife. Once she got used to the idea, once he'd taken her to bed, she'd change her mind. It might be his money and looks that initially attracted women, but he knew how to satisfy them.

Pleasure stirred at the memory of Emma on their wedding day. Her breathless anticipation. The flurry of nerves that barely concealed her desire for him.

All he needed was patience, time to remind her how much she wanted him.

There'd be pleasure too in having what she'd denied him when she'd run off, leaving him to explain the inexplicable to her friends and family. Runaway bride, indeed! Did she really think she could make a fool of him and not pay? Did she think he had no pride?

'I have every intention of developing a relationship with her.' Though the thought of it made him feel…

No. Better not to examine that too closely. He knew his duty and he'd do it.

'Well, you haven't got off to a good start.'

Christo shrugged. 'Some things take time.' Such as seducing a woman who needed the reassurance of a gentle touch. He read more than anger in Emma's obstinate stance and quickened breathing. There was awareness. How could he not notice when it crackled in the air between them?

'They'd go far better without your girlfriend here.' The words emerged through clenched teeth. Emma bit the words out.

Jealousy?

Despite the tension he'd fought these last hours, Christo felt delight unfurl.

'She's not my girlfriend.'

'She sure fooled me.'

Emma's chin swung higher. It wasn't Christo's companion who'd made a fool of her. It was her own husband. How she hated that word. Husband. Almost as much as she hated the fact she'd been stupid enough to marry him. She must have been out of her mind!

Now he'd brought his lover here. She'd heard about open marriages but this was the man who just days ago had demanded sex as his marital right!

As if all that weren't enough, there was yet another sting in the tail.

Despite the different colouring, one brunette and one redheaded, there was a strong similarity between the woman who'd stepped out of the limo and Emma's cousin, Maia. The gorgeous cousin with whom Christo had admitted he'd like to have an affair.

Both women were tall, sexy in a sultry, almost earthy way, yet with a sophistication Emma couldn't hope to match.

Plain Emma. Ordinary Emma. Emma the 'nice' girl. Emma who played by the rules and didn't like to upset people who cared for her.

She dug her fingers into her upper arms, fighting a wave of reckless anger. Losing her temper wouldn't help.

Yet, now she'd met Christo's 'type' and realised how far she was from the sort of woman he wanted, it was a battle to retain some surface calm. Because it brought home how ridiculous her dreams of happy-ever-after had been.

'Emma?' He straightened from the tree and moved closer, forging a path through scarlet poppies and smaller wildflowers. In the dappled light of the olive grove she almost believed that was regret on Christo's face. Except she'd had enough of self-delusion.

'That's far enough.'

He halted before her, his gaze clear and open, as if he'd never deceived her.

'She's Anthea's nanny, not my lover.'

Emma snorted. 'Even I'm not that gullible.'

'But I was. Or at least, the recruitment expert was.'

Something about his tone of voice, the jarring note that sounded like discomfort, as well as annoyance, stopped Emma's scornful reply.

This was the first time Christo Karides had admitted being anything other than in control. Was it a trick?

He curled his hand around the back of his neck. The action dragged his casual shirt up, stretching it across his wide chest.

Emma stared then raised her gaze to his face, telling herself it was the drowsy afternoon heat of the sheltered grove that made her feel warm.

'You're telling me she really is a nanny? She doesn't look or act like one.'

'The only other time I met them, she wore flat shoes, hair pulled back and her outfit was sensible, not—'

'Sexy?' Emma arched her eyebrows. 'Surely you noticed she couldn't take her eyes off you? She didn't even glance at Anthea.' Outrage on behalf of the bereaved little girl cut through Emma's hurt. They were both victims of this man.

'Oh, I noticed. *Today.*' His tone was grim. 'But she wasn't like that the other time. Then she was wonderful with

Anthea. Attentive and reassuring. She perfectly matched her excellent references.'

Emma frowned, finally registering what Christo had said a moment ago. *The only other time he'd met them.*

It wasn't just the nanny he'd met only once. It was his niece too. No wonder Christo and Anthea behaved like complete strangers. Yet did that explain his grim expression as he'd surveyed the little girl?

Slate-blue eyes caught and held hers. 'Today I saw a different side to her.' He lifted one shoulder in a half-shrug and Emma realised he was still talking about Anthea's nanny. 'It happens. Women deciding to make a play for a rich man who'll be a meal ticket. But I confess this time I was taken completely by surprise.'

Emma stared back at this man who took such things in his stride. A light breeze riffled his jet-black hair and the shifting shadows cast those high, carved cheekbones in stark relief, accentuating his hard male beauty.

She knew they came from different worlds but to accept such games as inevitable? 'If that's normal in your world, then I pity you.'

Something shifted in his face. His expression closed, turned still. For just a second Emma sensed she'd hit a nerve. Or had she imagined it?

'I'm not interested in sleeping with the hired help.' His voice was chill, sending a shiver tracking over her bare arms and neck. 'I never mix sex and business. Besides, I have a wife. Remember?' The way his voice dipped suddenly took Emma's stomach with it, diving low in a giddy swoop. 'What I want is someone I can trust to care for Anthea. She needs it, poor kid, after what she's been through.' He paused, as if side-tracked by his thoughts.

'You mean more than losing her mother?' Emma didn't know what prompted her words. A parent's loss would make any kid withdrawn and wary. Emma was certain her own early losses had affected her that way too. Yet after just a short time with Anthea she wondered at her level of self-containment, and the bruised expression in her eyes, as if expecting the worst at any moment.

Christo fixed her with a hard stare, as if daring her to go on. For answer she simply stared back.

Finally he sighed and shoved his hands deep in his trouser pockets. 'It's as well you know.' He paused and paced away, as if too restless to stand still. 'Anthea was living with her mother, my stepsister, in the USA.'

'Not in Greece?' But then that would explain why Anthea had responded easily when Emma had spoken to her in English.

'My stepmother and stepsister were American. It was decided Greece didn't suit my stepsister.' To Emma's astonishment, she saw Christo's mouth work, tugging down in a grimace before flattening into a grim line.

Her curiosity rose. She was about to ask what that meant when Christo continued. 'She went to live with relatives in the States.'

'Instead of staying with her mother and your father?' It seemed odd.

'Yes.' His tone put off further questions. 'She lived there till she died recently. Sadly, it wasn't a settled life. She was...troubled.' There it was again, that slight hesitation that made Emma more rather than less curious about his choice of words.

'Put plainly, she became addicted to drugs and alcohol. As far as I can tell, she never lived with Anthea's father, whoever he was.'

'You weren't in contact with her?'

Christo shook his head and turned to survey the villa through the trees. Was it her imagination or did he deliberately avoid her eyes?

'I only ever saw her once, years ago. I never heard from

her after she left.' He opened his mouth then closed it again. Had he been going to add something?

Emma pushed the idea aside. The issue now was Anthea, not Christo's relationship with her mother.

'Anthea lived with an addict?' Her heart sank as she imagined the sort of life the little girl had experienced.

Christo nodded, the movement abrupt. 'They moved a lot and I suspect she was neglected.'

Emma looked at that hard face, the profile made severe by tension, and realised that behind the adamantine stillness of his features Christo was distressed.

It made him suddenly, unexpectedly, human.

A flurry of warmth rushed through her. An unwanted stirring of sympathy.

She'd thought of him as a liar and a cheat. Seeing evidence of a softer side was unsettling.

'I should have followed up. I shouldn't have assumed she was okay.' The words were so quiet they melded with the sigh of the breeze through the silvered olive leaves.

Emma was puzzled. She'd assumed Christo and his stepsister had been young when they'd met. That Christo hadn't been responsible for her.

He turned back, those dark blue eyes searing in their intensity. 'Anthea hasn't had the advantage of a stable home or family. That's one of the reasons I want her settled with someone who can nurture her.'

Emma, in other words.

Indignation stirred anew. She wasn't some mail-order bride to be brought in to fill a gap. Yet her anger was muffled this time by the story she'd heard.

She understood Christo's desire to look after his niece. She even applauded it. Except for the ruthless way he'd lied to her, making her believe he wanted *her*.

'In that case, you need an excellent nanny. You can't rely on me long term.'

To her surprise, Christo inclined his head. 'Before you arrived I was debating whether to dismiss this nanny immediately. But that would leave you in the lurch when I go back to Athens.'

'You were concerned about me?' His consideration surprised her. Hadn't he acquired her for that very purpose?

Familiar hurt jabbed her. That was all she was to him, a convenient business acquisition, bringing him property and the mothering he wanted for Anthea. Even his demand for sex had been an afterthought, driven by annoyance that she'd defied him. She knew one thing for sure. She wasn't his type.

'Of course.' His gaze held hers. 'I never expected just to foist Anthea onto you. It would be unreasonable to expect you to care for her twenty-four hours a day. As my wife, you'll have other things to do with your time. And Dora is already busy enough.'

For a moment there Emma had actually started to warm to Christo. Until the reference to her being his wife. As if she had no other purpose in life.

'Actually, I'm going to be busy setting up my business. I won't have time for much else.'

Those penetrating eyes surveyed her for silent seconds and Emma wondered what he read in her face.

'All the more reason to find reliable help for Anthea.' Emma couldn't argue with that. 'The difficulty is that when I dismiss this nanny it will take time to find someone suitable.'

'You could look after her yourself.'

Black eyebrows winged up that broad forehead. 'I'm many things, Emma, but experienced in caring for traumatised children isn't one of them. Even if I trashed my schedule for the next several weeks to be with her, I wouldn't be suitable.'

'It's not a matter of being suitable. It's about providing warmth and love.'

Christo didn't answer. Didn't so much as blink.

He was right, Emma realised with icy clarity. Christo didn't do love. Little Anthea needed more than he could provide.

'Don't sack the woman. Give her another chance.' She surprised herself with the words.

'Are you serious?'

'You said yourself that she did a good job before. Maybe today was an aberration she's already regretting. We all make mistakes.'

Emma should know. This man had been the biggest mistake of her life. She knew how he could turn a woman's head.

'I could put her on notice. Spell out the boundaries to her,' he said slowly, as if thinking through Emma's suggestion. 'After all, she's the only one of us that Anthea has known for more than a couple of hours.'

'In that case, definitely give her a second chance. For Anthea's sake.'

He frowned. 'We'll have to keep a close eye on the situation. I won't allow Anthea to be neglected again.'

Did he notice that he'd said 'we'? It sounded as if he intended to take an active role in monitoring the situation. Perhaps he wasn't as cold-hearted as he seemed.

'If she doesn't live up to expectations, you can hire someone else. You could even tell your recruitment people that you may need a replacement if this one doesn't work out so they can check their books.'

'This time I'll vet the applicants personally.' Christo nodded. 'Thanks, Emma. It's a good, practical suggestion.'

Suddenly he smiled, a grin that transformed his features from sombre to breathtakingly attractive. It made Emma's pulse trip and stumble, then continue erratically.

'See how well we work together when we try? It just proves how perfectly matched we are.'

CHAPTER SIX

PERFECTLY MATCHED!

How dared Christo pretend they were any such thing?

Emma lay on her bed, fuming. No matter how she'd tried, she hadn't been able to sleep.

To her dismay she'd shared dinner alone with Christo. Anthea was too little to stay up and, after an interview with Christo, her nanny had elected to stay and watch over her. Dora had refused, point blank, to break a lifetime's habit and join them in the dining room.

Christo had been all easy charm, reminding her of their courtship in Australia. He'd complimented Emma on the villa and won Dora over with praise of her food and her home-made kumquat liqueur. It was hard to believe he was the same man who'd threatened blackmail to get Emma into his bed.

But she'd been taken in by him before. She refused to fall for that charade again. He might seem considerate but beneath lay a heart as cold as a steel trap.

Except where his niece was concerned. And, Emma suspected, his stepsister. There'd been something about his expression when he'd spoken of her...

Emma rolled her eyes, disgusted at her eagerness to find good in the man. She turned over and punched her pillow, trying to get comfortable.

It was impossible. Christo Karides kept invading her brain. It was bad enough when he'd been in another country, or on the mainland. Having him under the same roof made her edgy.

She told herself she felt indignant at him making himself at home, as if he were an invited guest instead of an unwanted husband.

There it was again. That shudder of repugnance at the word 'husband'.

But Emma was always brutally honest with herself, even if she'd spent years smoothing over prickly issues with her *papou*. That wasn't all she felt. There was a sliver of something else.

It had been satisfying this afternoon, discussing Anthea and her needs with him, hearing his thoughts and having him take her input seriously. That reminded her of their time in Melbourne, when he'd been not only solicitous but interested. She'd thought that had all been false. Now she wondered.

Emma bit her lip. She was going around in circles. She couldn't trust Christo Karides. The truly unnerving thing was that, despite everything, part of her wanted to.

On a surge of impatience, she flung back the covers and got up, grabbing the robe from the bottom of the bed.

Her mouth twisted as she put it on and cinched it around her waist. Steph had helped her choose it, and the matching nightgown of champagne silk and gossamer-fine lace for her trousseau. Emma had never owned anything like them in her life.

She'd imagined wearing this on her wedding night. Imagined Christo peeling it off as he kissed her in places she'd never been kissed before.

The thought raised gooseflesh on her skin, from her thighs to her hips and abdomen.

Spinning on her heel, Emma marched across the room and wrenched open the door to the balcony. She needed to think about something other than Christo. She'd count stars. That would keep her busy for the next hour or two.

There wasn't much moon and as the village was around the headland there was no light pollution. Just the inky-dark sky, the sigh of the sea and thousands upon thousands of stars.

Emma crossed to the railing and breathed deep. Funny that she'd never realised how much she missed this place till she returned. The scent of the sea was so evocative, mingling with the perfume of blossom and something else she couldn't name. A spicy aroma that tugged a cord low in her belly. She closed her eyes and inhaled through her nose, her brow crinkling in concentration. It was tantalisingly familiar and deeply attractive. She just couldn't place it.

'Hello, Emma.' Christo's voice, warm as melted chocolate, enveloped her. 'Couldn't sleep?'

She spun, one hand grabbing the railing for support, the other automatically closing the neck of her robe.

He stood a little way along the balcony. The private balcony accessed only by the master suite and one extra room where Papou had occasionally slept when Grandma had been ill and easily disturbed.

Emma blinked, but he was still there. Christo Karides, looking as she'd never seen him before. The light was too dim to read his expression but there was still a lot to see. A lot of naked flesh. He wore only loose, low-slung trousers that rode his hips and looked on the verge of sliding down long, hard thighs.

She swallowed abruptly and yanked her gaze up. But there was his bare torso. The starlight picked out sculpted lines and curves that spoke of power and pure eroticism.

He looked wonderful fully clothed. But half-naked, he was stunning. She'd dreamed of him nude so often but it was a shock to discover how compelling the sight of that bare body was. How it smashed through her anger and drilled down to the burning truth within her. That physically, at least, she'd never stopped craving this man. Even the rounded angles, from shoulders to arms and the symmetry of that tall, muscular frame, were too much.

Emma's breath disintegrated in an audible sigh and she swung away to stare at the sea. But her precarious calm was gone. She heard nothing over her pulse's catapulting rhythm.

And the tiny voice in her brain that spoke of want.

'What are you doing here?' She turned her head in his general direction, but not far enough to see him. This blast of weakness was too appalling. She refused to feed it.

'Like you, I had trouble sleeping.' He paused but only for a fraction. 'Perhaps we should find something to do together that will tire us out.'

Emma ignored the amusement in his tone and the blatant innuendo. That didn't deserve an answer.

But she couldn't ignore the unnerving hollow ache low in her body. Or the spiralling heat. It was as if at twenty-two her body had suddenly lost all connection with her brain, or with that part of it devoted to rational thought. She despised this man. She never wanted to see him again. But her long-dormant libido hadn't got the message yet. Once roused by him, it was still alive and eager.

'I mean, what are you doing here, in this part of the house? We prepared a different suite for you.'

'And it was charming. But totally unsuitable.'

Emma was on the point of swinging round to look at him when she changed her mind. Instead she anchored her fingers on the decorative ironwork railing and clenched her teeth.

'Why?'

'Because I asked Dora where your room was and told her I wanted to be next door. I refuse to sleep in the wing furthest from my wife. As you said, we have a relationship to forge.'

'I was talking about you and Anthea.' Her fingers tightened till they felt numb.

'Us too, Emma.' His voice slid easily to that *faux* intimate note that in the past had drawn her in so easily. The note that she'd innocently thought signalled genuine caring. She knew better now.

'There's no need for that. It's a marriage in name only and it will last just twelve months.'

'You know that's not true. You know there's more between us.'

Unable to contain herself, she spun round to face him. He'd moved closer, so close she could almost touch him. She jerked her gaze up and caught the glitter in his eyes.

'There won't be anything more. I'm not signing that contract.'

Slowly, annoyingly, he shook his head. 'I wasn't talking about the contract. I was talking about the fact that we want each other.'

'Not any more.' Emma curled her fingers, fighting the restless urge to reach out.

'Liar.' It was the merest whisper yet the accusation tolled through her body like a chiming bell.

He was right. That was the horrible truth.

Here in the intimate darkness, Emma felt the thousand proofs of it. The thrust of her pebbled nipples against the silk of her nightgown. The way that fine fabric grazed her bare flesh as if every nerve ending was suddenly too sensitive. The liquid heat between her legs. The edginess that made her want to shift and wriggle and, worse, press herself up against that hard body and discover how it would feel to…

'I don't want you, Christo.' It was the first bald-faced lie she could remember telling. But she refused to let him think she was so pathetic.

'Really?' He didn't sound at all dismayed. 'I could prove you wrong.' He shifted his weight, as if to step nearer, and Emma's heart leapt.

'No closer!' Emma flung her arm up, palm out. It took

everything she had to draw air into her lungs and find her voice but she did it. She'd learn to resist him if it killed her. 'I don't want to go to bed with you.'

Could he hear the lie?

At least he didn't move closer. In fact, to her astonishment, he turned and leaned his weight on the balustrade, looking out to sea. Her gaze roved his profile, from that strong nose to the hard angle of his jaw and up to the dark hair that looked rumpled, as if he'd dragged his hands through it.

Christo in a suit had been handsome. Christo pared back to basics and ever so slightly dishevelled made Emma's belly squeeze in longing.

Abruptly she turned away, sucking in a deep breath and placing her hands on the same railing.

'Don't look so scared. I told you I'd never force a woman. I'll wait till you come to me.'

She opened her mouth, to say that would never happen, then closed it again. The words would wash off him like water off a rock. She'd just have to demonstrate she meant what she said.

'So you don't want a contract now?' He sounded mildly curious, as if the issue of her sleeping with him was only of minor interest.

That, surely, would feed her determination? She'd never been brash or loud, demanding attention, but he'd already made her feel insignificant and taken for granted. She refused to settle for that.

'I don't want *that* contract.'

'Ah. But you still want everything else.'

'"Everything else" being property that's mine by right.' Adrenalin pumped through her blood. 'Or should have been if you hadn't inveigled your way into my grandfather's trust.'

How a wily businessman like Papou had been taken in

by Christo Karides, Emma would never understand. His health might have been failing but his mind had been sharp right till the end. It was he who'd warned her uncle that he'd over-extended, expanding his construction business so rapidly.

'Tell me about this place.' Christo's low voice drew her back to the present.

Instantly Emma stiffened as suspicion reared. 'Why do you want to know? I thought your company handled commercial property. Isn't that where you invest?'

'Relax. I only want to know because it's important to you. I heard it in your voice when you talked about it in Australia.' He paused. 'And you seem different here.'

She frowned. 'Different?'

'More assured. More confident.'

Emma shook her head and, standing straighter, turned to face her nemesis. 'I'm the same woman I always was. Nothing's changed.' Except she'd lost the last person she held dear. 'You were looking for a quiet mouse so you believed everything Papou told you about me.' Maybe *this* time he'd believe her.

'And your grandfather didn't get it right?' Instead of sounding annoyed, Christo's tone was merely curious.

She shrugged. 'He thought I was more delicate than I am.' Emma paused, wondering how much to share. But maybe this would convince Christo he was mistaken in thinking she could ever be the sort of wife he wanted. 'I had asthma badly as a kid and I was on the small side. Even though I grew out of the asthma, Papou never quite believed it. He was over-protective. He used to worry, so I learned not to confront him over things that didn't matter.'

Which had led to her taking the path of least resistance a lot of the time. Maybe if she'd stood up to him more often he wouldn't have persuaded Christo that she'd make the perfect homebody.

'I'm not a dutiful doormat.'

'So I've discovered.' Was that approval in his voice? She had to be imagining it. 'Now, about the villa…'

Emma stared up into that bold, shadowy face and wondered why he really wanted to know. On the other hand, talking with Christo was better than fighting him. Even with right on her side she found that unsettling.

She'd never enjoyed confrontation, but arguing with him was simultaneously frustrating and—Emma hated to admit it—exhilarating. As if the pulse of energy between them gave her a rush she'd never experienced before.

That was just plain crazy.

Finding her gaze straying down to those broad, straight shoulders and the muscled body limned by starlight, Emma swung away. She planted her palms on the railing and fixed her eyes on the view.

Which wasn't nearly as fascinating as the view of the man standing beside her.

She closed her eyes, willing herself to find the resolve she needed to pretend he didn't affect her.

Yet when she spoke her voice had a hoarse edge that she feared betrayed her. 'My grandparents met on Corfu. Papou had come back for a friend's wedding and my grandmother was on holiday from Australia. After a week, they were engaged. Three months later they were married.'

'Your grandfather was a decisive man.'

'Love at first sight is a family tradition. My aunt and uncle married after four months and my parents after two.' Emma snapped her mouth shut, belatedly seeing the connection to her own disastrous wedding. She'd fallen for Christo in record time. Because she genuinely believed in him, or because she'd been programmed to think love at first sight was utterly reasonable?

Now she knew to her cost how perilous that illusion was.

'And your grandfather owned this place?'

'It was his grandfather's.' She opened her eyes to survey the familiar coastline, the fragrant garden and behind it the silvery sweep of olive trees rising up the slope towards the hills. 'My grandmother adored it from the moment he brought her here. She was a horticulturalist and loved seeing what she could grow.'

'So they lived here.'

Emma shook her head. 'Only for a short time. Mainly they lived in Athens, then Australia. Papou was a businessman with interests on the mainland. In those days telecommuting wasn't an option. But this was always their favourite place. They'd come here several times a year. Even when they moved to Australia they came back regularly. We all did.'

'It had sentimental value, then.' He paused. 'For you too.'

Silently she nodded, surprised at the understanding in Christo's voice. She couldn't believe he had a sentimental bone in his body. Some of her happiest memories centred around this place. Of those precious years before her parents died. Of course there were other memories of them, of their day-to-day lives in Australia, but here at the villa there'd always been more time together as a family. Time Emma treasured.

She drew a breath and made herself focus on the present. 'It's a nice old place.' She wouldn't admit exactly how much it meant to her. Who knew how Christo would try to use that to his advantage? 'It's also an asset I can use to support myself.'

'Because you're determined to be independent.' His tone was non-committal but Emma heard the question.

'That's always been the plan.' Though she hadn't originally envisaged herself building a business here, in Greece. 'I've got a degree in business and event management. Plus experience in the field.' Okay, it was part-time experience, first with a major event organiser and later with a small but up-and-coming wedding planner. But full-time work had been impossible while she studied and looked after Papou. 'Of course I'll work.'

'Some would say marrying a wealthy man is a great career move. You need never lift a finger to support yourself.'

Emma's breath sucked in so sharply, pain shafted behind her ribs to radiate out and fill her chest.

She swivelled to face him, outrage obliterating caution. 'You...' She was so furious, the words backed up in her throat. In frustration she pointed a finger at his chest. 'You...'

Warm fingers enclosed hers and a thread of fire traced from his touch along to her elbow, then up to her shoulder, making her quiver.

'You're accusing me of marrying you for money?' Finally the words poured out, high and harsh.

'It's not unknown.' Christo's voice was matter-of-fact. His utter lack of expression was fuel to the fire of her anger. Did he think she'd been on the *make*?

'My family might not be as wealthy as yours, but we're not stony broke. At least, we weren't, before you weaselled your way into my grandfather's good graces.' For now Christo controlled her assets. 'But even if I didn't have a cent to my name—' scarily, she wasn't too far off that now '—I would never marry a man just to get his money.'

Vaguely Emma was aware of heat encasing her fingers as his big hand surrounded hers. But she was more concerned with convincing Christo he was utterly wrong about her.

'What proof have you got?' His tone was infuriatingly calm. 'Women do it all the time.'

That, Emma realised with a jolt, was the second time he'd referred to women cold-bloodedly targeting men as meal tickets. Suddenly she had a glimpse of the down side of being a mega-wealthy bachelor. Christo would never know how much of his appeal was down to his bank balance.

Tough! That didn't give him the right to use her for his convenience. Or accuse her of being a liar.

'Well, I don't. *I* didn't come looking for *you*, Christo Karides. *I* didn't deliberately set out to con you into marriage.' That had been him, targeting her and playing up to her hopes and vulnerabilities.

'So, if you didn't marry me for my money...' his words were slow and warm, like sun-drenched honey dropping onto her skin '...why *did* you marry me, Emma?'

It was only as the darkness pulsed between them and the silence grew heavy with waiting that Emma recognised his trap. To tell the truth meant admitting that she'd fallen in love with him. Or at least fallen for the mirage of love.

'This conversation's getting us nowhere. That's in the past and—'

'On the contrary, this conversation is just getting interesting.' He lowered his head, as if trying to read her face in the darkness. 'Tell me why you married me, Emma.'

That voice, honey now mixed with rumbling gravel, scraped through her insides. But, instead of leaving painful grazes, it stirred something altogether unwanted. Something she needed to banish. If only she knew how!

Suddenly she realised the danger of being this close to him. Of his flesh on hers. 'I want to go inside.'

'Could it be,' he went on as if she hadn't spoken, 'Because of *this*...?'

He tugged her hand, pulling her against him. Emma's hissed breath was loud as she planted her other palm on his chest to push him away.

But before she could he'd raised her captured hand to his face and pressed his lips to her palm. She felt surprisingly soft lips and the delicious abrasion of his hair-roughened jaw, a reminder of his masculinity, as if she needed it!

Instantly sensation juddered through her.

Desire.

Delight.

Weakness.

Shivers reverberated through her and Emma knew she had to fight this. But then Christo moved, bending lower to kiss the sensitive flesh of her wrist, creating a shower of sparks in her blood.

The trouble was Emma had so little experience. There'd been a guy at university when she'd been eighteen but that had never progressed beyond a few kisses, because her grandmother had died and suddenly, more than ever, she'd been needed at home. She had no experience withstanding such powerfully erotic caresses. Or the demands of her own body, finally woken after so long.

Firming her mouth, she pushed that unyielding chest with her free hand. It made no impact.

Or perhaps she didn't push very hard. For now Christo was kissing his way along the bare flesh of her forearm where the wide sleeve of her robe fell back.

His grip wasn't tight. She could yank her hand free. If only she could find the willpower to do it.

But, oh, the lush sensations spreading from those tiny yet incredibly intimate kisses.

Her breath sawed and in her ears blood rushed helter-skelter.

He'd reached her elbow and she stiffened like a yacht's sail snapping taut in the wind. Taut but trembling too, at the sensations he evoked. Her hand on his chest no longer pushed. Instead it splayed, fingers wide, absorbing the sultry heat of his hard chest and the teasing friction of the smudge of dark hair on his pectorals.

'Stop that now.' Because, heaven help her, she couldn't. 'I'm not sleeping with you, Christo.'

That caught his attention. He looked up and even in the

gloom she caught the brilliance of his eyes as he looked down at her. Then, without uttering a word, he put his mouth to her arm and slowly licked her inner elbow.

Emma's knees all but gave way as a frighteningly potent shot of lust punched her. She made a sound, a soft, keening noise that she wouldn't have thought possible if she hadn't heard it slide from her lips.

She cleared her throat, ready to demand he release her, when she felt the scrape of teeth nipping the soft flesh in the crease of her elbow. Then almost immediately the strong draw against her skin as he sucked the spot.

Emma bit down hard on her lip to prevent a groan escaping into the night. She'd had no idea something as ordinary as an elbow could be so sensitive. That it could make her feel...

Ready for sex. That was how she felt. With her trembling limbs and that pulsing point down between her thighs that urged her to move closer to Christo. There was an aching hollowness inside and her breasts seemed fuller than before, eager for contact, her nipples impossibly hard. If she followed that animal instinct she would rub herself against him, purring and pleading for follow through.

Her own weakness terrified her.

'I said I don't want to go to bed with you.' Her voice was too loud and too wobbly.

For answer he released her hand which wavered uselessly in the air then slowly dropped to her side. Instead of moving back he stroked his fingertips over her cheek. All she had to do was pull her head back a couple of centimetres to sever the contact but she couldn't do it. Instead she stood as if mesmerised by the caress of long, hard fingers that worked magic with each touch.

'I don't believe you.'

Why should he?

That was what terrified her. Not Christo's practised seduction but the fact that, after all he'd done, she still had no defences against him, or more precisely against her wilful body's craving for satisfaction.

The breath shuddered through her lungs. She felt herself sway, but managed to pull back at the last moment.

Christo followed.

Emma felt his warm breath on her cheek, the heat of his frame close to hers. She dragged in that leather, wood and male spice scent that made something inside her fizz like champagne bubbles.

Then those warm lips brushed her jaw. So lightly she almost wondered if she'd imagined it. But there was no mistaking the scorching trail of heat curling from her chin to her ear and then along to her mouth.

Emma had stopped breathing, stopped thinking. Her hands pressed to Christo's bare body which was part of the spell he wove. His smooth flesh and springy muscle invited exploration.

He kissed his way to the corner of her mouth then paused, hovering half a breath away.

Her lips tingled with want as she waited for him to kiss her properly. Not as he'd kissed her in the church, just a brief salutation to satisfy custom. Not as he'd kissed her when they'd got engaged, tenderly but too short and too chaste.

What Emma wanted, what she craved, was full-blown passion. She wanted to fall into that whirlwind of rapture she'd read about, and that her body assured her was waiting for her if she'd just let go and give herself to Christo.

She might detest him but she had no doubt he could allay the terrible gnawing hunger inside. The hunger *he'd* created. All she had to do was…

'Say it, Emma. Invite me into your bed. You're aching for me. I'll make it good for you.'

Of course he would.

But then, afterwards, what about her self-respect?

How could she hold her head up?

She'd let this man sweep her off her feet into a hazy romantic cloud that had about as much link to reality as unicorns prancing along the white sand of the beach below.

Seconds later Emma found herself in the doorway to her room, hands braced as if to stop herself reaching for Christo. She couldn't remember telling herself to step back. It must have been some primal survival instinct so deeply buried as to be almost automatic.

For there was no doubt now that Christo was the most dangerous man she'd ever met. He wasn't just cunning and ruthless, he'd introduced her to desire, and now her frustrated body had imprinted on him as the one man who could satisfy her.

It was ludicrous and appalling.

It scared her witless.

She grabbed the handle of the French door.

'I don't want you. I'll never want you.'

He stood, arms folded, watching as she tugged the door closed. In the instant before it snicked shut, she heard his voice, soft, deep and, oh, so sure.

'We both know that's a lie, Emma. But take your time. When we finally have sex it will be worth the wait.'

CHAPTER SEVEN

CHRISTO PULLED HARD through the water, forcing his body to the limit in an effort to weary himself. Anything to douse the frustration that had him wound so tight.

How had he ever thought winning Emma over would be simple? She had more determination, more sheer obstinacy, than any negotiator he'd ever confronted.

Her insistence on resisting him, despite the fact she clearly wanted him, was infuriating. He told himself if it weren't for the fact he was committed to her he'd walk away.

Christo had given her more than he'd ever given any woman. His name, his word, his promise for the future. Yet she looked at him with those glittering hazel eyes as if he were the devil incarnate.

Christo gritted his teeth and quickened his stroke till his shoulders and legs ached and his lungs were ready to burst.

Treading water, he hauled in a needy gulp of air and turned. In the distance the villa nestled into the curve of the bay, gracious and charming.

He'd thought Emma was just like that too, a mix of gentle ways and unobtrusive prettiness. An easy fit for his needs.

His harsh laugh echoed across the water.

Easy!

Anyone less easy he had yet to meet.

Oh, she certainly did her best to avoid direct confrontation. These last three weekends, whenever he'd arrived from Athens, she'd been the perfect hostess.

Christo ground his teeth. It was true he'd wanted a woman who could do him proud when entertaining, but it was something far more personal he wanted from her.

Far more personal. Despite the cool water and his fatigue after the sprint swim, he still felt that frustration low in his body.

Three weeks! He couldn't believe she'd held out for three weeks. He'd thought she'd break by now. For, try as she might, she couldn't hide her desire for him.

That first night here he'd almost had her in his arms and in his bed. She'd been like a fragrant summer rosebud, unfurling into his hand, velvet-soft and exquisite. His groin throbbed at the memory. But his little bride had an unexpectedly thorny resolve. Besides, he'd given his word. He'd promised to wait till she was ready.

The taut weight in his lower body testified to the toll his self-imposed patience was taking on him.

At least in one area she'd lived up to expectations. Her relationship with Anthea. Whenever he saw them together the brittle aura of containment around his niece chipped a little more. As for Emma, her policy of not getting involved had lasted about two seconds. Increasingly Anthea turned to Emma rather than the nanny paid to care for her.

Despite her obstinacy, Emma had a soft side. She was ruled by emotions. Plus she suffered from the same sexual frustration he did.

Christo's mouth curled up. All he had to do was take advantage of the opportunities that arose. Ignore his pride and chagrin that she hadn't already come to him and *make* those opportunities happen. Remind her again of the unfulfilled desire sizzling between them.

He lowered his head and began a steady overarm stroke towards the shore.

Half an hour later, a towel slung over his shoulder and his body warm from the sun, he strolled up the path from the cove and through the garden. A fat bee droned in the sunshine and the smell of roses caught his nostrils.

The irony of it didn't escape him. The drowsing villa

with its secluded garden and scented roses might have been Sleeping Beauty's bower. Somewhere inside was Emma, his bride, waiting to be woken by his touch.

She'd never admitted it but he suspected she was a virgin. Those tell-tale blushes and the slight clumsiness of her kisses had raised his suspicions. Which was one of the reasons he hadn't pressed her too hard.

Once they were lovers, once they'd shared intimate physical pleasure, he knew there'd be no more holding back.

He rounded a corner and stopped. It seemed his imagination was more accurate than he'd suspected. For there was Sleeping Beauty herself.

Emma lay fast asleep on a sun lounger.

His gaze tracked her from her honey-toned hair splayed around her shoulders to her bare feet. Afternoon sun gilded her toned legs where her lacy white skirt rucked up high above her knees. Christo's pulse quickened and his throat dried as he imagined exploring that satiny skin.

With each gentle breath her breasts swelled up against the vivid red of her sleeveless top, riveting his attention.

Even in sleep she was more striking than she'd been in Australia.

Because of her bright clothes? Or because he'd begun to appreciate she was far more than the docile bride he'd assumed?

A couple of children's books were tumbled across her lap, making her look as if she hadn't intended to fall asleep.

That was when he saw movement beside her and stiffened. At the same moment little Anthea, who'd been sitting on the flagstones half-hidden by the sun lounger, looked up.

Big brown eyes met his and Christo felt again that stifling sensation in his chest. It was as if the years scrolled back and he was looking into the wary eyes of his new stepsister, Cassie. Cassie had been older, almost a teenager, yet those eyes were the same. And so was the suffocating shadow of guilt that chilled his belly.

He hadn't been able to help Cassie all those years ago. In fact his casual attempt at kindness to the nervous little girl had backfired spectacularly. Because of him her whole future had been blighted. Was it any wonder he found it difficult being with Anthea? She might be tiny, but she was so like Cassie he couldn't look at her without remembering.

Christo waited for Anthea to turn away as she usually did. Proof again that he'd done the right thing organising a new mother and a nanny to care for her, since patently he wasn't cut out for it.

To his surprise, instead of shrinking back, his step-niece took her time frowning down at something she held then looked up at him again. Her eyes were bright and her look trembled between excited and tentative. As if she wanted to share with him but was afraid of being rebuffed.

Slowly she lifted a large piece of paper for him to see. It was covered in green crayon scrawls.

Christo felt something give deep in his chest, like a knot suddenly loosening, cutting the tension that stiffened his body. His breath drifted out, making him realise he'd been holding it.

He told himself he should leave her be, simply walk away. For he knew, even if she didn't, that he wasn't the person she needed.

But her expression, turning now from expectation to disappointment at his lack of response, slashed through his caution.

How could he resist?

He padded barefoot across the warm flagstones to Anthea. Her brow wrinkled in concentration as she tilted her head up to look at him.

Christo's heart gave an unsteady thump. How his business competitors would laugh if they could see him now, scared of a little girl, or more precisely of somehow doing the wrong thing for her. He didn't know children. He had virtually no experience of them. And the one time he'd actually bonded with one it had ended in disaster.

Breathing deep through his nostrils, he hunkered down before her. It was a relief to look away from that intense brown stare and focus on her drawing.

Amongst the swirl of circles he discovered four downward strokes that might have been legs. 'You drew this?' he said, buying time. He still hadn't a clue what it was.

Gravely Anthea nodded, watching expectantly.

Christo frowned, his brain racing. Clearly she expected more.

'It's very good.' Did he sound as stilted as he feared?

'Nice dat.' They were the first words Anthea had spoken directly to him and he should have celebrated this sign of thawing, except he had no idea what she meant.

Till she lifted one dimpled hand and pointed. 'Dat.'

Christo followed her hand and saw a white cat stretched out in the shade of a tree, one ear twitching, as if following their conversation. He looked back at the drawing and enlightenment dawned. There, he spied two triangles that might have been feline ears and a curling line that could be a tail.

'You drew the cat?'

She nodded emphatically.

'Do you like cats?'

Another nod.

Now what? Clearly he was meant to contribute more.

Briefly Christo thought of the work he could be doing, the calls he should make. Of waking Emma or rousting out Anthea's nanny to take over.

Was he really so craven?

'Would you like me to draw a cat for you?' He wasn't consciously aware of forming the words but suddenly they were out and she was nodding again, a hint of a smile curving her mouth. Warmth trickled through Christo's chest.

He settled more comfortably on the flagstones and took the drawing she held out. But, instead of turning it over and drawing on the back of it, he chose a purple crayon from those scattered nearby and wrote her name on one corner, sounding out the letters as he went.

'There, now everyone will know it's yours.'

Fascinated, Anthea traced the letters with her finger, one dark plait falling forward and brushing his arm. It seemed she'd forgotten to be wary of him.

'Now you.' She pointed to the blank pages nearby. 'A dat.'

Once more Christo was rocked by a moment of déjà vu. It had been years since he'd drawn. Since that weekend when he'd amused his shy young stepsister with sketches and cartoons to make her smile. In those days drawing—or doodling, as his father had scathingly called it—had been a habit. A hobby that had distracted him from the pressures of his father's demands and their uncomfortable family life.

But not after that weekend.

Christo swallowed the sour tang of bile as old memories stirred. Setting his jaw, he shoved all that aside. It was over, dead and buried.

He took a sheet, glanced at the cat, now sitting up watching them, and began to draw.

At his side, Anthea watched, apparently entranced, as a few swift lines became a cat half-asleep in the sun. Another couple of lines and the cat was dozing over a book that looked rather like the picture book beside Anthea's stack of crayons.

Christo heard a childish giggle and added a striped sun umbrella similar to the one behind Emma. Anthea giggled again but shook her head when he went to give it to her.

'Put your name.'

This conversation was the most she'd ever said to him

and it felt like a victory. Not that he had any illusions about ever being particularly close to Anthea. She'd already bonded with Emma and that relationship would strengthen with time.

Christo would provide a comfortable home, protection and support, but as for being a close father figure... He shook his head even as he wrote his name in clear letters for Anthea.

He'd never known love from either of his parents. To one he'd been a convenience and to the other something to be moulded into the perfect heir to the Karides commercial empire. The heir to a man who married trophy wives and expected his son to be as ruthless and successful as he.

Christo's lips twisted in a shadow of a smile as he thought how proud the old man would be if he were still alive. For Christo was far more successful than his father had ever been, having expanded the family business to a completely new level. As for ruthless—he'd always tried to be more humanitarian than his father. But when the pressure was on, when he really needed something, like a mother for Anthea, it turned out he was every bit as unrelenting as the old man.

The knowledge was a cold, hard lump in his belly.

He ignored it, for there was no point pining over things that could never change. Instead he leaned over the paper and concentrated on a new drawing for his eager audience.

Emma drifted out of her doze to the sound of Anthea's excited voice. She heard another voice answer, a deep, reassuring blur of sound that soothed her back towards slumber.

Blearily Emma tried to summon the strength to move, fighting the fog that enveloped her. She never napped during the day but last night, knowing Christo was in the room next to hers, she'd been unable to sleep.

It was like that each weekend when he returned to the island. In the beginning she'd wondered if he'd break his word, try to 'persuade' her into his bed. But as the days and nights had passed and he'd kept his word that fear had subsided.

Yet she was still on tenterhooks.

Because it's not Christo you're afraid of.

It was herself. She hadn't yet been able to banish that simmering attraction she felt. The physical awareness whenever he was near. For, despite his promise to wait, Christo was often near, not crowding her or touching her, but *close*. She'd feel his stare and look up to discover she had little defence against the heat in his eyes. Inevitably answering need flared.

She told herself again and again he didn't really want *her*, except as a convenient child minder. But her besotted self, the one who'd once tumbled headlong into the romantic mirage he'd created, refused to listen.

Finally she forced her eyelids open to squint at the sunlight. She moved and the books on her lap slid sideways. Panic stirred. Anthea. Was she okay? Emma was supposed to be minding her while the nanny had her afternoon off.

'Dog now. *Pease.*'

Emma turned towards the little girl's voice and would have fallen off the lounge if she hadn't been lying down.

For there was big, bad Christo Karides, down on the pavement with his niece.

Emma blinked and rubbed her eyes, wondering if this was some hard-to-shake dream. But the image remained. The little girl in her shorts and T-shirt, looking up earnestly at the man beside her.

Christo Karides in nothing but damp, black swim shorts and acres of bare, muscled body, was spectacular. A shot of adrenalin hit Emma's blood, making her heart kick into a frantic rhythm. Ever since the night on her balcony she'd been haunted by thoughts of his body. But he looked even more impossibly delicious in broad daylight.

It struck her that for the first time he didn't wear the closed expression that usually clamped his features when he was around Anthea. He seemed at ease.

Almost. He leaned over a sheet of paper, his brow furrowed in concentration, his expression intent.

Moving slowly, not wanting to draw his attention, Emma sat higher to get a better view. What she saw held her spellbound. Using a crayon, Christo deftly sketched a couple of lines that turned into a whiskery, canine face wearing an almost comical expression of longing. A few more sure strokes and a body emerged with short legs and a curling tail. Finally he completed the picture by adding a large bone, almost as big as the dog, which explained the animal's hungry look.

He was good. Very good. The dog had such character, she could imagine it trotting around the corner of the villa, dragging that oversized bone with it.

Anthea laughed with delight, the sound as bright as sunshine. Emma's lips curved in response. The little girl was gradually relaxing here in Corfu and smiled more often. But she was still withdrawn and shy. Hearing her so exuberant was wonderful.

Emma shafted a curious glance back to Christo.

For once he wasn't aware of her scrutiny, focused instead on the girl beside him.

'More!' Anthea was so excited she knelt beside him, her tiny hands on one muscled knee as she leaned over to look at the drawing.

'Why don't you draw a friend for the dog?' He pushed the paper towards her and held out the crayon.

After a moment's consideration she nodded, her small fingers plucking the crayon from his broad palm.

Emma's chest squeezed at the sight of them together. It

wasn't that she was eager for a baby, but she *had* imagined
Christo as the father of her children some time in the future.
Had imagined those powerful arms cradling their baby.

Seeing him now, gentle and patient as Anthea scribbled
what looked like a woolly sheep across the rest of the page,
Emma couldn't prevent a pang of loss. Silly to pine for
a man who wasn't real. The Christo Karides she'd fallen
for was a façade, deliberately constructed to gull her into
marriage.

Yet, watching her husband, she couldn't help mourn-
ing the loss of what might have been. If only Christo had
been genuine.

'Tell me about what you've drawn,' Christo murmured.

''Nother dog. See?' Anthea leaned in, the tip of her
tongue showing between her teeth as she added another
figure, this time with an oversized head and stick legs.
'And me.' Another lop-sided figure appeared. 'And you.'

She sat back, beaming, and Emma had a perfect view of
Christo. His face changed, an expression of surprise and
pleasure making him look years younger than thirty-one. It
made her realise how often he looked older than he was—
still devastatingly attractive, but as if he carried an unseen
burden that kept him too serious. That was, she supposed,
what came of running a successful multinational company.

Then he seemed to collect himself. 'Wonderful! Should
we put in anything else?' He looked across the terrace to
where Dora's old cat watched them.

'Emma!' Anthea leaned across Christo, chose a blue
crayon and held it up. 'Put in Emma.'

At the little girl's words, he lifted his head, his gaze col-
liding with Emma's.

This time the impact wasn't so much a sizzle as an im-
mediate burst of ignition. Emma felt it like a whoosh of
flame exploding deep in her belly.

But now there was more too. For Anthea followed his

gaze and saw her awake. Immediately she grabbed the picture and brought it over, excitedly pointing out the dog and identifying the figures she'd added. As Emma smiled, nodded and praised the little girl, her gaze met Christo's in a shared look of understanding and pleasure. A mutual relief that Anthea was starting to come out of her shell.

Perhaps it was crazy, but to Emma it felt like a rare, precious moment of connection.

As if, for once, she and Christo were on the same side. As if their shared purpose in providing for Anthea drew them together.

As if they weren't really enemies.

Except thinking like that had got her into this mess in the first place.

The spell was broken as Anthea held out the paper to him. After a moment he took it. But, instead of adding another figure to the crowded page, he turned it over.

She watched, fascinated, as he began to draw. Random lines coalesced and separated. Shapes appeared, familiar features. When he was done Anthea clapped her hands.

'Nice Emma.' The little girl crooned the words and held the page up.

It was a remarkable piece, considering it was executed with a thick child's crayon on cheap paper. Christo really was talented. But what held Emma's attention was the unexpected beauty of what he'd drawn. Not merely that the portrait was well-executed and recognisable as her. But that, for the first time in her life, Emma *looked* beautiful.

Her brow crinkled. What had he done to make her appear different? It looked so like her and yet on the page she was...more.

'Beautiful Emma.' His words feathered across her bare arms and wound themselves down her spine.

'Hardly.' She lifted her eyes to his, angling her chin. 'There's no need to exaggerate.'

He didn't so much as blink. 'I never exaggerate.'

No. He just implied more than was true. Such as making out he cared for her to get her to agree to marry him.

Swinging her legs over the side of the lounger, Emma got up, belatedly catching the spill of Anthea's books.

'It's a lovely picture, Anthea, but I like the one you drew better. Perhaps you could make another one for me to keep while I go inside and work? I'm sure Christo would love to help you.'

She didn't even look at him, just waited to see Anthea happily settled down with another sheet of paper, then turned on her heel and headed indoors.

Christo could look after his niece for once. Emma needed to work on her plans if she was ever going to turn the villa into a viable business.

But it wasn't business on her mind as she walked away. It was that strange moment of connection she and Christo had shared over Anthea's head. The instance of common purpose and understanding. It had felt profound. Even now Emma felt its echo tremble through her, making her skin shiver and her insides warm.

Or perhaps, more dangerously, it was a reaction to Christo's assessing stare that she felt trawl down her body as she walked.

She told herself she imagined it, yet her step quickened. She needed to get inside. Away from the temptation to turn back and see if she'd imagined the spark of something new in Christo's eyes.

To Emma's surprise, he stayed with Anthea for the next hour. Whatever had held the little girl back from him earlier had vanished. Whenever Emma looked out—and, to her chagrin, that was often—the pair had their heads together, poring over drawings then Anthea's books.

She heard the deep murmur of Christo's voice, a rich

velvet counterpoint to Anthea's higher voice, and satisfaction stirred. In the couple of weeks Anthea had been there, Emma had grown fond of the girl. It was good to think that she was beginning to build a relationship with her only relative.

Curiosity stirred about that family. Emma sensed there was more to their story than the death of Anthea's mother. She recalled the dark edge to Christo's voice as he'd talked of his stepsister and couldn't douse her desire to know more.

Desire. There it was again. That word summed up too many of her feelings for Christo.

'Emma?' She jerked round to find the man himself in the doorway, still almost naked in black swim shorts. Why didn't he put on some clothes? Emma hated the way her heartbeat revved at the sight of all that bare, masculine flesh.

She looked past him but saw no sign of Anthea. Instantly she was on alert, hyperaware that her visceral response to him made her vulnerable. Emma tried to spend as little time as possible alone with Christo but somehow that never quite worked.

'Anthea is with Dora, having a snack.'

Had he read her nerves? The thought was intolerable. Emma got up from the desk where she'd been working on her business plan but Christo was already padding across the room towards her.

'We need to talk.'

Her brow pinched. His tone and his watchful expression told her she wasn't going to like this.

'About Anthea?' A couple of weeks ago her thoughts would have gone instantly to their tenuous marriage arrangement. Strange how even the outrageous could seem almost normal after a while.

'No.' He paused and she sensed he marshalled his words carefully. The idea sent a premonition of trouble skittering through her. 'About our marriage. The paparazzi has got hold of the story.'

Surely he'd been prepared for that? Christo had insisted on fencing the estate with high-tech security infrastructure to keep out trespassers. He'd been convinced news of their very private wedding would score media attention. When she'd protested he'd spoken of protecting her and Anthea, which had ended her arguments. The little girl had been through enough without being hunted by the press.

'Is that all? It had to happen some time.' The tension pinching Emma's shoulders eased.

Christo stopped so close, she saw herself in his eyes. She hitched a silent breath and shoved her hands into the pockets of her skirt.

'Unfortunately it's not just the wedding they know about. There are reports that you ran away before the honeymoon and that we've separated.'

Storm-dark eyes bored into her and Emma realised Christo had just received this news. The last three weeks he'd been annoyingly at ease while she'd fretted about their impossible relationship. Now he hadn't had time to bury his anger under a façade of calm.

'It's close enough to the truth.'

His mouth tightened. '*Not* the story we're going to give them.'

Emma frowned. 'Do we have to give them any story? Surely you don't have to comment? You're Christo Karides. I thought you were above worrying about gossip.'

'I will *not* be pilloried in public as a deserted husband, or as some sort of Bluebeard who frightened off his bride.'

Even if you did?

The words danced on Emma's tongue but she didn't say them. She read his implacable expression and knew there was no point saying it. It would only inflame the situation.

Papou had taught her that no Greek male worth his salt

would allow a slight to his masculinity. Being seen as an undesirable husband clearly fitted under that heading.

'You'll need to start wearing your rings.' His gaze dropped to her bare left hand.

Emma froze on the spot, remembering the day she'd last worn them. Her wedding day.

'That's not necessary. Besides,' she hurried on when he opened his mouth to speak, 'I can't. I left them in Melbourne.' She'd dragged off the dainty gold band and the enormous solitaire diamond and left them with Steph for safekeeping. The memory of that moment of disillusionment and despair left a rancid taste in her mouth.

Christo's eyes narrowed but instead of berating her he merely paused. 'They can be replaced.'

Which proved just how little those symbols of their vows to each other meant to him.

Emma swallowed, hating the scratchy sensation as her throat closed convulsively.

'Me wearing a wedding ring won't be enough to convince anyone all's well with our marriage.'

'Of course not.'

The look of calculation on his face made her nervous. Emma crossed her arms.

'So how are you going to convince everyone?'

Christo's mouth curled up in a slow smile that simultaneously set her hormones jangling and sent a cold chill across her nape.

'Not me. *We*.' He paused, watching her reaction. 'You're coming with me to Athens this week. Together we're going to present a united front as a pair of deliriously happy newlyweds.'

As Christo's words sank in, Emma realised two things. That he was utterly serious. And that it wasn't just determination she read in his face—it was anticipation.

CHAPTER EIGHT

EMMA PROTESTED. SHE flat out refused to go.

But Christo was as immovable as Mount Pantokrator looming imperiously over the island. He refused to countenance her refusal.

She'd been ready to fight him over his need to appear macho and perfect. The adoring public saw him as a shining light in difficult economic times, a beacon of hope for the future. Frankly she'd enjoy seeing him taken down a peg.

But to her chagrin he cut off her arguments quickly. His character and status were inseparable from the success of his company. Especially now he'd turned from his usual international focus to concentrate on a major redevelopment in Athens. Persuading investors to come in with him was tough when Greece still suffered hard economic times, but he was determined to contribute to a resurgence.

If it came out that she'd run from him, the scandal could undermine confidence in his character and decision-making. His business would be affected. So would the livelihoods of his employees and contractors. As would others who relied on his continued success. Like her uncle.

But if they gave the paparazzi opportunities to see them as a couple the press would soon shift to other stories.

The prospect of being hounded wherever she went chilled her blood. And Anthea would be caught in the media circus too. It was in everyone's interest to minimise gossip.

Which was how Emma found herself staring across the Athens skyline from Christo's penthouse. The silhouette of the Acropolis was reassuringly familiar, as was the distant bright metal shimmer of the sea in the early evening light.

Yet Christo's Athens bore little resemblance to hers.

First there'd been the private jet. Then the discreet security detail. Emma had been prepared for the plush limousine, but not to have it waved through a stationary traffic snarl by a policeman who'd all but saluted as they'd passed. Then the no-expenses-spared shopping trip which had made Emma's eyes bulge.

Now this. The expansive sitting room seemed all glass and marble against that multi-million-dollar backdrop.

Emma had been into luxurious homes, assisting with lavish celebrations. She knew quality, and this was it.

Everything spoke of wealth, but not ostentatiously. No over-gilded ornamentation or fussiness here. Just the best of the best, from the soft furnishings to the custom-made furniture and original art.

She wandered through the room, past a modern fireplace which was in itself a work of art, to stop before a wall hanging that turned out to be a traditionally woven rug in deep crimson and jewel colours. The richness of its tones and tactile weave drew her hand. But she didn't touch. It was probably worth a fortune.

Emma's pulse skipped. Speaking of fortunes...

The hand she'd raised dropped to the delicate fabric of her dress. She'd never worn a designer original.

Involuntarily her gaze darted to the mirror above the fireplace. A stranger looked back.

The sheen of dark green silk accentuated the dress's close fit. Emma blinked. The change wasn't just that, or her newly styled hair. Nor the prohibitively expensive shoes.

She tilted her head. Was it the subtle smokiness of her new eye make-up? Or the lustre of the almost nude lipstick she'd never have chosen on her own?

When Christo had mentioned shopping for clothes, Emma had wanted to refuse anything bought with his funds.

But she knew the importance of appearances. The casual

clothes she'd packed for her honeymoon would look rustic in a sophisticated city venue. She wanted to scotch the stories about their mismatched marriage, not add to them.

Yet she'd resented being foisted on a cousin of Damen, Christo's best friend, whom Christo had lined up to take her shopping. But for once her husband had been right. She'd needed someone like Clio, with an eye for fashion and experience navigating Athens' most exclusive boutiques.

To Emma's surprise the other woman, despite her dauntingly glamorous appearance, had proved to have an irreverent sense of humour, a warm heart plus an unerring eye. She…

Her thoughts skittered to a halt as footsteps sounded from the corridor. Firm, masculine footsteps.

Everything inside Emma stilled, except her fluttery pulse that beat shallow and fast, like a moth trapped against glass. She spun round, lifting her chin.

Christo was a tall figure in the shadows at the far edge of the room, his expression unreadable. Was it a trick of the light that made that firm jaw look tense?

The air surged with sudden energy, like a giant heartbeat. She felt her nerves quicken, waiting.

Till she realised this was all her reaction to Christo. Freshly shaven and wearing a made-to-measure tuxedo, he looked good enough to eat. Her mouth dried as her imagination detoured in that direction and she forced herself to concentrate.

Did he like what he saw?

Furiously she told herself it didn't matter whether he did or not. While she wouldn't adopt this look every day, *she* liked it. That was what mattered. And that she looked sophisticated enough to pass as the wife of Greece's sexiest billionaire.

Christo had refused to be made a laughing stock in public. But how much worse for her to be the woman everyone knew he'd married for convenience, not love?

The thought sent a judder of revulsion through her. Come hell or high water, she'd play her part in this masquerade. She refused to be a figure of pity.

Still Christo said nothing. That brooding silence got on her nerves.

She turned towards the lounge where she'd put the wispy wrap and tiny evening bag that matched her jewelled green shoes. 'Are you ready to go?'

'Unless you want a drink to fortify yourself?' Out of her peripheral vision she saw him step into the room.

'I'd rather have a clear head, thank you.' Emma felt the familiar knife-twist of pain in her middle. The pang of hurt that even now she couldn't kill her attraction to him.

'I have something for you.'

Emma turned sharply, alerted by a note of something she hadn't heard before in Christo's voice. She couldn't place it.

But she did recognise the flare of heat in those dark blue-grey eyes. A thrill shot past her guard to resonate deep within her core. Her fingers curled into her purse, digging like talons into the fragile silk.

'A gift?' Emma strove for an insouciant tone. She already wore a new wedding band and a stunning gold filigree and diamond engagement ring. The latter was beautiful but felt like a brand of ownership. 'Not divorce papers, by any chance?'

One coal black eyebrow rose in a look that should have been annoyingly superior but, in her flustered state, seemed appallingly sexy.

Emma shut her eyes, praying for strength. This physical infatuation was supposed to disintegrate the longer she was exposed to him, not intensify.

'Emma?' The low burr of his voice rippled to her womb.

Opening her eyes, she fixed her gaze near his bow tie. But that was a mistake because above it was that oh-so-masculine jaw and stern chin with just a hint of an intriguing cleft.

'Are you all right?'

Surprised at his concern, Emma jerked her eyes up to his. A mistake, for she was instantly captured by a steely stare that this time seemed softer, like dawn mist over mountains.

'Of course. Why wouldn't I be?'

Christo read doubt behind the defiance in her fine eyes and felt protectiveness stir. He knew how tough it could be to maintain a smiling façade when in private all was turmoil. But he'd had a lifetime to master the art. He'd plucked Emma from the shelter of her home and thrust her into his world. He owed her his support.

'How about a truce for tonight? I'll keep the wolves at bay. All you need to do is smile and follow my lead. I'll look after you.'

Her head tilted to one side. 'That's supposed to make me feel better?'

It was a cheap jibe that should have annoyed him. Yet, like the crack about divorce papers, it had the opposite effect. Christo could weather a little snarkiness and he'd developed an appreciation for Emma's resilience.

Once he'd thought he wanted a quiet, docile wife. Now he discovered he preferred spirit to automatic obedience. Emma's eyes blazed brilliantly and he was pleased to see there was colour in her cheeks.

When he'd walked in, she'd looked pale. Beautiful, surprisingly so, but a cool stranger.

Even now he was unsettled by that first impression of her, standing like a glamorous stranger in his home. She'd looked sexy, svelte and sophisticated in the strapless fitted dress. He'd known in that instant she'd be accepted without question by his acquaintances and the press, for she had the appearance of so many other women in that milieu. Glossy. Confident. Gorgeous.

Strangely, that knowledge was undercut by disappointment. Even concern. That the Emma he'd begun to discover on Corfu had disappeared.

Tonight was about public perception, yet Christo hated the idea of the real Emma being lost or transformed into just another glamorous socialite.

'I may not be Prince Charming, but this time you can rely on me. I promise.'

Her gaze snagged on his and something beat hard in his belly. Something more than sexual desire or anticipation about tonight's performance.

Christo's breath frayed as he read her expression, saw defiance and annoyance and—could it be yearning?

Abruptly she turned away, as if to leave. 'Well, I can't promise this Cinderella won't turn into a pumpkin at midnight, but I'll do my best.'

Relief buzzed through him. Any fear that Emma had been subsumed by her new, sophisticated look died at her words.

'Wait. Don't you want your gift?'

'Gift?' She was half-turned away, but he saw her frown.

'For tonight. I want you to shine.' He withdrew a flat box and held it out to her.

Weird that he actually felt nervous, giving Emma jewellery. As if he hadn't given girlfriends jewellery before. Only this time it felt imperative that he got it right.

Maybe he was still smarting over the perfunctory glance she'd given the new rings he'd ordered. As if the exquisite filigree work, modelled on ancient designs and studded with flawless diamonds, hadn't impressed her in the slightest.

Annoyance flared. Christo wasn't used to questioning his emotions. He held out the leather box and flipped the lid open.

His anger died at Emma's long sigh of appreciation.

'I've never seen anything like it. What sort of stones are they?'

'Tourmaline.' The dark green was richer than emeralds, in his opinion. As soon as Clio had called him to describe Emma's dress, he'd known what he wanted. Finding it had been another matter. This set had just been flown into Athens for him.

'They're stunning. But I don't wear much jewellery. I don't want to look—'

'You'll look perfect,' Christo urged. Why wasn't he surprised that Emma, of all the women he'd known, should hesitate to accept beautiful jewels? 'Everyone will expect you to wear something spectacular. I'm supposed to be doting on you, remember?'

He watched as his words had their inevitable effect, cutting through her hesitation and stiffening her spine. For a second he regretted the loss of that misty smile of wonder on Emma's face. But, as she put on the long tourmaline and diamond eardrops, he was too busy maintaining his expression of gentle teasing when everything inside turned hot and urgent.

The elegant Art Deco style earrings swung against her slender throat. The colour intensified the green in her hazel eyes, making them glow.

Or was that something else in her expression?

Need pulsed through him. Not the need to put an end to public gossip, but the need to haul his pretty wife close and bury his face in the scented hollow of her pale throat. To smash down the barriers between them and make love to her.

'Now the necklace.' His voice hit a gravelly note.

'No.' She shook her head. 'It would be too much. On some other woman maybe, but not me. I'm not…'

The furrow of uncertainty in Emma's brow cut through his libidinous thoughts.

'Not what?'

Emma looked away and he sensed she was going to prevaricate. Then, instead, she shrugged and met his eye. 'I'm not a model or a sophisticate. I'm not…' Again that telling pause. 'Gorgeous and glamorous.'

Christo heard the hitch of her breath and realised that despite her defiant stare, as if daring him to judge her, Emma really couldn't see her own attractiveness.

But then, he hadn't in the beginning. Originally he'd thought her pretty and charming, but not in a league with the beauties he knew. Somewhere along the line, though, Christo had come to appreciate his wife's character and fire, her unique beauty.

'Who'd want a model?' he murmured, stroking a fingertip down her cheek. 'Most of them are scrawny and too afraid to enjoy a proper meal.' He paused, holding her eyes. 'You're beautiful, Emma. I defy any woman tonight to outshine you.'

Her eyes widened and a flush rose up her throat and into her cheeks. She swung away. 'Don't lie, Christo.' Her voice sounded muffled, twisting something in his belly. 'I've had enough lies from you to last a lifetime.'

Stymied, Christo stared at her profile, proud and, he realised, hurt. He was damned if he told the truth about her beauty and damned if he didn't. He should drop the subject, yet he was reluctant to leave it.

Emma hadn't struck him as a woman with hang-ups about her looks. Then memory pierced him. She'd admitted some time ago that she'd heard his conversation with Damen about why he'd married her. He recalled saying she wasn't his type. That her cousin was more his style, sexy and flamboyant.

Christo dragged in a slow breath, battling self-loathing. He plucked the necklace from the case and stepped behind his wife. Carefully he draped it around her neck, feeling her shiver as his hands brushed her nape. His own hands were unsteady. From the thwarted lust that had stalked him for weeks, or something else?

The clasp closed, he palmed her bare shoulders, fingers splaying across warm, satiny skin, and turned her to face the mirror.

'Look.'

Her chin jerked up, her narrowed eyes meeting his in the mirror.

'Not at me.' He let his gaze drift over the woman before him. 'You're stunning, Emma.' And it wasn't just because of the magnificent tourmaline and diamond collar around her slender throat. It was because of the woman who stood before him, trembling but as stiff as a soldier on parade.

Emma's eyes locked on the reflection of the man behind her as she battled not to lean back against all that delicious heat.

Christo Karides had treated her appallingly. He'd used her for his own advantage. Yet sometimes, like tonight, she fought to remember he was the enemy. He seemed too much like the caring lover she'd once believed him to be.

Take the expression in his eyes. Despite his stern tone, his eyes caressed her, made her feel warm and fuzzy inside. It wasn't the glaze of sexual possessiveness she'd seen in the past but something more tender.

Her thoughts terrified her. Hadn't she learned her lesson, reading emotions and motivations into Christo's actions that just weren't there?

She made to pull away but his hands stopped her. Not because his grip was hard, but because at that very moment those long fingers swept wide over the bare curve of her shoulders, massaging gently.

'Look, Emma.' His voice was soft.

Oh, she was looking. Her gaze swept from those broad shoulders to that solid jaw, past the tiny nick of a scar to his mobile mouth. Then up that decisive nose to eyes that glowed the colour of the sky at dusk.

Emma dragged in an abrupt breath and found herself inhaling that heady signature of cedar, leather and spice with that underlying note of male skin.

The scent shot to her brain, and her womb, and suddenly Emma wasn't looking just at Christo but at the pair of them. He with his hands on her body, she canting back towards him as if drawn to a magnet.

Suddenly she saw herself as others would. Wearing couture clothes and fabulous gems because Christo Karides demanded the best. A swift glance confirmed what she'd seen before. The makeover turned her into someone else. Someone glossy enough to match a billionaire, if only for an evening.

Heart hammering, Emma broke away. Tonight she'd play the doting bride and counter any negative press stories. But she'd be herself, not some puppet on a string dancing to Christo's tune. If he didn't like that, then that was entirely his problem.

CHAPTER NINE

CHRISTO COUNTED THE final items to be auctioned as the charity event drew to a close. Only half a dozen more.

He set his jaw and concentrated on keeping his touch light as he drew his fingertips across the soft skin of Emma's shoulder. She leaned close, her tantalising honey scent teasing his nostrils. The press of her hip on the seat next to his and the rounded contour of her breast against his side stirred a libido already at breaking point.

Telling himself she only did it to play the besotted bride didn't help. His body didn't care about her motivations, just the imprint of her warm curves and how much closer they could get once they left here.

No one bid on the next item. Christo frowned at the delay as Emma turned from speaking to the entrepreneur sitting on her other side and eased back into his embrace.

Fire stormed through his body, drenching him in heat.

Still no bids. Christo raised his hand, nodding to the auctioneer, who beamed back. It was past time they moved on to the final items and ended this. The event had dragged intolerably.

It had begun well enough. Emma had played her part admirably, sticking by his side and not flinching when he pulled her close. The fact she trembled when he did, Christo read as a positive sign. Emma had always been responsive to him and that hadn't changed. Did she know her body's reaction gave her away every time?

She'd been an enormous hit with his acquaintances. Far from being a shy mouse, she'd been quietly assured, conversing easily with everyone. She had the knack of drawing people out, truly listening to what they had to say and keeping the conversation rolling, even when it wasn't about her. She'd been everything he could have hoped for and more. As well as being articulate and sociable, she was…nice.

It seemed such a paltry word. But to Christo, having grown up in a world where appearances were everything, where trust was rare and self-interest dominated, Emma's sweet honesty and generous spirit felt precious.

He wasn't the only one to think so. All night he'd been congratulated and envied. In fact, he'd noted a few guys considering her a little too warmly. Till Christo had warned them off with a speaking stare.

Now he was heartily sick of the crowd. Of being congratulated on his lovely bride when that bride still kept her guard up against him. When this nearness was for show and she'd re-erect the barriers between them as soon as they were alone.

He wanted more. Much more.

He wanted his wife. Frustration grew with every minute and every brush of his hand against silky bare skin.

'You're bidding? I didn't think you'd be interested in this item.' Emma sounded surprised and he shrugged, willing the auctioneer to hurry.

'It's an important cause and no one else was bidding.'

Finally someone else did. The auctioneer caught Christo's eye and he read a mix of doubt and expectancy that indicated the man would drag this out in the hope of securing a much bigger profit. So much for Christo's scheme to end this quickly.

Supressing a sigh, he raised his hand and made a bid calculated to win. Whispers rippled around the room.

The auctioneer looked stunned, but recovered quickly to ask for more bids. There were none. Christo's price was too high for anyone else.

With a slam of the gavel, bidding closed.

Five more items to go. Christo stretched his legs and

tried to stifle his impatience. Emma moved, her body twisting against his, and the molten heat through his lower body turned to forged steel. His skin felt too tight and his lungs cramped.

'What are you going to do with it?'

'Sorry?' He turned to meet her eyes and felt the pause in her breathing as their gazes meshed.

Oh, yes. This desire was definitely mutual. She couldn't conceal the minute, give-away proof of her body's reaction to his.

All the more reason to get out of here as soon as possible and persuade her to put an end to this intolerable sexual frustration.

'The prize. Are you going to use it?'

Despite the confusion in Emma's expression, Christo read the glaze of heat in her eyes. Anticipation slammed into him. Tonight the waiting would end.

Strange to think that originally he'd viewed her as passably pretty. Merely a convenient spouse. She was anything but convenient and far, far beyond merely passable. Had he ever wanted a woman like this?

'Christo?'

'I'm not sure.'

Suspicion dawned in her fine eyes. The corner of her mouth curved into the tiniest hint of amusement. Christo's gaze locked on those glossy lips that had driven him to distraction all night.

Emma leaned close, her words whispering heat across his face as she murmured, 'You do *know* what you bought, don't you?'

He shrugged. 'I was more interested in helping them get through the programme quickly.'

Her breath hitched, her eyes widened and then she was laughing. The sound brought an answering smile to his mouth and an intense feeling of wellbeing. But at the same time that husky chuckle curled around his belly like a lasso, drawing tense nerves even tighter.

Beyond Emma heads turned. People leaned forward to hear the joke but she was totally focused on him. Just the way he liked her.

'That's very noble of you.' Still she smiled. No shadows in her expression now, just mirth and approval.

Christo was surprised at how good it felt when Emma looked at him that way. With shared understanding and humour.

'Don't you want to know what you spent all that money on?'

He shrugged. 'A car?' There'd been a sports car coming up for auction. When she shook her head he tried again. 'A boat?' Not that he needed another cruiser.

Emma shook her head, amusement and approval continuing to dance in her eyes. It struck him he could get used to her approval. It made him feel good.

'So, enlighten me, Emma.' His voice slowed on her name, savouring it. Or, more correctly, savouring the flicker of awareness in those bright eyes that shone tonight more green than brown.

She tilted her head down, whether to keep their conversation private or to avoid his eyes, he couldn't tell. 'An all-expenses-paid trip for a family of four to France, including a couple of days at Euro Disney.' Abruptly she looked up, her eyebrows rising. 'Are you excited to go on all the rides?'

His laughter shouldn't affect her like this. As if he'd turned her insides to melted caramel and added a huge dollop of sexual desire.

People laughed all the time. But Christo's deep, uninhibited chuckle affected her in the strangest way.

Not so strange. You've lusted after him all night.

All night? Far longer!

Just because he could afford to donate a small fortune to a children's charity didn't make him a decent man. Just as his smile didn't make him any less dangerous.

But it was hard to keep him in a box marked 'ogre' or 'blackmailer' when she saw him like this. Or head down with Anthea, working together on a crayon drawing.

Emma released a silent sigh and felt another layer of her defences slip away.

Face it. You've enjoyed being with him tonight. You like snuggling up against him, feeling his arm around you.

You like the admiration in his eyes.

Even if the admiration was for a glossy façade that wasn't the real Emma. Underneath the couture gown and priceless gems she was the same as always—ordinary. No makeover could change that.

'Hey.' A warm finger curled under her chin, tilting her face up. 'What's wrong?'

For the briefest moment, Emma contemplated telling her husband the truth. That she still cared for him despite her attempts not to. That part of her wanted him to care for *her*, not because she brushed up well enough to attend a gala social event but because he found her interesting, because he liked her for who she really was.

'Nothing.' She paused and summoned a smile, pulling back a little till his hand fell away. 'What are you going to do about the prize?'

For a long moment Christo studied her, as if probing to discover what went on inside her head.

'Give it to Giorgos.'

'Giorgos?'

'Our building's concierge. I introduced you to him today. His wife lost her job two weeks ago and their youngest is just out of hospital. They could do with a treat.'

Emma nodded as Christo turned to the event organiser who'd come up to talk with him.

Every time she reminded herself Christo wasn't worth pining over, he surprised her. Such as now, with his plan to give the holiday to his concierge. How many people who lived in the luxury apartment building even knew the man's name? Christo knew it and far more. He was genuinely interested in people. It wasn't the attitude of a man who viewed others as pawns.

Then there was his willingness to give Anthea's nanny a second chance. His patience with his little niece, despite his initial reserve. Plus there'd been his surprise gift for Dora, a bright-red motor scooter she now used whenever she needed to travel the several kilometres between the villa and the nearest town.

Emma had been stunned by his thoughtfulness. And by her lack of perception. Dora had mentioned she didn't like driving Papou's big car that sat gleaming in the garage. But Emma had forgotten the local bus only went by twice a day. Nor had she noticed the older woman was often fatigued or that she often made the trip on foot. Being distracted by her own problems was no excuse. Nor was the fact she'd grown up thinking Dora indomitable. That she'd come to rely on the housekeeper too much. It was Christo who'd arranged extra staff to assist Dora now the villa was occupied.

It was discomfiting, discovering her husband was more perceptive and generous than she'd credited. That he'd taken it upon himself to help out with something she should have dealt with.

The trouble was, Christo wasn't just a ruthless tycoon. There were times when he was plain likeable. That made him hard to resist. Especially when tonight all her not so dormant longings reawakened.

His arm tightened around her shoulders and he leaned in, breath tickling her ear and sending shivers of erotic awareness rippling through her.

'Ready to go?'

'But the auction?' She swung around towards the stage, belatedly registering the wave of applause that signalled the end of the event.

'We can skip the final speeches. I want to be alone with you.' Christo's eyes locked onto hers and the sizzle in her blood became a burst of fire.

Emma opened her mouth to protest. But what was the point? She'd tried and tried but resisting had become impossible.

Maybe it was time to reach out and take what she wanted. She was a woman with a woman's needs. Surely she could satisfy this physical craving and reduce the stress of trying to resist the irresistible?

She couldn't love Christo after what he'd done but she wanted him. She had nothing to lose by sleeping with him.

In fact, that contract he'd signed made it a condition of her escaping his influence. Though right now she had no thoughts of escape.

Nervous, she licked her lips. Instantly his attention dropped to the movement. Emma heard his breath catch.

Suddenly it was so easy. Because for the first time they were equals.

'I'd like that.'

The words were barely out of her mouth when he scooped her up to stand against him. Their farewells were rushed and she saw knowing glances as she grabbed her bag and wrap and said goodnight.

She'd liked the people at their table and enjoyed their conversation, but she was as eager as Christo to leave. So eager that she didn't protest as he guided her through the crowd with one arm still round her, his broad palm on her hip. Heat splayed from the spot, up her side, round to her breasts and straight down to her achy, hollow core.

Emma didn't even mind when photographers pressed close as they left the building and got into a waiting car.

All her attention was on Christo and the charge of erotic energy sparking between them.

Finally they were alone, a privacy screen cutting them off from the driver.

'At last.' The words were a groan, as if from a man exhausted. But Christo didn't look worn out. He looked taut, thrumming with energy.

When he reached out his hand, palm up, she put her fingers in his and felt that pulse of power race through her. It was like thunder rolling in from a massive storm front, a deep vibration heavy with building promise.

Emma couldn't prevent a shiver of reaction. She'd never experienced the like.

Christo nodded as his fingers clamped round her hand, as if he too felt that overwhelming inevitability. His smile of understanding looked strained.

That strain on his severely sculpted features flattened any final hesitation. This wasn't Christo seducing her. This was the pair of them caught in something elemental and all-consuming.

'Come here.' His voice was a rough whisper that did crazy things to her insides. Yet, despite the peremptory command, even now Christo didn't haul her close or try to force her. This was Emma's choice, as he'd promised.

She slid across the seat till she came up against the steamy heat of his big frame. One long arm wrapped around her, turning her towards him. She needed no urging. Her palm slipped under his jacket, moulding the rigid swell of his chest muscles through his fine shirt. Emma shivered at how good that felt. How much more she wanted to feel.

For a second those thundercloud eyes held hers, then Christo lowered his head and took her mouth.

Despite the urgency thrumming through them, his kiss was restrained, as if he fought to control the elemental storm that threatened to sweep them away.

He tasted of black coffee and something indefinable that set Emma's senses ablaze. Her hands clutched and she leaned in, needing more, far more than this gentle caress. Inside she was a threshing mass of need.

'Kiss me properly,' she hissed against his lips. She'd craved this so long. All that time he'd been carefully courting her she'd yearned for the taste of his unbridled passion. 'Please.'

Christo pulled back just enough to look deep into her eyes. Then, as if reading the hunger she could barely express, he planted his hands at her waist and hoisted her up to sit sideways across his lap. Emma had a bare moment to register his formidable strength, to lift her so easily in such a confined space. Then he kissed her again and nothing else existed but Christo and the magic he wrought.

There was fire. Emma felt it lick her insides, flaring brighter by the second. Frenzy. Rough demand and eager response. Tongues sliding together and mouths fused. Hearts thundering in tune. The roar of blood in her ears and bliss in her soul. Steely arms binding her to him.

This was the kiss she'd dreamed about in her virginal bed. No wonder she'd been frustrated and jittery all this time, unable to settle to anything useful after nights with too little rest and too many hours imagining Christo making love to her.

He tasted glorious. He felt even better. But there was more. Passion far beyond her experience, beckoning her deeper, simultaneously satisfying her desire and increasing it.

Emma's ribs tightened around her lungs as she forgot to breathe. But she couldn't have stopped if her life had depended on it. She clutched him as if she could meld their bodies through sheer force of will. She twisted closer, stymied by her fitted dress. There was something she needed even more than his lips on hers and those satisfyingly hard arms pinioning her close.

Emma shifted on Christo's lap, trying to ease that compelling restlessness.

Then without warning he tilted her back so she was no longer upright but supported only by his arm. Foggily she wondered why this felt so insanely perfect when at any other time she'd chafe at a show of superiority by her husband.

Her husband.

The word snapped her brain into a belated stir of worry, till Christo's hand on her bare knee obliterated extraneous thoughts.

Instantly that restless, needy feeling between her legs intensified. Her breath stalled as Christo plunged his tongue into her mouth in a lascivious swirl that made her nipples ache and tighten. At the same time his big, warm hand stroked up her thigh, rucking the silk dress higher and higher till air wafted...

A sudden hubbub erupted. Christo jolted upright, taking her with him as he ripped his hand free of her dress. She heard strange voices, questions and, like a dark undercurrent to the unfamiliar noise, the sound of Christo cursing quietly but ferociously.

For a second nothing made sense. Then out of the darkness a light flashed and then another.

Emma realised the back door of the limo was open. An attendant stood holding it wide. Behind him a huddle of people surged close, cameras snapping.

Paparazzi. Taking photos of her lying sprawled across Christo, his tongue down her throat and his hand up her dress.

In that instant glorious elation turned to wordless embarrassment. She shrivelled and couldn't quite get her body to move, to cover herself.

But Christo was already doing that. Not covering her, since there was nothing at hand to drape over her, but leaning forward, putting himself between her and those avid faces.

He said something she didn't hear and moments later the door slammed.

As if that movement released her from her shocked stasis, Emma suddenly found the strength to slither off his lap and onto the seat, scrambling to put some distance between them.

Eyes wide, she stared up at Christo. They were parked outside a brightly lit building and there was enough light to see his face. Far from being distressed or self-conscious at finding himself photographed in the act of making love in the back seat, he looked as solid and calm as ever.

As if making love to her *had* been an *act*?

Pain stabbed her heaving chest, transfixing her. Desperately she searched for some sign of annoyance or embarrassment on those proud features. She found none.

Had he *expected* the intrusion on their privacy?

Could he really be so calculating?

Everything inside Emma froze. She'd have sworn the moisture in her mouth turned to icicles as the idea hit.

Christo was breathing heavily, but that was understandable, given how their mouths had just been fused together. His hair was rumpled where she'd tunnelled her fingers along his scalp. His bow tie was undone and his shirt askew. But he looked unfazed by the furore outside the car. Unfazed and insanely hot.

Eyes on her, he pressed a button and gave instructions to the driver. His voice was crisp. Emma knew if she tried to talk right now it would emerge as a breathless squawk.

He watched her closely, as if trying to read her reaction. Was he wondering if she realised this had been a set up? Just like their wedding?

Had he really used her so callously? But then, given his track record...

The last shreds of heat inside Emma disintegrated, leaving her chilled to the marrow.

Even her fury, emerging from that white-hot sear of mortification, was cold. It whipped through her like the icy winter wind that swept Melbourne from the Antarctic.

'I apologise, Emma. The driver's original instructions were to take us to a restaurant where the press would be waiting to take photos.' Christo lifted his wide shoulders a scant centimetre. 'I was distracted when we left the auction and forgot to tell him to take us straight home instead. It was my mistake.'

'How very convenient.'

'Pardon?'

Emma lifted her hand to her hair, hauling up the soft waves he'd dislodged as he'd kissed her and jabbing in pins so hard Christo almost winced, imagining the grazes on her scalp. He wanted to reach out and grab her wrists, tell her the haphazard attempts to rectify the sophisticated hairstyle weren't working, and that besides he preferred it down. But she was upset enough. She wouldn't thank him.

The horror on her face smote his conscience. He shouldn't have let it happen. Should have protected her better. Even a woman who'd grown up in the public eye would cringe at the sort of pictures he knew would cover the tabloids in the morning.

Emma had looked wanton, beautiful and thoroughly aroused and the thought of anyone but him seeing her that way was like a knife to his gut. She was *his* and his alone.

'How incredibly convenient that you should *forget* to change the instructions. And that the doorman from the restaurant should open the car without a signal we were ready.'

Christo registered the acid in her tone and frowned. 'That's what doormen do. They open doors.'

He tamped down annoyance at her implication. She'd had a shock.

Emma's mouth turned mulish and her chin reared high in an attitude he knew too well. Stubborn defiance. 'And I suppose you had no idea we were outside the restaurant, even though you know Athens so well?' Her voice dripped shards of sarcasm that grazed his already smarting conscience.

'Let me get this straight. You're accusing me of luring you into a compromising situation just to embarrass you publicly?' Christo picked the words out slowly, barely crediting her implication.

'Of course not.' The vein of righteous indignation pulsing through him slowed. He'd been mistaken to think Emma could believe... 'Not to embarrass me specifically. I'm sure that was just collateral damage as far as you're concerned.' She dropped her hands to her lap and belatedly snicked her seatbelt closed as if to reinforce the distance between them. 'You did it to prove we're hot for each other, didn't you? That all's well between the bride and groom and any rumours that I'd left you were laughable.'

Her voice wobbled on the last word, but Christo couldn't feel sympathy.

Her accusation impugned his integrity. What sort of man did she think he was? So desperate he'd let the world into such a private moment?

A ripple of distaste coursed through him, starting from the bitterness filling his mouth and ending down at the soles of his feet.

He'd been vilified and taunted by his father whenever the old man thought he wasn't callous or committed enough to shoulder the mantle of the Karides corporation. He'd grown accustomed to press reports that misinterpreted or even invented facts about him. He accepted as inevitable that there were probably only a handful of people in the world, like his PA and his old friend Damen, who really knew him. But that didn't mean he'd shrug off such a deliberate insult.

An insult from the woman who, fifteen minutes ago, had all but begged him to take her in the back of this car.

A woman who'd driven him crazy these last weeks with lust and frustration.

A woman whose actions in running from him after their wedding had left him using all his influence and ingenuity to avoid a scandal that would damage them both.

The limo glided down into the underground car park of his apartment building. The increased lighting showed Christo a woman who was not only defiant but sneering.

Something cracked inside him.

'We'll continue this in the apartment.' He opened his door and got out, leaving the driver to get Emma's door.

The trip to the penthouse was completed in thick silence. The sort that wrapped around the lungs and squeezed mercilessly.

What was it about this woman that made him feel so furious, so resentful, so blindsided?

So *gutted*. As if, despite being in the right, he could have done better?

Christo had spent a lifetime learning to be top of his game, top of *any* game he played. He'd survived thirty-one years riding the rough with the smooth, learning never to expect too much. But nothing had prepared him for Emma.

Christo held the front door open to let her sweep past, nose in the air, green jewels swinging from her ears with each step. She crossed the foyer and entered the sitting room with an undulating sashay of her hips in that tight dress that might have been due to her high heels but which instinct told him was a deliberate provocation.

Did she know she played with fire?

In the car she'd driven him to the brink of insanity with her untrammelled eagerness. His wife kissed like an angel, but a woefully inexperienced one. He'd bet his last dollar Emma hadn't thought through the effect of such blatant sexual challenge. If she had, she'd probably run and lock herself in her bedroom.

The separate bedroom he'd arranged because he'd foolishly agreed to let her make the first move.

Christo gritted his teeth but made himself close the door quietly before following her.

She swung around, face flushed, eyes febrile and hair a delectable mess that made her look as though she'd just got out of bed.

His belly clenched painfully, re-igniting frustration. Even now his wife couldn't conceal the fact she wanted him. She devoured him with her eyes, her tongue darting out to slick her lips. Her breasts rose so high with each breath they strained the strapless bodice and her hard nipples signalled arousal. Anger, yes, but desire too.

It struck him that her indignation was a convenient shield for other emotions.

Christo shoved his hands in his pockets, rocking back on his heels. 'I've had enough, Emma.'

'*You've* had enough? I—'

'It's my turn to talk.' His tone was even but held the note of authority he'd honed over years as a CEO.

She took another hefty breath that made him wonder if her breasts might pop free of the green silk, then nodded.

'Maybe I should have been more upfront with you.'

Emma's eyes rounded, as if stunned at his admission.

'Maybe I should have spelled out exactly why I wanted to marry you.'

Not that it would have changed anything. He'd been determined to find the right woman and Emma was definitely it, despite her annoying habit of throwing up obstacles and questioning his motives.

'Maybe I shouldn't have assumed you knew there was

a business element to the arrangement. I shouldn't have assumed, wrongly, that your grandfather had discussed that with you.' He paused. 'I could have told you myself about Anthea.'

Except he'd been worried news of a ready-made family might deter Emma and he'd been utterly focused on putting his ring on her finger.

'But since then I've been completely upfront. From the moment I found you in Corfu I've been utterly honest with you.' Christo felt a bubble of mirthless humour rise. 'So honest, it shocked you.' The look of horror on her face when he'd mentioned sharing a bed had been both a blow to his ego and a spur to his determination.

Emma opened her mouth to speak but he shook his head. 'I told you we were going to the auction then to an exclusive restaurant so we could be seen together.' Christo drew a slow breath, still finding it hard to believe he'd so lost control that he'd been unprepared when the limo door had opened.

He never lost control. Never.

'I also apologised and explained how it happened. I forgot to tell the driver to bring us here because I was concentrating on you. Specifically, how I was going to strip you bare and make love to every centimetre of that delectable body.'

Emma's shocked hiss was loud in the quiet room, reminding him that she was a sexual innocent. That didn't excuse her accusations. Except that it was convenient for her to distort the truth.

Christo stalked closer. She couldn't hide the shimmer of nervous excitement in her eyes. But he wasn't in the mood to play to her tune any more.

'Tonight was an honest mistake. I have no more interest than you in having compromising pictures of us spread across the news. I prefer to keep my love life private.'

Not that he *had* a love life now. Because he'd given his word not to push her. This woman drove him mad!

'Don't imagine conspiracies where there are none. I don't operate like that, as you'd know if you'd paid attention lately.' Christo drew in a calming breath, but to little effect. He was past the point of no return.

'What's between us is real, Emma, and I'm not talking about a marriage certificate. I'm talking about desire, lust, attraction—whatever you want to call it. You can't run from it, though that seems to be your style. Instead of facing me after the wedding, you ran off like a hurt child.'

Her mouth dropped open at the jibe but he kept going, driven by the need to slash through all the pretence.

Christo closed the space between them, feeling the inevitable shimmer of awareness as he stepped up against her. It intensified to a riotous clamour as he touched his fingertip to her chin and tilted it up.

Bewildered eyes met his and he might have felt sorry for her if her games weren't driving him to the edge. It took every scintilla of control not to haul her close and kiss her into mindless abandon. No doubt then she'd claim he'd forced her. That she hadn't really wanted him.

'It's time you faced what's between us instead of pretending it doesn't exist or inventing excuses not to trust me.' Christo's voice ground low as his patience frayed. 'I've been patient. I've given you my name and my word. I want to give you my body too. But I won't be the butt of your lame excuses or manufactured obstacles because you're too scared to take what we both know you want.'

He stepped away, ignoring the confusion in her face.

'When you grow up, when you're ready to follow through, let me know.' Christo turned on his heel and strode away.

CHAPTER TEN

EMMA WRENCHED OFF the taps and grabbed an oversized towel. The shower had done nothing to relieve her distress. Warm water usually relaxed her. But tonight the fine spray had needled her skin like Christo's words needled her conscience.

She hadn't run away like a child!

Had she?

But why should she have stayed? He'd behaved monstrously, making her believe he loved her.

Except most of that had been wishful thinking. He'd been considerate and kind to her, so she'd *wanted* him to love her because she'd fallen for him.

As for making excuses or throwing up obstacles...

Emma briskly rubbed the towel over her body. But instead of expensive plush fabric, it felt like sandpaper. Like the graze of Christo's accusations.

Firming her mouth, she stepped out and dragged off her shower cap. Her hair fell around her shoulders but, instead of its familiar weight, she imagined his touch, so strong yet so tender, as he held her to him and kissed her.

Breathing heavily, she slung the towel over a rail and turned to get her nightwear. Except she'd been so furious and distressed, she'd stomped into the bathroom without grabbing anything to wear.

As she turned the beautiful green dress, discarded over a chair, caught her eye. Then the exquisite jewellery on the marble bathroom counter, sparkling under the light so much she could almost imagine it winked mockingly. As if reminding her that tonight's outfit wasn't her style. She was no glamorous sophisticate. She and Christo didn't fit.

Or was she doing it again? Making excuses and manufacturing obstacles?

Emma's mouth crumpled and her heart dived towards the honey-toned marble floor as suspicion solidified into something like certainty.

Christo had done the wrong thing, no doubt about that.

But shouldn't she at least have faced him and called him on that straight away? Shouldn't she have had more gumption than to run and hide like a child?

Misery curdled her belly. Her disappointment had been so acute, her heartbreak so painful, she'd needed to escape. But there was no escaping the complicated truth between them now.

Christo was right. Remarkably, she wanted him every bit as much as he seemed to want her, physically at any rate.

Desire fizzed in her blood whenever she saw him, or thought about him. But instead of doing something about it she'd looked for distractions to avoid facing it. Taking umbrage when she'd thought he'd brought a lover to the villa, though if she'd thought about it for even a second she'd have known Christo had more class than that. Accusing him of engineering that scene for the press tonight when that was laughable. Especially as she had perfect recall of his erection, steely hard against her hip.

Christo hadn't pretended to desire her. And she knew how vigorously he protected his privacy. One of his first actions after having found her in Corfu was to arrange perimeter security to stop intruders and prying press.

He'd wanted her. Plus he'd made her feel wonderful tonight in so many ways. His interest in what she had to say. The pride in his voice as he'd introduced her, and the way he'd kept steering conversations away from people she didn't know and into general areas so she could contribute. The warmth in his eyes as they'd shared amusement at some of tonight's auction items.

His possessiveness when men had got too close.

Emma shivered despite the warmth of the steamy bathroom and realised she was still naked.

Her gaze caught her reflection in the mirror that took up one wall. She was still the same old Emma. Not stupendous in any way. An average body and an ordinary face. Nice legs, she'd been told, but she'd always wished they were longer. As she'd wished for wheat-blonde hair and an elegant nose instead of one too close to being snub.

The only real difference she saw, apart from hair a shade lighter from the Greek sun, was the way her eyes glowed. Had they been so bright before?

It didn't matter. What mattered was why they glowed.

Christo. He had a talent for getting under her skin and making her feel more for him than she should. Once it had been love. She hurried to assure herself she was cured of that. What she felt was simple animal attraction.

Inevitably her mind turned to the salacious, outrageous demand he'd made that first day on Corfu. That she spend at least one night in his bed to claim her inheritance.

No matter how she'd told herself he couldn't force her, she'd never been able to forget it completely. She wanted to be with him and that need to discover how it would be grew daily. As if the seed, once planted in her mind, had grown till it obliterated all else. Now was her chance to satisfying her craving and her curiosity. Then afterwards, if she wanted to, she could walk away.

She shook her head. This wasn't about her inheritance or Christo's outlandish proposition. It was about satisfying her needs.

What would she do? Run and hide, as he expected? Play safe and try to avoid him?

Or throw herself into the fire and hope she survived?

Emma knew a moment's terrible self-doubt as inclination fought a determination to stand up for herself, not with words this time, but action.

Then she grabbed a plush robe from a hook and shrugged it on, cinching it around her waist.

The rap of her knuckles on the door of the master suite sounded over-loud. Emma waited, heart pounding, head tilted forward to listen. Nothing. Was Christo asleep?

Surely not. They'd only parted twenty minutes ago.

Firming her lips, she turned the doorknob and entered. Predictably the master suite was vast and luxurious. What surprised her was how comfortable it felt. She had an impression of parchment walls and splashes of rich teal that reminded her of the deep sea off Corfu on a sunny day. There was a book-lined wall and a leather lounge.

But what drew her eye was the filmy curtain riffling in the breeze at the open door, and beyond it the tall shadow on the terrace.

'Christo?' With numb fingers she shut the door behind her. That was all the time it took for him to step inside.

He still wore dress trousers but his tie was gone and his feet bare. Rolled sleeves revealed strong forearms that looked so good, her insides gave a needy leap. His formal white shirt gaped to reveal a slice of dark olive skin dusted with black hair that made her mouth dry.

Emma had seen him almost naked in his swim shorts, but somehow that V of tantalising flesh seemed just as decadently tempting. She gulped and lifted her gaze, noting the way his hair stood up, as if he'd clutched it. And the glitter of dark, assessing eyes.

'What is it, Emma?'

'I came to apologise.' She sucked in a quick breath. 'I was wrong to accuse you the way I did. I'm sorry.'

He pushed his hands into his trouser pockets, drawing her attention to his powerful thighs.

'Apology accepted. Thank you.'

Still he stood, simply watching.

She couldn't work out if that was anger emanating from him or something else. A voice in her head told her it was time to leave before she made a fool of herself or did something irreversibly dangerous.

Instead she stood her ground. Adrenalin shot through her blood in a classic 'fight or flight' response to this big, bold, provoking man who watched her as if he had all the time in the world.

'I didn't think before I spoke,' she offered.

He inclined his head, as if that was obvious.

Emma shifted her weight from one foot to another. He wasn't going to make this easy for her, was he?

Finally he spoke. 'It's late. Was there anything else?' His tone wasn't encouraging. He made no move towards her and Emma knew a craven urge to whip round and escape to the guest room.

But she was stronger than that.

Or perhaps just needier.

'Yes.' The word emerged too loud. 'I came because I want you to make lo—' She stopped. That wasn't what either of them wanted to hear. 'I want to have sex with you.'

Emma didn't know what she'd expected but it was more than she got. Christo didn't seem to move a muscle. Did he even blink?

What was he waiting for?

Then it struck her. She'd already said yes to him once tonight, only to turn on him after that mistake at the restaurant.

Maybe words weren't enough.

Or—the devastating thought sliced through her—maybe he'd changed his mind.

'If you still want me?' Ignoring the slight unevenness in her voice, she lifted her chin.

'I do.' The two words in that slow, deep voice sounded like a vow. Her nape prickled as she recalled their wedding vows. Then she shoved the recollection aside. This was different. She felt that here, now, there was only honesty between them.

Gathering her nerve, Emma paced forward, not stopping till they stood toe to toe.

The heady scent of virile male tantalised her nostrils and the breeze through the open door stirred her hair. What she read in those smoky eyes made heat flare across her skin. The dazzle of hunger was so potent, so raw, it dried her mouth and made her tremble.

Christo read Emma's nerves in her wide eyes and the racing pulse at her neck. She swallowed and he wanted to lick his way down her throat. He'd hungered for her for so long. He'd made allowances for her inexperience and hurt. He'd denied himself because he'd understood she needed time. Tonight his patience had reached its limit.

Which was why he wouldn't make a move till he knew she was absolutely committed. That she wouldn't change her mind again.

Swathed in an oversized bathrobe, Emma looked vulnerable, yet sexy and determined. It was a contradiction he didn't understand but he was fast losing the capacity for thought as she stared up with that provocative pout and her body clearly naked beneath the towelling.

He was torn between protectiveness and rampant lust.

'Show me.' His voice was a harsh whisper through lips that barely moved. His whole body ached from being held in check. From fighting the need to take.

He blinked when she stepped closer. He felt her warmth against him, her breath a puff of heat against his chest as she reached for his shirt and began to undo it.

Christo sucked in a desperate breath as her knuckles brushed his skin in a delicate, moving pattern designed to unstring his tendons and loosen his resolve. She leaned in and the honey scent of her hair infiltrated his brain, sending it into overload.

Abdominal muscles spasmed at she reached his trousers and paused.

Glowing eyes met his. Questioning eyes.

'Are you sure?' It cost him to speak. 'If we start this there'll be no turning back.'

She dropped her hands and stepped away. Disappointment smote him, so severe, he tasted it like poison on his tongue.

Christo was silently cursing his restraint when Emma tugged the belt of her robe. With a defiant tilt of her head, and a sensuous little shimmy that undid him, she let the material drop.

Naked, she was perfection.

Christo's heart beat so fast, it tripped and stole his breath.

Pale skin, pink nipples, and a V of darker hair nestling between her slender thighs, accentuating the impossibly sweet curve from waist to hips.

He'd wanted her when she was a convenient bride, acquired for purely practical reasons.

He'd been hot for her as she'd confronted him wearing only attitude and a blue bikini.

These last three weeks he'd ached for her at an even deeper level, haunted by her laugh, her sweetness with Anthea and Dora and, tonight, with him. Even when she defied him and drove him crazy, it only raised the scale of his wanting.

'Christo?'

He dragged his gaze up and saw her bottom lip caught between her teeth. Hesitation in her eyes.

Emma was about to turn away when his eyes met hers and blue fire welded her soles to the floor. Heat drenched her and suddenly doubt fled.

Big hands took hers and hooked them into the front of his trousers above the zip.

'Don't stop now,' he drawled as he dragged that snowy shirt up from his trousers and shrugged it off, leaving her in possession of a view that dried her mouth.

For ages she stared at the shift and play of bare, taut flesh over muscle. Then her brain kicked into gear and onto the task of undoing his trousers. It was tricky, possibly because her hands shook.

Finally, with a sigh that swelled her chest, she got them undone, but not before her knuckles brushed the tantalising length of his erection. She shivered, trying to imagine herself accommodating all that hardness. But the shiver wasn't all anxiety. Mostly it was excitement.

His trousers fell to the floor and still Christo stood, unmoving. Swallowing, Emma crooked her fingers into the top of his boxers and slid them down. The place between her legs throbbed with heat as she watched the reveal of yet more golden skin. Then his shaft sprang free and she jumped, staring.

As if reading her moment of panic, Christo lifted his hand to her cheek in a butterfly caress that eased her riot of nerves. But the riot started again as his finger trawled down, over her chin and collarbone to her breast, where delicately he circled her nipple. Emma shifted, trying to assuage the edgy sensation inside when his other hand captured hers and brought it against him.

'There's nothing here to be afraid of.' His voice wound around her as his eyes held hers.

Instinctively her fingers curled round his length, slowly exploring the fascinating velvet over steel combination. At the movement, Christo's eyes flickered, the corners of his mouth pulling down as if with tension. Gripping a little tighter, she slid her hand again and watched that tell-tale drag of his lips.

The realisation that she did that to him boosted Emma's confidence.

'I'm not afraid.'

But her smile ended in a gasp as his other hand flirted across her thighs, then slipped between her legs, right up against folds that felt swollen and wet. Gently he slid his fingers down, arrowing to the exact spot where sensation centred. He pressed, and she jolted as a current of electricity snapped through her.

Emma swayed forward, needing more, almost sighing with relief when his hand at her breast opened to mould her more firmly. In answer her fingers tightened around Christo till he murmured, 'Easy,' and she loosened her hold. Needing more, she planted her left hand on his chest, solid with muscle and tickly with that smattering of dark hair.

His heart beat steadily beneath her touch, the rhythm reassuring as she found herself in completely new territory.

The big hand between her legs moved again, sending sparks showering through her, then dipping even further till one finger slid home and Emma gasped at the shocking unfamiliarity of it. But shock turned to eagerness as he withdrew, then slid home again, evoking wonderful sensations. She found her pelvis rocking with the movement.

Another slide and the friction made her breath stop. Stunned, she stared into Christo's eyes and couldn't look away. Surely they should be in bed, lying down before...?

'We can't.' Her words faded as his thumb pressed that sensitive nub and she trembled all over.

'Believe me, sweetheart, we can. We can do whatever you like.' His words would have reassured Emma, except she read excitement in his dark eyes and determination in the angle of his jaw and knew he was as aroused as she. 'Hang on to me.'

He took his hand from her breast and lifted her fingers from his erection to his shoulder. Instinctively she held tight there. Just as well, because her knees threatened to buckle as he returned to caressing her breast, his other hand working between her legs.

Now she moved with every slide of his hand, finding the rhythm and forgetting her inhibitions. This felt so good, so perfect, she…

'Christo!' It was a desperate shout, half-muffled by the wave of ecstasy enveloping her.

She had half a second to see him smile, then he bent his head to hers. His kiss was lavish, demanding yet reassuring, connecting them even as she shattered, her soul shooting towards the heavens as her body shuddered and almost collapsed.

Christo took her weight, drawing her against him and hugging her tight. His warmth enveloped her and soft words rained down, soothing her gradual descent from that acute peak of pleasure.

Finally the shudders became random trembles and the burning white light dissipated as she clung to him, limp with satiation. Dimly Emma wondered that she felt no embarrassment at climaxing in front of him. She'd imagined finding release with Christo in bed with the lights off, not flaunting her pleasure before him. But it had felt perfect.

'Thank you. That was…'

Emma couldn't find the right words so gave up. Instead she smiled against his muscled chest and let herself sag in his arms, knowing he had her.

His erection hard against her belly reminded her that Christo hadn't found satisfaction. She wanted him to enjoy what she had and slid her hand between them.

'Not yet, *glyka mou*. Let's get you somewhere comfortable.' He stepped clear of his clothes, then scooped her up in his arms.

Emma's eyes snapped open and she fell into his slate-blue gaze. Was that satisfaction she saw? Or anticipation?

As he laid her on the bed a shiver shot through her at the prospect of what lay ahead. Still languid from that intense orgasm, she felt a scurry of nerves as Christo opened a nearby drawer then rolled on a condom.

'I haven't done this before.' The words jerked out of her and she licked her lips, torn between fascination, eagerness and just a touch of apprehension.

He paused, kneeling on the bed, arms braced beside her. Something flared in his eyes, something she couldn't decipher. 'But you want to?'

It was the second time he'd asked. It struck her that, far from being the domineering, macho bully she'd pegged him for when he'd made that demand about her living as his wife, Christo was careful with her. The tension riding his bunched shoulders and clenched jaw was obvious, but he held back. Did he feel the urgency she'd felt just minutes ago? Her mind boggled at his control.

Emma lifted her hand towards him and nodded. 'Show me how to make it good for you.'

Zeus preserve him. How to make it good for him!

Christo grimaced. 'It's already far too good.' He'd been so close to the brink that, even when he'd removed her hand, he'd almost come just watching and feeling her climax. And when she'd snuggled into him like a living blanket...

'But it could be better.' Her eyes were enormous but he read that obstinate mouth and felt his own curve.

'Oh, definitely.' He moved to straddle her legs, getting high just from the sight of her lithe, beautiful body laid out for his enjoyment.

Christo wanted Emma badly. He needed to possess her, fill her and claim her as his own. The urge to spread her legs and take her was so strong. But she was a virgin. He had no experience of virgins but he knew he needed to make this as easy for her as possible.

Instead of pushing her legs apart, he bent and pressed a light kiss to her hip bone. She jolted, as if still wired from her orgasm. The scent of feminine arousal wafted to him and he smiled. He'd give her a first time she'd never forget.

With that silent vow, Christo set about learning her body.

Emma protested. In between her sighs and gasps as he found a particularly sensitive spot to kiss or lick or stroke. He discovered a place at her ankle that undid her. A spot near the small of her back. Her inner elbow where he'd driven her to the edge that night on Corfu. And the more obvious places. Her breasts that filled his palms so sweetly. The sweep from neck to shoulder. And her inner thighs. By the time he'd finished she was trembling with need and he felt as if he'd been forged from pure, burning steel.

When he nudged his knee between her legs they fell open instantly and elation surged. He'd waited so long. He braced himself on one arm and, sliding his other hand beneath her, tilted her.

Blazing eyes met his. 'Finally!'

'Don't tell me you didn't enjoy yourself.' His mouth rucked up at one side at the memory of exactly how much Emma had enjoyed his caresses. Her skin was flushed and there was a dreamy look in her eyes that contradicted her attempt at brusqueness.

'It was wonderful.' She sighed. 'But I want *you*.'

Strange how her words reverberated within him. How long had he wanted to hear that? Emma wanting him, not running or fighting him.

Her fingers curled around him and his breath hissed. He'd done his best to prepare her but, at her touch, he could hold back no longer.

Christo leaned in, letting her guide him till he was positioned at her slick entrance. She gave a little wriggle at the contact and he rolled his eyes. He was never going to last; that was a given.

'Lift your knees.' His voice was as rough as gravel, but she understood, and he felt her legs lift to cradle his hips. He pressed into the most exquisite, firm heat. His breath stalled and he had to fight not to pump hard. Instead he kept his eyes on Emma and saw her brow wrinkle, as if in confusion.

'Okay?'

She blinked up at him but he saw no sign of pain. 'Odd but okay.'

'Odd?' He shook his head as he allowed himself to slip a little further. The sensations were overwhelming now. The feel of Emma taking him was so good Christo shook with the effort of restraint.

A soft hand touched his face. 'Are you all right?'

Christo grimaced. 'That's my line.' Clearly he wasn't doing this right if Emma felt nothing but concern for him.

Lifting one hand, he cupped her breast then bent to lower his head and suck at her nipple.

'Ah!' She lifted off the bed, drawing him further into that enticing heat. Fingernails dug into his shoulders as he caressed her and inexorably drove home.

Christo lifted his head and read Emma's glazed eyes. No pain there, no fear, just the same wonder he felt as he withdrew and forged home again.

With slow deliberation, Christo set a pace that had her rocking against him. Then, as she licked her lips and said his name, he reached his limit. Christo felt the bunch of tightening muscles in his arms, legs and backside. His rhythm changed, became urgent and inescapable, and the tingling began, racing down his spine and round to his groin.

There was just time to recognise the convulsive clasp of

Emma's tight muscles around him when rapture slammed into him, a rolling tidal wave that went on and on. She curled up, her climaxing body jerking and trembling in unison with his.

Blindly he dropped to one elbow, protectively scooping her close as together they plunged off the edge into oblivion.

CHAPTER ELEVEN

EMMA WOKE TO a sense of luxury and warmth. She lay, savouring the feeling of wellbeing. Opening her eyes, she discovered it was early morning, pale, rosy light spilling through the open window.

She was in Christo's bed.

Unreadable eyes watched her and she discovered that luscious sense of comfort came from the fact she was cuddled against him, lying on her side with one knee hooked over his hip and his arms around her.

'How are you?' His words caressed her mouth and, strangely, that seemed almost as intimate as the way their lower bodies were aligned, his powerful erection a reminder of what they'd shared last night.

Her face flushed. Even her ears tingled. What they'd shared went beyond everything she'd imagined.

'Fantastic.'

His mouth crooked at one corner. 'You are that.' Then dark eyebrows angled down. 'Not hurting at all?'

'I don't think so.' Emma shifted slightly, registering a slight heaviness between her legs, more an awareness than anything.

It wasn't any change in her body that concerned her. It was the consequence of sharing Christo's bed.

She couldn't pretend any more that he was a despicable monster. Yet was sex any solution to their convoluted relationship?

'So you got your wedding night after all. Just as you specified in the contract.' What made her say it, Emma didn't know. Except belatedly she realised she didn't have a clue where they went from here.

That hint of a smile vanished in an instant.

Christo's muscles stiffened around her. 'You're saying last night was about the contract? Giving yourself for a piece of property?' The abrupt change in him was shocking, his tone scathing.

'It was you who insisted I owed you a night in your bed!' Emma pushed against that solid chest and reared back, but he kept her where she was. Close enough to read, for a second, what seemed like disappointment in those smoky eyes.

She stilled, intrigued, telling herself it couldn't be. Christo wore that look again, the steely one that spoke of severe disapproval. His mouth was tight and the pulse at his temple drummed too fast. Yet still there was something in his eyes…

'Why did you sleep with me, then?' she challenged, her throat tight. 'Because I *owed* you? Was I some trophy? Was last night payback for me leaving you?'

'You think I collected a debt for pride's sake?' Christo's nostrils flared. 'I slept with you because you drive me crazy with wanting.' The words carried the lash of accusation. As if he held her responsible. 'Because there's a connection between us. You felt it too. Don't tell me you didn't.' He drew in a deep breath. 'Last night was about you and me, nothing else.'

Emma's breath jammed in her lungs. She couldn't doubt his sincerity, not when she was so close she read every change in his body.

'Why did you come to my bed, Emma?' The look in his eyes told her the answer was important to him.

She didn't want to reply but what was the point in trying to hide the truth?

'I couldn't fight myself any more,' she finally admitted. 'You're right. There *is* a connection.' It was growing stronger all the time. Emma tried to tell herself it was just sex but it was more complicated than that.

'You want to be with me.' He pulled her closer and she let him, because this was where she wanted to be, even if she had no idea where it would lead.

'I do.' She sighed. Once that would have been an admission of defeat. Now it was the simple truth. She was tired of hiding from it.

'And I want to be with you.' He nudged her chin up and she read his sincerity.

Excitement pulsed through her. Whether this was a mistake or not, at least in this they were equals. Emma couldn't find it in herself to turn away from him again.

She shrugged, feeling a little foolish. 'I only mentioned the contract because I'm a bit out of my depth.'

At her words he lifted his hand to stroke her hair back from her face. The gesture was so tender, almost loving. Emma felt a pang of regret that this could never be love. But she was an adult. She'd accept reality. Take the pleasure they both wanted and move on when it ended.

'I'm sorry. I overreacted.' Christo's mouth compressed to a crooked line. 'It's my own fault for spelling it out on paper. That *was* hurt pride.' Emma blinked at the admission and the apology. More and more, the Christo Karides she'd despised was transforming into a man she liked.

Emma nestled against that solid chest, inhaling his rich, salty male scent. After just one night she feared she was addicted to his body. His hugs banished the loneliness she'd felt since Papou's death. But it wasn't only that. In Christo's arms she felt wanted, cherished.

'It's a hot button of mine,' he continued. 'Women who trade their bodies for gain.'

'I suppose you've met a few, being rich.' And handsome.

'Enough.' Then, to her surprise, he went on. 'My mother was like that. She married my father for his money.'

Emma pulled back, searching Christo's face. Behind the scowl she was sure she saw hurt. It made her insides twist.

'Are you sure? Maybe she just—'

'No mistake.' Slate-blue eyes held hers. 'My father was good-looking and successful but he didn't have a loving nature.' Again that quirk of Christo's lips that looked more like pain than amusement. 'He had an eye for stunning women and my mother was a beauty queen. They married because she got pregnant with me.' Christo shook his head. 'He was a hard man, but honourable and faithful, whereas her main interest was spending. She admitted she'd never wanted me. Pregnancy was just her way to secure her future.'

'That's appalling! How could any mother say that to her child?' The thought sickened Emma.

Christo shrugged. 'She was furious at the time. She blamed me for my father finding out she'd cheated on him.' At Emma's questioning look, he added, 'I walked in on her with her lover and didn't react well. My father eventually heard about the fuss, I assume from the staff.'

Emma tried to imagine what it would be like, discovering your parent with a lover. She wondered what Christo meant by her not reacting well but, given the stark line of his clamped jaw, thought it best not to ask.

'So she spoke in the heat of the moment.' Emma didn't like the sound of Christo's mother but she hated seeing the lines of pain bracketing his mouth when he spoke of her.

'You're trying to excuse her? Don't bother. She never spoke to me after that. I haven't seen her since. She's living in Brazil now, married to a mining magnate, probably pretending she doesn't have an adult son.'

Emma digested that in silence. With a mother like that, and a father he'd described as hard, Christo began to make more sense. He was an only child and love had clearly been in short supply in his family. She wondered with a pang if he'd ever had tenderness from his father. Or anything approaching a happy family life.

Was it surprising he'd held back from Anthea, admitting he didn't have the skills to care for a child? There was even a lop-sided logic to his plan to acquire a convenient bride to fill that role, if he had no experience of a loving family.

What mattered, she realised, was that he hadn't shirked his responsibility. He was determined to make a good home for Anthea. She couldn't fault him for that.

Honourable, he'd called his father. Surely Christo had inherited that trait, or at least a strong sense of responsibility?

Emma surveyed him under her lashes. He could be a hard man. Look at the way he'd set about acquiring a wife. But there was more to him. Christo felt deeply. That was clear from everything she saw in his face and from the tightly contained voice as he'd relayed that horrible story about his mother. Obviously he held back a dam of painful emotions.

He didn't just feel responsible for his niece, either. He cared for her, even if he was just learning how to express it. That was why the sight of them bonding had fascinated Emma. It was as if he got as much out of being with Anthea as she did.

Plus, he cared for Emma. Last night at the reception he'd smoothed her way, ensuring she was at ease. His smiles and laughter had been genuine. She'd *liked* him as well as desired him. Then there was the way he'd taken time to ensure her first experience of sex was spectacular. Emma knew that wasn't always the case. Christo had put her needs above his own.

Perhaps the man she'd fallen for in Australia hadn't been a total mirage. Christo Karides was more complex than she'd credited.

'What are you thinking about?'

His words drew her attention back to his face. Their eyes meshed and heat simmered beneath her skin. How could he do that with just a look?

She shifted, the movement making her breathtakingly aware that she was still wrapped in his arms, naked, her lower body coming up against Christo's erection.

She saw his pulse throb at the contact. The simmer became a scorching blaze, running like wildfire along her veins and over her skin.

'I was thinking you're not the man I imagined you were.'

'Really?' His eyebrows rose, his body tensing.

'There's more to you than I thought,' Emma admitted. 'More to like.'

Christo's features eased and the corner of his mouth curled up. 'You certainly seemed to like me well enough last night,' he murmured in a drawl that dragged through her body like fingers ruffling velvet. She felt a tremor ripple through her belly.

One large hand traced an arabesque along her spine, slowing as it drew low towards her buttocks. Emma's breath stilled as her body thrummed into needy awareness.

'I did, didn't I?' Her voice was husky.

'And *I* like *you*.'

Emma swallowed hard. The words weren't fancy. Yet the way he said them, teamed with the way he looked at her, made them sound like something profound. Something significant.

For a second anxiety gripped her. She'd vowed not to fall for romantic fantasy again. Except this was no extravagant, gilded compliment designed to turn her head. This was plain and unvarnished...and she believed him.

There was tenderness in his touch and in his expression, as well as a good dollop of anticipation. An anticipation she shared.

Mutual attraction was simple and straightforward. She just had to remain clear-headed. Never again would she make the mistake of imagining there was love between them.

'So,' he murmured, 'If you like me and I like you...'

That roving hand palmed her bottom and tugged her flush against him. Emma's breath snagged as his rigid length slid up against that needy spot between her legs. Automatically she curved closer, seeking more.

'Then maybe,' she finished for him, 'we should spend more time together.' On the final word he nudged so close, she felt her flesh part to accommodate him.

Emma's eyes widened at how easy it was and how very, very good. She was just wrapping her fingers around his shoulder to pull even herself closer when Christo shook his head, a grimace, as if of pain, tugging at his mouth.

'Wait.'

Then he was gone, turning away for a condom, leaving her shocked to the core that she hadn't thought about protection. Giving herself to her husband was becoming the easiest thing in the world.

Emma chewed on that fact, wondering what heartache that boded for the future.

It wasn't just heat building inside her. She told herself it was arousal, hunger for the magic he'd shared with her last night. Emma blocked her mind to the possibility it might be anything more.

Then Christo was back, wrapping her close, meeting her eyes with a blazing look that banished all doubts. It was, she decided, time to quit worrying and go with the flow.

He smiled and it was like a light going on in the darkness. The radiance mesmerised her.

'Now, about spending more time together. I have a plan to bring us *very* close together.'

'You do?' Her voice was breathless. For his hand was already skimming her thigh, urging her to lift her knee higher over his waist.

The action spread her open against his groin where furnace-like heat beckoned. Emma shuffled closer and the friction of their bodies aligning sent a zap of energy to every sense receptor. He bumped his hips forward and her breath stopped.

'That feels so good.'

'We haven't even started yet.' The devil was in his eyes as he rubbed against her. Then he claimed her mouth in a slow, sultry, seductive kiss that led to a world of bliss. And from there to a whole morning spent in his arms and a haze of delicious wellbeing.

The haze lingered.

For four days they stayed in Athens, satisfying the public hunger for sightings of Greece's favourite billionaire and his new bride.

It wasn't as difficult as Emma had expected. Christo made everything easy, diverting her when she felt nervous, introducing her to people who were genuinely pleasant and interesting. Never leaving her side. She grew accustomed to the weight of his arm around her waist, or his long fingers threaded through hers, as if it were the most natural thing in the world.

As if her husband enjoyed touching her as much as she delighted in his touch.

They mingled with the rich and famous at exclusive restaurants, a gala gallery opening and a couple of parties. They had cocktails on the luxury yacht of an Italian billionaire who was interested in Christo's Athens redevelopment plan. Instead of leaving her to talk business with their host, Christo drew her in and mentioned that the property in question had been owned by her family for years. That she had a commercial interest in it. Emma had been stunned by the acknowledgement, feeling a flush of satisfaction and pride that her Papou's far-sighted purchase was now to be the centrepiece of a significant development.

She felt almost sophisticated in a daring designer outfit of white silk trousers and a vibrant red top with a deeply slashed V down the back that Christo couldn't resist. As they stood talking to their host, Christo kept running his fingers down her bare skin, making her tingle all over.

A week earlier she'd have thought he was doing it for the benefit of the paparazzi who were settled in small boats with telephoto lenses trained on the cruiser.

Now she knew better. For if Christo was attentive in public it was nothing to what he was like when they were alone. He was always touching her, always close, always finding new ways to bring her pleasure. She spent all night in his arms. They showered together, ate together, yet the urgent hunger between them grew more, not less, intense.

It was as if, that first night in Athens, they'd pulled down the barriers to reveal a need that couldn't be assuaged. Each day it increased. As if this were a proper marriage and they really were honeymooners.

When Emma let slip that despite her stop-overs in Athens she'd never visited the Acropolis, Christo arranged a special tour. One of the site's archaeological experts guided them around the ancient hilltop on their final afternoon. It was a wonderful experience. Even the throng of tourists, some of whom were as interested in her and Christo as in the marble temples, didn't detract from it.

Standing at the perimeter wall—watching the sunset wash the city apricot, gold then finally deep violet, as their guide told them tales of long ago—Christo pulled her back against his powerful frame, arms wrapped around her, his breath stroking her hair.

Emma felt such contentment, such joy, that for a moment it frightened her. Until she remembered she was taking one day at a time. That what they shared was based on desire, not love, and as such it couldn't last.

Strange that the knowledge wasn't as comforting as before.

CHAPTER TWELVE

THREE WEEKS AFTER their time together in Athens and things were excellent. Satisfaction filled Christo as he strode from the car park towards the old part of Corfu Town.

Anthea was growing into a happy kid instead of an apprehensive one. She adored Emma who, far from keeping her distance with a stranger's child, gave her all the warmth and encouragement she craved. Pleasure filled him, thinking of the pair together. He couldn't have asked for more.

The nanny's recent resignation on the grounds that life at the villa was too quiet was a relief. Her play for his attention still rankled. Now he had to secure a new carer but meanwhile Dora's niece filled the role admirably.

There'd been no more innuendo in the world's press about a runaway bride. Instead he and Emma had been dubbed the world's most besotted newlyweds.

Business proceeded on schedule with none of the expected negative fallout. Actually, there was more potential investor interest in his latest project than before, thanks to the Athens publicity. His bride had been a massive hit.

And the fireworks between him and Emma were now only of the sexual sort. No more flare-ups of indignation or accusation.

Heat smote his belly. Emma was so passionate, so eager.

The one thing that surprised him was how their intimacy wasn't confined to sex. It simmered between them, as if some invisible filament bound them together—their bodies but also their minds, their thoughts, even their amusement at the same things.

Christo slung his jacket over his shoulder and quickened his step through the late-afternoon throng. Emma wasn't expecting him and he looked forward to her welcome. Sex was phenomenal with his virgin bride, a quick learner who drove him to the brink with a mere touch. But just as alluring was the way her hazel eyes widened with delight whenever she saw him. Then they glittered more green than brown, a sign, he'd learned, that she was excited or happy.

Making Emma happy was fast becoming one of his favourite things.

He strode along the Liston, the wide, marble-paved pedestrian street edging the old town. On one side graceful colonnaded buildings lined the road, housing restaurants. On the other, the restaurants' shady outdoor seating gave onto the park with its unexpected cricket pitch, a quirk dating from the years of British rule. There was an elegance to the beautiful street, now full of promenading visitors, locals and waiters hurrying past with loaded trays. But he didn't have time to linger. He was here to find his wife.

As usual the word 'wife' stirred a zap of anticipation.

He'd left Athens a day early, arriving in Corfu on Thursday, because after four days of long hours in Athens he wanted Emma.

Once the idea of rearranging his schedule to be with a woman would have perturbed him. Now he viewed it as a perk of marriage. He had a desirable wife. Why wouldn't he spend time with her? He was CEO, after all. Careful planning, a couple of extra-long days and a little delegation meant everything was under control.

He turned left into one of the narrow lanes that snaked between tall Venetian-style buildings with their pastel colours and long shutters. Small shops did a brisk trade and he dodged souvenir hunters and families with ice-creams, delighted at the anonymity he found so hard to achieve in Athens.

Since his youth Christo's actions had been reported and scrutinised. He'd spent his life carrying the weight of expectation, first of his demanding father, then of the business world and, latterly, the public with its unending appetite for gossip about the rich and famous.

Maybe that was why he liked this island so much. With a few precautions he was generally free to do as he liked.

Right now he liked the idea of surprising his wife.

Consulting his phone, he took a turning, then another, passing a small square with a tiny church and a vibrant burst of pink bougainvillea shading patrons at a café. Another turn and...

Christo pulled up mid-stride.

His breath hissed between his teeth as a phantom fist landed a punch to his gut. He rocked back then found his balance in the wide-set stance of a man ready to defend what was his.

For there was Emma, hair high in an elegant style that left her slender, sexy neck bare. She wore one of her new outfits, cream trousers that clung to the curves of her rump and hips before falling loosely to jewelled sandals that exactly matched the amber of her sleeveless top.

She looked delicious enough to sink his teeth into. But Christo's attention zeroed in on the man with her. The man standing too close, his hand on her arm, his smiling face bent towards her.

Emma didn't mind. She smiled and nodded, listening as he leaned in to murmur in her ear.

Christo surged forward, ignoring the strange sensation, as if both his lungs and his throat constricted.

A bevy of chattering teenagers came in from a side-street, impeding his progress. By the time he reached the doorway where Emma had stood, the guy was gone and she was a glow of colour further ahead.

Impatient, he strode to catch up with her, his hand curling around her elbow.

'Christo! What are you doing here?'

Watching the excited green spark in her eyes, basking in the warmth of her smile, the fierce blaze in his belly dimmed and he found himself smiling back.

'Looking for you.' Her soft skin felt so good. Her lush honey scent was rich as nectar.

Christo's chest filled with a wild riot of feelings. He recognised pleasure and relief and refused to go further. Yet even a man committed to avoiding extreme emotion registered the depth of his relief.

Had he been *scared* Emma was more interested in the stranger than him? It didn't take a psychologist to read the scars of his mother's behaviour there.

To Emma he'd implied he hadn't known about his mother's betrayal till the end. Actually, he'd known most of his life. It was only when he'd found her with a teenager from his own high school, just two years older than himself, that Christo had finally cracked. There'd been no hiding from his father the smashed furniture or his bruised knuckles as he'd taken the other guy down. His mother had hated him for that and his father had withdrawn even further.

Christo had learned not to trust women, even when they came at a high price. Not to expect love or even companionship. He'd thought of a wife only as an asset, a commodity.

Looking into Emma's open features and the genuine smile curling her lips, Christo had a revelation.

He didn't want it to be that way.

The chains of the past were too restrictive. He wanted…

The idea of what he wanted stunned him.

'Where are we going?' Emma couldn't suppress the smile that kept breaking out. She'd missed Christo ever since he'd left for Athens on Monday morning. Here he was, back early.

For her? A shiver of excitement tugged through her belly and she strove to suppress it.

'Somewhere we can talk.' He threaded a way through the maze of alleys, emerging on the road behind the neo-classical Palace of St Michael and St George. Minutes later they descended a ramp built into the city walls to the tiny Faleraki beach.

It was one of her favourite places. Quiet and cut off from the bustle, the little bay looked across the water to the city ramparts, the towering Old Fortress, and beneath it the marina packed with yachts. Further down the beach a ramshackle pier provided a platform for local kids who were fooling around and jumping into the depths.

Christo led her to the point at the end of the small beach and the outdoor café. Unsurprisingly, a waiter emerged instantly, leading them to a shaded spot apart from other tables. It was the sort of thing that happened all the time with Christo, whether because they recognised his face or read him as a man who expected and happily paid for the best.

Instead of a table, they were installed on a comfortable couch under a wide umbrella. Their cool drinks and a platter of food arrived minutes later, set on the glass coffee table beyond which the aquamarine shallows gave way to deeper water the colour of lapis lazuli.

Emma sighed and sank back into the cushioned seat. She could get used to this.

Just as she'd grown used to the warmth of Christo's hand enfolding hers and the buzz of delight she got when he looked at her as if she were special. Those eyes…

Her heartbeat stuttered and seemed to pause before stumbling back into rhythm.

No. She wouldn't allow flights of fancy. This charge of excitement, like his heated expression, was about desire, attraction and physical pleasure. Nothing more.

'What brought you back from Athens?' He shrugged, those powerful shoulders riding high. Still he held her hand and it struck her that his expression was different, more guarded than she'd seen it in weeks. 'Is everything all right? Are you okay?'

She sensed something had changed. Something important.

His response proved her too fanciful. 'Everything's perfect. Just as it should be.' He leaned across to add ice to his ouzo, watching it cloud. 'I simply felt like taking a long weekend.'

Christo turned, lifting his glass. Automatically Emma raised her glass of tangy local ginger beer.

'Yia mas.' To us. A traditional toast, but when Christo leaned near, with that blazing look in his eyes, Emma felt...

She blanked that thought, wishing she'd ordered a shot of fiery ouzo instead of a soft drink. Something to jerk her out of useless imaginings.

'Who was that man?'

'Sorry?'

'The man you were with.' Emma caught the echo of something hard in Christo's tone, like steel hidden beneath velvet. For a moment she wondered if it could be jealousy. The possibility made something foolish within her swell.

'A local businessman.'

Christo sipped his drink then put it down and turned more fully towards her.

'And his business with you?' There it was again, a hint of sharpness.

Emma was torn between delight and disappointment. Just because Christo was possessive didn't mean anything. She was, for now, his wife. She'd seen how far he'd go to protect the public image of a happy couple.

The bubbling happiness she'd felt since the moment he'd sought her out in the old town faded.

'Emma?' Concern coloured his voice as he took her drink from her fingers then captured that hand too. 'What's wrong? What did he—?'

'Nothing! Nothing's wrong. He didn't do anything.' With a deep breath she pushed aside that silly sense of dissatisfaction and smiled. 'He runs a business decorating and catering for weddings. He interviewed me for a job.'

'A job?' She might have said she was flying to the moon, given his expression of blank surprise.

'Something to use my skills.' And earn an income. She needed funds to get her business off the ground. She didn't want to wait ten months till they went their separate ways and she received money from the Athens project.

'You're bored?'

Emma tilted her head, surveying him. 'I need to work, Christo. The villa is lovely and I have exciting plans to turn it into an exclusive resort. But that's longer term.' At least till she could get money to seed the first stages.

'This man—he offered you a job?'

Emma saw the tight angle of Christo's jaw and hesitated. 'He's consulting his partner first, but he was very positive.'

In fact, his enthusiasm had given Emma pause. The work had sounded good, despite the commuting time from the villa, but he'd been a little too friendly, his personal interest in her obvious. She hadn't really felt comfortable, had already decided…

'I don't want you working for him.'

'Sorry?'

'He's not trustworthy.'

'You know him?' Christo was a stranger to the area.

'I know his type. It wasn't business he had in mind.'

Exactly what Emma had thought. Yet Christo's assertion, implying he had the final say over her actions, stirred indignation. She tugged a hand from his and picked up her glass, taking a long swallow, then putting it down with a click on the table.

'*I* will decide whether or not to take the job.'

The glint in his eyes told her he wanted to disagree. 'You're my wife. You don't need to work.'

Emma arched her eyebrows. 'You're worried what people will think?' She could just about forgive his attempted intervention, given her own concerns about the guy who'd interviewed her. But to be told she couldn't work because of Christo's image...

Christo shook his head. 'I'm not trying to trap you at home. I have nothing against you having a job. I'll help you find one, if you like. I just don't want someone trying to take advantage of you.'

Perhaps that should sound strange coming from the man who'd traded on her besotted naivety to trap her into marriage. Instead it sounded *caring*. Not merely the result of macho possessiveness. There was a good dose of that, judging from the jut of his jaw. But there was more too.

For a second it reminded her of the old days, with her family, and particularly Papou, being over-protective. In the past Emma had found that trying, but she realised it felt good to know someone cared. She'd missed that.

'Emma.' Christo bent closer, as if trying to decipher her thoughts.

'You're not worried the press would say a billionaire's wife shouldn't work?'

A crack of laughter sounded. 'As if that's relevant!' Then, just as suddenly, he turned sombre. 'But I'm serious about that guy. The way he looked at you, he definitely wasn't thinking about work.'

Emma looked into Christo's strikingly handsome face, looking for self-interest, for some hint of manipulation. All she read was concern.

Once more that glow of warmth filled her.

She squeezed the big hand that held hers just a fraction too tight. 'Okay, I'll bear that in mind.' She'd already decided not to take the job, but she didn't want Christo thinking he could order and she'd immediately obey. He was domineering enough without further encouragement.

For long seconds he said nothing. Then he nodded and Emma released a pent-up breath. This felt like a victory. More. It felt like caring and respect.

Deep inside something tight and knotted frayed.

Christo gathered her against him, shifting so they both faced the glorious view. A shoal of fish glinted, turning in the crystalline shallows a few metres away. A yacht appeared around the promontory, its sail pristine white against the deep blue of sea and distant land.

Emma felt the comforting thud of Christo's heart and the warm weight of his arm around her. His breath feathered her hair and she inhaled his unique cedar, leather and spice scent. Elation rose.

'I'm glad to be back on Corfu, Emma.'

She smiled up at him, surprised to hear herself admit, 'I'm glad too.'

'Busy?' The deep voice came from behind Emma next morning as she sat in the courtyard loggia. Warm hands covered her shoulders and slid down her bare arms.

The pencil spilled from her hand onto the table. Her eyelids flickered as tingling heat rushed through her. She breathed deep, inhaling the familiar scent of Christo mingling with the last wisteria blooms. It was a heady mix.

Did he pull her close or did she lean back? Either way, as usual, she melted.

It was less than an hour since she'd left him and a giggling Anthea playing hide and seek in the garden. Two hours since Christo had held Emma pinioned against the wall of the shower, water sluicing over the pair of them, lips soldered together as he'd pumped into her, bringing them both to rapturous completion.

Thinking of it made her nipples peak and awareness tighten her inner muscles.

She sighed as he bent, nuzzled the hair from her neck and grazed his teeth where her neck curved into her shoulder. Emma shuddered. He knew all her sensitive spots.

'You're too distracting. I'm supposed to be working.'

Yesterday's conversation had reminded her how much she still had to do to get her business off the ground. She'd researched the market and competitors, checked local government approval processes and developed a business plan. She'd begun a website, scouted local suppliers and made plans for changes to the villa. But her non-existent cash flow meant she couldn't proceed as fast as she'd like.

Christo lifted his head and Emma bit her tongue rather than voice the protest that rose to her lips.

'On the weekend?'

She opened her mouth to say that was what he did, spent the weekends working, but it was no longer true. Last weekend there'd been a couple of calls to the Italian they'd met in Athens to discuss their joint venture. But that was all.

What had happened to the busy entrepreneur who'd initially seemed out of place at the villa?

'What are the drawings for?' Christo sat beside her at the table, pulling his chair so close his leg brushed hers and her shoulder nudged his upper arm.

She sighed and closed the papers. 'It's a long-term vision for the villa next door. But my main focus right now really needs to be on getting this place ready.'

'You're sure you want to do that?'

'Of course.' She needed the income and she had the skills to make it work. Eventually, when she and Christo divorced, this place would be hers free and clear.

Strange how the thought of being free of Christo no longer held the allure it once had. In fact, it chilled her to the bone despite the morning's warmth.

* * *

Christo had problems with the idea of outsiders here. Security would be a nightmare but, more than that, the place was their private haven. It wasn't modern like his Athens apartment but it felt like home. More than the ostentatious house where he'd grown up ever had.

'You won't mind sharing your home with strangers?'

Christo felt Emma's muscles tighten almost imperceptibly at his words. Yet she'd seemed rapt in the idea when she talked about it before.

Because she needs to support herself. Because you robbed her of the inheritance that should be hers, at least temporarily.

A decent man would give Emma back everything he'd taken.

Christo considered himself decent, if tough. He dismissed a pang of conscience.

'It's either that or move out completely. I'd rather be on hand when there are guests, to deal with their needs.'

'What about your privacy?'

'That's not a luxury I can afford.'

Christo stilled. He felt like a heel. 'Care to show me the drawings for next door?' When Emma hesitated, he reached forward. 'May I?'

She shrugged. 'Why not? Papou bought the neighbouring property, but it needed a lot of work, and he got sick not long afterwards so he never got around to doing anything with it.'

Christo surveyed the drawings. 'You have a good eye,' he murmured, lifting the top page to look at the next and the next. 'This could be something special. Even better than developing this place.'

'You think so?'

He met her stare, noting the excitement in her eyes at

odds with the press of her lips. As if she were scared to expect too much.

'I like the combination of modern and traditional. And extending the outdoor living space next to this—' he pointed '—is it a sunken garden?'

'It is, with a fabulous view over its own cove.'

'It would make a perfect venue for exclusive celebrations.'

'Weddings in particular.' She was enthusiastic now. 'I could lure a lot of people from overseas for a romantic wedding in Greece. Or anniversaries, or private holidays. One day, when I'm solvent, I'll tackle the remodelling.'

'I could help with that. My company specialises in property development.' Though on a much larger scale.

Emma spun round in her seat, her eyes huge. 'You threatened to withdraw your money from my uncle's business unless I stayed married to you. Yet you're *offering* it to me now?'

Not Christo's finest hour. He'd been desperate to convince Emma to stay with him. That need hadn't gone. It was just tempered by other things.

Feelings. It's tempered by what you feel for her. What you want her to feel for you.

Christo's pulse hammered high in his throat. Suddenly he didn't feel as invincible as usual.

'You agreed to my terms and I trust you to keep them,' he said, as if that was all he wanted, her presence for another ten months.

Christo paused, wondering if she had any notion how significant that admission was. Trust didn't come easily to him. Yet he'd discovered in Emma a woman unlike any he'd known. A woman who might disagree with him, but who, he was sure, wouldn't lie. She was sexy and passionate, gentle and emotional, practical and forthright. She cared for orphans and ageing housekeepers and maybe even for him.

Everything within him stilled as he acknowledged how much he wanted that.

'I want you to be happy and fulfilled, Emma.'

His words clearly took her by surprise, despite all they'd shared. But why shouldn't she be surprised? He'd couched their intimacy only in terms of sex. He'd let her imagine their connection was all about desire and satisfying carnal appetites. The truth, he'd discovered, ran far, far deeper.

Still she hesitated.

'Look on it as an advance against the money I owe you from the Athens property.' Not that he intended to use her funds for this. It would be his gift, but she didn't need to know that now.

Emma tilted her head to one side, as if trying to see him better. 'That would virtually dismantle the hold you have over me. You do realise that?'

Christo shrugged as if it were a small thing. As if his heart wasn't pummelling his ribs sickeningly and his neck wasn't prickling at the thought of her slipping away from him. But it wouldn't come to that.

'Until the year's up I still have ultimate say over the property.' He couldn't relinquish total control yet.

Slowly she nodded. But the reminder of that ace up his sleeve didn't dim the wonder in those hazel eyes. Her expression made him glow. As he had when he'd found her yesterday and she'd looked at him with such patent delight.

Had anyone ever looked at him as Emma did? For sure, he'd never felt this way about any other woman.

He lifted his hand to her satiny cheek, brushing it with the back of his knuckle. Something welled high in his chest and he opened his mouth to tell her...

'Emma!' A child's voice rang out and they turned to see Anthea and Dora's niece step out of the house. The new nanny released the girl's hand and predictably she flew across the courtyard to Emma's side like a bullet.

Emma gathered her up, settling her on her lap and nodding as Anthea told her how she'd helped tidy up.

Seeing the two together, the sensation in Christo's chest twisted into something powerful and barely familiar. This was how he'd imagined them, even better than he'd imagined. Yet it wasn't mere satisfaction he experienced.

Abruptly Anthea stopped chattering and turned to him, holding her arms out. 'Cwisto!' Inevitably her lisp made him smile. 'Up, pease. Up!'

It still stunned him that he'd built a rapport with Cassie's daughter. That he hadn't inadvertently hurt her because of his lack of experience. Guilt and the shadow of the past had persuaded him it wouldn't be possible. That he didn't deserve her trust.

Christo looked from Anthea to Emma and absorbed a barrage of emotions. Who'd have believed his world would be upended by two females? One tiny and demanding. The other feisty yet sweet. Both vulnerable. Both adorable.

Emma passed the little girl over to him, and he read in Emma's expression something he hadn't seen before. He wanted to freeze that moment, analyse that look, question her. But Anthea was wriggling, demanding he take her to see the baby birds in the nest they'd found in the garden.

He got up, slanting a look at Emma. But she turned away, folding the plans that riffled in the breeze.

Later, he told himself. This was too important to ignore.

CHAPTER THIRTEEN

'THE PLACE DEFINITELY has excellent potential,' Christo said as they left the empty villa and headed down the path to a private cove, smaller but no less beautiful than theirs next door. With each step their view of the jewel-toned water improved. Drifts of wildflowers, pink, white, blue and yellow, frothed up against the boles of massive olive trees and iconic tall cypresses.

Emma nodded, trying to stifle bubbling excitement that Christo was so positive about the place. All through their inspection Christo had asked tough, insightful questions. He'd closely examined the house and outbuildings which Emma hoped to turn into extra accommodation.

'It would take a lot of money to renovate,' she said. The more they inspected, the more she feared she'd underestimated costs. Emma knew events management but nothing about building. That was Christo's field.

He took her hand, weaving his fingers through hers. Emma's breath stalled then accelerated to a gallop. Ever since Athens he took every chance to touch her, to be close. The attraction between them was real, not manufactured for the press.

Was that why her heart sang when he touched her?

It might not be love but this…fling felt wonderful. As if she'd undone the shackles of grief, self-doubt and anger and had stepped free of them. She felt lighter at heart than she could ever remember.

See? She could enjoy the moment. Take pleasure like a sophisticated adult and…

Christo smiled and her thoughts frayed. He tugged her hand, leading her off the path and onto the deserted crescent of fine sand. Metres away the sun glinted off shallow water that sparkled like gems. It was a private paradise, screened at this end of the beach from open water by a tumble of rocks. There was just the shush of the sea on sand, a song-bird in the trees above and Christo.

Yearning trembled through her.

'Marketed right and run well, it would be worth the in-vestment. It can't be left. A vacant property will just de-grade. And with this—' he gestured to the private beach '—you're onto a winner.'

Emma nodded, struggling to focus on the property, not on the man. 'I've tried to calculate how much it would cost but I haven't got very far.'

He turned back, his grey-blue eyes snaring hers. 'Leave that to me. I'll get someone onto it.'

'You will?' Was he serious about helping with the place?

'Of course.' He released her fingers and instead wrapped both hands around her waist. 'I'll release the resources so you can remodel. My staff will chase up the best local builders.'

Emma was so stunned it took a second to register what he was doing with his hands. Until air wafted around her torso as he urged her arms up, pulling her top over her head.

'Christo!' She darted a look around the empty beach. 'We can't.' Yet her breathlessness proved she was more excited than outraged. Especially when, with one swift movement, he hauled his shirt over his head and dumped it on the sand.

Emma's heart beat too fast as she took in his muscled body. She'd discovered one of her favourite things was to lay her head on his chest, feeling the strong thud of his heart beneath her ear and listening to it hammer as she flicked his nipple with her tongue, or slid her hand down to squeeze his shaft and tease him till he growled and rolled her beneath him.

No growling now. Christo shucked his shoes and the rest of his clothes while she stood staring. She'd thought herself accustomed to the sight of him, all taut muscle and proud virility. But she'd never seen him under the bright blue sky, stark-naked and mightily aroused.

He looked like some Greek god, perfectly proportioned, formidably sexy and utterly intent. Her body softened in anticipation. Involuntarily her inner muscles squeezed and she felt the slick wetness of arousal.

'Believe me, Emma, we can.'

In seconds he'd undone her bra and tossed it onto his clothes. The sun warmed her bare flesh but it was nothing to the blaze of heat as his gaze licked her. She thrilled at the ardour she read in his face, yet they were outdoors and...

'Don't cover yourself, sweet Emma.' She hadn't realised she'd made to cover her breasts till warm hands shackled her wrists. 'Please? I want to see you. You know we're private here. You can trust me.'

Standing there half-naked, feeling totally exposed, Emma realised she *did* trust her husband. More than she'd once believed possible.

'You want sex on the beach?' Emma felt a ripple of shock. But then, despite weeks of passionate sex, she'd been a virgin just a short time ago. This was still new.

He smiled, and her heart took up Zumba behind her ribs. 'With you, I want sex everywhere.'

Christo's gaze snared hers. Arousal beat hard and low in her pelvis. She told herself this was merely physical. Nothing else, nothing to worry about. Conveniently she silenced the part of her that said this felt like far more than sex.

'If you want,' he added. His hands hung, fisted, by his sides and Emma read tension in the line of his jaw.

He meant it. He'd leave her be if she chose. Contrarily, the realisation conquered her natural reserve. She toed off her sandals, her hands going to the zip of her skirt. Then she paused, one last doubt surfacing.

'If we have sex it's not because you've promised to help refit the villa.' She held his gaze, willing him to believe. 'I'm not like your mother. I don't do sex for money.'

Christo stood unmoving so long, she wondered if she'd said the wrong thing. But how could it be wrong when it was the truth?

Finally he unlocked frozen muscles and shook his head. 'You're nothing like her, Emma. You think I don't know that?'

She lifted her shoulders. 'I don't want any misunderstandings between us.'

'Good.' He stepped so close his erection brushed her skirt and she shivered as need corkscrewed through her lower body. 'Just honesty between us now. That's what I want. And you, sweet Emma. I want you so badly.'

Christo's words set off a chain reaction inside, making internal muscles spasm needily and her heart thrum wildly. 'In that case, I hope you have a condom.'

He did. By the time Emma was naked he was sheathed and she was on her back on the warm sand, Christo kneeling like a conquering hero between her legs. His eyes had that glazed look he got when aroused and, when he nudged her, she automatically rose to meet him, the sensation so exquisite, she stifled a cry of delight.

'Don't hold back, *glyka mou*. I like hearing you.'

With a tilt of his hips Christo slowly drove in till she felt him lodged right at her heart. Emma told herself that was impossible, but that was how it felt when he tenderly kissed her on the lips and gently rocked against her, evoking sensations that should be just physical but which felt profoundly emotional too.

Like caring, homecoming, sharing, lo...

Warning bells clamoured and Emma knew she had to

break the spell of his tenderness. It was enough to make
her believe in things she shouldn't.

Holding tight to his shoulders, she lifted her head and
grazed his ear with her teeth. Then, as he'd said he liked
hearing her, she whispered to Christo just what she wanted
him to do next.

It was like igniting gunpowder. For a millisecond there
was breathless stillness, then he erupted in a surge of powerful energy, driving against her in an erotic rhythm that
stole her breath as his hand moved first to her breast, then
to the sensitive bud between her legs and…

'Christo!' His name was a hoarse shout over and over
again that faded to a gasp as he took her to a peak, then
another, shattering with her in a cataclysmic orgasm that
engulfed them in rapture.

When she was back in her body, Emma felt filled to the
brim, sated and spent yet emotional and needy, blinking
back tears of reaction to the most astounding experience
of her life. All she knew as she hugged Christo close was
that she wanted to stay this way for ever.

Gradually her breathing eased and her heartbeat too.
Still she clung tight, absorbing the scent of sweat and sex
and maleness, feeling the slippery silk of her lover's skin
against her.

Not her lover. Her husband.

Or maybe more.

Her breath tore from her throat.

'Come on, let's wash the sand away.' The deep voice
murmured in her ear as Christo moved, ignoring her protest and lifting her into his arms.

The water, though not cold, was chilly enough to shock
her into full alertness. He waded into the water, carrying
her in his arms, and Emma clung to him as if she hadn't
spent her childhood swimming several times a week. She
didn't want to think about why she felt so needy.

Later, as they lay sprawled on flat rocks at the end of the beach drying in the sun, Emma found herself doing what she'd told herself she wouldn't—seeking more from Christo.

It wasn't his money she wanted and, while he made her feel like a goddess when he took her in his arms and made love to her, Emma wanted to understand him.

Because she loved him.

She'd tried to stifle the knowledge but it wouldn't be silenced any more. She'd told herself it was just sex between them, sex and a business arrangement. But she'd deluded herself. The Christo she'd discovered in Greece was the same man she'd fallen for in Australia. It was only the aberration of the loveless marriage that didn't fit the man she'd come to know and like all over again.

Except, after having heard him describe his parents, she had an inkling about how he could separate love and marriage.

Unfortunately she couldn't do that and the realisation terrified her. Was she fooling herself again, tumbling into love with this man? Did she really know him or did she only think so?

And, if she did, what did she do next?

'Tell me about Cassie.'

'Sorry?' Christo opened one eye and squinted down at the damp honey-brown hair on his chest where Emma rested her head. He enjoyed the feel of her there, her body soft against him, one thigh over his so the intimate heat between her legs was tantalisingly close.

'I wondered about your stepsister.'

Christo frowned. 'Why?'

Emma lifted her head, her palm on his chest. Her eyes were sombre. As if, while he'd been lazing on a cloud of wellbeing, she'd been in a bleaker place altogether.

'*Glyka mou!* What's wrong?' Concern rose instantly.

She shook her head. 'Nothing. I was just thinking...' She shrugged then looked at him almost defiantly. 'How much I don't know about you. You never mention Cassie. But I feel she was important to you.'

Christo stared, stunned at the woman who, once again, turned his world upside down. Any other lover would be snuggled bonelessly against him, enjoying the comedown from that amazing high they'd shared. But not his Emma.

Why was he surprised? Emma was unlike any other woman.

'You said we'd be honest with each other.'

'That doesn't mean I want you prying into ancient history.'

'I see.' She didn't pull away but her luscious body stiffened. Her eyes grew shuttered, no longer reflecting the green of the sea but turning a flat, muddy brown. She turned her head away and guilt stirred in his gullet. He should have tempered his response, not barked at her because she'd touched on what he hated to think about.

Christo's heart thumped as he waited for Emma to roll away but she simply subsided where she'd been. Though the way she held herself reminded him of an animal nursing a wound, stillness betraying pain.

He lifted a hand to stroke her, then stopped.

Christo had spent half a lifetime not thinking about this. He baulked at opening up the past. Yet this was the first time Emma had asked him for anything.

Except a divorce.

He huffed an amused breath at the memory of her breathing fire as she'd demanded he release her from their marriage. She'd been so outrageously, provocatively sexy. At that moment he'd thought he'd die if he didn't have her.

Just as suddenly Christo's amusement faded.

He had her for now. But for how long? He wanted her

permanently, and not because of Anthea or words on a legal document. He just…wanted her for himself.

He dropped his hand to her hair, feeling the suck of her indrawn breath against his chest. For some obscure reason, this mattered to her.

And since Emma mattered to him…

Christo turned his head, his gaze drifting across the blue-green sea.

'She was eleven or twelve when she came to the house. A shy little thing with freckles, plaits and the biggest brown eyes you've ever seen.' Eyes just like Anthea's.

Against his chest Emma stirred but said nothing.

'My father and his second wife had just returned from their honeymoon. Cassie had stayed with relatives in the States while they travelled.'

'How old were you?'

'Almost eighteen.' Two years older than when he'd discovered his mother with her teenage lover. At eighteen Christo had worked in the family business and studied, living up to his father's demand that he excel at both.

'You really only met her once?'

'For a weekend. She arrived on Friday and left on Sunday.' Christo swallowed, the action hurting, as if something sharp had lodged in his throat.

Emma sat up. 'Christo? What's wrong?'

He jerked his gaze round to her, biting the urge to say *he* was wrong.

Get a grip, Karides.

He levered himself up to sit, draping his arms over his knees. 'Nothing. It's okay.'

Was he reassuring himself or her? Despite the sun, his nape prickled with cold.

'She was shy, even with her own mother, and with my father…' He shook his head. 'I think I mentioned he was a tough man. He hadn't a sentimental bone in his body. As for being kind to little girls...

'She tried to avoid him as much as possible and I helped her.'

He'd felt sorry for the kid, given her mother had seemed more concerned about placating her new husband than helping her daughter acclimatise to a new country and a new family. Christo, used to being alone, had been charmed by Cassie's hesitant smiles and shy interest. For the first time in his life, he'd felt he could make a difference.

There was a terrible irony there, if only he'd known.

'I took her swimming and sailing.' Getting her out of his father's way. 'And she used to watch me draw. She found my cartoons amusing.' That, if only he'd realised, had been his worst mistake. His father was annoyed enough at him 'wasting' his time with Cassie, but to have her encourage his scribbling wasn't to be borne. The old man viewed his interest in art with suspicion, a sign of weakness in his heir, who had to be tough and ruthlessly efficient. Real men didn't draw or play games. They closed deals, kept a tight rein on business and took hard decisions.

'She must have enjoyed being with you.'

Christo nodded. 'Yes. She even laughed, when she thought my father wasn't around.' He noticed a pebble on the rock at his feet and threw it, watching it arc over the water, then disappear as if it had never been.

Just like Cassie.

'But my father noticed.' Christo found another pebble and threw it. 'He was concerned about me. Apparently, with my stepsister I was soft and lacking seriousness. He was trying to make a man of me. Not someone who frittered away his time playing games or being sentimental over a kid.'

'I don't think I'd have liked your father.'

Christo turned to see Emma sitting, arms wrapped around her legs, chin resting on her knees. Even scowling she made his pulse quicken.

'He was moulding me so I could face whatever the commercial world threw at me. He lost his own father early and didn't want me struggling as he had.'

Emma's eyes met his and something thumped deep in his chest. 'The world isn't just commerce. There's love and friendship and family.'

Not as far as his father had been concerned. 'The upshot was he decided Cassie wasn't a good influence.'

'But she was only a little girl!' Emma's gaze widened.

Christo spread his hands. 'He felt I wasn't acting like a man.'

That had cut deep, especially as Christo had spent his life living up to his father's expectations.

'There's nothing manly about making a little kid feel alone and scared.'

Christo nodded. 'I agree. But he didn't see it that way. He'd never been one for close relationships. His marriages were about possessing beautiful women who enhanced his kudos.' He paused. 'Anyway, he decided Cassie couldn't stay. She was shipped back to relatives in the States.'

Emma looked aghast. 'Just because you'd been nice to her?'

At last she understood. 'Because I had to be tough. He wouldn't allow anything else and I...' Christo sighed and looked away '...accepted that.' Which made it even worse. 'So she went to America and I never heard from her again. After a while, I forgot about her. Occasionally I'd wonder what she was doing but I never followed up.' Bitterness was sharp on his tongue. 'So I didn't know the relatives who took her in later decided they didn't want another kid to look after. She ended up in foster care, shunted from one place to another.'

'It wasn't your fault.' Emma's whisper slid through him like the serpent in Eden, so tempting.

'Because of me she was banished to live her life with people who didn't want her. Meanwhile, I got on with *my* life as if she didn't matter at all.'

Christo threw another stone out into the water with such force, he almost wrenched his shoulder. 'If I'd done the honourable thing, if I'd bothered to check up on her, things might have turned out differently. She might still be alive.' He dragged in air to fill tight lungs. 'But I'm stronger now. I didn't do right by Cassie, but you can be sure I *will* do my duty by her daughter.'

Emma curled her arms tight around her knees and stared out to sea. Beside her Christo did the same, clearly not wanting to talk further.

Who'd have thought a simple question about his step-sister would reveal so much? Combined with what he'd told her before, it painted a picture that made her heart lurch with sympathy and pain. It was even worse than she'd thought.

A cold, controlling father and a distant, self-absorbed mother. His family hadn't been a family at all. It was re-markable they'd produced a man with as much decency as Christo.

Emma had heard his self-reproach as he'd spoken of Cassie. As if he, as a teenager, could have gone against the girl's mother and stepfather to provide a home for her.

Who'd provided a home for him?

He spoke of doing the honourable thing and about duty. Was that what drove Christo? Emma recalled his words when he'd found her in Corfu. About giving her his name and his word, as if that pledge was more important than love.

Which made sense for a man who didn't know love at all.

For a man who possibly never would.

The experts said what you experienced as a child co-loured your character for life. That lack of caring in a child's life stunted their emotional growth.

Emma's abdominal muscles spasmed as the pain intensified. She'd convinced herself she was over Christo, that she could enjoy uncomplicated sex then move on. But she'd given her heart to him in Australia and hadn't stopped loving him, despite anger and disillusionment.

Contrary to what she'd told herself, she'd secretly hoped Christo would come to love her. She'd taken his kindness, passion and ability to make her feel special as signs he'd begun to feel for her what she did for him.

Emma gritted her teeth as the pain settled into a cold, hard ache in her belly and chest.

She'd thought he was softening towards her. That they'd shared more than sex. There'd been companionship and caring, humour, a sense that they were building something together.

In a flash of blinding clarity she realised she'd seen what she wanted to see.

Christo was driven by an unshakeable sense of duty. It was there in his determination to care for his step-niece. To look to the needs of Dora, of all his staff, and Emma too.

No matter how much she admired him for the honour-able man he'd become despite the odds, duty was no re-placement for love.

She shut her eyes and pictured him with Anthea, re-membering his hesitation. True, his wariness was easing, and hopefully that relationship would blossom even more.

But Emma couldn't expect miracles. A man driven by duty, who had no experience of love, would never give her what she needed.

They'd found common ground but that was based on sex. Everything, even his desire to be here on the island, hinged on that and his need to portray the fiction of a happy family to the watching world.

Look at the way he'd snapped at her question about Cassie. Christo hated sharing anything personal. Her status as his wife didn't give her special privileges there.

Her husband was as likely to fall in love with her as snow falling in summer.

Even if theoretically it were possible, could she live with him in a one-sided relationship for the rest of the year, hoping for a miracle?

Emma had never thought of herself as greedy. Yet the idea of giving her all to the man she loved, knowing he felt only a sense of responsibility and lust for her, made her crumple inside.

What if the lust faded? What if someone else caught his eye? That was likely given the glamorous circles he moved in. Emma knew part of the reason he desired her was because she was a novelty to him. Despite the makeover in Athens, she wasn't cut out for his world.

With a hiss of indrawn air Emma shot to her feet. Seconds later she was stumbling across the sand to the scatter of discarded clothes.

'Emma? What's wrong?'

She swayed, struck by a blow of need so strong it almost felled her. The perverse, futile need to turn around and run straight back to Christo.

But what would that achieve? She needed distance. Time to think, to sort out her head and her heart.

'I've just remembered…something.' She grabbed the froth of her cotton lace skirt and stepped into it, yanking up the zip. 'I need to get back to the villa.' Her head spun uselessly as she tried to come up with an excuse. 'There's something I need to do.'

'What is it?'

He was behind her, so close his breath kissed her bare

neck and hair as she wrestled with her clothes. She forced herself to take a deep breath and drag the top on, feeling the material abrade her nipples. But she didn't have time for a bra. She had to get away.

A warm hand closed on her elbow and she jumped so violently, he let go. But now he was before her, those penetrating eyes concerned. It was a terrible temptation to think she was wrong. That maybe Christo did feel...

Emma reared back. Her lovesick heart wanted to believe in a happy ending when she *knew*, when he'd already spelled it out as clearly as he could, that he only wanted sex, and stability for his niece. She'd already fallen for wishful thinking once. She knew better now.

He stood before her, naked and powerfully built, and her longing was so great she had to avert her eyes.

'Talk to me, Emma.' His voice was warm velvet, enfolding her.

She stepped back, almost tripping over a sandal. 'Not now. I have to go—'

'I'm not letting you go anywhere when you're clearly upset.' He crossed his arms over that powerful chest, the picture of masculine obstinacy, and fear crested. Fear that if she wasn't careful she'd convince herself to stay, to settle for being a mere convenient wife rather than someone he cherished.

'It's not up to you to *let* me go anywhere.' Emma took refuge in anger, though it was only surface deep. She was too miserable to muster real outrage.

Then he did what she'd feared. Instead of blustering he turned gentle. As if he really cared about her.

'I'm worried about you, *glyka mou*. What's happened?'

Emma drew a slow breath and raised her eyes to his. 'I can't go on like this. I can't—' she waved one hand in the air '—keep up the pretence for a whole twelve months. This isn't going to work.'

From concerned, his proud features immediately turned stony. 'How can you say that? It's working beautifully.'

She shook her head, tugging her gaze away, feeling the instant ease in tension as she did. 'For you. For Anthea maybe. But not for me. I just can't do it any more.'

Emma registered a ripple of movement in his big frame, as if from a rising tide of energy. 'But you will. You gave your word.'

His voice was cooler than she'd heard in ages, each word clipped. The voice of a stranger.

'No! You forced me into a situation where I had no choice. I took your devil's bargain because that's all I could do. But it's impossible.'

Christo stepped towards her and she shrank back. Instantly he froze.

'Please.' Her voice wobbled and she had to work to get the words out. 'I need to be alone.'

Emma's breath came in laboured gasps. She swung around and fumbled for her sandals. But as she scrambled towards the path a hard hand closed around her elbow.

'Not so fast.'

CHAPTER FOURTEEN

CHRISTO REELED. HALF an hour ago they'd been wrapped in each other, lost in a blast of ecstasy so intense he was sure it had marked him for life.

Emma had marked him. Her sweet generosity. Her fiery strength. Her gentle caring.

He'd never known a woman like her. Had never expected to and had certainly never anticipated the effect she'd have on him.

Now he was entangled, caught so fast in the net of his own longing that there was no escape.

She couldn't expect him to let her go. Not now. Not when he'd glimpsed paradise with her. Christo had learned never to expect miracles. Everything in his world always came at a price.

But, despite everything, Emma had given herself to him freely, unstintingly. Not just in bed, but in so many other ways, ways that made him think the boundaries he'd known all his life could be broken. That if he made the effort perhaps there could be *more*.

He wanted that more so badly. He wanted Emma.

'Talk to me, Emma.' Nausea stirred at the thought of her so distressed. Of *him* distressing her. She trembled in his hold but didn't try to escape.

'What is it? Is it because of what I did? Because I didn't save Cassie?' Before he'd shared that, Emma had been content in his arms.

Guilt over his stepsister lay heavily, only lightening occasionally. When Anthea smiled her increasingly cheeky grin or put her hand in his. Or when Emma gave him that glowing look that made his heart stop.

'What?' Emma turned and his gut contracted when he saw that her lashes were spiked with tears.

'You despise me, don't you?' The words ground from him, revealing the depths of his fear.

Once he'd never have admitted that to anyone, even himself. He'd learned, almost before he could walk, to conceal weakness. But Emma stripped away his ability to pretend. Self-preservation should have kept his mouth shut about the past, but for once he'd wanted to share everything because it was Emma wanting to know.

Look where that had got him.

'I don't despise you.' Her words were choked and unconvincing.

Christo's pulse beat raggedly. He knew he'd guessed right. Yet still he couldn't release her. He slid his hand to her wrist, feeling the tumultuous pulse there.

'Then what? You weren't in a hurry to leave before I told you about Cassie.'

'It's not that.' Her gaze slid from his and Christo felt the lie like a blow to the back of his legs severing his tendons.

Now he found the willpower to release her and step back.

'Don't lie to me, Emma.' That was one of the things he treasured about her. She always told him the truth.

'I'm not—' He felt her gaze on him. 'Christo? Are you all right?'

He grimaced. Even now, when she knew the worst of his faults, Emma could find it in her to be concerned for him. She was too caring for her own good.

'No. I'm not.' He hefted a breath, trying to fill lungs that had seized. Looking down into drenched hazel eyes Christo realised he had no option but to tell *her* the truth. The whole truth, that he'd been grappling with for weeks now. 'I can't let you go.'

She stepped back and Christo felt as if he'd cracked right through the middle, seeing her retreat.

'You have to.' He heard her desperation and knew this was his last chance.

Pride be damned. He couldn't let her go without a fight. 'I need you, Emma. Please. I…love you.'

He'd never thought to hear, much less say, those words. They were foreign on his tongue but as soon as he said them something that felt remarkably like peace settled around him.

It was short-lived.

Emma flung up her hand as if to ward him off. 'Don't, please. That's too cruel.'

Gently Christo captured her hand and pulled it down, resisting the impulse to tug her to him and never let her go. 'Why is it cruel?'

He was the one being rejected. But seeing Emma so distraught tempered his reaction.

Sad brown eyes met his. 'You're just saying that because you know that I…' Her chin came up. 'I was in love with you when we married. You think you can make me stay if you pretend to love me now.'

Christo shook his head, ignoring the dart of pain at the fact she spoke of loving him in the past tense.

'I'm not pretending, *karthia mou*. I promised to be honest with you.' He paused, watching her eyes widen. 'I want more than a convenient marriage. I want you as my partner, my love, the one that I cherish for the rest of my days.'

Instead of the response he'd hoped for, Emma's mouth turned down at the corners. Pain clouded her expression.

'It's too late, Christo. Once I might have fallen for that, but not now.'

'I see. You don't trust me after all.' He couldn't blame her. He'd set about winning her with ruthless efficiency. Now, looking back on his determination to put his ring on Emma's finger, he understood it was because he'd been falling for her from the very first. At the time he hadn't had the emotional understanding to recognise he was falling in love, yet he'd known instinctively he needed this woman in his life.

Emma shook her head, her hair a tangle around her shoulders. Her red top was inside out, her skirt drooping on one side where the zip hadn't pulled up all the way, and her nose was pink. She was still the most beautiful woman he knew. Christo's heart gave a mighty thud, as if trying to leap free of his rib cage and throw itself on her mercy.

'I won't hold you to our agreement.' It killed him to say it but how could he keep her by force? 'Your uncle's business is safe. Your assets are too.'

He read surprise on her face and pushed harder.

'That's what I was going to tell you today. That I want this to be a real marriage. That I want more from you than just a legal agreement and a home for Anthea.'

Her chin tilted. 'And sex.'

He nodded. 'And sex.' The thought had an inevitable effect with a surge of blood to the groin. 'I want more, Emma. I'm greedy. I want *you*. The whole of you. I want to be the one you care for because I care for you. I *love* you.' The words came easier this time, despite the fact he felt stretched on a torture rack by her lack of response.

Christo stood, waiting for her to capitulate, to admit she cared for him even a little. To give him hope.

Nothing. Just that frozen look of shock.

Defeat was a boulder crushing his chest, flattening his very being. Yet he couldn't give up. His feelings for her were too vital.

Finally he dragged out the words. 'I won't stand in your way, Emma. But, wherever you go, I'll be there. Hoping you change your mind. If you go to Melbourne, I'll buy a home there. If you stay in the Corfu villa, I'll look for a place nearby.' He dragged his hand through his hair, silently admitting his desperation. 'After all, you'll want to see Anthea from time to time.' He prayed she did. It looked like being the only way he'd get to see Emma.

'But your business is based in Athens!'

Christo huffed out a terse laugh. 'You think that will stop me?' He shook his head. 'For you I'd give that up. I've got more than enough money for a lifetime.' As he said it Christo felt an unexpected sense of freedom. Never in his life had he contemplated a world without Karides Enterprises. 'There's more to life than business.'

His father would be spinning in his grave.

But this was his life. Not his father's.

Emma faltered back a step, her hand going to her throat. 'You couldn't. It's your life.'

'*Part* of my life,' he said slowly. 'A part that I enjoy, most of the time. But there are more important things in my life now. Like you.'

Emma heard his words and told herself this was a trap to keep her in a convenient marriage.

But when she saw the excitement and wonder in Christo's eyes it was hard not to believe him.

'I'm not my father, Emma. I saw his life and I didn't want it, even as I spent my time learning how to be him.'

'No,' she whispered, unable to stop herself. 'You aren't him. You sent Cassie away. You tried to help her. You're helping her daughter.'

That had to count for something. Christo was a better man than his father.

'I love you, *karthia mou*.' There were those words again. He called her 'his heart'. How was a woman supposed to resist that? 'Ah, Emma, don't cry.' He lifted a finger to her face, brushing away the single tear that had spilled down her cheek. 'I didn't mean to hurt you.'

'I just don't know what to believe.'

His hand dropped. 'If nothing else, believe I'll never intentionally hurt you again.' Christo swallowed. 'I've got a lot to learn, like how to care for a family. Maybe that's why I was so determined to win you and keep you. For my own selfish reasons and not for Anthea at all. I understood, though I couldn't admit it, that I needed you. For your beautiful, loving heart.'

To Emma's amazement he took a step away. A chill enveloped her.

'If I thought it would work I'd promise you jewels and designer clothes. There's a luxury yacht off Santorini, a ski chalet at St Moritz and a chateau in the Loire.' As she watched, his intent gaze grew cloudy. 'But I know you, Emma. You care about people more than things. There's nothing more I can say. Words alone won't convince you.'

His eyes were bleak, his sensual mouth a grim line. Every line of that strong, superb body spoke of pain.

And it struck her that she believed him. These weren't empty words. He really would change his life to win her, move to Australia to be with her.

Even in the days of their courtship Christo hadn't actively lied. She'd been the one spinning fairy tales out of his kindness and gentle wooing, building them into far more than he'd ever implied.

She stared into those smoky eyes, feeling the depth of pain he didn't bother to conceal. Christo stood there, uncaring about his nakedness, as if nothing mattered but convincing her.

'You'd really give up the business for me?'

Fire sparked in those eyes. Emma saw blue flames ignite. 'I'll do whatever it takes. Just say the word.'

Abruptly the dreadful tightness wrapping her ribs eased and she took a shuddery breath of relief. Of hope.

'I might still want those designer clothes if I'm going to look like a billionaire's woman.'

The fire in his eyes became a blaze of heat as he absorbed her words. 'Clothes don't make the woman, Emma.'

'Or the man.' She nodded at his naked body and he shrugged, a smile flickering at the corner of his mouth.

'I'm hoping you'll decide it's what's inside that counts.'

If Emma hadn't been so close she'd never have seen the shadow of self-doubt in his expression. Never have noticed the way his pulse thundered too hard at his temple. As if, despite all his experience bringing off hugely profitable deals, Christo still feared he wasn't good enough for her.

Emma stepped up to him, putting her hand to his pounding chest. 'There's something you should know.'

Christo's hand clamped hers to him. His jaw tightened, as if expecting the worst. 'Tell me.'

'I tried but I never fell out of love with you.'

It took long seconds for her words to sink in. 'You still love me?' Beneath her hand Christo's heart took up a helter-skelter rhythm that matched hers.

Emma nodded and suddenly they were both grinning. His hands framed her face. 'You love me.' This time he said it as if he believed it.

'And you love me.' Now she could see it in his face, feel it in the rippling tremor that passed through him. How wrong she'd been, imagining Christo incapable of deep emotion. For there it was, clear as day.

Then his hands were on her, not undressing her or seducing her, but lifting her high and swirling her round and round till the world spun and the only solid thing in it was Christo.

Finally he stopped, panting, and collapsed on the sand, cushioning her as she landed on him.

'My own Emma.' He wrapped his arms around her. 'You give me heart to be the man I never thought I could be.'

'And you give me courage to be more than I'd ever thought possible.' The moment felt so huge, so momentous.

'Stop talking and kiss me, wife.'

Instead of taking offence at his command, Emma gladly complied. Then she made a demand of her own, which provoked one of Christo's trademark sexy smiles and kept them on the beach for hours celebrating.

EPILOGUE

AFTER MONTHS OF detailed planning and intense work the neighbouring villa was finally open. The residence was elegant and well-appointed and the gardens a triumph. Christo's staff had provided expert assistance but it was Emma and her team of locals who'd pulled it all together.

Christo stood in the sunken garden, redolent with the velvet scent of roses, cypresses and the salt tang of the sea. The days grew shorter but, as if ordained by fate, or perhaps his wife's sheer positivity, the afternoon sun shone bright in a cloudless sky.

His gaze wandered from the draperies of sea-green gauze and silk that led from the shallow steps, past the flowering shrubs, to the pergola where he stood. The place had a festive air.

'You look like the cat who swallowed the cream.'

Christo turned to Damen, grinning beside him.

'Can you blame me?'

His friend shook his head. 'The transformation is stunning.'

Christo knew he was talking about the villa, once sad and neglected, now an inviting showpiece. But the real change, he knew, was within himself. He was a different man from the one who'd flown to Melbourne to secure a commercial property and a convenient wife.

Not for the first time he paused to wonder at old man Katsoyiannis agreeing to the deal. He'd been as sharp as a tack, nobody's fool, and so protective of his granddaughter. Had he seen what Christo hadn't? That Emma was the perfect woman for him?

'Emma's the one responsible.' Not just for the renovation, but for the change in him.

'She's a miracle worker, and not only with bricks and mortar.' Damen clapped him on the shoulder. 'I've never seen you looking so relaxed, or so happy.'

Christo shrugged, not bothering to conceal a smile. 'What can I say? Marriage agrees with me.' It wasn't just the fact that he delegated more and worked mainly from their home in Corfu. The life he shared with Emma and little Anthea was filled with joy. 'You should try it.'

Ignoring Damen's choke of shock, he turned away.

There was Dora, surrounded by relatives and friends. The familiar faces he'd come to know from Corfu. A scattering of invitees from Athens. On the other side of the garden Emma's cousin Maia chatted to Clio, both looking effortlessly chic, and both ignoring the attempts of men aged from seventeen to seventy to catch their attention.

Neither woman could hold a candle to his Emma.

'There she is.' Damen's voice made him look past the crowd.

At first all he saw was Emma's friend Steph descending the steps to the garden. Did that explain the breathless quality of Damen's voice? Christo hadn't missed the undercurrent between them.

Then he forgot all else as he caught sight of Emma.

Once again she wore the slim-fitting gown of cream that made her waist look impossibly small and she as fragile as gossamer.

Except his wife was anything but fragile. She was strong and determined, but kind and caring too. *Loving.*

His breath escaped on the thought.

Loving. That was Emma.

Her head was up, an antique lace veil framing her features. With every step the tourmaline eardrops he'd given her swung and gleamed, but they couldn't outshine the happiness on her face. As Emma's eyes met his Christo felt that familiar thump, as if their two hearts beat as one. Then she smiled and the world turned radiant.

Her uncle walked beside her, beaming. And…

'Cwisto!' Anthea barrelled into his legs, wrapping her arms around his thighs and crushing her posy of flowers.

'Here, sweetie, stand with me.' Steph, in her green bridesmaid's dress, beckoned the little girl, but Anthea shook her head.

'Can't I stay with you, Cwisto?' Big brown eyes met his. He knew he was being manipulated but did he care?

'Of course.' He took her hand in his. 'You're part of this too.'

For, in renewing their vows, Emma committed herself to both of them. As he committed himself to her.

Then Emma's uncle led her forward and Christo took his bride's hand, drawing her close. Never had he felt such profound emotion as when he saw the love in her clear gaze.

'You take my breath away, *karthia mou*.' He bent his head and gathered her to him, kissing her until he felt her turn satisfyingly boneless.

A small hand tugged his trouser leg and Anthea's piercing whisper penetrated. 'Not *now*, Cwisto. Be good. You have to wait till *after* the pwomises.'

The crowd laughed and Emma's eyes danced as she leaned back, breathless, in his embrace. 'Yes, there's plenty of time for kisses later.'

'I'll hold you to that, *agapi mou*.' Then, grinning, he lifted Anthea in his other arm and turned to the celebrant.

* * * * *

BILLIONAIRE'S MEDITERRANEAN PROPOSAL

JULIA JAMES

For Joyce

CHAPTER ONE

TARA SASHAYED INTO the opulent function room at the prestigious West End hotel along with the rest of the models fresh off the catwalk. They were still gowned in their couture evening dresses, and their purpose now was to show them off up close to the private fashion show's wealthy guests.

As she passed the sumptuous buffet she felt her stomach rumble, but ignored it. Like it or not—and she didn't—modelling required gruelling calorie restriction to keep her body racehorse-slender. Eating normally again would be one of the first joys of chucking in her career and finally moving to the countryside, as she was longing to do. And that dream of escape was getting closer and closer—escape to the chocolate-box, roses-round-the-door thatched cottage in deepest Dorset that had belonged to her grandparents and now, since their deaths, belonged to her.

In her grandparents' day it had been the only home she'd ever really had. With her parents in the armed forces, serving abroad, and herself packed off to boarding school at the age of eight, it had been her grandparents who had provided the home comforts and stability that her parents had not been in a position to provide. Now, determined to make it her own 'for ever' home, she was spending every penny she earned in undertaking the essential repairs and restoration that were required for such an old house—from a new thatched roof, to new drains…it all had to be done.

And now it nearly was. It only lacked a new kitchen and bathroom to replace the very ancient and decrepit units and sanitary ware and she could move in! All she needed was another ten thousand pounds to cover the cost.

That was why she was taking on all the modelling assignments she could—including this evening one now—squirrelling away every penny she could to get the cottage ready for moving in to.

She could hardly wait for that day. The glamour of being a fashion model had worn off long ago, and now it was only tiring and tedious. Besides, she had increasingly come to resent being constantly on show, all too often attracting the attention of men she had learned were only interested in her because she was a model.

She sheered her mind away from her thoughts. Jules had been a long time ago, and she was long over him. She'd been young and stupid and had believed that it was herself he'd cared for—when all along she'd simply been a trophy female to be wheeled out to impress his mates…

It had taught her a lesson though and had made her wary. She didn't want to be any man's trophy.

Her wariness gave her a degree of edginess towards men which she knew could put men off, however striking her looks. Sometimes she welcomed it. She wasn't one to put up with any hassle. Maybe something of her parents' emotional distance had rubbed off on her, she sometimes thought. They'd always taught her to stand up for herself, not to be cowed, overawed or over-impressed by anyone.

She certainly wasn't going to be overawed by the kind of people here tonight, knocking back champagne and snapping up couture clothes as if they were as cheap as chips! Just because they were stinking rich it didn't make them better than her in any way whatsoever—no way was anyone going to look down on her as some kind of walking clotheshorse!

Head held high, poker-faced, she kept on parading around, as she was being paid to do. The evening would end soon, and then she could clear off and get home.

Marc Derenz took a mouthful of champagne and shifted his weight restlessly, making some polite reply to whatever Hans Neuberger had just said to him. His mood was grim, and getting worse with every passing minute, but that was something he would never show to Hans.

A close friend of Marc's late father, Hans had been at his side during that bleak period after Marc's parents had been killed in a helicopter crash, when their only offspring had still been in his early twenties. It had been Hans who'd guided him through the complexities of mastering his formidable inheritance at so young an age.

Hans's business experience, as the owner of a major German engineering company, as well as his wisdom and kindness, were not things Marc would ever forget. He felt a bond of loyalty to the older man that was rare in his life, untrammelled by emotional ties as he had been since losing his parents.

It was a loyalty that was causing him problems right now, though. Only eighteen months ago Hans, then recently widowed following his wife's death from cancer, had been inveigled into a rash second marriage by a woman whom Marc had no hesitation in castigating as a gold-digger. And worse.

Celine Neuberger, here tonight to add to her already plentiful collection of couture gowns, had made no secret to Marc of the fact that she was finding her wealthy but middle-aged husband dull and uninteresting, now that she had him in her noose. And she had made no secret of the fact that she thought the opposite about Marc...

Marc's mouth tightened. Celine's eyes were hungry on him now, even though Marc was blanking her, but that did not seem to deter her. Had she been anyone other than Hans's wife Marc would have had no hesitation in ruthlessly sending her packing. It was a ruthlessness he'd had to learn early—first as heir to the Derenz billions, and then even more so after his parents' deaths.

Women were very, *very* keen on getting as close to those billions of his as possible. Ideally, by becoming Madame Marc Derenz.

Oh, at some point in his life, he acknowledged, there *would* be a Madame Derenz—when the time was right for him to marry and start a family. But she would be someone from the same wealthy background as himself.

It was advice his father had given him: to do what he himself had done. Marc's mother had been an heiress in her own right. And even for mere *affaires*, his father had warned him, it was best never to risk any liaison with anyone not from their own world of wealth and privilege. It was safer that way.

Mark knew the truth of it—only once had he made the mistake of ignoring his father's advice.

Celine Neuberger was addressing him now, her voice eager, and he was glad of the interruption to his thoughts. He had been recalling a time he did not care to remember, for he had been young and trusting then, and he had paid for that misplaced trust with a heartache he never wanted to experience again.

But what Celine had to say only worsened his mood sharply.

'Marc, have I told you that Hans has promised to buy

a villa on the Côte d'Azur! And I've had the most *wonderful* idea!'

Celine's gushing voice grated on him.

'We could house-hunt from *your* gorgeous, gorgeous villa on Cap Pierre! *Do* say yes!'

Every instinct in Marc rebelled at the prospect, but he was being put on the spot. In his parents' time Hans and his first wife had often been guests at the Villa Derenz—convivial occasions when the young Marc had had the company of Hans's son, Bernhardt, and had made enthusiastic use of the pool and gone sea bathing off the rocky shoreline of Cap Pierre. Good memories…

Marc felt a pang of nostalgic loss for those carefree days. Now, all he could say, resignedly, and with a forced smile, was, '*Bien sûr!* That would be delightful.' He tried to make the lie convincing. 'Delightful' was the last word to describe spending more time with Celine making eyes at him. Having to hold her at bay.

A triumphant Celine now pushed even further in a direction Marc had no intention of letting her advance. She turned to her husband. 'Darling, don't feel you have to stay any longer—Marc can see me back to our hotel.'

Hans turned to Marc, a grateful expression on his face. 'That would be so kind of you, Marc. I have to phone Bernhardt—matters to do with the forthcoming board meeting.'

Again, how could Marc object without giving Hans the reason?

The moment Hans had left Celine was, predictably, off the leash. 'Now, tell me,' she gushed, smiling warmly up at him, 'which would suit me best?' She gestured at the perambulating models.

Marc, knowing his mood was worsening with every passing moment in this impossible situation he'd been dumped in, lanced his gaze around to find the nearest model, whatever she was wearing, determined to give Celine the least opportunity for lingering.

But, as he did so, suddenly all thoughts of Celine went right out of his head.

During the fashion show itself he'd paid no attention to the endless parade of females striding up and down the catwalk, focussing instead on his phone. So now, as his eyes caught the figure of the model closest to where they stood, he felt his gaze riveted.

Tall, ultra-slender—yes. But then all the models were like that. None like this one, though, with rich chestnut hair glinting auburn, loosely pinned into an uplift that exposed a face he simply could not take his eyes from.

The perfect profile—and then, as she turned to change direction, he saw a strikingly beautiful face with sculpted cheekbones, magnificent eyes shot with sea-green, and a wide, lush mouth that was, at this moment, tight-set. The expression on her amazing face was professionally blank, but as his eyes focussed on her he felt his male antennae react instinctively—and on every frequency. She was quite incredible.

Without conscious volition he raised his free hand, summoning her over. For a second he thought she had not seen his gesture, for she was moving as if to keep stalking around as the rest of the models were doing. Then, tensing, she strode towards him. He could not take his eyes from her...

The thoughts in his head were flashing wildly. OK, so she was a model—and that put her out of reach from the off, because models were nearly always *not* from the kind of privileged background he insisted that any woman he showed interest in be from. But this one...

Whatever she had—and he was still analysing it, with his male antennae registering her on every frequency—it was making it dangerously hard for him to remember the rules of engagement he lived by.

As she approached, the impact she was making on him strengthened like a magnet drawing tempered steel. *Dieu*, but she was stunning! And now she was standing in front of him, a bare metre or so away.

He scrutinised her shamelessly, taking in her breathtaking beauty. And then he caught a flash in her eyes—as if she resented his scrutiny.

His own eyes narrowed reactively—what was her problem? She was a model; she was being paid to be looked at in the clothes she was wearing. OK, so in fact she might have been wearing a sack, for all he cared—it was her amazing beauty that was drawing his attention, not her gown.

But, abruptly, he veiled his appreciative scrutiny. It didn't matter how stunningly beautiful she was. He had not summoned her for any reason other than the one he gave voice to now. The *only* reason he would show any interest in her.

'So, what about this one?'

He turned to Celine. The sooner he could get the wretched woman to spend Hans's money on a gown— any gown!—the sooner he would be able to get her back to her hotel and finally be done with her for the evening.

His eyes went back to the model. The number she was wearing was purple—a kind of dark grape—in raw silk, draped over her slight breasts, slithering down her slender body. Again Marc felt that unstoppable reaction to her spectacular beauty. Again he did his best to stop it—and again he failed.

'Hmm...' said Celine doubtfully. 'The colour is too sombre for me, Marc. No.' She waved the model away, dismissing her.

But Marc stayed her. 'Please turn around,' he instructed. The gown was a masterpiece—as was she—and he wanted to see what she looked like from the back.

The flash in those blue-green eyes came again, and again Marc wondered at it as she executed a single revolution, revealing how the gown was almost backless, exposing the sculpted contours of her spine, the superb sheen of her pale skin. And as she came back to face them he saw an expression of what could only be hostility.

What is it with her? he found himself thinking. Annoyance flickered through him. Why that reaction? It wasn't one he was used to when he paid attention to a woman—in his long experience women *wanted* to draw his attention to them! His problem was keeping women away from him, and without vanity he knew that it was not only his wealth that lured them. Nature had bestowed upon him gifts that money could not buy—a six-foot-plus frame, and looks that usually had a powerful impact on women.

But not on this one, it seemed, and he felt that flicker of annoyance again as his gaze rested on her professionally blank face once more.

For a second—a fraction of a second—he thought he saw something behind that professional blankness. Something that was not that hostile flash either...

But then it was gone, and Celine was saying pettishly, 'Marc, *cherie*, I really don't like it.'

She waved the model away again, and she strode off with quickened stride, her body stiff. Marc's eyes followed her, unwilling to lose her in the throng which swallowed her up.

A pity she was a model...

For all her amazing looks, which were capable of piercing the black mood possessing him at having been landed with Hans's wretched adultery-minded wife, the stunning, flashing-eyed beauty was not someone, he knew perfectly well, he should allow himself to pursue...

She isn't from my world—let her go.

But a single word echoed in his head, all the same. *Domage...*

A pity...

Tara wheeled away, gaining the far side of the room as fast as she could. Her heart-rate was up and she knew why. Oh, she *knew* why!

She shut her eyes, wanting to blank the room. To blank the oh-so-conflicting reactions battling inside her head right now. She could feel them still, behind her closed eyes, slashing away at each other, fighting for supremacy.

Two overpowering emotions.

Impossible to tell which was uppermost!

The first—that instinctive, breath-catching one—had come the moment she'd seen that man looking at her... seen him for the first time. She certainly hadn't seen him at the fashion show, but then she never looked at the audience when she was on the catwalk. If she had—oh, she'd have remembered him all right...

No man had ever impacted on her as powerfully—as instantly. Talk about tall, dark and devastating! Sable-hair, cut short, a hard, tough-looking face with a blade of a nose, a strong jaw, a mouth set in a tight line. And eyes that could strip paint.

Or that could rest on her with a look in them that told her that he liked what he was seeing...

She felt a kind of electricity flicker through her and her expression darkened abruptly. The complete opposite emotion was scything through her head, cutting off the electricity.

Liked it so much he just saw fit to click his fingers and summon me over so he could inspect me!

She fought for reason. OK, so he hadn't actually clicked his fingers—but that imperious beckoning of his had been just as bad! Just as bad as the way he'd so blatantly looked her over...

And it wasn't the damn gown he was interested in.

That opposite emotion, with a jacking up of its voltage, shot through her again. As if she was once again feeling the impact of that dark, assessing inspection...

She threw the switch once more. *No—stop this, right now!* she told herself. So what if he'd put her back up? Why should she care? That over-made-up blonde he'd been with had treated her just as offhandedly, waving her away. So why get uptight about the man doing so?

And so what, she added for good measure, that she'd had that ridiculously OTT reaction to the man's physical impact on her? He and Blondie came from a world she wasn't part of and only ever saw from the outside—like at this private fashion show. Speaking of which...

She gave herself a mental shake, opened her eyes and continued with her blank-faced perambulations, showing off a gown she could never in all her life afford herself. She was here to work, to earn money, and she'd better get on with it.

Oh, and if she could to stay on this far side of the room... Well away from the source of those emotions in her head.

'Marc, *cherie*, now, *this* one is ideal! Don't you think?'

Celine's voice was a purr, but it grated on Marc like nails on a blackboard. However, at last, it seemed, Hans's wife had found a gown she liked and was stroking the gold satin material lovingly, not even looking at the model wearing it. This model was smiling hopefully at Marc, but he ignored her. He was not the slightest bit interested.

Not like that other one.

He cut his inappropriate thoughts off. Focussed on the problem at hand. How to divest himself of Hans's wife at last.

'Perfect!' he agreed, with relief in his voice. *Could they finally get out of here?*

His relief proved short-lived. Celine's scarlet-tipped fingers curled possessively around his arm.

'I've seen all I want here. I'll arrange a fitting for that gold dress while Hans and I are in London. But right now...' she smiled winningly at Marc '...do be an angel and take me to dinner! We could go to a club afterwards!'

Marc cut short her attempts to commandeer him for the rest of the evening. Never one to suffer irritation gladly, he knew his temper had been on a shortening fuse all evening. It was galling to see his father's old friend in the clutches of this appalling woman. How on earth could Hans not have seen through her?

But then dark memory came, though he wished it would not. Hadn't *he* been similarly blinded once himself?

Oh, he could tell himself he'd been young, and naïve, and far too trusting, but he'd been made a fool of all the same! Marianne had strung him along, playing on his youthful adoration of her, carefully cultivating his devotion to her—a devotion that had exploded in an instant.

Walking into that restaurant in Lyons, Marianne thinking I was still in Paris, seeing her there—

With another man. Older than Marc's barely two and twenty. Older and far wealthier.

Marc's father had still been alive then, and Marc only the prospective heir to the Derenz fortune. The man Marianne had been all over, cooing at, had been in his forties, and richer even than Marc's father. Marc had stared, the blood draining from his face, and had felt something dying inside him.

Then Marianne had seen him, and instead of trying to make any apology to him she had simply lifted her glass of champagne, tilted it mockingly at Marc, so the light would catch the huge diamond on her finger.

Shortly afterwards she had become the third wife of the man she'd been dining with. And Marc had learnt a lesson he had never, never forgotten.

Now, his tone terse, he spoke bluntly. 'Celine, I already have a dinner engagement tonight.'

Hans's wife was undeterred. 'Oh, if it's business I'll be good as gold,' she assured him airily, not relinquishing her hold on his arm. 'I sit through enough of Hans's deadly dull dinner meetings to know how!' she added waspishly. 'And we could still go clubbing afterwards...'

Marc shook his head. Time to stop Celine in her tracks. 'No, it's *not* business,' he told her, making the implication clear.

Celine's eyes narrowed. 'You're not seeing anyone at the moment. I know that,' she began, 'because I'd have heard about it otherwise.'

'And I'm sure you will,' Marc replied, jaw set.

He did *not* want a debate over this. He just wanted to get Celine off his hands before his temper reached snapping point.

'Well, who is it?' Celine demanded.

Marc felt his already short fuse shortening even more. He wanted to get out of here—now—and get shot of Celine. Any way he could. The fastest way he could.

He said the first thing that came into his head in this infuriating and wretched situation. 'One of the models here,' he answered tersely.

'*Models?*'

She said the word as if he'd said *waitresses* or *cleaners.* In Celine's eyes women who weren't rich—or weren't married to rich men—simply didn't exist. Let alone women who might possibly interest the likes of Marc Derenz.

Her eyes flashed petulantly. 'Well, which one, then?' she demanded. She was thwarted, and she was challenging him.

It was a challenge he could not help but meet—and he called her bluff with the first words that came into his head. 'The one in the dress you didn't like—'

'*Her?* But she looked right through you!' Celine exclaimed.

'She's not supposed to fraternise while she's working.'

Even as he spoke he was cursing himself. Why the hell had he said it was *that* model? The one who had stiffened up like a poker?

But he knew why. Because he was still trying to put her out of his head, that was why—trying and failing. He'd been conscious of his eyes sifting through the crowded room even as Celine was cooing over the gown she was selecting, idly searching for the model again. Irritated both that he was doing so and that he could not see her.

She was keeping to the far side of the room. Not coming anywhere near his eyeline again.

Because she is avoiding me?

The thought was in his head, bringing with it emotions that were at war with each other. He shouldn't damn well be interested in her in the first place! For all the reasons he always stuck to in his life. But he could remind himself of those reasons all he liked—he still wanted to catch another glimpse of her.

More than a glimpse.

Another thought flickered. Was it because she hadn't

immediately—eagerly!—returned his clear look of interest in her that she was occupying his thoughts like this? Had that intrigued him as well as surprised him?

He didn't have time to think further, for Celine was counter-calling *his* bluff.

'Well, *do* introduce me, *cherie*!' she challenged.

It was clear she didn't believe him, and Marc's mouth tightened. He was not about to be outmanoeuvred by Hans's scheming wife. Nor was he going to spend a minute longer in her company.

With a smile that strained his jaw, he murmured, 'Of course! One moment.' And he strode away across the room with one purpose only, his mood grimmer than ever. Whatever it took to shed the clinging Celine, he'd do it!

His eyes sliced through the throng, incisively seeking his target. And there she was. He felt the same kick go through him as had when he'd first summoned her across to him. That racehorse grace, that perfect profile—and those blue-green eyes which now, as he accosted her, were suddenly on him. And immediately, instantly blank.

And not in the least friendly.

Marc didn't give a damn—not now. His temper was at snapping point after what he'd put up with all evening.

He stood in front of her, blocking Celine's view of her from the other side of the room. Without preamble, he cut to the chase. Whether this was a moment of insanely stupid impulse, or the way out of a hole, he just did not care.

'How would you like,' he said to the model who was now staring at him with a closed, stony look on her stunningly beautiful face, 'to make five hundred pounds tonight?'

CHAPTER TWO

TARA HEARD THE WORDS, but they took a moment to register. She knew only that they'd been spoken with the slightest trace of an accent that she hadn't noticed in his curt instruction to her before.

She had still been trying to quench her reaction to the man who had just appeared out of nowhere in front of her. Blocking her. Demanding her attention. Just as he'd demanded she walk across to him and Blondie and twirl at his command.

OK, so that was her job here tonight, but it was the *way* he'd done it that had put her back up!

As now he was doing all over again—and worse. Because she did not *want* to feel that kick of high voltage again, that unwelcome quickening of her pulse as her eyes focussed, however determinedly she tried to resist, on that planed hard face and the dark eyes that were like cut obsidian.

The sense of what he'd just said belatedly reached her brain, as insulting as it was offensive.

She started to open her mouth, to skewer him with her reply—no *way* was she going to tolerate such an approach, whoever the hell this man was!—but he was speaking again. An irritated expression flashed across his face.

'Do *not*,' she heard him say, and there was a distinct

tinge of boredom in his voice, as well as curt irritation, 'jump to the tediously predictable assumption you are clearly about to make. All I require is this. That you accompany myself and my guest back to her hotel, where—' he held up a silencing hand as Tara's mind raced ahead to envisage unspeakable debaucheries '—she will get out and you will stay in the car with me and then return here.'

The words were clipped from him, and then his eyes were going past her towards one of the fashion designer's hovering aides. He summoned him over with the same imperious gesture he'd used to draw her over to show off the gown she was wearing.

The man came scuttling forward. 'Monsieur Derenz, is there anything you require?' he asked eagerly.

Tara heard the obsequiousness in the man's voice and deplored it. The last thing rich guys like this one needed—let alone those with the kind of tough-looking face that he had, who expected everyone to jump at their bidding—was anyone kow-towing to them. It only encouraged them.

'Yes,' came the curt reply. 'I'd like to borrow your model for a very temporary engagement. I require a chaperone for my guest, Mrs Neuberger, as I escort her to her hotel. Your model will be away for no more than half an hour. Obviously I'll pay you for her time and take full financial liability for her gown. I take it there'll be no problem?'

The last was not a question—it was a statement. The aide nodded immediately. 'Of course, Monsieur Derenz.' His eyes snapped to Tara. 'Well? Don't just stand there! Monsieur Derenz is waiting!'

And that was that.

Fulminating, Tara knew she didn't have a choice. She needed the money. If she kicked off and refused then her agency would be told, and as this particular fashion designer was highly influential, there would be no hope that her objection to being shanghaied in this manner would be upheld.

All the same, she glared at the man shanghaiing her as the aide scuttled off again. 'What *is* this?' she demanded.

The man—this Monsieur Derenz, whoever he was, she thought tautly—looked at her impatiently. She'd never heard of him, and all the name did was confirm that he was not British—a deduction that went not just with his name and slight accent, but also with the air of Continental style that added something to his stance, and to the way he wore the clearly hand-made tuxedo that moulded his powerful frame in ways she knew she must not pay any attention to...

'You heard me—my guest needs a chaperone. And so do I!'

Tara could see his irritation deepen as he spoke.

'I want you to behave as if you know me. As if —' his mouth set '—we are having an affair.'

This time Tara did explode. *'What?'*

That dark flash of impatient irritation seared across his face again. 'Cool it,' he said tersely. 'I merely need my guest to be...disabused...of any expectations she may have of me.'

'She'd be welcome to you!' Tara muttered, hardly bothering to be inaudible.

How had she managed to get inveigled into this? Then something pinged back into her mind.

'Did you say five hundred pounds?' she demanded. No way was she going to come out of this empty-handed—not for putting up with this man commandeering her like this.

'Yes,' came the indifferent reply. 'Providing you don't waste any more of my time than this is already taking.'

Without waiting, he helped himself to her arm and started to walk back with her across the room, to where

Tara could see the blonde woman who, apparently, had the idiotic idea that this man being tall, dark, handsome—and presumably, judging by how obsequious the aide had been, very rich—in any way compensated for his high-handed behaviour and peremptory manner.

As he walked her towards the unwanted blonde he bent his head to her. 'We have been together only a short while...you are reluctant to leave your work early, being highly conscientious—and if you pull away from me like that one more time your money is halved. Do you understand me?'

There was a grim note in his voice that put Tara's back up even more. But he was still talking.

'Now, tell me your name.'

It was another of those orders he clearly liked giving.

'Tara,' she said tightly. 'Tara Mackenzie. And I need to get my bag and coat first—'

'Unnecessary.' He cut her off. 'You'll be back here soon enough.'

They had reached the blonde, who was looking, Tara could see, like curdled milk at their approach.

'Ah, Celine—this is Tara. Tara—Frau Neuberger.'

His voice was more fulsome, and there might well be relief in it, Tara thought.

'Tara's been given the all-clear to leave early, so we can drop you off at your hotel. *Alors, allons-y.*'

He cupped a hand around Celine's elbow and drew them both forward simultaneously, his guiding grip allowing no delay. Moments later they were on the pavement outside the hotel, and Tara found herself stepping into a swish chauffeured limo. She settled herself carefully, mindful of her horrendously expensive gown, arranging the skirts so they did not crush.

The man she was supposed to be giving the impression

that she was having an affair with—however absurd!—sat himself down heavily between her and the blonde—who, Tara was acidly amused to see, was faffing about with her seatbelt in order to get the man she wanted to make some form of body contact and fasten it for her. Sadly for her, it seemed he did not return the desire.

'Marc, *cherie*, thank you!' Tara heard the woman gush.

OK, Tara connected, Marc Derenz. She still had no idea who he might be, but then so many of the richest of the rich were completely unknown to the wider world. To the plebs in it like herself. Well, what did it matter *who* he was? Nor did it matter that he seemed to possess the kind of physical appeal that was so annoyingly able to compete with her resistance to his peremptory and quite frankly dislikeable personality.

She glanced at him now, as the car moved off into the London evening traffic. His profile was just as tough-looking as his face—and the clear set of his jaw indicated that his mood had not improved in the slightest. She heard him make some terse reply in German to the blonde at his side, and then suddenly he was turning to Tara.

Something flickered in his eyes. Something that made Tara's insides go gulp even though she didn't want them to. Suddenly, out of nowhere, she felt the close physical proximity of this man—felt, of all things, that it wasn't Blondie who needed a chaperone, it was *her*…

That flicker in those dark, dark eyes came again. And this time it was more than just a flicker. It was a glint. A glint that went with the set of that tough jawline.

'Tara, *mon ange*—your seatbelt…'

His voice was a low murmur, nothing like as brusque as it had been when he'd spoken to Blondie, and there was only one word for its tone.

Intimate…

Out of nowhere, Tara felt herself catch her breath. She heard her thoughts scramble in her brain. *Oh, dear God, don't look at me like that! Don't speak to me like that! Because if you do...*

But there was something that was even more of an ordeal for her than the husky, intimate tone of his accented voice that was doing things to her that she did not want them to do—because the only reason she was here in this plush limo was to provide fleeting cover in a situation that was none of her making and that would be over and done with inside half an hour, tops...

Only it seemed that Marc Derenz was utterly oblivious to what she didn't want him to do to her—to the effect he was having on her that she *must* not let him see! Because her reaction to him was totally irrelevant! Totally and absolutely nothing to do with her real life. And totally at odds with the way she *should* think of him—as nothing but a rich man moving other people around for his own convenience and not even bothering to be polite about it!

But it was impossible to remember that as he leant across her, reaching for her seatbelt, invading her body space just as he invaded her senses. She could feel the hardness of his chest wall against her arm, see the cords of his strong neck, the sable feathering of his hair, the hard-edged jawline and the incised lines around his mouth. She could catch the expensive masculine scent of his aftershave. His own masculine scent...

Then, in a swift, assured movement, he was reaching for the seatbelt and pulling it across her. And in those few brief seconds the breath stopped in her lungs.

Oh, God, what has he got—what has he got?

But it was a futile question. She knew exactly what he had.

Raw, overpowering sexuality. Effortless, unconscious, and knocking her for six.

It was all over in a moment and he was back in his position in the middle of the wide, capacious seat, turning his attention to Blondie, who was relentlessly talking away to him in rapid French. Tara could see her long red nails pressed over Marc Derenz's sleeve, her face upturned to his—claiming his attention. Ignoring Tara.

The woman's rudeness started to annoy her—adding to her resentment of the way she'd been commandeered for this uninvited role. Well, if she was supposed to be riding shotgun, she had better behave as if she were!

Cutting right across Blondie's voluble chatter, she deliberately brushed her hand down Marc Derenz's sleeve. It was an effort to do so, but she forced herself. She had to recover from her ludicrous reaction to his fastening her seatbelt for her. She had to recover from her ludicrous reaction to his overpowering masculinity full-stop.

After all, she told herself robustly, she'd lived with her looks all her life and had been a model for years—she was a hardened operator, able to give short shrift to men importuning her. No way was this guy going to cow her just because he had the looks to melt her bones. No, it was time to prove to herself—and, damn it, to him too!—that she wasn't just going to meekly and mildly put up and shut up. Whatever it was about him that riled her so, she wasn't going to let him call all the shots.

In which case…

'Marc, baby, I'm sorry I gave you a hard time over leaving early. Forgive me?' She leant into him just a fraction, quite deliberately, and put a husky, cajoling note into her voice.

His head swivelled. For a moment she saw an expres-

sion in his eyes that should have been a warning to her.
But it was too late to regret drawing his attention to her.

'You'll have to accept, *mon ange*, that I have severe
time constraints in my life. *Hélas*, I have to be in Geneva
tomorrow, so I wanted to make the most of tonight.'

He sounded regretful. And intimate. It was an intimacy
that curled right down her body. He didn't have a strong
French accent, but, boy, what he had worked...

And then Blondie was jabbering in German, and he
turned to her to reply.

Relief drenched through Tara. If that was him simply
acting the role of attentive lover...

She dragged her mind away, steadied her breathing.
Oh, sweet Lord, whatever he had, he definitely had what
it took to get past her defences.

Her expression changed. It was just as well that his personality didn't match his looks—he had all the winning
charm of a ten-ton boulder, crushing everyone around him!
And it was even more just as well, she was honest enough
to admit, that her acquaintance with this man was going
to be extremely short-lived.

She'd see this exercise through, get back to work, and be
a useful five hundred pounds the richer for it. All feeding
into the Escape to My Cottage in the Country fund. She
made herself focus on that subject for the remainder of the
thankfully short journey, doing her best to ignore the very
difficult to ignore presence of the man sitting next to her,
and grateful that he was being monopolised by Blondie,
who was clearly making the most of him.

As the car pulled up under the portico of the woman's
hotel Tara sat meekly while the other two got out. Marc
Derenz escorted Blondie indoors, to emerge some minutes
later and throw himself back into the car, this time on the
far side vacated by Blondie.

'Thank God!' Tara heard him say—and he sounded as if he meant it.

Tara couldn't resist. He was such a charmless specimen, however ludicrously good-looking. 'Such a bore, aren't they?' she said sweetly. 'Women who don't get the message.'

Dark eyes immediately swivelled to her, and Tara reeled inwardly with the impact. It was like being seared by a laser set to stun. Despite the effort it cost her, she gritted her teeth, refusing to blink or back down.

He didn't deign to answer, merely flicked out his phone and jabbed at it. A moment later he was in full flood to someone he clearly wanted to talk to—unlike herself—and Tara assumed from his businesslike tone, that business was what it was.

She leant back, not sure if she was feeling irritated by his manner or just glad the whole escapade was almost over. Even so, she unconsciously felt her head twist slightly as the car moved back out into the traffic, so she could behold his profile. Again, she felt that annoyingly vulnerable reaction to him, that skip in her pulse. She jerked her head away.

Oh, damn the man! He might radiate raw sexuality on every wavelength, but his granite personality was a total turn-off. The minute she was out of here and had the money he'd promised her she would never think about him again.

Five minutes later they were back at the hotel where the fashion show was being held and she was climbing out of the limo. Pointedly, she held her door open—no way was he driving off without paying her.

'You said five hundred,' she said, holding out her hand expectantly. The only reason, she reminded herself grimly, that she had anything to do with this man was for money! No other reason.

For a moment he just looked at her, his face closed. Then he got out of the car, standing in front of her. He was taller than her, even with her high heels, and it wasn't something she was accustomed to in men.

She felt her jaw set. There was something about the way he was looking at her. As if he were considering something. She lifted her chin that much higher, eyeballing him, hand still outstretched for her pay-off.

His dark eyes were veiled, unreadable.

'My money, please,' she said crisply. What was going on? Was he going to try and welch on the deal? For a sum that would be utterly trivial to a man like him?

Then, abruptly, she realised why he was not reaching for his wallet. Because he was reaching for her hand.

Before she could stop him, or step away, he'd taken hold of it and was raising it to his mouth. His expression as he did so had changed. Changed devastatingly.

Tara felt her lungs seize—felt everything seize.

Oh, God, she heard her inner voice say, silently and faintly and with absolute dismay, *don't do this to me...*

But it was too late. With a glint in his obsidian eyes, as if he knew perfectly well that what he was doing would sideswipe her totally, he turned her hand over in his, exposing the tender skin of her wrist.

Eyelashes far too long for a man with a face that tough swept down, veiling those dark, mordant eyes of his. And then his mouth, like silken velvet, was brushing that oh-so-delicate skin, gliding across it with deliberate slowness. Soft, sensuous, devastating.

She felt her eyelids flutter shut, felt a ludicrous weakness flood her body. Desperately she tried to negate it. It was just skin touching skin! But her attempt to reduce it to such banality was futile. Totally futile. The warm, grazing caress of his mouth on the sensitive surface of her skin focussed every nerve-ending in her entire body just on her wrist. She was melting, dissolving…

He dropped her hand, straightened. 'Thank you,' he murmured, his voice low, his eyes holding hers. The darkling glint in them was still there, but there was something more to it—something that kept her lungs immobile. 'Thank you for your co-operation this evening.'

There was the merest hint of amusement in his voice. She snatched her hand away, as if it had been touched by a red-hot bar of iron, not by the sensuous, seductive glide of his mouth.

She had to recover—any way she could. 'I only did it for the money!' she gritted, going back to eyeballing him, defying him to think otherwise.

She saw his expression harden. Close. Whatever had been there, even if only to taunt her, had vanished. Now there was only the personality of that crushing boulder back in evidence.

With a clearly deliberate gesture he reached for his wallet in the inner pocket of his tailored dinner jacket, and an equally deliberately flicked it open. Stone-faced—determinedly so—Tara watched him peel off the requisite number of fifty-pound notes and hold them out to her.

She took them from him, her colour heightened. There was something about standing here and having a man handing her money—any man, let alone this damn one!

He was looking at her with that deliberately impassive expression on his face, but there was something in the depths of those dark veiled eyes of his that made her react on total impulse. The man was so totally charmless, so totally forbidding, and yet he had so *totally* shot to pieces her usual cool-as-ice reaction to any kind of physical contact with a man. She'd *let* him do all that wrist-kissing, *let* him taunt her as he had and hadn't even *tried* to pull away from him.

Now, in an overpowering impulse to get some kind of retaliation, she lifted the topmost fifty-pound note from the wad in her hand. Stepping forward, she gave her saccharine smile again and with deliberate insolence tucked the fifty-pound note into his front jacket pocket and patted it.

'Buy yourself a drink, Mr Derenz,' she told him sweetly. 'You look like you could use one!'

She turned on her high heel, stalking away back into the hotel, not caring about his reaction. If she never saw Marc Derenz again it would be too soon! A man like him could only be bad, bad news.

A man who, like no other man she'd ever met, could turn her into melting ice-cream with a taunting wrist-kiss and a veiled glance from those dark eyes—and who could equally swiftly make her mad as fire with his imperious manner and rock-like personality.

Yes, she thought darkly, *definitely* bad news.

On *so* many counts.

Behind her, stock-still on the pavement, knowing the doorman had been covertly observing the exchange and not giving a damn, Marc watched her disappear from sight, the skirts of her gown billowing around her long, long legs, that glorious chestnut hair catching the light. In his memory he could still taste the silken scent of the pale skin at her wrist, the warmth of the pulse beneath the surface.

Then, his expression still mask-like, he turned away to climb back into his car, and be driven to his own hotel.

As if mentally rousing himself, he reached for the crumpled note in his breast pocket. He slipped it back into his wallet, depleted now of the four hundred and fifty pounds that were in her possession. As his wallet held his gaze, he felt as if the contents were reminding him of something important to him. That he would be wise not to forget.

How much he had wanted to silence that acidly saccharine mouth of hers, taunting him in a way that right now, in the mood he'd been in all evening, had *not* been wise at all… Silence it in the only way he wanted…

No. Tara Mackenzie was not for him—not on any terms. All his life he'd played the game of romance by the rules he'd set out for himself, to keep himself safe, and it was out of the question to consider breaking them. Not even for a woman like that.

After all, he mused, had it not been for the wretched Celine he would never even have encountered her. Now all he wanted was to put both of them behind him. For good.

It would be less than a fortnight later, however, that he would be forced to do neither. And it would blacken his mood to new depths of exasperatedly irate displeasure…

Tara was looking at kitchens and bathrooms online, trying to budget for the best bargains. However she calculated it, she still definitely needed at least another ten thousand pounds to get it all done. And even living in London as cheaply as she could—including staying in this run-down flat-share—it would take, she reckoned, a good six months to save that much.

What I need is some nice source of quick, easy dosh!

She gave a wry twist of a smile tinged with acerbity. Well, she'd made that five hundred pounds quickly enough—just for keeping the oh-so-charmless Marc Derenz safe from Blondie.

Memory swooped on her—that velvet touch of his mouth on the tender inside of her wrist…

A rasp of annoyance broke from her—with herself, for

remembering it, for feeling that tremor that it had aroused go through her again now.

He only did it to taunt you! No other reason.

With an impatient resolve to put the wretched man out of her thoughts, she went back to her online perusal. Moving to Dorset—*that* was important to her. Not some obnoxious zillionaire who'd put her back up from the very first. Nor some man who could set her pulse racing…a man who was so, so wrong for her…

A thought sifted across her mind. Would there ever be a man who *was* right for her, though?

Yes, she thought determinedly—one day there *would* be. But she wasn't going to find him here in London, in her life as a model. No, it would be someone she'd meet when she'd started her new life in the country. Someone who didn't know her as a model at all, and who didn't see her as a trophy to show off with. Her thoughts ran on. Someone who was, oh, maybe a vet—or a farmer, even—at home in the countryside…

She pressed her lips together, giving a smothered snort. Well, one thing was for sure, it would not be Marc Derenz. And, anyway, she was never going to set eyes on him again.

A sharp rapping on the front door of the flat made her jump. She gave a sigh of irritation. Probably one of her flatmates had forgotten her keys.

She put her laptop aside, padded to the door, and opened it.

And stepped back in total shock.

It was the last person on earth she'd ever expected to see again.

Marc Derenz.

CHAPTER THREE

MARC'S MOOD WAS BLACK. Blacker even than it had been that torturous evening at the fashion show, with Celine trying to corner him. He'd hoped the brush-off he'd given her would mean she'd give up. He'd been wrong.

She was still plaguing him—still set on inviting herself to the Villa Derenz on the blatant pretext of house-hunting. It had been impossible to refuse Hans's apologetic request—and now he'd been landed with them arriving this week.

Marc's reaction had been instant—and implacable. He'd blocked her before—he would just have to do it again. However damn irritating it was to have to do so.

His eyes rested now on the means he was going to have to use. Tara Mackenzie.

He knew her name, and it had been easy enough to find out where she lived. He cast a disparaging eye around the dingy apartment. The front door opened on to the lounge, which was cheaply furnished and messy—belongings were scattered on battered settees, and a rack of washing was drying in front of the window.

His gaze swept round to the woman he'd tracked down.

And he veiled it immediately.

Even casually dressed, in jeans and a loose shirt, Tara Mackenzie was a complete knockout. Every bit as stunning as he remembered her. The same insistent, visceral response to her that he'd felt at that fashion show, that he'd been doing his damnedest to expel from his memory, flared in him again. Deplorable, but powerful. Far too powerful.

He crushed it down.

She was staring at him now, with those amazing blue-green eyes of hers, and had opened her mouth to speak. He pre-empted her. He wanted this sorted as swiftly as possible.

'I need to talk to you. I have a business proposition to put to you.'

His voice was clipped to the point of curtness. Just as it had been before at the fashion show. Tara's hackles rose automatically. She was still reeling from seeing him again—still reeling from the overpowering impact he was having on her, that seemed to be jacking up the voltage of her body's electricity as if she'd suddenly been plugged into the mains.

This time he was not in a hand-made tux, but in a dark grey killer business suit that screamed *Mr Rich and Powerful! Don't mess me about!*

Just as the look on his face did. That closed expression on his hard-planed, utterly unfairly devastating features and the obvious aura of impatience about him. His automatic expectation that she would meekly listen to whatever it was he was about to say.

He went on in the same curt, clipped voice, his faint accent almost totally supressed. 'Extend the role you adopted at the fashion show and you can make five thousand pounds out of it,' he said, not bothering with any preamble.

Tara frowned, and then she smiled, enlightenment dawning. It wasn't a genuine smile, but it helped her control that voltage hammering through her.

'Blondie still pestering you, is she?' she put to him.

She saw his expression tighten at her sardonic observation. Obviously he was annoyed, but he was acknowledging, tacitly, what she had said.

'Well?' It was his only response.

'Tell me more.' Tara smiled sweetly.

The electricity kindled by his utterly unexpected arrival had sparked a kind of exhilaration in her. It dawned on her that he was resenting having to approach her. And that, she knew, feeling another spark inside her, was really quite gratifying...

Just why that should be so she did not pause to examine.

He took a short breath, his eyes still like lasers on her. 'A week of your time—ten days at the most. It would be... residential,' he said, 'but entirely...' His eyes suddenly closed over their previous expression. 'Entirely synthetically so. In other words, on the same basis as before.' A tight, non-humorous smile tightened his mouth. 'For appearances only.'

Was there a warning in the way he'd said 'only'? Tara didn't know and didn't care. It was entirely irrelevant. Of course it was 'appearances only'. No other possibility. Any woman thinking anything more of him would need her head examined!

'You would,' he continued, in that businesslike voice, 'be my house guest.'

Tara's eyebrows rose. 'Along with Blondie, I take it?'

He gave a brief nod. 'Precisely so.'

'And I get to run interference?'

He nodded again, impatience visible in his manner but saying nothing, only letting those laser eyes of his rest on her, as if trying to bend her to his implacable will.

And then suddenly, out of nowhere, there was something in them that was a like a kick in her system—something that flashed like a warning light in her head…as if she stood upon the brink of a precipice she hadn't even realised was there.

Just as suddenly it was gone. Had she imagined it? That sudden change somewhere at the back of those unreadable slate-dark eyes? Something he'd swiftly blanked? She must have, she decided. There was nothing in his expression now but impatience. He wanted an answer. And fast.

But she did not like being hustled. She took a breath and met his eyes, though she was conscious of the way she'd crossed her arms firmly over her chest, as if keeping him and his imposing, utterly out of place presence at bay.

'OK, do I have this right? You will pay me five thousand pounds to spend up to ten days, max, as your house guest, and behave—strictly in public only—' she made sure she emphasised that part '—as if I am your current squeeze, just as I did on that limo ride the other night, while your *other* house guest—Blondie—gets the message that, sadly for her, you are not available for whatever adulterous purpose she would like you to be. Is that it?' She raised her eyebrows again questioningly.

His expression did not change. He merely inclined his sable-haired head minutely.

Tara thought about it. 'Half up front,' she said.

He didn't blink. 'No. You might not show up,' he said flatly.

His eyes flicked around their shabby surroundings and Tara got the message. Someone who had to live in a place like this might indeed walk off with two and a half thousand pounds.

She made herself look at him. The man was loaded. He had to be, the way he behaved, the lifestyle he had— chauffeur-driven limo, hanging around at couture fashion shows in swanky hotels. No way was she going to be short-changed by him. After all, pro rata, the five hundred pounds for the bare half-hour previously was *way* more generous than this offer.

'Ten thousand,' she said bluntly.

It would be chicken-feed to a man like him, but a huge sum for herself. And exactly what she needed for her cottage. For a moment she wondered if she'd overplayed her hand. But then, maybe she should be glad if she had. Could she *really* face spending any more time in the company of this man? The reasons not to were not just her resistance to his rock-like personality...

Caution started to backfill the ridiculously heady sense of sparking exhilaration she had felt. Caution that came too late.

The voltage in those eyes seared. Then abruptly cut out. 'OK. Ten thousand,' he gritted out. As if she'd just pulled a tooth from his steeled jaw.

That spark of exhilaration surged again inside her, overriding the vanished and defeated caution. Boy, was he mad she'd pushed the price up!

She felt herself smile—a genuine one this time. And then, abruptly, her triumph crashed. With a gesture that was vivid in her memory, he was coolly extracting his gold-monogrammed leather wallet from his jacket, peeling off a fifty-pound note. Then a second one.

Reaching forward, with a glint in his eye that gave her utterly insufficient warning, even though it should have, he tucked the two notes into the front pocket of the shirt she was wearing.

'A little something on account,' he said, and there was a purr in his voice that told her that this was exactly what she knew it was.

His comeback for her daring to tip him with his own money.

She opened her mouth to spit something at him but he was turning on his heel. Striding from the room. Informing her, as he rapidly took his leave, that arrangements would be made via her agency.

Then he was gone.

Taking a long, deliberate breath, she removed the two fifty-pound notes from her breast pocket and stared at them. That, she reminded herself bluntly, was the nature of her relationship with Marc Derenz. And she had better not lose sight of it. The only reason he'd sought her out was to buy her time, because she could be useful to him. No other reason.

And I wouldn't want it to be for any other reason!

Her adjuration to herself was stern. Just why it was that Marc Derenz, of all the men she'd ever encountered in her life, could have this devastating effect on her, she didn't know. She knew only that no good could come of it. Her world was not his, and never would be.

It was hard to remember her warning to herself as, a week later, she turned to look out through the porthole of the plane heading for the Côte d'Azur. Their destination had been a little detail Marc Derenz had omitted to inform her of, but she had no complaint. Just the opposite. Her mood was soaring. To spend a whole week at least on the fabled French Riviera—and be paid for doing so! Life didn't get any better.

She didn't even care that she was being flown out Economy, in spite of how rich the man was. And, boy, was he *rich*! She'd looked him up—and her eyebrows had gone up as well.

Marc Derenz, Chairman of Banc Derenz. She'd never heard of it, but then, why would she have? It was head-quartered in Paris, for a start, and it was not a bank for the likes of her, thank you very much! Oh, no, if you banked at Banc Derenz you were rich—very, *very* rich. You had investment managers and fund managers and portfolio managers and high net worth individual account managers—all entirely at your disposal to ensure you got the very highest returns on your millions and zillions.

As for her destination—the Villa Derenz was featured in architectural journals and was apparently famous as being a perfect example of Art Deco style.

It was something she could agree with a few hours later, as she was conducted across a marble-floored hall and up a sweeping marble staircase like something out of a nineteen-thirties Hollywood movie.

She was shown into a bedroom, its décor pale grey and with silvered furniture. She looked about her appreciatively. This was *fabulous*. It was a sentiment she echoed when she walked out onto the balcony that ran the length of the frontage of the villa. Her breath caught, her eyes lighting up. Verdant green lawns surrounded the brilliant white building, pierced only by a turquoise circular pool and edged by greenery up to the rocky shoreline of the Cap. Beyond, the brilliant azure of the Mediterranean confirmed the name of this coastline.

She gazed with pleasure. No wonder the rich liked being rich if it got them a place like this.

And I get to stay here!

She went back inside to help the pair of maids unpacking her clothes. They weren't her own clothes—a stylist had selected them, on Marc Derenz's orders, Tara assumed, as being suitable for the role she was going to play. For all that, she would definitely enjoy wearing them. Actually wearing them for herself, not for other women to buy—it would be a novelty she would make the most of.

She would make the most of everything about her time

here. Starting with relishing the delicious lunch about to be served to her out on the balcony, under a shady parasol, followed by a relaxing siesta on a conveniently placed sun lounger in the warm early summer sunshine.

Where Marc Derenz was she didn't know—presumably he'd turn up at some point and she would go on duty. Till then…

'Don't burn.'

The voice that woke Tara was deep and familiar, and its abrupt tone told her instantly that concern for her well-being was not behind the statement.

Her eyes flared open, and for a moment the tall figure of the man who was going to pay her ten thousand pounds for staying in his luxury villa in the South of France loomed darkly over her.

She levered herself up on her elbows. 'I've got sun cream on,' she replied.

'Yes, well, I don't want you looking like a boiled lobster,' Marc Derenz said disparagingly. 'And it's time for you to start work.'

She sat up straight, feeling her arms for the thin straps of her swimsuit, which she'd pushed down to avoid tan marks on her shoulders. As she did so she felt the suit dip dangerously low over her breasts. And she felt suddenly, out of nowhere, a burning consciousness of the fact that those hard, dark eyes were targeted on her, and that all that concealed her nakedness was a single piece of thin stretchy material.

Deliberately, she busied herself picking up her wrap, studiedly winding it around herself without looking at him. Whether he was looking at her still she did not care.

I'm going to have to get used to this—to the impact he

has on me. And fast. I can't go on feeling so ridiculously self-conscious. I've got to learn to blank him.

With that instruction firmly in mind, she finished knotting her wrap securely and looked across at him. Against the sun he seemed even taller and darker. He was wearing another of his killer business suits, pale grey this time, with a sharp silk tie and what would obviously be twenty-four-carat gold cufflinks and tiepin.

Tara made herself look and sound equally businesslike. 'OK,' she said. 'What's the next thing on the agenda, then?'

'Your briefing,' Marc Derenz replied succinctly.

His pose altered slightly and he nodded his head at a chair by the table, seating himself on a second chair, crossing one perfectly creased trouser leg over the other.

'Right,' he started in a brisk voice as she sat where he'd bade her. 'There are some ground rules. This, Ms Mackenzie, is a *job*. Not a holiday.'

Marc rested his eyes on her impassively. But he was masking a distinctly less impassive emotion. Arriving here from Paris to find her sunning herself on the balcony had not impressed him. Or, to be precise, she had not impressed him with her lack of recognition that she was here to fulfil a contractual obligation. In every other respect he'd been very, *very* impressed...

Dieu, but she possessed a body! He'd known she did, but to see it displayed for him like that, before she'd become aware of his presence, had been a pleasure he had indulged in for longer than was prudent.

Because it didn't matter how spectacular her figure was, let alone her face, this was—as he was now reminding her so brusquely—a job, not a holiday.

Certainly not anything else.

His thoughts cut out like a guillotine slicing down. In

the days since he had hired her to keep Celine Neuberger at bay he'd had plenty of second thoughts. And third thoughts. Had he been incredibly rash to bring her here? Was he playing with matches near gunpowder?

Seeing her again now, viewing that fantastic body of hers, seeing her stunning beauty right in front of him again, and not only in the memories he'd done his best to crush, was...*unsettling*.

Abruptly he reminded himself that she was not a woman from his world, but a woman he'd admitted into his life briefly, under duress only, and not by free choice. That that did not mean he could now break the rules of a lifetime—rules that had served him well ever since the youthful fiasco over Marianne that had cost him so dearly. Oh, not in money—in heartache that he never wanted to feel again.

But I was young then! A stripling! It was calf love, nothing more than that, and that's why it hit me so hard.

Now he was a stripling no longer, but a seasoned man, in his thirties, sure of himself, and sure of what he wanted and how to get it. Sure of his relationships with the women he selected for his *amours*. Women who were nothing like the one now sitting opposite him, taking money for her time here.

That was what he must remember. *She* would—that was for certain. It was the reason she was here...the reason she'd accompanied him from the fashion show. She'd made it perfectly clear then—and again when she'd so brazenly upped what he'd been prepared to offer her to come out here now. That was warning enough, surely?

However stunning her face and figure—however powerful her appeal—his relationship with Tara Mackenzie must be strictly professional only. She was here, as he reminded himself yet again, only to do a job.

It was, therefore, in a brisk, businesslike tone that he

continued now. 'The Neubergers are arriving this evening. From then on, until they leave, you will assume the role you are here to play. What is essential, however,' he went on, 'is that you understand you are here to *act* the part only. You are *not* to imagine we actually have a relationship of any kind whatsoever or that one is possible at all. Do you understand me?'

Tara felt herself bridling as his dark eyes bored into hers. He was doing it again! Putting her back *right* up. And not just in the way he'd said things—in *what* he had said.

Warning me off him. Telling me not to get ideas about him. Oh, thank you—yes, thank you so much, Monsieur Derenz. It was so *necessary to warn me off you! Not.*

Would she really ever consider a man with the personality of a lump of granite, who clearly thought every woman in the world was after him?

Indignation sparked furiously in her. 'Of course, Monsieur Derenz. I understand perfectly, Monsieur Derenz. Whatever you say, Monsieur Derenz,' Tara intoned fulsomely, venting her objection to his high-handed warning.

His eyes flashed darkly and his arched eyebrows snapped together in displeasure. 'Don't irritate me more than you already have, Ms Mackenzie,' he said witheringly.

'And don't *you*, Monsieur Derenz,' she shot back, bridling even more at his impatient put-down, 'entertain the totally unwarranted assumption that I have *any* desire to do anything more than *act* the part I am here to play! And,' she continued, refusing to be cowed by the increasingly black look on his face, 'I expect *you* to do likewise. There is to be *no* repeat of that little wrist-kissing stunt you pulled just before I went back into the fashion show!' She saw his expression stiffen and ploughed on. 'No unwarranted body contact at all. I appreciate that my role must be convincing—but it is for *public* view only.'

Even just *pretending* to be on intimate terms with him was going to be a challenge. A challenge that, now she was seeing him again, was making a hollow form inside her. Oh, *what* did the wretched man have that got to her like this?

Deliberately, she made herself think not about how drop-dead devastating he was, sitting there in his killer suit, drawing her hapless gaze to his hard-featured face with the night-dark eyes, but of how obnoxious his manner was. Yes, that was a much safer way to think of him!

The best way of all, though, would be to do what he was doing, annoying though it was to admit it—treat this entire matter as simply a professional engagement.

So, with a deep breath, and a resumption of her cool tone, she asked in a no-nonsense, businesslike way, 'OK—so, the Neubergers… You'd better tell me what I'll be expected to know.'

He didn't seem to like it that she'd taken control of the conversation—but then, she thought acidly, Marc Derenz was clearly used to calling all the shots, all the time. Maybe his employees—and she was one herself, after all, however temporary—were not expected to speak before the august chairman of Banc Derenz.

However, he answered her readily enough, in a no-nonsense tone matching her own.

'Hans Neuberger is head of Neuberger Fabrik—a major German engineering company based in Frankfurt. He is a long-standing family friend and he knows this villa well from many previous visits. Celine is his second wife—Hans was a widower—and their marriage is a relatively recent one…less than two years. He has adult children from his first marriage—'

'Who hate Celine's guts,' put in Tara knowingly.

He made no reply, only continued as if she had not spoken. 'Celine has persuaded her husband to house-hunt for a villa here, and on that pretext she has invited herself to stay, with predictably obvious intent.'

His tone was icy and Tara found herself chilled by it. Even more so as he continued in the same cold voice.

'I will not conceal from you the fact that I consider Hans's marriage to Celine…ill-advised. The woman targeted him for his wealth, and she presumes to target myself—' his tone dropped from cold to Arctic '—as a source of…*entertainment*.' His voice plunged to absolute zero. 'This demonstrates just how ill-advised their marriage is. Were Hans Neuberger anything other than, as I have said, a long-standing family friend, there would be absolutely no question. I would have no hesitation in sending her packing.'

Tara took a slicing breath. 'No, no question at all…' she muttered.

It was unnerving to see just how cold Marc Derenz could be—and how ruthless. Imperious in manner, intemperate in mood—yes, she'd seen that already—but this display of icy ruthlessness was something else…

He got to his feet. 'As it is, however, I am required, for Hans's sake, to proceed by taking a more…*subtle* approach.'

Tara gave a tight smile. 'To demonstrate to her that the…*vacancy* in your life is fully occupied?'

His eyes rested on her, dark and unreadable. 'Precisely,' he said.

He got to his feet. He seemed taller than ever, looming over her. He glanced at his watch—doubtless one of those custom-made jobs, she assumed, that cost more than a house. Then his eyes flicked back to her. She got the feeling that he'd suddenly veiled them, and found herself doing likewise with her own. Instinctively she reached for her discarded sunglasses, as if for protection.

'Cocktails at eight, Ms Mackenzie. Do not be late. I don't appreciate tardiness,' he instructed brusquely.

With that, he left her. And as she watched him stride across the balcony Tara suddenly felt as if she'd gone six rounds with a heavyweight.

She picked up her book, conscious that her heart-rate was elevated. One thing was for sure—she was going to earn her money here.

As she settled back in her lounger a stray thought flickered. *I should have asked for danger money—I think I'm going to need it.*

But whether that would protect her from Marc Derenz's unyieldingly flinty manner, or from his much more devastating impact on her, she did not care to examine...

CHAPTER FOUR

MARC WAS IN his office, staring moodily at his computer screen, paying the display no attention. He kept a fully kitted-out office in all his properties, so that he could keep constant tabs on his business affairs.

It had been his habit to do so ever since his vast inheritance had landed on his too-young shoulders. If he hadn't kept a tight grip on everything, shown everyone he was capable of running the bank, he'd have been sidelined by his own board. Doing so had made him appear hard-nosed, even arrogant sometimes, he was aware, but imposing his will on men a generation older than him had been essential. Even now, over a decade on, the habit of command was ingrained in him, whoever he was dealing with.

Including women who were being paid handsomely to do a very simple job, and yet who seemed to find it impossible not to simply take on board his very clear instructions without constantly answering him back!

His mouth tightened. This nonsense with Hans's wife was causing him quite enough grief as it was. To have Tara Mackenzie constantly interrupting him, gainsaying him, answering him back, was just intolerable!

He gave a sigh of exasperation. She had better adopt a more gracious and compliant attitude once the Neubergers arrived, or she would never convince the wretched Celine that they were an item.

Why can't she just be like other women are with me? he demanded of himself in exasperation. All his life women had been eager to please him. So why was this one so damn *un*-eager? With her stunning looks, she could have made him far better disposed towards her.

Maybe I should win her over...

Whatever her self-righteous protestations, she had, he knew with his every well-honed male instinct, reacted just the way he'd intended when he'd kissed that tender spot inside her wrist that evening of the fashion show... It had had exactly the effect on her he'd wanted. Started to melt her...

So maybe I should do more of that, not less...

The thought played in his mind. It was tempting...oh, so tempting...to turn that obstreperous antagonism towards him to something much more...*co-operative*...

It would be a challenge, certainly—he had no doubt of that. But maybe he would welcome such a challenge. It would be an intriguing novelty, after all. So different from being besieged by over-eager females...

He thrust the thought from him, steeling his jaw. No, that would *not* be a good idea! Did he *really* have to run through all the reasons why Tara Mackenzie, whatever her allure, was out of bounds to him?

No, he did not. He pulled his keyboard decisively towards him. All he had to do was get through this coming week, using the woman he was paying an exorbitant amount of money, to keep the wretched Celine off his case.

Tara Mackenzie was here to do a job, and then leave. That was all.

All.

Decision reaffirmed, he went back to his work.

* * *

Tara cast a professionally critical eye over her reflection. And *professional* was the word she had to keep upper-most in her mind. This, she reminded herself sternly, was just as much a job as striding down a catwalk. And Marc Derenz was simply her employer. She frowned momen-tarily. Thankfully only for a week or so.

For a week I can put up with his overbearing manner!

And, of course, for the ten thousand pounds he was paying her.

She nodded at her reflection, that showed her in a knee-length royal blue cocktail dress, from a very exclusive luxury label, her make-up immaculate, hair in a French pleat, and one of the pieces of top-brand costume jewel-lery she'd found in the suitcases around her neck. Yes, she looked the part—the latest woman in Marc Derenz's life. Couture-dressed and expensive.

So—time to go onstage. One of the maids had told her she was being waited for downstairs, so she made her way to the head of the Hollywood-style staircase. From the top she could see a white-jacketed staff member opening the huge front doors and stepping aside to let Marc Derenz's guests enter, just as Marc himself issued forth from an-other ground-floor room.

And stopped dead.

Immediately Tara could see why. This was not the Neu-bergers arriving—this was Frau Neuberger *toute seule*.

Celine—*sans mari*—was dressed to kill in a tailored silk suit in crème-de-menthe, five-inch heels, and a hand-bag that Tara knew, from her modelling expertise, had a waiting list of over a year and wouldn't give you change from twenty thousand pounds...

'Marc, *cherie*!' Celine cooed as she came up to her host,

who was still standing frozen, and lavished air kisses upon him. 'How *wonderful* to be here!'

'Where is Hans?' Tara heard him ask bluntly, at which Celine gave an airy wave.

'Oh, I told him we had no need of him! We'll do *perfectly* well on our own!' She patted Marc's cheek insouciantly with her bare hand, lingering over the contact with her varnished fingernails.

Tara wanted to laugh. Celine was in high fettle, despite the thunderous expression on her quarry's face. Well, time to disabuse her of her hopes.

She started forward, heels tapping on the marble stairs. A wide, welcoming smile parted her lips. 'Celine, how lovely to meet you again!' she exclaimed. 'We're so glad you were able to come!'

She reached the hallway, marshalling herself alongside Marc Derenz. Her pulse was not entirely steady—and that was nothing to do with Celine Neuberger and everything to do with the way Marc Derenz had looked at her as she'd walked down towards them. The way his hard dark eyes had focussed totally on her, as if pinning her with his gaze. A gaze that this time was not like a laser, but more… Appreciative. Liking what it saw. More than liking…

She felt a flush of heat go through her limbs, and then, collecting herself, reminded herself that of *course* Marc Derenz had looked at her like that—*he* was in role-play just as much as she was! She bestowed an air kiss upon Celine, whose face had contorted in fury at Tara's appearance.

'I just *adore* house-hunting! We'll have *such* fun together! I can't wait!' she gushed, ignoring the other woman's obvious anger at her presence there. 'Why not describe what you're after by way of a villa over drinks?' she invited Celine cordially, hoping that Marc Derenz would lead them to wherever it was that cocktails were going to be served. She hadn't a clue—and if Celine realised that it might give the game away.

Thankfully, he did just that, ushering them both into a sumptuous Art Deco salon, where wide French windows opened onto a terrace bathed in late sunshine. Celine, all but snatching her glass, immediately started to talk animatedly in German to Marc, clearly intent on cutting out Tara as much as she could.

Marc's expression was still radiating the same thunderous displeasure it had been since he had seen Celine arrive without her husband. For her part, Tara cast a jaundiced eye at the woman.

Honey, you'd be welcome to him! He's arrogant and bad-tempered and totally charmless! Help yourself, do!

But of course that was out of the question. So, knowing she had to act—quite literally—she stepped forward, a determined smile on her face, placing a quite clearly possessive, hand on Marc Derenz's arm.

'I'm hopeless at German!' she announced insouciantly. 'And my French is only schoolgirl, alas. Are you telling Marc what you're looking for in a house here?'

As she spoke she was aware that the arm beneath her fingertips had steeled, and his whole body had tensed at her moving so closely into his body space. She pressed her hand on his sleeve warningly. Celine was never going to be fooled if she stayed a mile distant from him.

And he needn't think she *wanted* to be in his body space! His utterly unnecessary warning from the afternoon echoed in her head, informing her that she was to remember she was only here to *act* a part. Not to believe it was real.

I wouldn't want it to be real anyway, sunshine, she said tartly but silently to him.

In her head—treacherously—a single word hovered. *Liar.*
You might not like him, the voice went on, *but for some
damn reason he has the ability to turn your knees to jelly,
so you just be careful, my girl!*

She pushed it out. It had no place in her thoughts. None
at all. She was *not* looking for Marc Derenz to pay her
what he so clearly imagined would be the immense compliment of desiring her for real. So there was no need at
all for him to have warned her off.

And all this—all she was going to have to act out for
the duration—was just that. An act. Nothing more.

An act it might be, but it was hard going for all that.

All through dinner she made a relentless effort to be
Marc Derenz's charming hostess—attentive to his guest,
endlessly gushing and smiling about the delights of searching for zillion-dollar homes on the French Riviera to this
woman who clearly wished her at the bottom of the ocean.

Tara was doggedly undeterred by Celine's barely civil
treatment. Far more exasperating to her was Marc Derenz's
stony attitude.

OK, so maybe he was still blazingly furious that Celine
had turned up on her own, but that didn't mean he could
get away with monosyllabic responses and a total lack
of interest in the conversation Tara was so determinedly
keeping going.

As they finally returned to the salon for coffee and liqueurs, she hissed at him, 'I can't do this all on my own!
For heaven's sake, play *your* part as well!'

She slipped her hand into his arm and sat herself down
with him on an elegant sofa, deliberately placing a hand
on his muscled thigh. She felt him flinch, as if she'd burnt
him, and a spurt of renewed irritation went through her. If
she could do this, damn it, so could he!

She turned to him, liqueur glass in her hand. 'Marc,

darling, you're being such a grouch! *Do* lighten up!' she cooed cajolingly.

Her reward was a dark, forbidding flash of his eyes, and an obvious increase in the reading on his displeasure meter as his expression hardened. Her mood changed abruptly. Actually, she realised, there was something very satisfying in winding up Marc Derenz! He was so *easy* to annoy.

A little frisson went through her. She might be playing with fire, but it was enticing all the same...

She turned back to Celine, who was fussing over her coffee. 'Marc's just sulking because he doesn't want to go house-hunting,' she said lightly. 'Men hate that sort of thing—let's leave him behind and do it ourselves!'

But Celine was having none of this. 'You know nothing about the area,' she said dismissively. 'I need Marc's expertise. Of course ideally,' she went on, 'we'd love to buy here, on Cap Pierre—it's *so* exclusive.'

'So much so that there is nothing changing hands,' was Marc's dampening reply.

Dieu, the last thing he wanted was Celine Neuberger anywhere on the Cap. And the next last thing he wanted, he thought, his mood darkening even more, was Tara's hand on his thigh.

It was taking all his resolve to ignore it. To ignore her, as he had been trying to do ever since his eyes had gone to her, descending the staircase with show-stopping impact, and he'd caught his breath at her beauty, completely unable to drag his eyes away from her.

All his adjurations to himself that Tara Mackenzie was out of bounds to him had vanished in an instant, and he'd spent the rest of the evening striving to remember them. But with every invasion by her of his personal space it had proved impossible to do so. As for her hissing at him like that just now—did she not realise how hard it was for him to have to remember this was only a part he was playing? And then, dear God, she had placed a hand on his thigh…

How the hell am I going to get through this week? Was I insane to bring her here?

But it didn't matter whether he had been insane or not—he was stuck with this now. And, tormenting or not, she was right. He had to behave as if he were, indeed, in the throes of a torrid affair with her—or else what was the point of her being here at all?

So, now, trying to make the gesture casual, he placed his free hand over hers. Was it her turn to tense suddenly? Well, *tough*.

To take his mind off the feel of her slender fingers beneath the square palm of his hand, he said, making his voice a tad more amenable, 'I'm sure you and Hans will find what you're looking for, though, Celine. How about higher on the coastline, with a view?'

Pleased at being addressed directly, even if did cast a sour look at him all but holding hands with Tara, Celine smiled engagingly.

'A view would be essential!' she stipulated, and then she was away, waxing lyrical about various houses she had details for, animatedly wanting to discuss them.

Marc let her run on, saying what was necessary when he had to, aware that the focus of his consciousness was actually the fact that his fingers had—of their own accord, it seemed—wound their way into Tara's… His thumb was idly stroking the back of her hand, which felt very pleasant to him, and her palm seemed be hot on his leg, which felt more than merely pleasant…

He could feel himself starting to wish Celine to perdition—and not for the reason that he had no interest whatsoever in a spot of adultery with his friend's wife…

Because he wanted Tara to himself...

He could feel his pulse quicken, arousal beckon...

Maybe the cocktail he'd imbibed, the wine he'd drunk over dinner, the brandy now swirling slowly in his glass, had loosened his inhibitions, faded the reminder he'd been imposing on himself all evening that he had not brought Tara here for any purpose other than to shield him from Hans's wife.

But what if I had?

The thought played in his mind, tantalising...tempting.

Then, with a douche of cold water, he hauled his thoughts away. He lifted his hand away too, restoring Tara's hand to her own lap with a casual-seeming move. He got to his feet. He needed to get out of here.

'Celine, forgive me. I have a call booked to a client in the Far East.' He hadn't, but he had to call time on this.

Celine looked put out, but he couldn't care less. Tara was looking up at him questioningly. Then she took the cue he was signalling. He saw her give a little yawn.

'We'd probably both better call it day,' she announced to Celine. 'I'm sure you're tired after your journey.'

She was making it impossible for Celine to linger, and Marc ushered them both from the room, bidding his unwanted guest goodnight.

Then he turned to the woman who was not his guest, but his temporary employee, however hard she was making it to remember that.

'I'll be about half an hour, *mon ange*,' he murmured, knowing he had to give just the right impression to Celine. Knowing, with a part of his mind to which he was not going to pay any attention, that, however much of a siren call it was, he did not want it to be a mere 'impression' at all...

He silenced his mind ruthlessly, by force of will, turning on his heel and heading for his office, where he was *not* about to make phone call to the Far East, but another, far more urgently needed communication.

The whole evening had been nothing but a gruelling ordeal—and not just for the reasons he'd thought it would be. Not just because of Celine.

Because of Tara.

And what she was tempting him to.

Which he must resist or risk breaking the most essential rule he lived by.

As Tara gained her bedroom relief filled her. Dear Lord, but that had backfired on her—big-time! Hissing like that at Marc to be more convincing in his role-play! Had she been nuts to demand that? To take the initiative he would not?

Memory was hot in her head, as if it were still happening—sitting up close and personal beside him, so that the heat from his body was palpable through the fine jersey of her dress. And then, after so stupidly getting a kick out of winding him up with her taunt about being a grouch, putting her hand on his thigh.

Hard muscle and sinew…and a strength beneath the material of his trousers that had made her want to snatch her hand away as if she'd touched white-hot metal. But she hadn't been able to, because his own hand had closed over hers, imprisoning it between the hard heat of his thigh and the soft heat of his palm.

And then she'd felt her throat catch as that casual meshing of his fingers with hers, that slow, sensual stroking of his thumb, had lit up a thousand trembling nerve-ends in her…

No! Don't think about it! Focus, instead, on getting to bed.
Tomorrow was going to be another long day. Just put-

ting up with Celine was ordeal enough—let alone Marc as well.

Putting him out of her mind as best she could, she got on with getting into her night attire, carefully hanging up the beautiful dress she'd been wearing, then removing her make-up and brushing out her hair. The familiar rituals were soothing to her jagged nerves—as much as they *could* be soothed.

Aware that she was still on edge, and knowing why and deploring it, but unable to calm herself any more, she headed for the palatial en suite bathroom to brush her teeth. As she did so she glanced askance at the door inset beside it. It was no surprise that she'd been put into a bedroom with what must be a communicating door to wherever it was that Marc Derenz slept, because otherwise it would look too obvious that she wasn't really there in the role she claimed. But all the same it was unnerving to think that only a flimsy door separated her from him.

Without thinking too much about what she was doing, let alone why, she went to test it. Locked—and from the other side. A caustic smile pulled at her mouth. Oh, it was definitely time to remind herself that whatever Marc Derenz did in public in order to put out the impression that they were having an affair, in private he was obviously keeping to the arrogant warning he'd given her—not to take his attentions for real...

Well, that was a two-way message, and it was time to remind him of it! She reached for the bolt on her own side, meaning to shoot it closed. And jumped back.

The door had been pulled open from the other side, and Marc Derenz was stepping through into her bedroom.

Her eyes flashed in alarm. 'What are you doing?' she demanded.

She saw his brows snap together in his customary displeased fashion, as if she had no business challenging his walking in unannounced to her bedroom. Quite illogically, she welcomed it.

It's better to dislike him than to—

Her disturbing thought was cut short.

'I need to speak to you,' he announced peremptorily.

He was still in his dinner trousers, but he'd taken off his jacket and his tie was loosened. It gave him a raffish look. As did the line of shadow clearly discernible along his jawline.

Tara felt her stomach hollow. It just did not matter how disagreeable he was. Marc Derenz really should not be so bone-meltingly attractive...

And he shouldn't be in your bedroom either.

The realisation hit her and she took a step back, suddenly aware that she was in her pyjamas. Oh, they might be modesty itself, with their wide silk trousers and high-collared *cheong-sang* top, but they were still nightwear.

'Well?' she prompted, lifting her chin. She didn't like the way his dark eyes had swept over her, then veiled instantly. Didn't like the way she was burningly aware that they had... Didn't like, most of all, the way her nerves had started to jangle all over again...

'I've been emailing Bernhardt—Hans's son.' Marc's voice was brusque, as if he wanted to get this over and done with. 'I've told him in no uncertain terms that he must make sure Hans joins us. I won't have Celine here on her own. Even with you here to—'

'To protect you,' completed Tara helpfully.

Another of his dark looks was his reply, before he continued as if she had not interrupted him. 'Thankfully Bernhardt agrees with me. He's going to tell his father he'll stand in for him at a board meeting so Hans can arrive tomorrow evening. It's all arranged.'

She could hear relief in his voice, and saw a snap of satisfaction in his eyes.

'So we just have to get through tomorrow, do we? Trailing along while Celine looks at houses?' Tara said.

She was trying to silence the jangling of her nerves at his unexpected presence—in her bedroom, with her only in her night attire. She fought to make her voice normal, as composed as she could make it.

'Or are you going to find a way of getting out of it? I don't mind coping with her on my own if you want to bottle it,' she added helpfully.

His expression darkened again. 'No, I'll have to come along as well. If I don't she'll end up landing Hans with some overpriced monstrosity!' He gave an exasperated sigh.

Tara couldn't help but give a laugh, though it earned her yet another darkling look. 'I'll take a bet she'll go for the most garish, opulent pile she can find,' she said, preferring to have a dig at Celine than let herself be distracted by Marc Derenz's overpowering, and utterly unfairly impactful presence in her bedroom. 'Gold bathrooms and crystal chandeliers in the kitchen.'

'Very likely,' he replied grimly. 'Oh, hell, why on earth did he marry the damn woman?' he muttered to himself.

'Well, she's certainly a looker,' Tara conceded, still trying to make normal conversation. 'Over-done-up, to my mind, but presumably it appeals to your friend.'

He shook his head. 'Not Hans,' he said. 'The last thing he wants is any kind of trophy wife.'

Tara couldn't keep the caustic note from her voice. 'Are you sure? Most men like to show off the fact that they can acquire a woman that other men will envy them for.'

Marc's eyes narrowed. 'Is that your experience?'

She shrugged her shoulders. 'It's pretty common in the

world I come from—models are, after all, the ultimate trophy females to make a man look successful.'

Was there bitterness in her voice? She hoped not, but being with Jules had made her wary. What would a man like Marc know, or care, about men like Jules, who needed to feel big by draping a model on their arm? *He* certainly wouldn't need to.

A man as rich and as drop-dead gorgeous as he is doesn't need to prove a thing to anyone!

The thought was in her head before she realised it was there.

Then it was wiped right from her mind. Marc Derenz had taken a step towards her.

'Can you blame them?'

There was something different in his voice, in his stance, in the way he was looking at her.

Suddenly, out of nowhere, every nerve in her body was jangling again—louder than ever. What the hell was she doing, talking to him like this? Standing here in her bedroom, wearing only her silk pyjamas, while Marc Derenz stood there far too close to her, looking so unutterably damn *sexy* with his loosened tie, his jacketless shirt, the hint of a shadowed jawline...

She caught the scent of his aftershave—something expensive, custom-designed, a signature creation made for him alone...

And his eyes—those deep, dark eyes—like slate, but suddenly not hard like slate, but as if a vein of gold had suddenly been exposed in their unyielding surface...

She couldn't drag her own eyes from them...

Couldn't drag breath into her lungs...

Could not focus on a single other thing in the universe than those dark, gold-lit eyes resting on her...

The room seemed to be shrinking—or was it the space between them?

He started towards her again, lifted a hand. She caught the glint of gold at his cuffs, echoing that same glint in those dark eyes of his that were now holding hers...holding her immobile, breathless, so she couldn't breathe, couldn't move...

She could only hear the blood surging in her veins, feel electricity crackle over her skin, as if all he had to do was touch her—make contact...

'Can you blame them?' he said again.

And now there was a husk in his voice, a timbre to it that did things to her insides even as his outstretched hand reached towards her, a single finger drawing down her cheek, lingering at her mouth.

His eyes were playing over her face and she felt a kind of drowning weakness slacken her limbs. Making it quite impossible for her to move a muscle, to do anything other than simply stand there...stand there and feel the slow drift of his fingertip move across the soft swell of her lips. Only his touch on her mouth existed...only the soft, sensuous caress...

'*Pourquoi es-tu si, si belle?*' His murmur was a low husk as he lifted his other hand to slide it slowly, sensuously, around the nape of her neck, through the tumbled masses of her loosened hair. 'Why is it that I cannot resist your beauty?'

She felt her eyelids flutter, felt her pulse beating in her throat, felt her lips parting even as his fingers splayed across her cheek, cupped her jaw to tilt her face to his lowering mouth which she could not, for all the world, resist...

Her eyelids dropped across her eyes, veiling him from sight. She was reduced only to the kiss he was easing across the mouth she lifted to his... Reduced only to the feathered silk of his touch, the hand at her nape cradling her skull, the fingers woven into her hair.

It was like that lingering wrist-kiss all over again, but a thousand times more so. A million sensations swirled within her at the sheer velvet sensuality of his kiss...his mouth moving on hers, tasting her, exploring her. She was helpless—helpless to resist. The heady scent of his aftershave, his body, was in her senses, in the closeness of him as he shaped her mouth to his.

She felt herself leaning into him, letting her own hands glide around the strong column of his back, feeling the play of muscle and sinew, with only the sheer cotton of his shirt to separate her palms from the warmth of his flesh.

She could not stop—would not. Blood was surging in her...her pulse was soaring. She was drowning in his kiss, unable to stop herself, unable to draw away, to find the sanity she needed to find...

And then, abruptly, he was pulling away from her. Stepping away so sharply that her hands fell from him, limp at her sides, just as her whole body felt limp.

Dazedly, Tara gazed blankly at him. She had no strength—none. All her limbs were slack and stricken. Inside her chest her heart was pounding, beating her down.

She heard him speak, but now there was no husk in his voice, no low, sensual timbre. Only a starkness that cut like a knife.

'That should not have happened.'

She felt it like a slap—but it was a sudden awakening from her deathly faint and her eyes flared back into vision, her mind into full consciousness of what she had permitted...given herself up to...

She saw him standing there, stepped back from him. There was a darkness in his face, in his eyes, and his features were pulled taut—as forbidding and shuttered as she had ever seen them.

Then, with the same sharp movement with which he'd pulled away from her, he was turning away, body rigid, his expression still tight as steel wire, walking with heavy, rapid strides to the door. Walking through. Snapping it shut behind him. Without another word.

Leaving her alone, heart pounding, lungs airless, his words echoing in her head—resonating as if it had been she who'd uttered them.

Dismay hollowed her.

Marc plunged down the staircase. *Dieu*, had he been insane to let that happen? Hadn't he warned himself repeatedly that he must keep his response to her hammered down, where it could not escape?

Anger with himself consumed him. Anger he welcomed—for it blotted out more than any other emotion could, blotted out the memory of that irresistible kiss.

Well, you should have resisted it! You should—and must—resist her! She is not here for such a purpose! It would be madness to indulge yourself. Indulge her...

Every reason for his warnings to himself about the dangerous folly of letting the desire that had seized him from the first moment her show-stopping beauty had hit upon his senses marched through his head at his command.

He kept them marching. He must allow nothing else to occupy his mind. Nothing except work. That would keep him on the straight and narrow.

Gaining the hallway, he yanked open the door to his office. The Far Eastern markets would soon be starting up. They would absorb him until he was sufficiently tired to risk heading for bed. *Tout seul.*

His mouth tightened. Most definitely alone.

And it must stay that way. Anything else was a folly he would not commit.

Would not.

CHAPTER FIVE

TARA STOOD IN the over-hot garden of the over-ornate villa they'd just toured, feigning an enthusiasm she did not feel in the slightest. But that was preferable to letting her thoughts go where she did not want them to go. To the memory of that disastrous kiss last night.

She gave a silent groan. Had she been crazy to let Marc Derenz kiss her? *Why* had she let him? Why hadn't she stopped him? Why hadn't she told him to go to hell? Why…?

Why did I kiss him back?

That was what was so disastrous—that she'd *let* him kiss her. And returned it!

Angrily, she catalogued all the reasons why she had been so insanely stupid as to have let that kiss happen. Capping it with the one she'd always had to remember, ever since she'd made the mistake of trusting Jules.

Men who see me only as a model are bad news! And I won't be any man's trophy to show off! I won't!

But even as she yanked that warning into her head she felt it wavering. Hadn't she already accepted that Marc Derenz had no need of a trophy female—not with his wealth, his looks.

Yes, and doesn't that just make him even worse? she shot back to herself. *Thinking every woman in the world is after him?*

She pressed her lips together. Well, not her! She had *not* needed that final warning from him in the slightest.

'*That should not have happened.*'

And it wasn't going to happen again—that was for certain! Somehow, whatever it took, she was going to get through the rest of this week, collect her money and get away—away from the wretched man.

Until then she had to keep going.

She put her mind back to the role she was supposed to be playing.

'Four of the bedrooms don't have balconies,' she pointed out to Celine helpfully. 'Do you think that rules this one out?'

Celine ignored her. It had been obvious to Tara that she'd been doing her best to do so all morning. Instead she turned to Marc.

'What do *you* think, Marc, *cherie*?' she posed with a little pout. 'Does it matter if not all the bedrooms have balconies?'

'No,' said Marc succinctly, his indifference to the issue blatant. He glanced at his watch impatiently. 'Look, would you not agree that it's time for lunch?' he demanded. He was clearly at the limit of his patience.

Tara found herself almost smiling, and welcomed the release from the self-punishing thoughts going round and round in her head. He was so visibly bored and irritated—and, whilst she could not blame him, she knew with a waspish satisfaction that this time it was not she who was drawing his ire. Besides, at least when he was being bad-tempered he wasn't being amorous...

His ill humour, she noted with another caustic smile, seemed completely lost on the armour-plated Celine however. All through lunch—at a very expensive restaurant in Nice—Tara watched the woman determinedly making up to him, constantly touching his sleeve with her long scarlet nails, making cooing noises at him, laughing in an intimate fashion and throwing fluttering little glances at him…

All to utterly no avail.

He sat there like a block of stone, his expression getting darker and darker, until Tara wanted to laugh out loud. She herself was doing her level best to drag Celine's attention towards her instead, chattering away brightly, waxing lyrical about the houses they'd viewed, the ones they might still view, obdurately not letting Celine blank her as the woman kept trying to do.

That her brightly banal chatter was only adding to the visible irritation on Marc's face did not bother her. What else did he expect her to do, after all? She was here to run interference, and that was what she was doing. And, after all, the way wretched Celine was behaving, the whole situation was just ridiculous! He really needed to lighten up about it.

As the woman turned away now, to complain about something or other to a hapless passing waiter, Tara could not suppress a roll of her eyes at Celine's endless plays for Marc's attention. Then, abruptly, his eyes snapped to hers, catching her in mid-eye-roll.

She saw his mouth tighten and one of his laser looks come her way. She gave a minute shake of her head in resignation, a sardonic twitch of her lips, and for a moment— just the slightest moment—she thought she saw something flicker in the slate-grey depths of his eyes. Something that went beyond a warning to her not to come out of role. Something that she had never seen before. A flicker so faint she could not believe she'd seen it.

Humour.

Good grief, did the wretched man actually have a sense

of humour? Somewhere buried in the recesses of his rock-like personality?

If he did she didn't catch any more sight of it. After lunch was finally over Celine gushingly begged Marc to head for Monte Carlo. With ill grace he complied, and Tara found herself glad of the excursion. Not only was it a lot better than looking at over-priced, over-decorated villas for sale, but she'd never seen Monte Carlo, and she looked around her with touristic scrutiny at the grandeur of the Place de Casino, her gaze lingering on the fabled casino itself.

'It's where fools go to lose their money,' a sardonic voice said at her side.

She glanced at Marc, whose expression mirrored his disparaging tone of voice. 'Now, *there* speaks the sober banker!' she exclaimed lightly. 'All the same,' she added, 'sometimes those fools come out millionaires.'

'The winners win from the other gamblers who lose.' His tone was even more crushing. 'There is no free money in this world.'

'Unless,' Tara could not resist saying, 'one marries it… That's always been a favourite way of getting free money.'

Her barb was wasted. Celine's attention was focussed only on the luxury shopping mall opposite the casino. Like a heat-seeking missile, she headed towards it. As Tara made to follow she caught a frown on Marc's face. She presumed it was because he was now facing a prospect every man loathed—shopping with women.

Impulsively, she tucked her hand into his elbow. *'Courage, mon brave!'* she murmured humorously, leaning into him.

She only meant to lighten him up, maybe even to catch a glimpse of that crack in his steel armour that she'd evoked so unexpectedly over lunch. But clearly his mood had worsened too much for that.

Her hand was abruptly removed and he strode forward, leaving her to hasten after him into the mall.

She gave a sigh. And a twist of her mouth. It had been stupid of her to do that. And not because it had annoyed him instead of lightening him up. Because *any* physical contact at all with the man was not a good idea in the least...

Not after last night. Not after that kiss—that disastrous, dangerous, completely *deranged* kiss that she should never have let happen!

No, any physical contact with him that wasn't forced on her by the necessity of playing the role he was paying her to play, was totally *défendu*. Totally forbidden. And she mustn't forget it. Not even to wind the man up. Or try and lighten him up. It was just too risky...

Because, however overbearing and obnoxious he could be, she was just too damned vulnerable to what he could make her feel.

Sobered, she followed him into the mall.

'*Fraulein*, how very good to meet you!'

Hans Neuberger was shaking Tara's hand genially, his face smiling. He had a nice face, Tara decided. Not in the least good-looking, and late middle-aged—a good twenty years older than his wife—but with kindly eyes.

She smiled warmly back. 'Herr Neuberger,' she returned.

'Hans, please!' he said immediately, and she liked him the more.

They were in the magnificent Art Deco salon once more, and Hans Neuberger had just arrived. He'd kissed Celine dutifully on the cheek, but she'd turned away impatiently. Tara thought her a fool to treat her kindly husband with such open indifference.

'Hans! I'm glad to see you!'

Tara turned. Marc was striding in, holding out his hand to his guest in greeting. She stared, disbelief etching her features.

Good God, the man could smile! As in *really* smile! Not the cynical, humourless indentation of his mouth she'd seen so far, or that infinitesimal chink she'd seen at lunchtime, but an actual smile! A smile that parted his mouth, reached his eyes to crinkle them at the edge. That lightened his entire face...

She felt her breath catch.

Gone, totally, was the hard-faced, bored, impatient, ill-tempered expression she was so used to. Just...gone. It made him a *completely* different person—

She reeled with it, still hardly believing what she was seeing. And she felt something shift inside her, rearrange itself. Marc Derenz...*smiling!* It was like the sun coming out after thunderclouds...

She stared on, bemused, aware that her pulse had suddenly quickened and that it had something to do with the way Marc's smile had softened his face, warmed his eyes... It warmed something in her as well, even though it was not directed at her in the least.

But what if it were—?

No. She shut her mind off. It was bad enough coping with the utterly unfair impact the man had on her when he was being his usual ill-humoured self. She could not possibly think how she would cope if he were capable of being *nice*, for heaven's sake!

It was a resolve she had to stick to throughout dinner. She was helped in that by focussing her attention on Celine's husband. Hans Neuberger really was far too nice to be landed with a shrew like Celine. He was clearly hurt and bewildered by her dismissiveness, and Tara did her best to divert him.

'I think Marc said you're based in Frankfurt? All I know about it is the huge annual book fair. Oh, and that it was the birthplace of Goethe.'

Hans's kindly face lit up. 'Indeed—our most famous son! And Germany's most famous poet—'

Celine's voice was sharp as she cut across him. 'Oh, for heaven's sake, Hans, don't start boring on about poetry! Who cares?'

The rudeness was so abrupt that Tara stared. Hans was silenced, looking stricken. Tara felt immensely sorry for him and rallied to his defence.

'I'm afraid I know very little about German poetry—it didn't really come into my English Literature course at university, alas,' she said politely.

'Speaking of university...' Marc's voice interjected now, as he picked up the baton. 'Has your youngest—Trudie—graduated yet?'

As Hans answered Tara saw Marc throw a glance at her. There was something in his eyes she'd never seen before. Appreciation. Appreciation, evidently, for coming to Hans's rescue as she had.

She blinked for a moment. Then gave a minute nod.

For the rest of the meal she did her best to shield Hans from his unpleasant wife, drawing him out about Goethe and the German Romantics, comparing them with the English Romantics of the same period. Marc joined in, widening the discussion to include French poetry too, keeping the conversation going.

Celine seemed to be in a foul mood—though whether that was because she was clearly being cut out of a conversation she was incapable of contributing to, or whether it was just because her husband had arrived, Tara wasn't sure and didn't care.

What *was* clear, though, was that Celine was not about to let her husband's presence get in the way of her determined pursuit of Marc Derenz, and she was still focusing her attention solely on him.

She continued to do so, quite blatantly, the following day. She dragged them all out for yet more house-viewings, then insisted on heading to Cannes, so she could trawl through the luxury brand-name boutiques strung out along the Croisette.

'She really is,' Tara heard herself say *sotto voce* to Marc, as Celine preened in front of a mirror, 'the most tiresome woman ever! Poor Hans can't possibly want to stay married to her!'

'She's like a leech,' he snapped shortly. 'And Hans is too damn soft-hearted for his own good!'

'Can he really not see her true character?' Tara mused disbelievingly.

Marc's face hardened. 'Men can be fools over women,' he said.

She glanced at him curiously. He couldn't possibly be referring to himself—she knew that. A man like Marc Derenz was made of granite. No woman could make an impact on him.

'Marc, *cherie*!' Celine's piercing call sought to summon his attention. 'Your taste is impeccable! Should I buy this?'

'That is for Hans to say, not me,' came his tight reply.

'Oh, Hans knows nothing about fashion at all!' was Celine's rudely dismissive retort.

Tara stepped forward, seizing a handbag from a stand. 'This would go perfectly with that outfit,' she said. And it was not for Celine's sake, but for the sake of her hapless spouse, hovering by her side.

Celine was hesitating between outright rejection of anything that Tara suggested and lust for the shiny gold bag. The latter triumphed, and she snatched it from her.

'Magpie, as well as leech,' Tara murmured, her head dipped towards Marc.

Did she hear a crack that might just be laughter break from him, before it was abruptly cut off? She stole a look at him, but the moment was gone.

At least, though, the handbag had clinched it and Celine was ready to depart.

It still took for ever, it seemed to Tara—and probably to Marc and Hans as well, she thought cynically—before they could finally return to the villa. Another grim evening loomed ahead of them, with Celine openly discontented because Marc had flatly vetoed her repeated suggestion that they head for the casino at Monte Carlo.

But her petulant mood improved markedly when, after dinner, she took a phone call that made her announce, 'That was the Astaris. They're on their yacht in Cannes. They're giving a party tomorrow.' A frown crossed her brow. 'I haven't got a *thing* to wear for it!' She turned towards Marc. '*Do* run me into Monte, tomorrow, *cherie*! I'm sure Tara can stay here and discuss poetry with Hans,' she added pettishly.

Not surprisingly, Celine's blatant ploy to get Marc to herself for yet another shopping expedition failed, and the following morning all four of them set out for Monaco.

This time, thankfully, Celine availed herself of a personal shopper, who read her client perfectly so that she could emerge triumphantly with a gown that would cost her husband an outrageous sum of money. Full of herself, Celine then demanded that they lunch at the principality's premier hotel, overlooking the marina packed with luxury yachts, and proceeded to plague her husband to buy something similar.

It was obvious to Tara that this was the last thing Hans wanted to do, and she took pity on him by deliberately interrupting the flow of his wife's importuning.

'Tell me,' she asked, 'what else is in Monte Carlo besides the casino, luxury shops and yachts?'

Hans's face brightened. 'The Botanic Gardens are world-famous,' he said.

'Have we time to visit?' Tara asked. It would be nice, after all, she thought, sighing inwardly, while she was here, actually to see something of the Côte d'Azur other than expensive villas, expensive shops and expensive restaurants.

'What a good idea!' Celine put in immediately. 'Hans, you take Tara to the gardens and Marc and I can—'

'I thought you wanted to talk to a yacht broker?' Marc cut across her brutally, pre-empting whatever scheme Celine was about to dream up to get him on his own.

Celine sulked visibly, then ordered Hans off to find out who the best yacht broker in the principality was. Dutifully the poor man went off to ask the hotel's concierge. Perking up at her husband's absence—however temporary—Celine leant across to Marc, resting her hand on his sleeve in her possessive fashion, stroking it seductively.

'A yacht is *so* essential these days—you must agree!' she oozed. '*Do* help me persuade Hans, *cherie*!'

There was a cajoling, caressing note in her voice, and her scarlet nails curved over his arm. Her over-made-up face was far too close to his, her eyes greedy for him, openly lascivious—and suddenly, out of nowhere, Tara had had enough. Just *enough*.

There was something in her that absolutely revolted at seeing Celine paw at Marc the way she did. Something that was the last thing she should feel about him—but feel it she did, and with a power that shook her.

Parting her lips in an acid grimace she leant forward. 'Celine,' she said, sweetly, but with a bite to her voice that could have cut through steel wire, 'call me old-fashioned, but I would prefer you, please, to take your hand *off* Marc!'

Immediately Celine's eyes snapped to Tara. There was venom in them. And in the words she snapped out too.

'Oh, my, how *very* possessive! Anyone might think you have *ideas* about him!'

It was a taunt—an obvious one—and Tara opened her mouth to retaliate. Except no words came. Only a spearing dart of emotion that should not be there…should not exist at all.

And then, suddenly, Marc's voice cut across her consciousness. She felt her hand being taken, turned over, exposing her wrist. Before she knew what he intended he had dipped his head, grazed his mouth across that tender skin, sending a million nerve-endings firing in her so that she could only stare at him, eyes widening…

'I very much hope Tara *does* have ideas about me…very possessive ideas!' she heard him say. 'For I most certainly do about her!'

His voice had dropped to a low purr, and now his gaze was holding Tara's with an expression of absolute intentness.

Was he trying to convey a message? She didn't know—could only feel all those nerve-endings still firing inside her like a hail of fireworks as the dark gaze on her suddenly lifted, shifting to Celine. Tara felt his hand, large and strong, enfold hers, meshing his fingers into hers… *possessively.*

She saw him smile—a smile, she suddenly thought, that

had a twist of ruthlessness to it. A ruthlessness that was entirely explained when she heard him speak.

'You can be the first to know, Celine.' That same deep, steely purr was in his voice. 'Tara is my fiancée,'

Fiancée? Tara heard the word, but could not credit it. Where had *that* come from?

Urgently, she looked at Marc, burningly conscious not just of what he had dropped like a concrete block on them all, but even more of the tightly meshed fingers enclosing hers. Possessively...very possessively.

With a corner of her consciousness she heard a hissing intake of breath from Celine.

'*Fiancée?* Don't be absurd!'

Her derision stung. Stung with an echo of Marc's voice telling her not to get ideas about him, telling her this was playacting only and for no other purpose.

And it stung with much more. With the way his mouth had felt like velvet on the tender skin of her wrist just now, taunting her...tempting her...

Of its own volition and entirely instinctively, with an instinct as old as time and as powerful as the desire she felt for the man who had brought her here, Tara felt her mouth curve into a derisive smile, a mocking laugh.

Because he did not desire her for himself, but only to block another woman's access to him.

She felt her hand lift to Marc's cheek, felt herself lean towards him. Felt her mouth reach for his, open to his, to feast on it, possessive with passion and naked desire...

How long she kissed him she did not know, for time had stopped, had ceased to exist. There was only the sensation of Marc's mouth, exploding within her, the taste of him, the scent of him, the weakening of every part of her body as desire flamed inside her...

Dazed, she drew back, gathering what senses she could,

knowing her heart was pounding in her breast but that she had to say something. Anything.

Deliberately she gave that mocking little laugh again. Clearly Celine had wanted proof of the engagement Marc had suddenly and out of nowhere imposed upon the scene.

'We were going to keep it secret—weren't we, darling?'

Her glance at Marc was brief. She did not meet his eyes…did not dare to. Then she looked back to Celine across the table. She had to stay in role, in character—that was essential, however hectic her pulse was after that insanely reckless kiss that she had been unable to prevent herself from taking from him.

'Don't say anything to Hans, will you?' she said to Celine. 'Marc wants to tell him himself—before we announce it formally.'

The expression on Celine's face was as if she had swallowed a scorpion—or a whole bucketful of them. Then Hans was coming back to the table. He started to say something about yacht brokers but Celine cut across him. She was furious—absolutely seething.

Tara's glance went treacherously to the man she had just kissed with such openly passionate abandon…

But then so was Marc…

CHAPTER SIX

MARC YANKED ON his DJ and strode to the connecting door, pulling it open and striding into Tara's bedroom. He still could not believe he'd done what he'd done. Telling Celine that Tara was his fiancée! And then letting her kiss him—*again*. Had he gone mad? He must have. But had there been *any* other way of getting Hans's damn wife to lay off him?

Even as he'd made that momentous announcement he'd been appalled at himself. Danger had shimmered all around. Every precept he'd lived his life by had been appalled.

And now he had to do what he was intent on doing—make it absolutely crystal-clear to Tara Mackenzie that he had spoken entirely on impulse, exasperated beyond the last of his patience by Celine. It was a final means to an end—nothing more than that. Being his fiancée was every bit as fictional as his original proposition.

His mouth set in a grim expression. That devastating kiss she'd given him had not been fictional in the least! It had been searingly, devastatingly *real*...

But he absolutely could *not* risk that. Risk anything like that at all! Not with Tara—the woman he should have nothing to do with whatsoever outside the playacting he was paying her for...

She can't be anything in my life—I can't risk it. And

I can't risk her thinking she can be anything in my life. Wanting any of this to be real...

His eyes went to her now. She was sitting at the dressing table, putting on her lipstick. She was quite at home in his villa, in this bedroom with its luxurious atmosphere, with its priceless pieces of Art Deco furniture, the silver dressing table set, the walls adorned with paintings from the thirties by artists whose prices in auction rooms were stratospheric.

Tara looked perfect in the setting—as if she belonged there...

But she doesn't belong. I hired her to play a part, and the fact that the part has suddenly become that of my fiancée changes nothing!

That was what he had to remember.

That the searing desire he felt for her was not something he could permit.

Part of him registered that, yet again, she was looking totally stunning. The russet silk halter-necked evening gown left her sculpted shoulders bare and skimmed the slender contours of her spectacular body, and her glorious hair waved lustrously over her shoulders in rich abandon.

Her head swivelled sharply as he strode in, and she dropped her lipstick on a silver tray.

'We need to talk!' Marc's voice was brusquer than he'd intended, but he did not care.

Tara's chin lifted, her eyes defiant. She got to her feet and got in first. 'Don't look at me like that!' she said. 'I know I was impulsive, kissing you like that, but—'

He strode up to her, took her shoulders. He'd had to wait *hours* for this moment! He'd had to endure babysitting Hans at the yacht broker's so he didn't end up buying a damn yacht for his appalling wife, then endure the car ride back to the villa, and then endure Tara disappearing up to her room to shower and dress for the evening. He was not going to wait a single interminable moment longer!

'It was *totally* unnecessary!' he barked.

'It was totally *necessary*!' Tara shot back. She wrenched herself free. 'Look, you'd just dropped that on me out of the blue! Saying I was your fiancée! I didn't know what to do—only that I had to follow your lead and make it look real!'

'*Dieu*, it looked real, all right! It damn near earned a round of applause from everyone there! And, worse, it nearly got seen by Hans.' He took a rasping breath. 'Hans must *not* know anything about this—do you understand? Because it isn't real! You *do* understand that, don't you?'

His eyes were skewering hers and his hand slashed the air for emphasis.

'There is *no* relationship between us! *No* engagement! Do *not* think otherwise!'

He saw her expression tighten, her eyes flash.

'Of course I do!' she snapped.

'Then *behave* like you understand it!' he shot back. He drew a deep, if ragged, breath to calm himself, get himself back under iron control. Because if he didn't…

She was standing there, breasts heaving, eyes fired with retaliation, looking so incredibly beautiful that with a single impulse he could have swept her up into his arms and buried his mouth in hers, feasting on those lush, silken lips…

And he dared not—dared not do anything of the sort. It would be madness. All he could do was what he did now. School his features, take another breath…

He held up a hand, silencing any utterance she might be going to say. He needed to say his piece first. 'OK, so I dropped a bombshell…went off-script. And OK…' his expression changed '…if I must I can accept that you acted on impulse to give credibility to what I'd just thrown at you.'

His breathing was still heavy, but he forced it back. Went on with what he had to say.

'But from now on, although we've told Celine we're engaged, we absolutely *must not* let Hans think so!' He took another ragged breath, ran his hand through his hair. 'Or he will believe it.'

His mind slewed away from the prospect of Hans believing that he and Tara were engaged to be married…the hassle and misunderstanding it would lead to…the absolute impossibility of it ever being real, Hans would not understand.

That was what he must cling to now—the fact that his outburst of sheer exasperated temper, when he had been goaded beyond endurance by Celine, was for *her* consumption only, serving only to convince her to give up any hopes of an adulterous affair with him.

'So,' he said now, 'are we clear on that? We've let Celine think we are engaged—that I've proposed to you and you've accepted—but, as you so adeptly persuaded her, that I am waiting to tell my old friend Hans myself, and we'll be announcing it formally later on. And on that basis…' he took a final heavy breath, his eyes skewering Tara '…we'll get on with the rest of this damn evening. Which I am *not* looking forward to—Celine's appalling friends and their even more appalling party to endure!'

He held out a hand to Tara, not wanting her to say a word…not wanting her to do anything but meekly go along with what he was paying her to do—acting the part of his fiancée.

For a moment it looked as if she was going to argue with him—something no employee of his had ever dared to do.

And Tara was no different from *any* other employee—that was what he had to remember. What *she* had to remember.

Then stiffly, ignoring his outstretched hand, she marched to the door, pulled it open.

He caught up with her, and they walked down the stairs. '*Smile*,' Marc urged grimly, *sotto voce*, 'you're my secret fiancée, remember!'

He saw her mouth set in a smile—tight, but there, even if it *was* totally at odds with the glacial expression in her eyes.

As they walked into the salon he saw Celine was already there, looking gaudy in a new gold lamé gown, Hans, totally ignored by her, stood dutifully at her side.

A basilisk glare shot from Celine to Tara beside him, far stronger than any animosity she'd displayed so far towards the woman she perceived as getting in her way. Marc's mouth compressed tightly. Well, maybe his announcement and Tara's outrageous kiss had hit home— even if he was still furious that she'd had the temerity to do such a thing off her own bat.

His simmering anger—and the prospect of a party with a bunch of Celine's friends—made him stiffer than ever in his manner, and his 'Shall we set off?' was made through gritted teeth. His jaw tightened even more when he felt Tara slip her hand into his arm. And nor did his black mood improve when they boarded a yacht lit up like a Christmas tree, music blaring and the deck heaving with just the kind of people he disliked most—those who showed off their money as conspicuously and tastelessly as possible.

Celine, however, was clearly in her element, and she swanned around, discarding Hans as soon as she could, knocking back champagne as if it was water. Marc watched her flirting openly with other men and did his best to keep talking to Hans and to avoid as much as possible any contact with anyone else.

Including Tara.

He was burningly conscious of her standing at his side, not saying a great deal—partly because of the noise of the party and partly because he was quite deliberately talking business with Hans, attempting to block his friend's view of his wife, currently cavorting on the small dance floor with unconcerned abandon with some man. He had no idea who and doubted Hans did either.

But, for all his efforts to ignore Tara, he could still catch her elusive fragrance, hear the rustle of her gown as she shifted position, and he knew that he wanted only to turn his head so his eyes could feast on her...

Was it the hypnotic rhythm of the music, or the champagne he'd imbibed to get him through this ordeal, or the oh-so-occasional brush of her bare arm against his that was building up inside him a pressure he was finding it harder and harder to resist?

He didn't know—only knew that Tara standing beside him was a torment.

I want her. I should not want her, but I do. It's madness to want her, and I know it—and it makes no difference. Whatever it is about her, she makes me forget all the rules I've lived my life by...

'Marc, *cherie*, dance with me!'

Celine had abandoned her partner, was sashaying up to him. Her eyes were glittering and the overpowering scent of her perfume was cloying. She leaned towards him, as if to lead him out onto the dance floor.

'Dance with Hans,' he answered shortly. 'I'm about to dance with Tara.'

The moment he said it he regretted it. The last thing he needed to endure was taking Tara out on the dance floor.

But it was too late. Celine's eyes flashed angrily at his blunt refusal as he turned to Tara.

'*Mon ange?* Shall we?' His voice was tight, and the expression in his eyes warned her not to refuse him.

He saw her stiffen, saw her obvious reluctance to be taken into his arms and danced with. It fuelled his anger. He reached out, helping himself to her bare arm, and guided her forward. Stiffly, she looped her arms around his neck, barely touching him, and his hands moved to rest on her slender hips.

He could feel the heat of her body through the thin fabric of her gown. Feel, too, how stiffly she was moving as they started to dance. He made himself look down at her face, which was set in stark lines, as if dancing with him were the most repugnant thing in the world.

'Celine is watching us,' he gritted. 'Let's make this a bit more believable, shall we? After all,' he added, 'we're an engaged couple now, aren't we? So give it all you've got, *mon ange.*'

His taunt was deliberate, and she knew it—he could see by the sudden flash in her eyes. It gave him a perverse satisfaction to see it, to know with every male instinct in him that there was only one reason why she was reluctant to make this look real.

And it was not because he repelled her...

It was time to make that clear to her—and if it helped convince Celine too...well, right now he didn't give a damn about Hans's benighted wife or keeping her away from him. Right now only one intention fuelled him. Consumed him...

His hands at her hips drew her towards him, closing the distance between them, and one palm slid to the small of her back to splay across her spine. The supple heat of her body was warm beneath his palm.

For a split second, he felt her resist—as if she would not give in to what he knew from the tremor that ran through her and the sudden flaring of her eyes her body was urging her to do. Then, with a little helpless sigh in her throat, her resistance was gone and she was folding against him, her hands tightening around his neck, her eyes gazing up at him.

He felt her breasts crest against his chest—felt his own body reacting as any male body would react to such a woman in his arms! A woman who was driving him crazy with wanting her, being denied her...

His splayed hand at her spine pinioned her to him and his thighs guided her in the slow, sensual rhythm of the dance. He heard her breath catch again. Her lips were close to his, so tantalisingly close. He felt his head dip...wanting so badly to feel that silken velvet he had tasted only once before. He hungered for it with a desire that was now surging in him, to taste her again...to sate himself on her...

He pulled her more closely against him, knowing that she knew—for how could she not know just how very much he desired her...?

His lashes dipped over his eyes. He said her name— low and husky with desire... Relief was flooding through him—relief that finally she was in his arms, in his embrace, that she was pressed as closely to him as her body would be were he making love to her...

The rest of the world had disappeared. Hans, Celine, the whole damn yacht had disappeared. Only Tara was here—the woman who had stopped the breath in his lungs the first time he'd set eyes on her. The woman he wanted now more than any other woman.

His eyes were holding hers, not relinquishing them, watching her pupils expanding, seeing the dilation of desire in those incredible blue-green eyes of hers...

His mouth lowered to hers, seeking the sweet, silk velvet of her lips…so hungry to feel them part for him…for her to yield the sweetness of her mouth to his once more… Desire was like molten lava in him…

And then, abruptly, she was yanking herself away from him, and there was something flaring in her eyes now that was not desire—that was the very opposite of that. She strained against him, dropping her arms from him, removing his hands from her body. She seemed to be swaying as he looked down at her, face dark with her rejection.

'The music has stopped.'

She got the words out as if each one were a stone. He stared at her blankly, then heard her go on, her eyes like knives now.

'And if you *ever* try that on again with me I'll… I'll…'

But she did not finish. Instead, with a sudden contortion of her face, she walked off the dance floor, seizing up a glass of champagne from a passing waiter and knocking it back.

'A lovers' tiff? Oh, dear!' Celine's voice was beside him, her false sympathy not concealing her spite.

He ignored her, his eyes only for Tara, clutching her flute, refusing to look at him. His senses were still aflame, afire, and yet as the noise of the party filled the air, as the thud of music started up again, faster this time, he turned to Hans.

'Let's get out of here,' he said bluntly.

Ruthlessly, he shepherded them ashore, summoning his driver as he did so, and then piling them all into the limo the moment it drew up.

Tara had got in first, and was making herself extremely busy with a seatbelt. Her colour was high, her mouth set tight, long legs slanted away from his direction. As he threw himself into his own seat—diagonally opposite

Tara—he saw Celine's gaze whip between the two of them. Speculation was in them as she took in Tara's withdrawal, her hostile body language.

Marc shut his eyes. He was beyond caring now. Let Celine think whatever the hell she wanted! His thoughts were elsewhere.

He wouldn't get any sleep that night—it would be impossible—but he didn't care about that either...

The moment they arrived back at the villa Tara all but bolted up the stairs, and he heard her bedroom door slam shut. Hans also took himself off. Marc made for the sanctuary of his office—anything to get away from Celine, who had gone to help herself from the drinks trolley in the salon.

He was just pushing open his office door when he heard her call out behind him.

'Marc, *cherie*—my poor, poor sweet!'

He hauled himself around. Celine was issuing towards him, a liqueur glass in her hand. Her eyes were glittering as she made for him. Every muscle in his body tensed. His black mood instantly tripled in intensity. Dear God, this was the last thing he needed now.

'Celine, I have work to do,' he ground out.

She ignored him. Came to him. Draped one bare arm around his shoulder. Her over-sweet scent was nauseating to him, her powdered half-exposed breasts in the skin-tight gold dress even more so.

He yanked her arm away, propelled her backwards. She was undeterred. He could smell alcohol mingling with her perfume.

The glitter in her eyes intensified. 'Don't marry that woman, Marc. You can't! She's not right for you. You know she isn't. She thinks she can treat you the way she did tonight. Push you away. You don't want a woman like that, Marc!'

She swayed towards him, trying to reach for him again. He seized her wrist, holding her at a distance. His face was thunderous, but she was still trying to touch him, to clutch at him with her scarlet nails.

'You want *me*, Marc! I know you do!' she cried, her voice slurring, 'I would be so, *so* good for you! Let me show you.' She swayed again, as if to throw herself into his arms.

'Celine, you are married to Hans,' he growled.

Dear God in heaven, was he to endure this now? On top of everything else? Fighting off Celine, with her rampant libido loosened by the alcohol she'd consumed all evening?

Her face twisted. 'Hans?' She all but spat out the name. 'He means nothing to me! *Nothing!* I should never have married him! I can't bear him. I can't bear him to touch me! He's old and pathetic and boring!' Her voice was vicious, cruel. 'I want to divorce him! Get him out of my life! I want a man like *you*, Marc—only you!'

Marc thrust her from him, stepping aside, filled with disgust at her. 'Get to bed, Celine. Sleep it off. You are the last woman on this earth I'd be interested in, and I wouldn't be even if you weren't married to Hans!'

He heard her gasp in stunned disbelief and outrage, but he was turning away from her, plunging inside his office. Slamming the door shut behind him. He leant back against it, slipping the lock. Not trusting Hans's unspeakable wife not to try and follow him in.

He swore fluently. Cursing her. Cursing the whole world. Cursing, most of all, the fact that upstairs, in a bedroom he must not let himself go anywhere near, was the one woman on earth that he wanted.

Who was tormenting him beyond endurance.

* * *

Tara woke. Instantly awake after dreams she dared not remember.

I can't bear this! I can't bear this any longer!

To have to act this role with Marc—only act it! Act it and keep him at bay at the same time. To tell herself over and over again that it was just role-play, nothing more than that!

Except it wasn't, was it? She could no more fool herself that she was acting than she could tell herself that *he* was!

Memory burned in her of that slow dance to end all slow dances... Their own bodies had betrayed them, shown them that neither of them were *acting*...

No! She mustn't think of it! Must not remember it!

She was here for one reason only: to protect Marc Derenz from another man's wife. And she was doing it for money, as a paid employee. *Anything* else was not real.

Whatever their bodies told them.

She hauled her mind away. So what? So what if she could not stop her body's reaction to him? If she could not stop that electricity surging within her whenever he looked at her, touched her? It didn't matter—not a jot—because none of this was real.

And even if it were real, she told herself, her thoughts bleak now, she could not let it be real. She was an outsider to this world. Her life was in England and she was moving to the country, starting afresh, getting out of the fashion world. Out of the orbit of men like Marc Derenz.

However powerful and devastating his impact on her...

With a heavy sigh she got up, went through into the en suite bathroom. There was another gruelling day ahead of her. She had better brace herself for it.

Yet as she headed downstairs a little while later she noticed there seemed to be a different atmosphere in the villa. It was quieter, for a start, and as she crossed the salon to reach the terrace where breakfast was always served she realised she could not hear Celine's dominating voice yapping away.

She walked out. There was only Marc, sitting in his usual place at the head of the table, drinking his coffee, perusing the morning newspapers.

Tara frowned. 'Where are Hans and Celine?' she asked as she took her seat. Her expected sense of awkwardness after the night before had vanished in her surprise at not seeing his guests there.

Marc looked up. He hadn't heard her step out on the terrace. His eyes went to her, riveting her like a magnet, then instantly veiling.

'They've gone,' he said.

Tara's frown deepened as she reached for the jug of orange juice. 'What do you mean? More house-viewing?'

Marc sat back, folded his newspaper and set it aside with a deliberate movement. His mood could not be more different from his mood when he had ploughed up the stairs last night, thrusting the vision of the drunken, vicious-mouthed harpy that was Celine from him, wanting only to seek oblivion from what Tara had so tormentingly aroused in him.

The news that had greeted him this morning had wiped all that from his mind, leaving only one emotion. And that had brought with it only one decision that now burned in him, just as the memory of Tara kissing him had, of how their bodies had clung to each other in that devastating slow dance...

With Celine and Hans gone, and Tara tormenting him with his desire for her, there was only *one* decision he now wanted to make—and to hell with all his endless damn warnings to himself! To hell with the lot of them!

She was gazing at him now… Tara with her sea-blue eyes set in that breathtakingly beautiful face of hers, her lush lips parted, a frown still on her brow as he answered her question.

'No,' he said.

The emotion he felt was in his voice, and he could see that it had registered with Tara as well, for her expression had changed.

'Gone,' he elaborated now. 'As in Hans has flown back to Frankfurt, where he will be consulting a divorce lawyer. As for Celine—I don't know and don't care. Presumably to find herself a divorce lawyer as well.'

Tara stared. *'Divorce?'*

'Yes.' Marc smiled.

And Tara, to her disbelief, realised that it was a genuine, hundred-carat smile.

It wasn't just the shock of what he'd said but the dazzling impact of his smile that froze the jug in her hand. 'I don't understand,' she said weakly.

He lifted his coffee cup again, tilted it towards her. 'Congratulations,' he said. 'To both of us! It did the trick—*my* announcement to Celine yesterday that you were my fiancée and *your* oh-so-convincing behaviour that went with it!'

He took a mouthful of coffee and continued in that voice that was so different from any she had heard from him before.

'It rattled Celine into making one last desperate attempt on me. When we got back last night she threw caution to the winds—and herself at me. Full-on. She told me she didn't want Hans any more, that she only wanted me. What I didn't realise at the time,' he went on, 'when I was disabusing her of her hopes, was that Hans overheard her saying she wanted to divorce him.' He took a breath. 'So he is going to oblige her and file for divorce himself.'

Tara's face lit. 'That's *wonderful*! I couldn't be happier for him!'

'Nor me,' said Marc. His expression changed again. 'Celine will try and take him to the cleaners, but Bernhardt will make sure she gets as little as possible. He's been on the phone to me already, thanking me profusely.'

His eyes rested on Tara. They were warm in a way she'd never seen before. So was his voice when he spoke again.

'And I have to thank you too, Tara.'

His expression was veiled suddenly and his voice suddenly changed again. Now there was something in it that sent flickers of electricity through her, that quickened her pulse, made her eyes fix on his.

'You don't need me to tell you how damnably tormenting this whole thing has been! But...' he gave a heartfelt sigh, rich with the profound relief that was the only emotion in him right now '...thank the Lord that is all over now!'

Inside his head Marc heard the very last of his life-long warnings to himself—heard it and dismissed it. He had not come this far, endured this much, to listen to it any more. Hans and Celine were gone—but Tara... Oh, Tara was here—and here was exactly where he wanted her...

And whatever else he wanted of her—well, he was damn well going to yield to it. Resisting it any longer, resisting *her*, was just beyond him now. Totally beyond him. Yes, she was a woman he would never usually have allowed himself to get this close to physically, but fate had brought them this far and he was not going to deny any longer what was between them.

Up till now it had been playacting—but from this morning onwards, he would make it searingly, blazingly *real*. It was all he wanted—all that consumed him.

She was gazing at him now, with uncertainty in her face—and something more than that. Something that told him he was not going to be the only one giving in to what had flamed between them right from the very start.

He smiled a smile warm with anticipation. With the relief he felt not just at Celine's departure but at the thought of his own yielding to what he so wanted.

He poured himself some more coffee, helped himself to a brioche. 'Now,' he went on, 'we just have to decide how we're going to celebrate the routing of the unspeakable Celine.'

Tara looked at him. Part of her was still reeling from the news that Hans was finally going to get rid of his dreadful wife, but that was paling into insignificance because she was reeling from the total change in Marc.

It was as if a different person sat there at the head of the table. Gone was the tight-faced, ill-humoured, short-fused man who could barely hide his constant displeasure and exasperation. Just gone. Now an air of total relaxation radiated from him, with good humour and satisfaction all round…

The difference could not be greater.

Nor the impact it was having on her.

She watched him sit back in his chair, one long leg crossed over the other, completely at his ease.

Was this really Marc Derenz of the frowning brows, the steel jaw, the constant darkling expression in his eyes?

'So,' he said, buttering his brioche, 'what would you like to do now that we have the day to ourselves?'

Tara started. 'What do you mean?' She tried to gather her thoughts. 'Um…if Celine and Hans have gone, I ought to go back to London.'

Suddenly the frown was back again on his face. 'Why?' he demanded.

'Well, I mean… I've done what you brought me out here to do, so there's no point me being here any longer.'

He cut across her. 'Oh, for God's sake—there's no need to rush off!' He took a breath, his stance altering subtly, as did the expression in his eyes. 'Look, let's just chill, shall we? We damn well deserve it, that's for sure! So, like I say, what would you like to do today?' His eyes rested on her. 'How well do you know the South of France—I mean apart from trailing around the damn shops with Celine and seeing those dire houses she dragged us to? Why don't I show you the South of France that's actually worth seeing?'

He seemed to want an answer, but she could not give one. How could she? This was a Marc Derenz she had never known existed. One who could smile—really smile. One who radiated good humour. Who seemed to be wanting her company for *herself*, not for keeping Celine Neuberger at bay.

She felt something flutter inside her. Something she ought to pay attention to.

'Um… I don't know. I mean…' She looked across at him. His expression was bland and she tried to make it out. 'Why?' she said bluntly. 'As in why do you want me to stay? As what?'

That strange feeling inside her was fluttering again, more strongly now.

'What do you mean, "As what?",' he countered.

'Am I still in your employ, or what? Am I supposed to have some sort of role? Am I—?'

He cut across her questions. 'Tara, don't make this complicated. Stay because you're here…because Celine and Hans have gone…because I want to celebrate their impending divorce. Stay for any damn reason you like!'

He was getting irritated, she could see. For some reason, it made her laugh. 'Oh, that's better,' she said dulcetly. 'I thought the new, improved Marc Derenz was too good to be true!'

For a second he seemed to glower at her. Then his face relaxed. 'You wind me up like no other woman,' he told her.

'You're so easy to wind up,' she said limpidly.

She could feel that flutter inside her getting stronger. Changing her mood. Filling her, suddenly, with a sense of freedom. Of adventure.

He shook his head, that rueful laugh coming again. 'I'm not used to being disagreed with,' he admitted.

Tara's eyes widened. 'No? I'd never have guessed.'

He threw her a look, then lifted both his hands in a gesture of submission. 'Truce time,' he said. He looked at her. 'You know, I'm not really a bear with a sore head most of the time. You've seen me at my worst because of Celine. And,' he admitted, 'you've caught the sharp edge of my ill-humour because of that. But I *can* be nice, you know. Why don't you stick around and find out just how nice, hmm…?'

She felt a hollow inside her, into which a million of the little flutters that had been butterflying inside her suddenly swooped.

Oh, Lord, this was a bad, *bad* idea! To 'stick around', as he'd put it! Yet she wanted to—oh, she wanted to! But on what terms? With what assumptions? That was what she had to get clear. Because otherwise…

She took a breath. 'Marc, these past days have been…' She tried to find a word to describe them and failed. 'Well, you know—the role-playing. It was…' she swallowed '… confusing.'

She didn't want to recount all the incidents, the memories she couldn't cope with, the times when all self-control had been ripped from her.

He nodded slowly. His dark eyes rested on her with something behind them she did not need a code-breaker to decipher.

'Yes,' he said. 'And it's time—way beyond time—to end that confusion.'

He did not spell it out—he did not have to. She knew that as he went on.

'So let's put the confusion behind us, shall we? And the acting and the role-playing? We'll just take it from here. See what happens.' He paused, those dark eyes unreadable—and yet oh-so-readable. 'What do you say?'

He was waiting for her answer.

She could feel those butterflies swooping around in that hollow space inside her, knew that she'd stopped breathing. Knew why. Knew, as she very slowly exhaled, that whatever she'd said to herself while being so 'confused'—dear God, that word was an understatement!—about the way this man could make her feel, that now, with just the two of them here, like this, finally free to make their own choices, that she was making a decision that was going to take her to a place with Marc Derenz that she did not know. Had never yet been.

But she wanted to go there with a part of her that she could not resist. She heard words frame themselves in her mind. Knew them to be true.

It's too late to say no to this—way too late.

As he'd said—no more role-play, no more acting. No more 'confusion'. Just her and Marc…seeing what happened…

And if 'what happened' was her yielding to that oh-so-powerful, never before experienced desire for him, would that really be so bad?

She glanced about her at this beautiful place, at the devastating man sitting there, drawing her so ineluctably.

Would it be so bad to experience all that she might with this man? Whatever it brought her?

I've never known a man like this—a man who makes me feel this way. So why should I say no to it? Why not say yes instead...?

She could feel the answer forming in her head, knowing it was the answer she would give him now. A tremor seemed to go through her as slowly she nodded her head.

She saw him smile a smile of satisfaction. Pleased...

His smile widened and he pushed a bowl of pastries towards her. 'Have a croissant,' he invited. 'While we plan our day.'

CHAPTER SEVEN

'So, WHAT DO you think?'

Marc slewed the car to a juddering halt at the viewpoint and killed the engine. This was the car he liked to drive when he was at the villa—a low-slung, high-powered beast that snaked up the *corniches*, ate up the road as they gained elevation way up here in the foothills of the Alpes-Maritimes.

He turned to look at the woman sitting beside him in the deep bucket passenger seat as the engine died. Satisfaction filled him. Yes, he had made the right decision. He knew he had—he was definite about it.

The discovery from a clearly upset Hans that morning that he had accepted his marriage was over, and that Celine was not happy with him, had been like a release from prison for Marc. He'd said what needed to be said, organised Hans's flight, then seen him off with a warm handshake.

Celine's departure he had left to his staff while he himself had gone off to phone a jubilant Bernhardt.

And after that there'd only been himself to think about. Basking in heartfelt relief, he'd gone to breakfast in peace, his glance automatically going to the upper balcony. To Tara's bedroom.

Tara.

He had known a decision had to be made.

What am I going to do? Pack her off back to London or...?

Even as he'd framed the question he'd felt the answer blazing in his head. For days now she'd haunted him…that amazing beauty of hers taunting him. His but only in illusion. His only reality, punching through every moment of his time with her, was that he wanted to say to hell with the role he'd hired her to play. He wanted *more*.

And when she'd walked out onto the terrace he'd taken one look at her and made his decision.

No, she wasn't from his world. And, had it not been for the insufferable Celine and his need to keep her away from him, he'd never have let Tara get anywhere near him. Yes, he was breaking all his rules never to get involved with someone like her.

And he just did not care.

Not any more.

I want her—and for whatever time we have together it will be good. I know that for absolute sure—

It was good already. Good to have had that relaxed, leisurely breakfast, deciding how to spend their day—a day to themselves, a day to enjoy. Good to have her sitting beside him now, her sandaled feet stretched out in the capacious footwell, wearing a casual top and skinny cotton leggings that hugged those fantastic legs of hers. Her hair was caught back with a barrette and her make-up was minimal. But her beauty didn't need make-up.

His eyes rested on her now, drinking her in.

'The view is fabulous,' she was exclaiming. Then she frowned. 'It's just a pity it's so built up all along the coastline.'

Marc nodded. 'Yes, it's a victim of overdevelopment.

Which is why I like being out on the Cap—it's more like the Riviera was before the war, when the villa was built.'

He gunned the engine again, to start their descent, telling her how the villa had been party central in the days of his great-grandfather.

It was a subject he continued over lunch, stopping off at a little *auberge* that he liked to go to when he wanted to get away from his usual plush lifestyle.

'He invited everyone who was anyone—painters, expat Americans, film-makers, novelists.'

'It sounds very glamorous.' Tara smiled as he regaled her with stories.

'My grandfather was much quieter in temperament—and my father too. When I was a boy we spent the summers here. Hans and his first wife and their children were often visitors, before my parents were killed—'

He broke off, aware that he was touching on something he did not usually talk about to the women in his life. But Tara was looking at him, the light of sympathy in her eyes.

'Killed?' she echoed.

'They both died in a helicopter crash when I was twenty-three,' he said starkly.

Her expression of sympathy deepened. 'That must have been so hard for you.'

His mouth tightened. 'Yes,' was all he said. All he could say.

He watched her take a slow forkful of food, then she looked at him again. 'It can't compare, I know, but I have some idea of what you went through.' She paused. 'My parents are both in the army, and part of me is always waiting to hear that…well, that they aren't going to come home again. That kind of fear is always there, at some level.'

It came to him that he knew very little about this

woman. He only knew the surface, that fabulous beauty of hers that so took his breath away.

'Did you—what is that old-fashioned phrase in English?—"follow the drum"?' he heard himself asking.

She shook her head. 'No, I was sent to boarding school at eight, and spent most of my holidays with my grandparents. Oh, I flew out to see my parents from time to time, and they came home on leave sometimes, but I didn't see a great deal of them when I was growing up. I still don't, really. We get on perfectly well, but I guess we're quite remote from one another in a way.'

He took a mouthful of wine. It was only a *vin de table*, made from the landlord's own grapes, but it went well with the simple fare they were eating. He found himself wondering whether Tara would have preferred a more expensive restaurant, but she seemed content enough.

She was relaxing more all the time, he could tell. It was strange to be with her on her own, without Celine and Hans to distort things. Strange and…

Good. It's good to be here with her. Getting to know her.

And why not? She came from a different world, and that was refreshing in itself. But it was about himself that he heard himself speaking next.

'I was very close to my parents,' he said. 'Which made it so hard when—' He broke off. Took another mouthful of wine. 'Hans was very kind—he stepped in, got me through it. He stood by me and his wife did too. I was… shell-shocked.' He frowned, not looking at her, but back into that nightmare time all those years ago. 'Hans helped me with the bank too. Not everyone on the board thought I could cope at so young an age. He guided me, advised me—made sure I took control of everything.'

'No wonder,' she said carefully, 'you're so loyal to him now.'

His eyes went to hers. 'Yes,' he said simply.

She smiled. 'Well, I hope his life will soon be a lot happier.' Her expression changed, softened. 'He's such a lovely man—it's so sad that he was widowed. Do you think he'll marry again eventually? I mean, someone *not* like Celine!'

'It would be good for him, I think,' Marc agreed. 'But, as I said to you, the trouble is he can be too kind-hearted for his own good—easy for him to be taken advantage of by an ambitious female.'

'Yes…' She nodded. 'He needs someone *much* nicer than Celine! Someone,' she mused, 'who really values him. And…' she gave a wry smile '…who enjoys German romantic poetry!'

Marc pushed his empty plate aside, wanting to change the subject. Of course he was glad for Hans that he'd freed himself from Celine's talons, but right now the only person he wanted to think about was Tara.

She had already finished her *plat du jour*, and she smiled at him as she reached for a crusty slice of baguette from the woven basket sitting on the chequered tablecloth.

'You've no idea how good it is to simply eat French bread!' she told him feelingly. 'Or that croissant I had at breakfast! So many models are on starvation diets—it's horrendous!'

He watched her busy herself, mopping up the last of the delicious homemade sauce on her empty plate, disposing of it with relish.

'Won't you have to starve extra to atone for this now?' he posed, a smile in his voice.

She shook her head. 'Nope. I'm going to be chucking in the modelling lark. It's been good to me, I can't deny that, but I haven't done anything since university that qualifies me for any other particular career—not that I want to work nine-to-five anyway. I've got other plans. In fact,' she added, 'it's thanks to being out here that I can make them real now.'

He started to ask what they were, but the owner of the *auberge* was approaching, asking what else they might like. They ordered cheese and coffee, changing the subject to what they would do in the afternoon. It was an easy conversation, relaxed and convivial.

Marc's eyes rested on her as they discussed what she might like to see. She was so different, he observed. That all too familiar argumentative antagonism was gone, that back-talking that had irritated him so much. Oh, from time to time there was a wicked gleam in her eye when she said something he knew was designed to try and wind him up, but his own mood was now so totally different it had no effect except to make him laugh.

She's easy to be with.

It was a strange thing to think about her after all the aggro, all the tension that had been between them.

We've both lightened up, he mused.

Only one area was generating any tension between them now. But it was at a low level, like a current of electricity running constantly between them, visible only in sudden veiled glances, in the casual brush of hands, in body contact that was not intentional or was simply necessary, such as handing her a menu, helping her back into the low-slung car as they set off again, catching the light floral fragrance of her scent.

His eyes wanted to linger on her rather than on the road twisting ahead. On their constant mutual awareness of each other. He let it run—low voltage, but there. This was not the time or the occasion to do anything about it. That was for later...for this evening. And then... Ah, then... He smiled inwardly, feeling sensual anticipation ease through him. Then he would give it free rein. And discover, to the full, all that he burned to find in her.

There would be no more drawing back—no more hauling himself away, castigating himself for his loss of self-control, no more anger at himself for wanting her so much…

I am simply not going to fight it any more.

He had not deliberately sought her out, or selected her for a relationship. She had come into his life almost accidentally, certainly unintentionally, because of his urgent need to protect himself from Hans's amoral wife—but she was here now. And after all he'd had to put up with over Celine, damn it, he deserved a reward!

He glanced sideways at her as they drove back down towards the coast. And she deserved something good too, didn't she? She'd done the job he'd set her—triumphantly!—so why shouldn't he make sure that now she had as enjoyable a time remaining as he could ensure?

He would do his best, his very best, to ensure that. It was impossible for her to deny the desire that flared between them, and now there was no more aggravation, no more frustration, no more confusion, no more role-playing and no more barriers.

As his eyes went back to the twisting road ahead, and he steered his powerful car round the hairpin bends, he felt his blood heat pleasurably in his veins. Whatever the risks of breaking the rules he lived his life by—Tara would be worth it.

Most definitely worth it…

Tara sat at the silvered Art Deco dressing table, carefully applying minimal eye make-up—just a touch of mascara tonight was all that was needed—and a sheen of lip gloss. Her mood was strange. Everything was so similar to the previous night, when she'd been making up her face and getting dressed for that yacht party with Celine's awful friends, and yet everything was totally different.

Marc was different.

That was the key to it, she knew. That 'bear with a sore head', as he had called himself with total accuracy, was simply gone. She couldn't help but make a face at how he'd railed at her. This time yesterday he'd laid into her furiously in this very room for daring to take matters into her own hands, and to damn well lay off him! But her ploy had worked—and he'd had to admit it had worked even better than either of them could have imagined!

And now, mission more than accomplished, they could both have their reward for freeing poor Hans from his ghastly wife.

Reward...

The word hovered in Tara's head. Beguiling, tempting. She knew just what that reward was going to be...

Impossible not to know...

And to know with a certainty that had been building up in her hour after hour, all day.

Marc was right—whatever was happening between them, it was powerful and irresistible. They wanted each other—had done since first seeing each other, and had gone on wanting each other all through those torturous days when they'd both been forced to pretend in public what they had tried so hopelessly to deny in private.

They wanted each other. It was the one undeniable truth between them.

It was as simple as that.

Her eyes flickered around the beautiful room and she looked out through the windows to the darkening view beyond, over the gardens and the sea. Her very first thought on arrival here had been how gorgeous it all was, and how she should make the most of it.

Well...a half-smile played around her mouth...now she *was* going to make the most of it. And of the man who came with it.

The man who, even when he was at his most overbearing, his most obnoxious, his most short-tempered, possessed the ability to set her pulse racing, her blood surging, her heart-rate quickening...

She could feel it now, and with another little flutter inside her, she got to her feet.

I can't resist him and there's no reason to. He wants me—I want him. I know it won't last—can't last—but I must simply enjoy this time with him.

He wasn't a man she'd ever have got involved with had it not been for him hiring her, but since he had, and she was—well, why not accept what was happening between them?

Why not—as she was doing now—slip into an ankle-length, fine cotton sundress in a vivid floral print of vibrant blues and crimsons that was nothing like the formal evening gowns and cocktail dresses she'd worn when the Neubergers were there. She was 'off duty' now, and she wanted only to feel comfortable.

It was a look that Marc had echoed, she saw as she joined him out on the terrace. He wore a plain white open-necked shirt with the cuffs turned back and dark blue chinos. Still devastatingly attractive, but relaxed.

The two of them were all set, ready for a comfortable and relaxed evening together...

She felt that little flutter inside her again.

But that was for later. For now there was just the warmth in Marc's eyes—a warmth that wasn't only male appreciation of her, but a side of him she hadn't seen in him before, except for when he had greeted Hans. A side of him that had so taken her aback as he'd dropped that perpetual ill-humour of his.

He was walking towards her, an open bottle of champagne and two flutes in his hands. He set the flutes on a table laid for dinner, with candles glowing in protective glass cases, and started to pour the champagne. Silently he handed her a softly effervescing glass, keeping the other for himself.

'It's a champagne evening,' he announced, a smile playing at his mouth. He raised his glass. 'To us,' he said softly, his eyes never leaving her. 'To our champagne evening. *Salut!*'

And it *was* a salute, Tara knew. It was a recognition of what was happening between them—what had been happening ever since their first encounter. An acknowledgement that neither of them could walk away now from the other…from this champagne evening.

I want this—I want everything about it. Even for the short while that it will be mine…

The words were in her head—unstoppable. And she didn't want to stop them, to silence them. All she wanted, on this evening of all evenings, was what there was and what was to come.

'*Salut…*' she said in soft reply, and took a mouthful of the delicate drink, her eyes still holding his. There was a glow in her body, a sweetness in her veins, a low pulse at her throat.

He drank as well, and then, with a smile, said, 'Walk with me.'

She did, and they strolled across the darkening garden to the edge of the lawn, where the manicured grass gave way to rougher land, and then a rocky shore tumbled down to the lapping sea below.

There was a little jetty, and steps cut into the rocky outcrop to take them there, and he led her down. They stood on the jetty awhile, looking out across the night-filled sea. From this point at the tip of the Cap there was no line of sight to the shoreline with all its bright lights. Even the villa behind them was not visible this low below the shoreline.

'We might be on a desert island…' Tara breathed, her voice still soft. 'All on our own.'

At her side, Marc gave a low laugh. 'The world vanished away,' he said.

He turned to her. Lifted the hand that was not holding his flute to trail a finger along the contours of her mouth.

'I want this time with you,' he said, and she could hear the husk in his voice now, feel the frisson in her veins that it engendered. 'We are free to have it—and I very much wish to share it with you.'

There was a question in his voice—and yet an answer too. For how could she refuse him? She knew she would not be here, standing with him out on the jetty, beneath the gathering night, if she did not want what he wanted too.

Marc felt desire creaming inside him, yet he knew he must not be precipitate. He had considered her out of bounds, was breaking all his rules by indulging himself with her, and as that was so he wanted to take from this forbidden *liaison d'amour* all that it could offer him.

And it will be worth it! She is promising everything I want—everything I have already so tantalisingly tasted.

Tara made no reply to what he had said, but she did not need to, she knew. Perhaps, it was unwise, letting herself be drawn into a world that was not hers, to a man who could never be hers for that reason, and she knew it must be brief, but she accepted it. Accepted all of it. This beautiful villa, this beautiful place, and the man whose domain it was.

She took another slow mouthful of her champagne, feeling its potency ease into her bloodstream, committing her to what she was doing.

They stood awhile, as the sky darkened to absolute night and one by one the stars began to shine. The low lapping of the water was seductive...as seductive as the warm, caressing breeze that lifted off the sea. Then, the sky dark, the champagne drunk, they made their way back to the terrace to dine together.

What they ate Tara would not afterwards remember. She knew only that it was delicious, and that the conversation flowed between them as effortlessly now as it had been fraught before. Had they really been so...so intemperate towards each other? So antagonistic, so irritated and exasperated by each other? It seemed impossible. Impossible to think of Marc as the man he had been when now his ready smile, his low laugh, his lambent eyes were warm upon her.

What they talked about she would not remember either. She only knew that another conversation was taking place as well—a conversation that, as the meal ended and liqueurs were consumed, the coffee pot drained, he suddenly brought to vivid life as he reached for her hand, drew her to her feet.

The staff were long gone, and they were here alone on the candlelit terrace. He stood in front of her, so dark against the night beyond. She caught his scent, felt herself sway and smile...

He said her name—a caress—and lifted his hand to her hair to draw her closer to him. But there was no need. With a little sigh, closing her eyelids, she let her body fold against his, let it rest, as it wanted so much to do, against the strong column of his. He took her weight against him effortlessly and her hand slid around his waist, resting on the cool leather of his belt, the tips of her fingers feeling the hard heat of his flesh beneath the thin fabric of his shirt.

She gave a soft, almost inaudible sigh in her throat. And then his mouth was silencing her. Moving with the velvet softness that had caused her sleepless nights, and which now sent a drowning bliss through her with every feathering touch.

She gave herself to it. This time... Ah, this time there was no barrier, no regret, no resistance to what was happening between them. She was giving herself utterly to it...

Their kiss was long, unhurried, for they had all the night before them... Then, as her breasts engorged, their peaks cresting against the hard wall of his muscled chest, she heard him growl, felt his mouth releasing hers. His eyes poured down into hers, and she felt with a frisson of arousal that he was responding as strongly as was she.

Was it wickedness that made her loop her hands around his neck and whisper, 'Shall we slow dance?'

For tonight they could—oh, yes, they could indeed— and with that came the knowledge that now there need be no more play-acting, that they could finally accept and revel in the desire that flamed between them. No more being thwarted, no more pulling away... At last they could give in to what they had wanted from the very first.

The growl came again—a low rasp—and instead of an answer she was suddenly, breathlessly, swept up into his arms.

'We can do better than that,' he told her, and the deep husk in his voice was telling her just what that 'better' was going to be.

She gave a half-cry, half-laugh, and then he was striding indoors, across the marble hall, up the marble stairs.

She clung to him, and she was held fast in his powerful grip as he carried her along the landing, to head inside a room she had never yet stepped into.

It was dark, but he knew the way. Knew the way to the wide bed waiting for them. And as he lowered her to its surface, coming down beside her, he knew there were no more questions to ask, no more answers. Their bodies had asked and answered all that was needed.

Desire—that was the question *and* the answer. And it flamed between them, powerful and unquenchable. They were to be aroused by all that it could offer, to savour it… to enjoy. In a sharing of slow, caressing pleasure, a banquet of the senses.

He leant over, dark against the dimness of the room, smoothing the tumbled mass of her glorious hair, spearing his fingers through the lush tresses as she gazed up at him, starlight from the undrawn drapes shining in her dilated eyes. Waiting for his possession. For her possession of him.

He kissed her again slowly, tasting, drawing from her every drop of nectar. Again he felt his body fill with desire, with wanting.

For a moment he held back, as if to give himself one last chance to draw away completely, but she caught his mouth again, arching her neck, her spine, putting her hands around his back, drawing him down to her to feel the swell of her breasts, to hear the soft moan of desire in her throat.

He gave a low, husky laugh, cut short as his kiss deepened, his arousal surged. His palm closed over one peak and her soft moan came again as she pressed against his caressing hand, wanting only what he could arouse in her. Heat filled her body—her limbs…the soft vee of her thighs.

Her dress was in the way, and restlessly she sought to free herself. But he was there before her. His hands slipped the material from her, cast it aside even as he cast aside his own clothing, freeing them both to come together now, as their bodies longed to do, with a will they could not stop, nor wanted to.

They wanted only to do as they were doing—to wind themselves around each other, pinioning and clasping. His mouth was gliding down the satin contours of her slender body, and again low moans came from her.

Her head twisted helplessly on the pillow as she gave herself to his silken touch. Desire soared within her and she wanted more—oh, she wanted all of him! She felt her thighs slacken, her body's heat flare, and her fingers clawed over his strong, muscled shoulders.

She drew him into her and he surged in full possession. She cried out, gasping at the power of him, the potency. Her hands clutched him tighter, and more tightly yet, as he moved on her, within her, releasing with every surge more and more of what was rising within her, unstoppable, unquenchable. A glory of sensation, a gasping of delight, of mounting urgency...

And then it broke within her, flooding out into every vein, every portion of her body, racing out from her pulsing core to the furthest extremity, her whole body burning in this furnace of ecstasy.

As she cried out he surged within her again, his body thrashing, fusing with hers like metal melting into metal, white-hot and searing.

And she was everything he desired—everything he wanted. She was fulfilling all her promise, pulsing around his body, her own body afire, until the fire consumed itself and he felt her hands at his shoulders slacken, felt her whole body slacken.

He felt his do so too, heavy now upon her, and he rolled her, with the last of his strength, so that she was beside him and he could fold her to him, feel her shuddering body calm, her racing heartbeat slow, her hectic breathing quieten. He held her as his own slugging heart steadied, his limbs heavy, inert.

Slowly he felt the lassitude of her body's repletion ease through her as he stroked her hair, murmuring to her he knew not what. He knew only that his soft caressing, his softer murmurs, brought her to stillness in his cradling arms.

He felt his eyelids droop, sleep rushing upon him. He knew he must yield to it—for now. But as consciousness slipped from him, and the warmth and the silken length of her body pressed against his, something told him his sleep would not be long...

Nor hers...

CHAPTER EIGHT

MORNING LIGHT WAS bathing them. Tara could feel it warm upon her back, which was partly covered by a single sheet. Her arm was flung across the bare torso of the man beside her, still asleep.

She herself was still drowsy and somnolent from the night that had passed. A night like no other she had ever known.

Memory drenched through her and she hugged her naked body more closely against the one she was entwined with. Had she ever imagined a night like that was possible?

Time and time again he had possessed her—each time a consummation of bliss that had caused her to cry out over and over again as her body had burned with his, in a heat that had been a consuming fire, bathing their straining muscles and sated flesh, her spine arched like a bowstring, his body plunging into hers, her hands clutching at the twisting contours of his shoulders, her head thrashing on the pillow as they reached their peaks together.

And then peace had blanketed down upon her, upon them both—an exhaustion, a sweeping sigh of exhalation as their bodies had closed upon each other, no space between them, pressed to each other in heated fastness, hers turned into his, folded against him, her limbs heavy, his yet heavier. And then, dazed and dazzled, she had sought the rest that had come—instant and obliterating.

Only for him to rouse her yet again…and for her to wake in an instant, to overpowering desire again…

Memories indeed…

She felt her mouth smile against his throat, her eyelids flutter, felt him stir in answer, his hand easing across her flank with soft caress.

For a while they simply lay there, letting the sun from the windows warm their entwined bodies, dozing and then waking slowly to full awareness of the day. Saying nothing, for there was no need.

Not until Marc, with a stretching of his limbs, turned his head to smile across at her. 'Breakfast? Or—?'

She laid a finger across his mouth. 'Breakfast!' she said, shaking her head. 'One night with you lasts a long, *long* time…'

He gave a laugh, pleased with her answer. Pleased with the entire universe. He had known women before—many women. But this one…

His mind sheered away. It wasn't necessary to think, to examine or analyse. It was only necessary to enjoy this gloriously sunny morning, here in the place he loved where he never seemed to have enough time to spend. It was only necessary to get himself up from his bed, reach for a grey silk robe and knot it around his waist.

His muscles felt stretched, fully used…

He reached a hand down to her. 'If you want breakfast,' he said, and there was a husk in his voice with which Tara had become very familiar with in the long, sensual reaches of the night, 'you had better use your own shower.'

He nodded towards the communicating door, then headed for his own en suite bathroom. At the door to it he turned. She was starting to stand up, and the sight of her fabulous racehorse body, full in the sunlight now, almost made him change his mind and carry her through to his own shower, where washing was *not* going to be a priority...

But his stomach gave a low grumble. He had expended a great deal of energy last night and it needed to be replenished.

So he said only, 'See you downstairs. And think about what you would like to do today—because if you can't come up with anything I have a very enticing idea of my own...'

He let his voice trail off and raised a hand in half-salute, leaving her to her own rising.

When they regrouped, out on the terrace, he threw himself into a chair. He was wearing shorts, and a striped top.

Tara, settling herself down opposite him, gave a laugh. 'You look like a *matelot*!' She smiled.

Marc's eyes glinted. 'The very thing,' he said. He sat back. 'It's a beautiful day and the wind is just right—let's take to the water.'

She laughed. 'Is *that* your enticing idea?' she returned. 'I was assuming something far more...*physical*...' she said wickedly.

'Depends where we drop anchor,' Marc returned, his expression deadpan.

She laughed again. She could have laughed at anything this morning—this glorious, *glorious* morning. The morning after the night before...and the night before had been like no other night had ever been...

Could ever be...

For just a moment she felt a dart pierce her. Would anything in all her life ever compare to the night she'd spent in the arms of this man she had so rashly committed herself to? A man she knew she should never have given herself to but had simply not been able to resist?

What if nothing could?

She pushed the question aside. This was not a morning for questions—for doubts of any kind. She was having this time with Marc, and if he was a million miles from her own normality—well, so be it. Too late for regrets now, even if she wanted to have them—which, right now, she did *not*.

She reached for a croissant, revelling in its yeasty temptation, in yielding to *all* temptations. 'That sounds fun.' She smiled. 'I didn't see a boat moored at the jetty, though.'

'It's kept at the dock in Pierre-les-Pins, at the head of the bay. I'm having it sailed to the jetty now.'

He said it casually, but the remark lingered in Tara's head as she busied herself with her breakfast. It was another reminder of just how hugely wealthy he was. Just as much as this villa was a reminder, with its manicured lawn and pool, and its complement of attentive staff, and the top-marque car he'd driven her about in yesterday, and the chauffeur-driven limo, the gourmet restaurants, and the designer wardrobe he'd snapped his fingers for, and every other element of his life.

Unease filtered through her. Before, while she'd been working for him, it hadn't bothered her, his vast wealth. But now… Was she wise to get personally involved with him in any way? Even for what must inevitably be only a brief time, in this mutually self-indulgent 'reward' for their torturous past week? With a man from a world so entirely different from her own?

It was difficult to remember that—to believe in all that fabulous wealth of his, in the bank that bore his name and was the source of all that wealth—when she was skimming over the azure waters of the Mediterranean, the breeze filling the billowing sails.

But the huge disparity in their wealth was harder to ignore that evening when, gowned once more in one of the fabulous couture evening dresses supplied for her by him for the role that was no longer a role, but real, for whatever short duration it would prove, he whisked her off in the sleek, chauffeured car, to dine out in another fearsomely expensive Michelin-starred restaurant, where every dish cost a fortune and the wines ten times as much.

She put it aside. For this evening, this time they would have together, it was just the two of them, lovers for real now. She felt a little shimmer of wonder at the transformation. She could actually enjoy it. She had Marc to herself, and it was 'new Marc'—Marc with his ready smile, his air of absolute relaxation, total well-being.

He raised his glass to her and she did likewise, taking a sip of the formidably pricey vintage wine, savouring it even as she savoured all the wonderful delicacies on offer from the menu.

'This is beyond heaven!' She sighed blissfully as whatever concoction he'd ordered for her slipped down her throat. 'I could really get used to this! How on earth am I going to go back to my usual humble fare after this?'

She expected to hear his low laugh, which she was getting used to hearing now, but it didn't come. Instead there was a flickering in his eyes, as if his thoughts were suddenly elsewhere. And in a place he did not care for.

She wondered at it, then set it aside. Nothing was going to spoil this evening. She gazed around the restaurant, taking it in, knowing that this was an experience she must make the most of. Once she was in her little cottage in Dorset, places like this would be a distant memory only.

A little pang went through her and her eyes moved back to the man sitting opposite her. He, too, one day, would be only a distant memory...

There was a tiny catch in her throat and she reached for her wine glass, made some deliberately light remark, to which Marc responded this time—as if he, too, had set aside something there was no point thinking about. Not now...not tonight. Not with the night ahead of them...

Anticipation thrummed through her, and a sudden sensual awareness. Her eyes went to him across the table, caught his, saw in them what she knew was in hers... What remained in them all through their long, leisurely and exquisite meal, as conversation flowed between them—easy now, when it had been impossible before.

It was nearly midnight before they left—but when they returned to the villa Tara discovered that the night was still young...

Their night lasted till dawn crept over the edge of the world, and brought with its first light the sleep her body was too exhausted to deny... The sleep that overtook their bodies, all passion finally spent, folded around each other as if parting could never come.

It was a false illusion...

Marc was in his office, attempting to catch up with work. But his mind wasn't on it. He gave a rueful grimace. Where his mind was right now was out by the pool—the pool beside which Tara would be sunning herself, turning her silken skin a deeper shade of delectable gold, all the more enticing to caress...

With a groan, he tore the seductive vision from his head and focussed on the computer screen, on the myriad complexities of his normal working life making their usual round-the-clock demands on him. Demands that he had no inclination to meet at the moment but that were piling up nevertheless.

He knew he could not postpone them indefinitely. That

at some point he'd have to knuckle down and deal with them. The truth was, he wasn't used to taking so much time out from work.

Work had dominated his life ever since he'd had to shoulder all the responsibilities of his inheritance at a painfully early age. Even when he set aside his workload for social engagements, or for his carefully considered forays into highly selective affairs, as was his habit, they never interfered with his primary task in life—to see Banc Derenz through to the next era of its survival in an ever-changing financial landscape. So why, he pondered now frowningly, the figures on the screen ignored still, was he being so careless of his responsibilities at this time?

At first he'd put his indulgence at giving in to his inconveniently overpowering attraction to Tara simply as relief at getting the wretched Celine off his case once and for all. But that had been two weeks ago—two weeks of pure self-indulgence, as he was well aware. Of indulging himself with Tara—giving himself to a sensual feast and to a time out of his customary highly disciplined and demanding lifestyle to simply…simply what?

To have a holiday.

That was what he was doing. Simply having a holiday with this irresistible woman! A holiday that was an endless drift of golden days here in the balmy weather of the Riviera. Lounging by the pool, taking out the sailboat, driving along the coast or up into the hills, making a foray across the border into Italy one day to explore San Remo, strolling around the perfumeries of Grasse another day, heading further still to St Raphael, with its ochre-red cliffs, and then St Tropez, with all the nostalgia of its fashionable heyday in the sixties. They had explored the villages and landscapes that had so beguiled the Impressionists, wandered around the narrow streets of the old town in Nice, strolled along the seafront in Cannes, lunched on one of the many private beaches, or out on the jetty over the water…

A procession of easy-going days, relaxed and carefree, before returning home to the villa…and all the sensual delights of the nights they shared.

He shifted in his seat. When would he tire of Tara? When would her allure grow stale? When would he not want to trouble himself with making conversation with her, engaging in repartee as she presumed to tease him and he returned as good as he got, volleying with her until they both were laughing…or kissing…

I must tire of her soon. Surely I must?

She wasn't from his world, so how could he think of her as anything other than a passing *amour*? Oh, she'd adapted to it easily enough—but then, what woman *wouldn't* find it easy to adapt to the wealthy ease of his highly privileged life.

Has she adapted too well? Got too used to it?

The thought was in his head before he could stop it. Reminding him of all the reasons why he never took up with women who did not share his own lifestyle in their own financial right.

His eyes went to his screen. No sum of money there was without a whole string of zeroes after it—it was the realm he worked in, that encompassed the accounts of his extremely rich clients. Sums of money that the likes of Tara would never see in her lifetime…

Memory scraped in his head. Unwelcome, but intruding all the same. How Tara had sat with Celine on that ultratedious afternoon in Monte Carlo, and made that casual comment that 'marrying money' was still a sure-fire way to help oneself to riches. He'd considered it a snipe at Celine, but now, his frown came again. But maybe it was something she believed herself?

More memories came...uglier and more intrusive, forcing their way in. Marianne...making up to him...enticing him and luring him, the young heir to Banc Derenz, only to callously abandon him for a much safer financial bet—a man with his own wealth already safely in his pockets.

Another image formed in his mind. Sitting in that restaurant with Tara—one of the most exclusive and expensive on the Riviera—the day after their first night together. *'I could really get used to this!'* she'd said, and sighed pleasurably...

More thoughts came to him—disturbing and uneasy. He had declared to Celine that Tara was his fiancée, and the sole purpose of the announcement had been to try and get Hans's wife's clutching claws off him. But had that impulsive proposal set thoughts running in Tara's head? Was she remembering them when they were together now? When they kissed...embraced...made love?

Does she think I might propose for real? Make her my wife?

Roughly, he pushed his chair away from his desk. He would not let such thoughts in. He glanced at his watch. She'd been sunning herself far too long—she must not burn her skin...her oh-so-delectable skin.

Again memory skimmed in his mind—of how irritated he'd been that first day here, to arrive and find the woman he had hired to keep Celine at bay behaving as if she were here on a free luxury holiday.

Well, now she really is here on a free luxury holiday...

Again the unwelcome thought was in his head. Again he dismissed it. For she could enjoy this time with him with his blessing—enjoy all the luxury he took for granted himself. His expression changed. After all, *she* was a luxury herself—to him. An indulgence like none he'd ever experienced. And he wanted to indulge himself...

An anticipatory smile played about his mouth. Her heated skin would need cooling down—and a shower together was the very thing to achieve that. He would lather her body all over with his own hands...every beautiful centimetre of her...

His mood much improved, he abandoned any fruitless attempt to work and strode impatiently from the room to make his anticipation reality.

Tara stretched languorously and rolled over so that it was her back—bare from neck to hip—that received the blessing of the sun's rays.

This really was *gorgeous.* To be basking here in the sun, after a late, leisurely breakfast, with nothing more strenuous to do than maybe take a cooling dip in the pool beside her and then, later on, drape herself in her chiffon sarong and drift across to where the staff were setting out their customary al fresco lunch.

She and Marc would make their *déjeuner* of the finest delicacies, all freshly prepared by hands other than theirs, and whisked away at the end of their meal by those other hands, leaving them nothing to do but laze the afternoon away or take the sailboat out, or swim off the jetty in the calm seas lapping the shore. Or maybe, if they were feeling energetic, head off in that powerful black beast of a car, purring like a contented tiger, to see yet more of the fabled Côte d'Azur.

And then they'd return as the sun was lowering, to sip sundowners by the pool and wait for yet another gourmet meal to be served to them by others' labour.

A pampered lifestyle indeed...

Idly she flexed her toes, eased the arms cushioning her head, utterly at ease. *I could get used to this...*

Oh, she could indeed! she thought, half-ruefully, half-languorously. No wonder the rich liked being rich…

But, for all the luxury of her surroundings and the ease of her days, she knew that not a single glass of vintage champagne, not a moment spent lounging like this beside the pool, would count for anything at all were she not here with Marc.

It was Marc and Marc alone who was turning this luxury into paradise for her. Marc—who only had to glance at her with those dark, knowing eyes of his and she would feel her whole body flicker as if with unseen electricity. All he had to do was touch her…

A shadow fell over her, and as if she'd conjured him from her thoughts he was hunkering down beside her, letting his index finger stroke sensuously down the long curve of her spine, arousing every bit of that flickering electricity.

She gave a little moan in her throat at the sensation and heard his low laugh. Then, suddenly, she was being caught in his arms, dizzyingly swept up. Her moan of sensuous pleasure turned into a squeal, and he laughed again.

'Time for a cool-down,' he informed her.

For a second she thought he was going to toss her into the pool, but he was striding indoors with her, heading upstairs. Suddenly mindful of her abandoned bikini top, she pressed herself hurriedly against his torso, lest they encounter one of the staff. She felt her breasts crest, and knew there was only one way that this was going to end…

Lunch was going to have to wait…

'What's the plan for this afternoon?' Tara enquired casually as, quite some time later, they settled down to the delicious *al fresco* lunch awaiting them on the vine-shaded terrace.

'What would you like to do?' Marc asked indulgently.

His mood was good—very good. Their refreshing shower had done a lot more than refresh him…

Have I ever known a woman like her?

The question played in his mind and he let it. So did the answer. But the answer was one that, unlike the question, he suddenly did not care to consider. Did he really want to accept that no other woman in his life had come anywhere close to how Tara made him feel? Accept how she could elicit his desire for her simply by glancing at him with those amazing blue-green eyes?

How long had this idyll here at the villa been so far? A fortnight? Longer still? The days were slipping by like pearls on a necklace…he'd given up counting them. He did not wish to count them. Did not wish to remember time, the days, the month progressing. He liked this timeless drift of day after day after day…

'You choose,' Tara said lazily, helping herself to some oozing Camembert, lavishing it on fresh crusty bread.

She must have put on pounds, she thought idly, but the thought did not trouble her. She didn't care. Didn't even want to think about going back to London, picking up on the last of her modelling assignments, giving notice on the flat-share, clearing her things and heading west to move into her thatched cottage and start the life she had planned for so long.

It seemed a long, long way away from here. From now.

Her eyes went to Marc, her gaze softening, just drinking him in as he helped himself to salad, poured mineral water for them both…

He caught her looking at him and his expression changed. 'Don't look at me like that…' There was the familiar husk in his voice.

She gave a small laugh. 'I haven't the strength for anything else but looking,' she said. Her voice lowered. 'And looking at you is all I want to do…just to gaze and gaze upon your manly perfection!'

There was a lazy teasing in her voice and his mouth twitched. He let his own gaze rest on her—on her feminine perfection…

Dimly, he became aware that his phone was ringing. Usually he put it on to silent, but he must have flicked it on when he'd attempted—so uselessly—to knuckle down to some work.

He glanced at it irately. He didn't want to be disturbed. When he saw the identity of the caller his irritation mounted. He picked up the phone. He might as well answer and get it over and done with…

Nodding his apologies to Tara, he went indoors. Disappeared inside his study. Behind him, at the table, Tara tucked in, unconcerned, turning her mind to how they might amuse themselves that afternoon.

But into her head came threads of thoughts she didn't want to let in. She might not want the time to pass, but it was passing all the same. How long ago had she flown out here from London? It plucked at her mind that she should check her diary—see when she had to be back there, get in touch with her booker. Show her face again…

I don't want to!

The protest was in her head, and it was nothing to do with her wanting to quit modelling and escape to her cottage. It was deeper than that—stronger. More disturbing.

I don't want this time with Marc to end.

That was the blunt truth of it. But end it must—how could it not? How could it *possibly* not? How could anything come of this beyond what they had here and now— this lotus-eating idyll of lazy days and sensual nights…?

She shifted restlessly in her chair, wanting Marc to

come back. Wanting her eyes to light upon him and him to smile, to resume their discussion about how to spend a lazy afternoon together...

But when he did walk out, only a handful of moments later, it was not relief that she felt when her eyes went to him. Not relief at all...

She'd wondered when this idyll would end. Well, she had her answer now, in the grim expression on Marc's face—an expression she had not seen since before the routing of Celine. It could presage nothing but ill.

She heard him speak, his voice terse.

'I'm sorry, I'm going to have to leave for New York. Something's come up that I can't avoid.' He took a breath, throwing himself into his chair. 'One of my clients—one of the bank's very wealthiest—wants to bring forward the date of his annual review. I always attend in person, and it's impossible for me to get out of it. Damned nuisance though it is!'

Tara looked at him. She kept her face carefully blank. 'When...when do you have to leave?' she asked.

'Tomorrow. I should really leave today, but...'

'Oh,' she said. It seemed, she thought, an inadequate thing to say. But the words she wanted to say, to cry out to him, she could not. *Should* not.

I don't want this time to end! Not yet!

Even as she heard the cry inside her head she knew it should not be there. Knew she should not be feeling what she was feeling now—as if she were being hollowed out from the inside. She had no right to feel that way.

Right from the start she had known that whatever it was she was going to indulge herself in with Marc, it was only that—an indulgence. They had come together only by circumstance, nothing more. Nothing had ever been intended to happen between them.

He never meant to have this time with me. Would never have chosen it freely. It was simply because of his need to use me to keep Celine away from him! He'd never have looked twice at me otherwise—not with any intent of making something of it.

Memory, harsh and undeniable, sprang into her head. Of the way Marc had stood there, that first day she'd arrived, telling her that her presence was just a job, that he was out of bounds to her, that she was there only to play-act and she was not to think otherwise. He could not have spelt out more clearly, more brutally, that she wasn't a woman he would choose for a romance, an affair, any relationship at all…

She knew it. Accepted it. Had no choice but to accept it. But even as she told herself she could hear other words crying out in her head.

He might ask me to go with him! He might—he could! He could say to me just casually, easily, Come to New York with me—let me show you the sights. Be with me there.

She looked at him now. His expression was remote. He was thinking about things other than her. Not asking her to go with him.

Then, abruptly, his eyes met hers. Veiled. He picked up his discarded napkin, resumed his meal. 'So,' he said, and his voice was nothing different from what it always was, 'if this is to be our last day, how would you like to spend it?'

She felt that hollow widening inside her. But she knew that all she could do was echo his light tone, though she could feel her fingers clenching on her knife and fork as she, too, resumed eating.

'Can we just stay here, at the villa?' she asked.

One last day. And one last night.

There was a pain inside her that she should not be feeling. Must not let herself feel.

But she felt it all the same.

* * *

Marc executed a fast, hard tack and brought the yacht about. His eyes went to Tara, ducking under the boom and then straightening. Her windblown hair was a halo around her face as she pushed it back with long fingers, refastening the loosened tendrils into a knot.

How beautiful she looked! Her face was alight, her fabulous body gracefully leaning back, and her eyes were the colour of the green-blue sea.

One thought and one thought alone burned in his head. *I don't want this time with her to end.*

How could he? How could he want it to end when it had been so good? All the promise that she had held for him, all that instant powerful allure she'd held for him from the very first moment he'd set eyes on her, had been fulfilled.

He knew, with the rational part of him, that had he never had to resort to employing her to keep Hans's wife at bay he would never have chosen to follow through on that initial rush of desire. He'd have quenched it, turned aside from it, walked away. Hell, he wouldn't even have known she existed, would he? He'd never have gone to that fashion show had it not been for Celine…

But he had gone, he had seen her, and he had used her to thwart Hans's wife…

He had brought her into his life.

Had rewarded himself with her.

His grip on the tiller tightened. *It's been good. Better than good. Like nothing else in my life has ever been.*

From the first he'd known he wanted her—but these days together had been so much more than he'd thought they could be! He watched as she leant back, elbows on the gunwale, lifting her face to the sun, eyes closed, face in repose as they skimmed over the water, her hair billowing in the wind, surrounding her face again.

He felt something move within him.

I don't want this to end.

Those words came again—stronger now. And bringing more with them.

So don't end it. Take her with you to New York.

His thoughts flickered. Why shouldn't he? She could be with him in New York as easily as she was here. It could be just as good as it was here.

So take her with you.

The thought stayed in his head, haunting him, for the rest of the day. As he moored the yacht at the villa's jetty, phoned for it to be taken back to harbour. As they washed off the salt spray in the pool, then showered and dressed for dinner. As they met on the terrace for their customary cocktails.

It was with him all the time, hovering like a background thought, always present. Always tempting.

It was there all through dinner—ordered by him to be the absolute best his chef could conjure up—and all through the night they spent together...the long, long night in each other's arms. It was there as he brought her time and time again to the ecstasy that burned within her like a living flame, and it seemed to him that it burned more fiercely than it ever had, that his own possession of her was more urgent than it ever had been, their passion more searing than he could bear...

Yet afterwards, as she lay trembling in his arms, as he soothed her, stroked her dampened hair, held her silk-soft body to his, his unseeing gaze was troubled. And later still, when in the chill before the dawn he rose from their bed, winding a towel around his hips and walking out onto the balcony, closing his hands over the cold metal rail, and looking out over the dark sea beyond, his thoughts were uncertain.

If he took her with him to New York, what then? Would

he take her back to France? To Paris? To stay with him at his hotel? Make her part of his life? His normal, working life?

And then what? What more would he want? And what more would *she* want…?

Again that same disturbing thought came to him—that she, too, might be remembering his impulsive declaration that afternoon, casting her as his intended wife, his fiancée, the future Madame Derenz.

Foreboding filled him. Unease. He did not know what she might want—could not know. All he knew was how he lived his life—and why. Just to have this time with her he'd already broken all the rules he lived by—rules that he'd had every reason to keep and none to break.

It had been good, this time he'd had with Tara—oh, so much more than good! But would it stay good? Or would danger start to lap at him…? Destroying what had been good?

Was it better simply to have this time—the memory of this time—and be content with that? Lest he live to regret a choice he should not have made…? Their time here had been idyllic—but could idylls last? *Should* they last?

He moved restlessly, unquiet in his mind.

He heard a sound behind him—bare feet—and turned. She was naked, her wanton hair half covering her breasts, half revealing them.

'Come back to bed,' she said, her voice low, full with desire.

She held out a hand to him—a hand he took—and he went with her.

To possess her one last time…

Their bodies lay entwined, enmeshed. He stroked back the tumbled mass of her hair, eased his body from hers. Tara reached out her hand, her fingertips grazing the contours of his face. The ecstasy he'd given her was ebbing, and in its place another emotion was flowing.

She felt her heart squeeze and longing fill her. A silent cry breaking from her. *Don't let this be the last time! Oh, let it not be the last time for ever!*

A longing not to lose him, to lose *this*, flooded through her. Her eyes searched his in the dim light. When she spoke her throat was tight, her words hesitant, infused with longing. 'I could come to New York with you…' she said.

The hand stroking her hair stilled. In the dim light she saw his expression change. Close. Felt a coldness go through her.

'That wouldn't work,' he answered her.

She heard the change in his voice. The note of withdrawal. She dropped her eyes, unable to bear seeing him now. Seeing his face close against her, shutting her out.

She took a narrowed breath and closed her eyes, saying no more. And as he drew her back against him, cradling her body, and she felt his breath warm on her bare shoulder, he knew that what they'd had, they had no longer. And never could again.

Behind her, with her long, slender back drawn against his chest, his arm thrown around her hips, Marc looked out over the darkened room. He had answered as he'd had to. With the only safe answer to give her. The answer that he had known must be his only answer from the very first.

CHAPTER NINE

TARA WOKE, STIRRING slowly to a consciousness she did not want. And as she roused herself from sleep and the world took shape around her she knew that it was already too late.

Marc was gone.

Cold filled her, like iced water flooding through her veins. A cry almost broke from her, but she suppressed it. What use to cry out? What use to cry at all?

This had always been going to happen—always!

But it was one thing to know that and another to feel it. To feel the empty place where he had been. To know that he would never come back to her. Never hold her in his arms again...

She felt her throat constrict, her face convulse. Slowly, with limbs like lead, she sat up, pushing her tangled hair from her face, shivering slightly, though the mid-morning sunlight poured into the room.

She looked around her blankly, as if Marc might suddenly materialise. But he never would again—and she knew that from the heaviness that was weighing her down. Knew it in the echo of his voice, telling her he did not want to take her with him. Knew it with even greater certainty as her eyes went to an envelope propped against the bedside lamp...and worse—oh, far worse—to the slim box propping it up.

She read the card first, the words blurring, then coming into focus.

You were asleep so I did not wake you. All is arranged for your flight to London. I wish you well—our time together has been good.

It was simply signed *Marc*. Nothing more.

Nothing except the cheque for ten thousand pounds at which she could only stare blankly, before replacing numbly into the envelope with the brief note.

Nothing except the ribbon of glittering emeralds in the jewellery case, catching the sunlight in a dazzle of gems. She let it slide through her fingers, knowing she should replace it in its velvet bed, leave it there on the bedside table. It was a gift far too valuable to accept. Impossible to accept.

But it was also impossible not to clutch it to her breast, to feel the precious gems indent her skin. To treasure it all her life.

How can I spurn his only gift to me? It's all that I will have to remember him by.

For a while she sat alone in the wide bed, as if making her farewells to it and all that had been there for her, with him. Then, at length, she knew she must move—must get up, must go back to her own bedroom, shower and dress, pack and leave. Go back to her own life. To her own reality.

The reality that did not have Marc in it. That *could* not have him in it.

I knew this moment would come. And now it has.

But what she had not known was how unbearable it would be… She had not been prepared for that. For the tearing ache in her throat. For the sense of loss. Of parting for ever.

It wasn't supposed to be like this! To feel like this!

The cry came from deep within her. From a place that should not exist, but did.

No, it was *not* supposed to be like this. It was supposed to have been nothing more than an indulgence of the senses…a yielding to her overpowering attraction to him…a time to be enjoyed, relished and revelled in, no more than that.

She should be leaving now, heading back to her own life, with a smile of fond remembrance on her face, with a friendly farewell and a little glow inside her after having had such a wonderful break from her reality!

That was what she was supposed to be feeling now. Not this crushing weight on her lungs…this constricted throat that choked her breath…this desperate sense of loss…

With a heavy heart she slipped through the connecting door. She had to go—leave. However hard, it had to be done.

Two maids were already in her room, carefully packing the expensive clothes Marc had provided for her—an eternity ago, it seemed to her. She frowned at the sight. She must not take them with her. They were couture numbers, worth a fortune, and they were not hers to take.

She said as much to the maids, who looked confused.

'Monsieur Derenz has instructed for them to go with you, *mademoiselle*,' one said.

Tara shook her head. She had the emerald necklace—that was the only memory of Marc she would take, and only because it was his gift to her. That was its value—nothing else.

On sudden impulse, she said to the two young girls, '*You* have the clothes! Share them between you! They can be altered to fit you… Or maybe you could sell them?'

Their faces lit up disbelievingly, and Tara knew she

could not take back her words. She was glad to have said them.

It was the only gladness she felt that day. What else had she to be glad about? That tearing feeling seemed to be clawing at her, ripping her apart, her throat was still choked, and that heaviness in her lungs, in her limbs weighing her down, was still there as she sat back in the chauffeured car, as she was whisked to the airport, as she boarded her flight.

He had booked her first-class.

The realisation made her throat clutch, telling her how much things had changed since her arrival.

My whole life has changed—because of Marc...

It was not until a fortnight later, as she checked her calendar with sudden, hollowing realisation, that she knew just how much...

Marc stood on the terrace of his penthouse residence in one of Manhattan's most luxurious hotels, staring out over the glittering city. His meeting was over, and the client was pleased and satisfied with what Bank Derenz had achieved for him. Now, with the evening ahead of him, Marc shifted restlessly.

There was something else he wanted.

Someone.

I want Tara—I want her here with me now. To enjoy the evening with me. I want to take her to dinner, to see her smile lighting up her eyes—sometimes dazzling, sometimes teasing, sometimes warm with laughter. I want to talk about whatever it was we used to talk about, in that conversation that seemed to flow so freely and naturally. And, yes, sometimes I want to spar with her, to hear her sometimes deadpan irony and those sardonic quips that draw a smile from me even now as I remember them...

And after dinner we'd come back here, and she'd be standing beside me, my arm around her, all of Manhattan glittering just for us. And she'd lift her face to mine, her eyes aglow, and I would catch her lips with mine and sweep her up, take her to my bed...

He could feel his body ache with desire for her, the blood heating in his veins.

With an effort of sheer will he tore his mind away from that beguiling scene so vivid in his head. He must not dwell on the woman he had left sleeping that morning, her oh-so-beautiful body naked in his bed, her glorious hair swathed across the pillow, her high, rounded breasts rising and falling with the gentle sound of her breathing.

It had been hard to leave her. Hard to reject her plea to come with him. Harder than he'd wanted it to be. Harder than it should have been. Harder than it was safe to have been—

But the safe thing for him to do had been to leave her. He knew that—knew it for all the reasons that had made him so wary of yielding as he had...yielding to his desire for her.

And the fact that he wanted to yield to it again, that his body so longed to do so, that he wanted to phone her now, tell her a flight was booked for her and that she should join him in New York, must make him even more wary.

It isn't safe to want her. It isn't safe because it's what she wants too. She asked outright—asked to come with me, wanted more than what we had in France. How much more would she have asked of me? Expected of me?

That was the truth of it. The harsh, necessary truth he'd always had to live his life by.

His eyes shadowed, thoughts turbid. He was making himself face what he did not want to face, but must—as he always had.

If I bring her here...keep her with me...how can I know if it's me she's choosing or Banc Derenz?

That was the reason he now turned away from the plate-glass window overlooking the city far below.

His thoughts went back to when he had last set eyes on her, sleeping so peacefully in his bed. He had slipped past her, to the bedside table, where he had placed the farewell note he had scrawled. And his gift for her.

The gift that would part him from her for ever. The gift that he'd left, quite deliberately, to tell her that what they'd had was over.

To tell *himself...*

Tara leant against the window frame of her bedroom at the cottage, breathing in the night air of the countryside. So sweet and fresh after the polluted traffic fumes of London. An owl hooted in the distance, and that was the only sound.

No ceaseless murmurings of cicadas, no sound of the sea lapping at the rocky shore, no scent of flowers too delicate for England...

No Marc beside her, gazing out over the wine-dark sea with her, listening to the soft Mediterranean night, his arm warm around her, drawing her against his body, before he turned her to him, lowered his mouth to hers, led her indoors to his bed, to his embrace...

She felt her heart twist, her body fill with longing.

But to what purpose?

Marc was gone from her life and she from his. She must accept it—accept what had happened and accept everything about the life she faced now.

Accept that what I feel for him, for the loss of him, is not what I thought I would feel. Accept that there is nothing I can do about it but what I am doing now. Accept that what I'm doing is all that I can do. All that can happen now.

Her expression changed as she gazed out over the shadowy garden edged by trees and the fields beyond.

How utterly her life had changed! How totally. All because of Marc...

She felt emotion crush within her. Should she regret what she had done? Wish that it had not happened? That it had not changed her so absolutely?

How *could* she regret it?

She gave a sigh—but not one of happiness. Nor of unhappiness. It was an exquisitely painful mix of both.

I can think of neither—feel neither. Not together.

Separately, yes, each one could fill her being. They were contradictory to one another. But they never cancelled each other out. Only...bewildered her. Tormented her.

She felt emotion buckling her. Oh, to have such joy and such pain combined!

She felt her hand clutch what she was holding, then made herself open her palm, gaze down at what was within. In the darkness the vivid colour of the precious gems was not visible, yet it still seemed to glow with a light of its own.

It was a complication she must shed.

I should never have taken it! Never kept it to remember him by!

She felt the emotion that was so unbearable, buckle her again. For one long moment she continued to gaze at what she held. Then slowly, very slowly, she closed her hand again.

She had kept it long enough—far too long. It must be returned. She must not keep it. Could not. Not now. *Especially not now.*

The emotion came again, convulsing her, stronger than ever. Oh, sense and rational thought and every other worldly consideration might cry out against what she was set on—but they could not prevail. *Must* not.

I know what I must do and I will do it.

With a slow, heavy movement she withdrew from the window, crossed over to the little old-fashioned dressing table that had once been her grandmother's and let fall what she held in her hand.

The noise of its fall was muffled by the piece of paper onto which it slithered. That, too, must be returned. And when it had been the last link with Marc would be severed. *Almost* the last…

She turned away, her empty hand slipping across her body. There was one thing that would always bind them, however much he no longer wanted her. But she must never tell him. For one overwhelming reason.

Because he does not want me. He is done with me. He has made that crystal-clear. His rejection of me is absolute.

So it did not matter, did it? Anything else could not matter.

However good it was, it was only ever meant to be for that brief time. I knew that, and so did he, and that is what we both intended. That is what I must hold in my head now. And what he gave me to show me that he had done with me, so that I understood and accepted it, must go back to him. Because it is the right and the only thing to do.

And when it was gone she would get on with the life that awaited her now. With all its pain and joy. Joy and pain. Mingling for ever now.

Marc was back in Paris. After New York he'd had the sudden urge to catch up with all his affairs in the Americas, making an extensive tour of branches of Banc Derenz from Quebec to Buenos Aires, which had taken several weeks. There had been no pressing need—at least not from a business perspective—but it had seemed a good idea to him, all the same, for reasons he'd had no wish to examine further.

The tour had served its purpose—putting space and time between those heady, carefree days at the villa and the rest of his life.

Now, once more in Paris, he was burying himself in work and an endless round of socialising in which he had no interest at all, but knew it was necessary.

And yet neither the tour of the Americas, nor his current punishing workload, nor the endless round of social engagements he was busying himself with were having the slightest effect.

He still wanted Tara. Wanted her back in his life. The one woman he wanted but should not want.

With the same restlessness that had dominated him since he'd flown to New York a few months ago he looked out over the Parisian cityscape, wanting Tara there with him.

He glanced at his watch without enthusiasm. His car would be waiting for him, ready to take him to the Paris Opera, where he was entertaining two of his clients and their daughter. His mouth tightened. The daughter was making it clear that she would be more than happy for him to pay her attention for reasons other than the fact that her parents banked at Banc Derenz. And she was not alone in her designs and hopes.

He gave an angry sigh. The whole damn circus was starting up again. Women in whom he had no interest at all, seeking his attention.

Women who were not Tara.

He shut his eyes. *I'll get over her. In time I'll forget her. I have to.*

He knew it must happen one day, but it was proving harder than he had thought it would. *Damnably* harder.

It was showing too, and he was grimly aware of that. Aware that, just as he'd been when Celine had plagued him, he was more short-tempered, having little patience either for demanding clients or fellow directors.

A bear with a sore head.

That was the expression he'd used to Tara.

Who was no longer in his life. And could never be again. However much he wanted her. *Because* he wanted her.

That was the danger, he knew. The danger that his desire for her would make him weak…make him ready to believe—want to believe—that his wealth was not the reason at all for her to be with him.

He'd believed that once before in his life—and it had been the biggest mistake he'd ever made. Thinking he was important to Marianne. When all along it had only been the Derenz money.

And the fact that Tara valued the Derenz money was evident. Right from the start she'd been keen on it—from that paltry five hundred pounds for chaperoning Celine back to her hotel to the ten thousand pounds she'd demanded for going to France.

And she had taken those emeralds he'd left for her. Helped herself to them as her due—just as readily as she'd helped herself to the couture wardrobe he'd supplied.

Oh, she might not be a gold-digger—nothing so repellent—but it was undeniable that she had enjoyed the luxury of his lifestyle, the valuable gifts he'd given her. And that was a danger sign—surely it was?

If I take her back she'll get used to that luxury lifestyle… start taking it for granted. Not wanting to lose it. It will become important to her. More important to her than I am.

And soon would it be me she wanted—or just the lifestyle I could provide for her?

He felt that old, familiar wariness filling him. Restlessly, he shifted again, tugging at the cuffs of his tuxedo.

What point was there in going over and over the reasons he must resist the urge to get back in touch with her, to resume what they had had, seek to extend it? However powerful that urge, he had to resist it. He must. Anything else was just too risky.

The doors of the elegant salon were opening and a staff member stood there, presumably to inform Marc that his car was awaiting him. But the man had a silver salver in his hand, upon which Marc could see an envelope.

With a murmur of thanks he took it, then stilled. Staring down at it. It had a UK stamp. And it was handwritten in a hand he had come to recognise.

He felt a clenching of his stomach, a tightening of his muscles. A sudden rush of blood.

What had Tara written? *Why?*

His face expressionless, belying a melee of thoughts behind its impassive mask, he opened it. Unfolded the single sheet of paper within and forced his eyes to read the contents.

The words leapt at him.

Marc,
I am not going to cash your cheque. What started out as a job did not end that way, and it would be very wrong of me to expect you to be bound by that original agreement.

Also, but for different reasons, I cannot keep the beautiful necklace you left for me. I am sure you only meant to be generous, but you must see how impossible it is for me to accept so very expensive a

*gift. Please do not be offended by this. I shall have
it couriered back to you.*

*By the same token, nor can I accept the gift of
all the couture clothes you provided for me. I hope
you do not mind, but I gave them to the maids—they
were so thrilled. Please do not be angry with them
for accepting.*

*I'm sorry this has taken me so long, but I've been
very busy working. My life is about to take me in a
quite different direction and I shall be leaving London, and modelling, far behind.*

It was simply signed with her name. Nothing more.

The words on the page seemed to blur and shift and
come again into focus. Slowly, very slowly, the hand holding the letter dropped to his side.

His heart seemed to be thumping in his chest as if he'd
just done a strenuous workout. As if a crushing weight
had been lifted off him. An impenetrable barrier just…
dissolved. Gone.

He stared out across the room. The member of staff was
standing in the doorway again.

'Your car is ready, Monsieur Derenz,' he intoned.

Marc frowned. He wasn't going to the opera. Not tonight. It was out of the question. A quite different destination beckoned.

The thud of his heartbeat was getting stronger. Deafening him. The letter in his hand seemed to be burning
his fingers. He looked across at the man, nodded at him.
Gave him his instructions. New instructions.

An overnight bag to prepare, a car to take him to Le
Bourget, not the Paris Opéra. Regrets to be sent to his
guests. And a flight to London to organise.

As the man departed only one word burned in Marc's head, seared in his body. *Tara!*

She had taken nothing from him—absolutely nothing. Not the money she'd earned, nor the couture wardrobe, nor the emerald necklace. Nothing at all! So what did that say about her?

Emotion held in check for so many punishing weeks, so many self-denying days and nights, exploded within him. Distilled into one single realisation. One overpowering impulse.

I can have her back.

Tara, the woman he wanted—*still* wanted!—and now he could have her again.

Nothing he had ever felt before had felt so good…

CHAPTER TEN

TARA WAS WALKING along the hard London pavements as briskly as she could in the heat. Summer had arrived with a vengeance, and the city was sticky and airless after the fresh country air. She was tired, and the changes in her body were starting to make themselves felt.

She'd travelled up from Dorset by train that morning and gone straight to her appointments. The first had been with a modelling agency specialising in the only shoots she'd be able to do soon, to see if they would take her on when that became necessary. The other, which she'd just come from, had been with her bank, to go through her finances.

Now that she could no longer count on the ten thousand pounds from Marc, it was going to be hard to move to Dorset immediately. Yet doing so was imperative—she had to settle into her new life as quickly as she could, while she was still unencumbered. She would need to buy a car, for a start—a second-hand one—for she would not be able to manage without one, and she still hadn't renovated the kitchen and the bathroom as planned.

She'd hoped that her bank might let her raise a small mortgage to tide her over, but the answer had not been encouraging—her future income to service the debt was going to be uncertain, to say the least. She was not a good risk.

It would have been so much easier if I could have kept that ten thousand pounds...

The thought hovered in her head and she had to dismiss it sharply. Yes, keeping it would have been the prudent thing to do—even if Marc would never know why—but as he *could* never know, she could not possibly keep it.

It was the same stricture that applied to her destination now, and her reason for going there. Yes, the prudent thing to do now would be to sell the necklace, realise its financial value, and bank that for all that she would need in the years ahead. But she had resisted that temptation, knowing what she must do. It was impossible for her to keep his parting gift!

Her letter to him, which he must have received now, for she had posted it from Dorset several days ago, had made that clear. Perhaps he was accustomed to gifting expensive jewellery to the women he had affairs with—but to such women, coming as they did from his über-rich world, something like that emerald necklace would be a mere bagatelle! To her, however, it was utterly beyond her horizon.

If he had only given me a token gift—of little monetary value. I could have kept that willingly, oh, so willingly, as a keepsake!

Her expression changed. More than a keepsake. A legacy...

She shied her mind away. She could see her destination—only a little way away now. The exclusive Mayfair jeweller she was going to ask to courier the necklace back to Marc. They would know how to do it—how to ensure the valuable item reached him securely, as she had written to him that it would.

Once it was gone she would feel easier in her mind. The temptation to keep it, against all her conscience, would be gone from her, no longer to be wrestled with. Her eyes shadowed, as they did so often now. And she need no longer wrestle with a temptation so much greater than merely keeping the emeralds.

She heard it echo now in her head—what had called to her so longingly… *Tell him—just tell him!*

Oh, how she wanted to! So much!

But she knew she was clutching at dreams—dreams she must not have. Dreams Marc had made *clear* she must not have.

Wearily, she put her thoughts aside. She had been through them, gone round and round, and there was no other conclusion to be drawn. Marc had finished with her and she must not hope for anything else.

Not even now.

Especially not now.

Deliberately she quickened her pace, walking up to the wide, imposing doors. A security guard stood there, very visibly, and as she approached moved to open the electronically controlled doors for her. But just as they opened, someone walked out.

'Fraulein Tara! *Was fur eine Uberraschung!*'

She halted, totally taken aback. Hans Neuberger came up to her, pleasure on his kindly face, as well as the surprise he'd just exclaimed over seeing her.

'How very good to see you again!' he said in his punctilious manner. 'And how glad I am to do so.' He smiled. 'This unexpected but delightful encounter provides me with an excellent opportunity! I wonder,' he went on, his voice politely enquiring, 'whether you would care to join me for lunch? I hope that you will say yes. Unless, of course,' he added, 'you have another engagement perhaps?'

'Um—no. I mean, that is…' Tara floundered, not really knowing what to say. She was trying to get her head around seeing Hans again, since the last time she'd seen him had been just after that party on the yacht in Cannes, with Celine's dreadful friends...

'Oh, then, please, it would be so very kind of you to indulge me in this request.'

His kindly face was smiling and expectant. It would be hard to say no, and she did not wish to hurt his feelings, however tumultuous hers were at seeing him again, which had plunged her head back to the time she'd spent in France. So, numbly, she let him guide her across the street where she saw, with a little frisson of recognition, the side entrance to a hotel that stung in her memory.

This was the hotel where Marc had deposited Celine that first fateful evening...

Emotion wove through her, but Hans was ushering her inside. His mood seemed buoyant, and he was far less crushed than he'd been at Marc's villa. Getting Celine out of his life clearly suited him.

And so he informed her—though far more generously than Celine deserved. 'I was not able to make her happy,' he said sadly as they took their places in the hotel restaurant. 'So it is good, I think, that she has now met another man who can. A Russian, this time! They are currently sailing the Black Sea on his new yacht. I am glad for her...'

Tactfully, Tara forbore to express her views on how the self-serving Celine had latched on to yet another rich man. Hans's face had brightened, and he was changing the subject.

'But that is quite enough about myself! Tell me, if you please, a little of what is happening with *you*?' His expression changed. 'I have, alas, been preoccupied with—well, all the business of setting Celine free, as she wishes to be. But I very much hope all is still well with you and Marc.'

There was only polite enquiry in his question, yet Tara

froze. Floundering, she struggled for something to say. Anything...

'No—that is to say Marc and I— Well, we are no longer together.'

She saw Hans's face fall. 'I am sorry to hear that,' he said. His eyes rested on her and there was more than his habitual kindness in them. 'You were, I think, very good for Marc.' He paused, as if finding the right words. 'He is possessed of a character that can be very...*forceful*, perhaps is the way to describe him. You were—how can I express this?—a good match for him.'

'Yes,' Tara said ruefully. 'I did stand up to him—it's not my nature to back down.'

Hans gave a little laugh. 'Two equal forces meeting,' he said.

She looked at him. 'Yes, and then parting. As we have. Whatever there was,' she said firmly, 'is now finished.'

Hans's eyes were on her still, and she wished they weren't.

'That is a pity,' he said. 'I wish it were otherwise,'

She took a breath. 'Yes, well, there it is. Marc and I had a...a lovely time together... But, well, it ran its course and that is that.'

She wanted to change the subject—any way she could. Her throat had tightened, and she didn't want it to. Seeing Hans again had brought everything back in vivid memory. And she didn't want that. Couldn't bear it. It just hurt too much.

'So,' she said, with determined brightness as the waiters brought over the menus, 'what brings you to London? Have you been here long?'

Thankfully, Hans took her lead. 'I arrived only this morning,' he said. 'My son Bernhardt will be joining me this evening with his fiancée. They are making a little holiday here. His mother-in-law-to-be is accompanying them. She was a close friend of my wife—my *late* wife—and, like me, was most sadly widowed a few years ago. We have always got on very well, both sharing the loss of our spouses, and now, with the engagement of our children, we have much in common. So much so that—well,' he went on in a little rush of open emotion, 'once my divorce from Celine is finalised, Ilse and I plan to make our future together. Our children could not be more delighted!'

A smile warmed Tara's expression. 'Oh, that's wonderful!' she exclaimed.

Just as she'd hoped, the kindly Hans would be marrying again—happily this time, surely? Such a match sounded ideal.

He leant forward. 'You may have wondered,' he said, 'why I was emerging from that so very elegant jeweller's when I encountered you—'

Tara hadn't wondered—had been too taken aback to do anything of the sort—but she didn't say so. Anyway, Hans was busy slipping a hand inside his jacket, removing from it a small cube of a box. Tara did not need X-ray vision to know what it would contain.

He held it towards her, opening it. 'Do you think she will like this?' he asked.

There was such warmth, such hope in his voice, that Tara could not help but let a smile of equal warmth light up her own face.

'It's *beautiful*!' she exclaimed, unable to resist touching the exquisite diamond engagement ring within. 'She will *adore* it!' Spontaneously, she reached her hand to his sleeve. 'She's a lucky, *lucky* woman!' she told him.

And then, because she was glad for him—glad for anyone who had found a happiness that for herself could never be—her expression softened.

'Let me be the very first to congratulate you,' she said. And she kissed him on the cheek, an expression of open delight on her face.

Marc sat in his chauffeured car, frustration etched into his expression. He was burning to find Tara—the imperative was driving him like an unstoppable tide, flooding over him.

He was free. Free to take her back. Free to claim her, to make her his again. There was nothing to stop him, to block him—not any more. Had she been anything like he'd feared she would never have written that letter to him—never have said what she had.

He took it out of his jacket pocket again now, read it again, as he had read it over and over, his eyes alight.

Their expression changed back to frustration. To know that he was free to take her back, to renew what had been between them and yet not to be able to find her…! It was intolerable—unbearable.

But she was not to be found.

He had gone to her flat last night, heading there the moment the private jet from Le Bourget had landed at City Airport, after urging the car through the traffic, to be told in an offhand fashion by a flatmate that she was away, and they had no idea where.

Thwarted, he had had to repair to his hotel, to kick his heels, and thence to interrogate her modelling agency first thing that morning—only to be informed that she had no modelling engagements that day and that they had no idea where she was and did not care. For reasons of confidentiality they would not give him her mobile number—which he, for reasons now utterly incomprehensible to him, had never known. They would let him know he was trying to contact her, and that was all.

He glowered, face dark, eyes flashing with frustration, as the car moved off into the London traffic. He had occupied himself by calling in on the branch of Banc Derenz in Mayfair, but now he was hungry.

He did not want the manager's company for lunch. He didn't want anyone's company. *Only one person.*

It burned within him…his sense of urgency, his mounting sense of frustration that he had come to London to find her—claim her. To throw lifelong caution to the winds and to ride the instinct that was driving him now, that her letter had let loose, like a tidal wave carrying him forward…

His car pulled up at his hotel. The very same hotel where he'd deposited Celine the first night that Tara had come into his life.

He'd wanted her then—had felt that kick of desire from the first moment of seeing her, so unwillingly responding to his impatient summons at that benighted fashion show, had felt it kick again when she'd sat beside him in the limo, and yet again creaming in his veins as, with a deliberate gesture, he'd taken her hand to kiss her wrist…to show her that she might be as hostile, as back-talking as she liked, but she was not immune to him, to what was flaring like marsh fire between them…

A smile played at his mouth, as his mind revolved those memories and so many more since then…

And all those yet to come.

Immediately his imagination leapt to the challenge. Their first night together again… The sensual bliss would burn between them as it always had, every time!

His mind ran on, leaping from image to image. And afterwards a holiday—only the two of them. Wherever she wanted to go. The Caribbean, or maybe the Maldives, the Seychelles? The South Seas? Wherever in the world she wanted. Wherever they could have a tropical island entirely to themselves...

Nights under the stars...days on silver beaches...disporting ourselves in turquoise lagoons...lazing beneath palm fronds waving gently in the tropical breeze...

Anticipation filled him, surging in his blood...

The chauffeur was opening his door and he vaulted out. He would grab lunch, and then interrogate that damn agency of hers again. He'd already sent one of his staff from the London branch of Derenz to doorstep her flat, lest she arrive there unexpectedly.

She's here somewhere. I just have to find her.

Find her and get her back. Back into his life—where she belonged.

He strode into the hotel, fuelled with the urgency now driving him...consuming him. Filled with elation—with an impatience to find her again that was burning in his veins. To have her unforgettable beauty before him once again...

'Mr Derenz, good afternoon. Will you be lunching with us today?'

The polite enquiry at the entrance to the restaurant interrupted his vision.

'Yes,' he said distractedly, impatiently.

His glance needled around the restaurant.

And froze.

The image in his head—the one his eyes had frozen on—solidified.

Tara—it was *Tara*. Here. Right in front of him. Across the dining room. Sitting at one of the tables.

There was someone with her—someone with his back to him.

Someone that Tara was looking at. Gazing at.

Smiling at, her face alight with pleasure and delight.

He saw the man she was smiling at offer something to

her, saw the flash as it caught the sunlight. Saw her lean forward a little, reach out a long, slender forearm. Saw what it was that she touched with her index finger, how the delight in her eyes lit her whole face.

Saw her lean closer now, across the table, saw her bestow a kiss upon the cheek of the man he now recognised.

Saw blackness fill his vision. Blinding him...

Memory seared into his blinded sight.

Marianne across that restaurant, sitting with another man, his diamond glittering on her finger, holding up her hand for Marc to see...

Still blinded, he lurched away.

There was blackness in his soul...

Just as she brushed her soft kiss of congratulation on Hans's lined cheek, Tara's gaze slipped past him.

And widened disbelievingly.

Marc?

For a second emotion leapt in her, soaring upwards. Then a fraction of a section later it crashed.

In that minute space of time she had registered two things. That he had seen her. And that he had turned on his heel and was walking out of the restaurant again as rapidly as the mesh of tables would allow him.

That told her one thing, and one thing only. He had not wanted to see her. Or acknowledge her presence there.

She felt a vice crushing her as she sat back in her seat, unable to breathe. She urgently had to regain control of herself. If Hans noticed her reaction he might wonder why. If he turned he might see Marc leaving the restaurant. Might go after him...drag him back to their table. She would have to encounter Marc again—Marc who had turned and bolted rather than speak to her.

If she'd ever wanted proof that he was over her—that

he wanted *nothing* more to do with her—she had it now. Brutally and incontrovertibly!

The vice around her lungs squeezed more tightly. *I've got to get out of here!*

She didn't dare risk it! Didn't dare risk an encounter with him that he so obviously did not want! It would be mortifying.

'Hans, I'm so sorry, but I'm afraid I don't have time for lunch after all.' The excuse sounded impolite, but she had to give it. 'Do please forgive me!'

She got to her feet; Hans promptly did the same.

'I'm so very pleased for you—you and Ilse.' She tried to infuse warmth into her voice but she was keeping an eye on the exit to the hotel lobby. Was it clear of Marc yet? If she could just get to the corridor leading to the side entrance Hans had brought her in by she could escape...

She got away from Hans. He looked slightly bewildered by her sudden departure, but it could not be helped. At the door to the restaurant she glanced towards the revolving doors at the main entrance, leading to the street, then whirled around to head towards the side entrance.

Just as a tall, immovable figure turned abruptly away from the reception desk, out of her eyeline.

She cannoned into it.

It was Marc.

CHAPTER ELEVEN

SHE GAVE AN audible cry—she couldn't stop it—and lurched backwards as quickly as she could. He automatically reached up his hands to steady her, then dropped them, as if he might scald himself on her.

She couldn't think straight—couldn't do anything at all except stumble another step backwards and blurt out, 'Marc—I... I thought you had left the hotel.'

Marc's face hardened. The livid emotion that had flashed through him as she'd bumped into him turning away from the reception desk was being hammered down inside him. He would not let it show. *Would not.* He'd been cancelling his reservation for that night. What point and what purpose to stay now? he thought savagely.

He knew he had to say something, but how could he? The only words he wanted to hurl at her were...pointless. So all he said, his voice as hard and as expressionless as his face was, 'I am just leaving.'

Had she come running after him?

But why should she? She has no need of me now!

The words seared across his naked synapses as if they were red-hot. No, Tara had no need of him now—no need at all!

Savage fury bit like a wolf.

Hans! God in heaven—Hans, of all men! Beaming like

a lovesick idiot, offering her that ring...that glittering, ir-idescent diamond ring! For her to reach for. To take for herself. Just as Marianne had.

Fury bit again, but its savagery was not just rage. It was worse than rage. Oh, *so* much worse...

Yet he would not let her see it. That, at least, he would deny her!

She was looking up at him, consternation in her face. Was she going to try and explain herself—justify herself? It sickened him even to think about it.

But she made no reference to the scene he knew she had seen him witness. Instead she seemed to be intent on attempting some kind of mockery of a conversation.

'So am I,' he heard her say. 'Just leaving the hotel.'

Tara heard her own words and paled. *Oh, God, don't let him think I'm angling for a lift! Please, please, no!*

Memory, hot and humiliating, came to her, of how she had asked to go to New York with him—and the unhesi-tating rejection she had received. She felt that same morti-fication burning in her again, that he might think she had come racing after him.

This whole encounter was a nightmare, an ordeal so ex-cruciating she couldn't bear it. He was radiating on every frequency the fact that seeing her again was the last thing he wanted. His stance was stiff and tense, his expression closed and forbidding. He could not have made it plainer to her that he did not want to talk to her. Did not want to have anything at all to do with her any more.

He wants nothing to do with me! He didn't even want to come over and say hello—not even to his friend Hans!

Could anything have rammed home to her just how much Marc Derenz did *not* want her any longer? That all he wanted was to be shot of her?

Her chin came up—it cost her all her strength, but she

did it. 'I must be on my way,' she said. She made her voice bright, but it was like squeezing it through a wringer inset with vicious spikes.

She paused. Swallowed. Thoughts and emotions tumbled violently within her, a feeling akin to panic. There was something she had to say to him. To make things clear to him. As crystal-clear as he was making them to her. That she, too, had moved on with her life. That she would make no claim on him at all. Not even as a casual acquaintance…

She felt emotion choke her, but forced herself to say what she had to. Reassure him that she knew, and accepted, that she was nothing to him any longer.

She had said as much in her letter to him and now she would say it again, to make sure he knew.

'I'll be moving away from London very soon. I'm getting out of modelling completely. I can't wait!' She forced enthusiasm into her voice, though every word was torn from her.

His stony expression did not change.

'I'm sure you will enjoy your future life,' he replied.

He spoke with absolute indifference, and it was like a blow.

'Thank you—yes, I shall. I have every intention of doing so!' she returned.

Pride came to her rescue. Ragged shreds of it, which she clutched around her for the pathetic protection she could get from it.

'Hans is still in the restaurant.' She made herself smile, forcing it across her face as if she were posing for a camera—putting it on, faking it, clinging to it as if it were a life raft. 'I'm sure that he will want to see you! He has such exciting news! Best you hear it from him…'

She was speaking almost at random, in staccato ramblings. She could not bear to see his face, his indifferent expression, as he so clearly waited for her to leave him alone, to take himself off. She shifted her handbag from one hand to the other, and as she did so she jolted. Remembering something.

Something she might as well do here and now. To make an end to what had been between them and was now nothing more than him waiting impatiently for her to leave him be.

She raised her bag, snapping open the fastener.

'Marc—this is most opportune!' The words were still staccato. 'I was going to ask the jeweller across the road to courier this to you, as I promised, but you might as well take it yourself.'

She delved into her bag, extracted the jewellery case. Held it out to him expectantly.

His eyes lanced the box, then wordlessly he took it. His mouth seemed to tighten and she wondered why. Expressionlessly, he slid it into his inside jacket pocket.

For a second—just a second—she went on staring up at him. As if she would imprint his face on her memory with indelible ink.

Words formed in her head, etching like acid. *This is the last time I shall see him...*

The knowledge was drowning her, draining the blood from her.

'Goodbye, Marc,' she said. Her voice was faint.

She turned, plunging down the corridor. Eyes blind. Fleeing the man who did not want her any longer. Who would never want her again.

Whom she would never see again.

Anguish crushed her heart, and hot, burning tears started to roll silently down her cheeks. Such useless tears...

Marc stood, nailing a smile of greeting to his face as his guests arrived. It was the bank's autumn party, for its most valued clients, held at one of Paris's most famous hotels, and he had no choice but to host it. But there was one client whose presence here this evening he dreaded the most. Hans Neuberger.

Would he show up? He was one of the bank's most long-standing clients and had never missed this annual occasion. But now…?

Marc felt his mind slide sideways, not wanting to articulate his thoughts. All he knew was that he could not face seeing Hans again.

Will he bring her here?

That was the question that burned in him now, as he greeted his guests. What he said to them he didn't know. All that was in his head—all there had been all these weeks, since that unbearable day in London—was the scene he had witnessed. That nightmare scene that was blazoned inside his skull in livid, sickening neon.

Ineradicable—indelible.

Tara, leaning forward, her face alight. Hans offering that tell-tale box, its lid showing the exclusive logo of a world-famous jeweller, revealing the flash of the diamond ring within. And Tara reaching for it. Tara bestowing a kiss of gratitude on Hans's cheek with that glow in her face, her eyes…

Bitter acid flooded his veins. Just as it had all those years ago as he'd watched Marianne declare her faithlessness to the world. Declare to the world what she wanted. A rich, older man to pamper her…shower her with jewellery.

His face twisted. To think he had *rejoiced* that Tara had declined to cash the cheque he'd left for her! Had returned his emeralds.

Well, why wouldn't she? Now she has all Hans's wealth to squander on herself!

He stoked the savage anger within him. Thanks to *his*

indulgence of her, she had got a taste for the high life! Had realised, when he'd left her, that she could not get that permanently from himself! So she'd targeted someone who could supply it permanently! Plying Hans with sympathy, with friendliness…

It was the very opposite of Celine's open scorn, but with the same end in mind. To get what she wanted—Hans's ring on her finger and his fortune hers to enjoy…

With a smothered oath he tore his mind away. What use to feel such fury? Such betrayal?

He had survived what Marianne had done to him. He would survive what Tara had inflicted upon him too.

Yet as the endless receiving line finally dwindled, with only a few late guests still arriving, he found his eyes going past the doors of the ornate function room to the head of the stairs leading up from the lobby.

Would she come here tonight with Hans?

He felt emotion churn within him.

But it was not anger. And with a sudden hollowing within him, he knew what the emotion was.

Longing.

He stilled. Closing his eyes momentarily. He knew that feeling. Knew its unbearable strength, its agony. Had felt it once before in his life.

After his parents had been killed.

The longing…the unbearable, agonising longing to see again those who were lost to him for ever.

As Tara was.

Tara who could never be his again…

'Marc—I am so sorry to arrive late!'

His eyes flashed open. It was Hans—alone.

He froze. Unable to say anything, anything at all. Unable to process any thoughts at all.

Hans was speaking again. 'We have been a little delayed.

Bernhardt is with me, and I hope you will not object but I have brought two other guests as well. Karin—Bernhardt's fiancée—and...' He smiled self-consciously as Marc stood, frozen. 'And one more.' And now Hans's smile broadened. 'One who has become very dear to me.'

Marc heard the words, saw Hans take a breath and then continue on, his eyes bright.

'Of course until my divorce is finalised no formal announcement can be made, and it has been necessary, therefore, to be discreet, so perhaps my news will be a surprise to you?'

Marc's expression darkened. 'No—I've known for weeks.' His voice was hard—as hard as tempered steel. His eyes flashed, vehemence filling his voice now, unable to stay silent. 'Hans, this is *madness*—to be caught again! Did you not learn enough from Celine? How can you possibly repeat the same disastrous mistake! For God's sake, man, however besotted you are, have the sense not to do this!'

He saw Hans's expression change from bewilderment to astonishment, and then to rejection. 'Marc,' he said stiffly, 'I am perfectly aware that Celine was, indeed, a very grave error of my judgement, but—'

'And so is *Tara*!' Marc's voice slashed across the other man's.

There was silence—complete silence. Around him Marc could hear the background chatter of voices, the clinking of glasses. And inside the thundering of his heartbeat, drowning out everything. Even his own voice.

'Did you think I hadn't seen you both, in London? You and Tara—' His voice twisted over her name. Choking on it. 'Did you think I didn't see the ring you were giving her? See how her face lit up? How she couldn't wait to take it from you? How eager she was to kiss you?'

Hans stared. Then spoke. *'Bist Du verukt?'*

Fury lashed across Marc's face. Insane? No, he was *not* insane! Filled with any number of violent emotions, but not that!

Then suddenly Hans's hand was closing over his sleeve with surprising force for a man his age. 'Marc—you could not *possibly* have thought—' He broke off, then spoke again. His tone brooked no contradiction. 'What you saw—whatever it is you *feared* you saw, Marc—was Tara's very kind reaction to the news I had just told her. Of my intention to remarry, yes, indeed. But if you think, for an instant, that *she* was the object of my intentions—'

Marc felt his arm released. Hans was turning aside, allowing three more people who had just entered the room to come up to them. Marc's eyes went to them. Bernhardt, a younger version of Hans, well-known to him, with a young, attractive woman on one arm. And on the other arm an older woman with similar looks to the younger one. A woman who was smiling at Hans with a fond, affectionate look on her face. And on the third finger of the hand tucked into Bernhardt's arm was a diamond ring...

Hans turned back to Marc and his tone was formal now. 'You will permit me to introduce to you Frau Ilse Holz and her daughter Karin?'

His eyes rested on Marc.

'Ilse,' Marc heard him say, as if from a long way away, 'has done me the very great honour of agreeing, when the time is right, to make me the happiest of men. I know,' he added, 'that you will wish us well.'

Marc might have acknowledged the introduction. He might have said whatever was required of him. Might have been aware of Hans's gaze becoming speculative.

But of all of those things he had absolutely no awareness at all. Only one thought was in his head. One blinding thought. One absolute realisation. Burning in him.

And then Bernhardt was leading away his fiancée, and the woman who was to be both his mother-in-law and his stepmother, into the throng.

Hans paused. His eyes were not speculative now. They were filled with compassion. 'Go,' he said quietly, to Marc alone. 'This…here…' he gestured to the party all around them '…is not important. You have others to see to it. So—go, my friend.'

And Marc went. Needing no further telling…

CHAPTER TWELVE

A BLACKBIRD WAS hopping about on the lawn, picking at the birdseed which Tara had started to scatter each day now that autumn was arriving. A few late bees could be heard buzzing on what was left of the lavender. There was a mild, drowsy feel to the day, as if summer were disinclined to pack its bags completely and leave the garden, preferring to make a graceful handover to its successive season.

Tara was glad of it. Sitting out here in the still warm sunshine, wearing only a light sweater and cotton trousers, her feet in canvas shoes, was really very pleasant. The trees bordering the large garden backing on to the fields beyond were flushed with rich autumnal copper, but still shot through with summer's green. A time of transition, indeed.

It echoed her own mood. *A time of transition.* She might have finally made the move from London to Dorset some weeks ago, but it was only now that she was really feeling her move was permanent. As was so much else.

She flexed her body, already less ultra-slim than she'd had to keep it during her modelling career. It was filling out, softening her features, rounding her abdomen, ripening her breasts.

Her mind seemed to be hovering, as the seasons were, between her old life and the one she was now embarked upon. She knew she must look ahead to the future—what else was there to do? She must embrace it—just as she must embrace the coming winter. Enjoy what it would offer her.

Her expression changed, her fingers tracing over her midriff absently. She must not regret the time that had gone and passed for ever—the brief, precious time she'd had during that summer idyll so long ago, so far away, beside that azure coast. No, she must never regret that time—even though she must accept that it was gone from her, never to return. That Marc was gone from her for ever.

A cry was stifled in her throat. Anguish bit deep within her.

I'll never see him again—never hear his voice again— never feel his mouth on mine, his hand in mine. Never see him smile, or laugh, or his eyes pool with desire... Never feel his body over mine, or hold him to me, or wind my arms around him...

Her eyes gazed out, wide and unseeing, over the autumnal garden. How had it happened that what she had entered into with Marc—something that had never been intended to be anything other than an indulgence of her overpowering physical response to him—had become what she now knew, with a clutching of her heart, to be what it would be for ever?

How had she come to fall in love with him?

She felt that silent cry in her throat again.

I fell in love with him and never knew it—not until he left me. Not until I knew I would never see him again. Never be part of his life...

Her hands spasmed over the arms of the padded garden chair and she felt that deep stab of anguish again.

But what point was there in feeling it? She had a future to make for herself—a future she *must* make. And not merely for her own sake. For the sake of the most precious gift Marc could have given her. Not the vast treasures of his wealth—that was dust and ashes to her! A gift so much more precious…

A gift he must never know he had given her…

Her grip on the arms of the chair slackened and she moved her hands across her body in a gesture as old as time…

She would never see Marc again, and the pain of that loss would never leave her. But his gift to her would be with her all her life… The only balm to the endless anguish of her heart.

In the branches of the gnarled apple tree a robin was singing. Far off she could hear a tractor ploughing a field. The hazy buzz of late bees seeking the last nectar of the year. All of them lulled her…

She felt her eyelids grow heavy, and the garden faded from sight and sound as sleep slipped over her like a soft veil.

Soon another garden filled her dreamscape…with verdant foliage, vivid bougainvillea, a glittering sunlit pool. And Marc was striding towards her. Tall, and strong, and outlined against the cloudless sky. She felt her heart leap with joy…

Her eyes flashed open. Something had woken her. An alien sound. The engine of a car, low and powerful. For a second—a fraction of a second—she remembered the throaty roar of Marc's low-slung monster…the car he'd loved to drive. Then another emotion speared her.

Alarm.

The cottage was down a dead-end lane, leading only to a gate to the fields at the far end. No traffic passed by. So who was it? She was expecting no visitors…

She twisted round to look at the path leading around the

side of the cottage to the lane beyond. There was a sudden dizziness in her head…a swirl of vertigo.

Had she turned too fast? Or was it that she had not woken at all, was still dreaming?

Because someone was walking towards her—*striding* towards her. Someone tall and strong, outlined against the cloudless sky. Someone who could not be here—someone she'd thought she would never see again.

But he was in her vision now—searing her retinas, the synapses of her stunned and disbelieving brain. She lurched to her feet and the vertigo hit again.

Or was it shock?

Or waking from the dream?

Or still being within the dream?

She swayed and Marc was there in an instant, steadying her. Then his hands dropped away.

Memory stabbed at her—how he'd made the same gesture in that nightmare encounter at the hotel, dropping his hands from her as if he could not bear to touch her. She clutched at the back of her chair, staring at him, hearing her heart pounding in her veins, feeling disbelief still in her head. And emotion—unbearable emotion—leaping in her heart.

She crushed it down. Whatever he was here for he would tell her and then he would leave.

For one unbearable moment dread knifed in her.

Does he know?

Oh, dear God, she prayed, please do not let him know! That would be the worst thing of all—the very worst! Because if he did…

She sheared her mind away, forced herself to speak. Heard words fall from her, uncomprehending. 'What… what are you doing here?'

He was standing there and she could see tension in

every line of his body. His face was carved as if from tempered steel. As closed as she had ever seen it.

Yet something was different about him—something she had never seen before. Something in the veiling of his eyes that had never been there before.

'I have something to give you,' he said.

His voice was remote. Dispassionate. But, as with the look on his face, she had never heard his voice sound like that.

She stared, confused. 'Wh-what?' she got out.

'This,' he said.

His hand was slipping inside his jacket pocket. He was wearing yet another of his killer suits, she registered abstractedly through the shattering of her mind. Registered, too, the quickening of her pulse, the weakening of her limbs that she always felt with him. Felt the power he had to make her feel like that... Felt the longing that went with it.

Longing she must not let herself feel. No matter that he was standing here, so real, so close...

He was drawing something out from his inner pocket and she caught the silken gleam of the grey lining, the brief flash of the gold fountain pen in the pocket. Then her eyes were only on what he was holding out to her. What she recognised only too well—the slim, elegant jewel case she had returned to him that dreadful day in London that had killed all the last remnants of her hope that he might ever want her again...

She shook her head. Automatically negating.

'Marc—I told you. I can't take it. I know...' She swallowed. 'I know you...you mean well...but you must see that I can't accept it!'

Consternation was filling her. Why was he here? To insist she take those emeralds? She stared at him. His face was still as shuttered as ever, his eyes veiled, unreadable. But a nerve was ticking just below his cheekbone and there were deep lines around his mouth, as though his jaw were steel, filled with tension.

She didn't understand it. All she understood—all that was searing through her like red-hot lava in her veins— was that seeing him again was agony... An agony that had leapt out of the deepest recesses of her being, escaping like a deranged monster to devour her whole.

Through the physical pain rocking her, from holding leashed every muscle in her body, as if she could hold in the anguish blinding her, she heard him speak.

'That is a pity.' He set the case with the emerald necklace in it down on the table beside her chair.

There was still that something different in his voice— that something she'd never heard before. She'd heard ill-humour, short temper, impatience and displeasure. She'd heard desire and passion and warmth and laughter.

But she'd never heard this before.

She stared at him.

He spoke again. 'A pity,' he said, 'because, you see, emeralds would suit you so much better than mere diamonds.'

'I don't understand...' The words fell from her. Bewildered. Hollow.

The very faintest ghost of what surely could not be a twisted smile curved the whipped line of his mouth for an instant. As if he was mocking himself with a savagery that made her take a breath.

'They would suit you so much better than the diamond ring which Hans presented to you.'

Tara struggled to speak. '*Presented?* He *showed* it to me! Dear God, Marc—you could not...? You could not have thought...?'

Disbelief rang in every word that fell from her. He could

not have thought that! How *could* he? Shock—more than shock—made her speechless.

A rasp sounded in his throat. It seemed to her that it was torn from somewhere very deep inside him.

'We see what we want to see,' he replied. The mockery was there again, in the twist of his mouth, but the target was only himself. And then there was another emotion in his face. His eyes. 'We see what we *fear* to see.'

She gazed at him, searching his face. Her heart was pounding within her, deafening her. 'I don't understand,' she said again. Her voice was fainter than ever.

'No more did I,' he said. 'I didn't understand at all. Did not understand how I was being made a fool of again. But this time by *myself.*'

She frowned. '"Again"?'

He moved suddenly, restlessly. Not answering her.

Here he was, standing and facing her in this place that had been almost impossible to find—hard to discover even by relentless enquiry.

It had taken him from a ruthless interrogation of her former flatmates, in which he had discovered that she had moved out…had hired a van to transport her belongings, to the tracking down of the hire company, finding out where they had delivered to, and then, finally, to hiring a car of his own and speeding down to that same destination.

All with the devil driving him.

The devil he was purging from himself now, after so many years of its malign possession. So much depended on it. *All* depended on it.

He took a breath—a ragged breath. 'When you look at me, Tara, what do you see?'

What do you see?

His words echoed in her skull. Crying out for an answer she must not give.

I see the man I love, who has never loved me! I see the man who did not want me, though I still want him—and always will, for all my days! That is the man I see—and I cannot tell you that! I cannot tell you because you don't want me as I want you, and I will not burden you with my wanting you. I will not burden you with the love you do not want from me... Nor with the gift you gave me.

But silence held her—as it must. Whatever he had come here for, it was not to hear her break the stricken silence that she must keep.

He spoke again, in that same low, demanding tone.

'Do you see a man rich and powerful in his own realm of worldly wealth? A man who can command the luxuries of life? Who has others to do his bidding, whatever he wants of them? Whose purpose is to protect the heritage he was born to—to protect the wealth he possesses, to guard it from all who might want to seize it from him?' His voice changed now. 'To guard it from all who might want to make a fool of him?'

He shifted again, restless still, then his voice continued. Eyes flashing back to her.

'You saw Celine with Hans—you saw how she took ruthless advantage of him, wanted him only for his wealth. You saw what she did to him—' He made a noise of scorn and disgust in his throat. 'I am richer than Hans—considerably so, if all our accounts were pitted one against the other! But...' He took a savage breath. 'I am as vulnerable as he is.' A twisted, self-mocking smile taunted his mouth. 'The only difference is that I know it. Know it and guard endlessly against it.' He shook his head. 'I guard myself against every woman I encounter.'

His expression changed.

'And the way I do it is very simple—I keep to women from my own world. Women who have wealth of their own…who therefore will not covet mine. It was a strategy that worked until—' he took a ravaged breath, his eyes boring into hers, to make her understand '—until I encountered you.'

A raw breath incised his lungs.

'I broke a lifetime's rules for you, Tara! I knew it was rash, unwise, but I could not resist it! Could not resist *you*. You taunted me with your beauty, with that mouthy lip of yours, daring to prick my *amour propre*! Answering me back…defying me! And your worst crime of all…' His voice was changing too, and he could not stop it doing so. It was softening into a sensual tone that was echoing the quickening of his pulse, the sweep of his lashes over his eyes. 'You denied me what I wanted—pushing me away, telling me it was only play-acting, tormenting me with it.'

His breath was ragged again, his eyes burning into hers.

'And so when we were *finally* alone together, free of that damnable role-play, I could only think that I should not make it real with you—that I should not break my lifetime's rules…'

He saw her face work, her eyes shadow.

'Not all women are like Celine, Marc.'

Her voice was sad. Almost pitying. It was a pity he could not bear.

He gave a harsh laugh. 'But they *could* be! And how am I to *tell*? How would I *know*?' He paused, and then with a hardening of his face continued. 'I thought I knew once. I was young, and arrogant and so, so sure of myself—and of the woman I wanted. Who seemed to want me too. Until…' He could not look at her, could see only the past, indelible in his memory, a warning throughout his life, 'Until the day I saw her across a restaurant, wearing the engagement ring of a man far older than I. Far richer—'

He tore his voice away and he forced his eyes to go back to the woman who stood in his present, not in his past.

'How could I *know*?' he repeated. His eyes rested on her, impassive, veiling what he would not show. 'That last night you asked to come with me to New York…'

She blenched, he could see the colour draining from her skin, but he could not stop now.

'But if you came to New York with me then where next? Back to Paris? To move in with me perhaps? For how long? What would you want? What would you start to take for granted?' His voice changed, and there was a coldness in it he could not keep out. 'What would you start to expect as your due?'

He drew breath again.

'That's why I ended it between us,' he said. 'That's why,' he went on, and he knew there was a deadness in his voice, 'I left you the emerald necklace. Sent you that cheque. To… to draw a line under whatever had been. What you might have thought there was—or could be.'

He fell silent.

Tara could hear his breathing, hear her own. Had heard the truth he'd spoken. She pulled her shoulders back, straightening her spine, letting her hands fall to her side. Lifted her chin. Looked him in the eye. She was not the daughter of soldiers for nothing.

'I never thought it, Marc.' Her voice was blank. Remote. 'I never thought there was anything more between us than what we had.'

She had said it. And it was not a lie. It was simply not all the truth. Between 'thought' and 'hope' was a distance so vast it shrank the universe to an atom.

'But I did,' he said. His jaw clenched. 'I did think it.' His expression changed. 'I didn't want to end it, Tara. I didn't want *us* to end. But…' Something flashed in his face. 'But I was afraid.'

She saw a frown crease his forehead, as if he had encountered a problem he had not envisaged. As if he were seeing it for the first time in his life.

'But what is the point of fear,' he asked, as if to the universe itself, 'if it destroys our only chance of happiness?'

His eyes went to her now, and in them, yet again, was something she had never seen before. She could not name it, yet it called to her from across a chasm as wide as all the world. And as narrow as the space between them.

She saw his hand go to the jewel case, flick it open. Green fire glittered within.

'Emeralds would suit you,' he said again, 'so much better than mere diamonds. Which is why—'

There was a constriction in his voice—she could hear it…could feel her heart start to slug within her. Hard and heavy beats, like a tattoo inside her body.

She saw him replace the necklace on the table, saw his hand slide once again within his breast pocket, draw out another object. A cube this time, with the same crest on it that the emerald necklace case held. She saw him flick it open. Saw what was within.

He extended his hand towards her, the ring in its box resting in his palm. 'It's yours if you want it,' he said. The casualness of the words belied the tautness of his jaw, the nerve flickering in his cheekbone, the sudden veiling of his eyes as if to protect himself. 'Along with one other item, should it be of any value to you.'

The drumming of her heartbeat was rising up inside her, deafening in volume. Her throat thickened so she could not breathe.

He glanced at her again, and there was a sudden tensing in his expression that hollowed his face, made it gaunt with strain. 'It's my heart, Tara. It comes with the ring if you want it—'

A hand flew to her mouth, stifling a cry in her tearing throat. 'Marc! No! Don't say it—oh, don't say it! Not if… not if you don't mean it!' Fear was in her face, terror. 'I couldn't bear it—'

Her fingers pressed against her mouth, making her words almost inaudible, but he could hear them all the same.

'It's too late,' he said. 'I've said it now. I can't take it back. I can't take back anything—anything at all! Not a single thing I've ever said to you—not a single kiss, a single heartbeat.' Emotion scythed across his face. 'It's too late for everything,' he said. 'Too late for fear.'

He lifted his free hand, gently drew back the fingers pressing against her mouth, folding his own around her, strong and warm.

'What good would it do me? Fear? I can gather all the proof I want—the fact that you returned my cheque, refused my emeralds, gave away a couture wardrobe! That my insane presumption that you had helped me dispose of Celine only to clear the path for your own attempt on Hans was nothing more than the absurd creation of my fears. But there *is* no proof! No proof that can withstand the one sure truth of all.'

He pressed her fingers, turning them over in his hand, exposing the delicate skin of her wrist. He dipped his head to let his lips graze like silken velvet, with sensuous softness… Then he lifted his head, poured his gaze into hers.

Her eyes glimmered with tears, emotion swelling within her like a wondrous wave. Could this be true? Really true?

'Will you take my heart?' he was saying now. 'For it holds the one sure truth of all.'

His eyes moved on her face, as if searching…finding.

'It's *love*, Tara. That's the only one sure truth. All that I can rely on—all that I need to rely on. For if you should love me then I am safe. Safe from all my fear.'

His eyes were filled with all she had longed to see in them.

'And if my love for you should be of any value to you—'

Another choking cry came from her and her arm flung itself around his neck, clutching him to her. Words flew from her. 'I've tried so hard—so desperately hard—to let you go! Oh, not from my life—I knew that you were over in my life—but in my heart. Oh, dear God, I could not tear you from my heart...'

The truth that she would have silenced all her life, never burdening him with it, broke from her now, and sobs—endless sobs that seemed to last for ever—discharged all that she had forced herself to keep buried deep within her, unacknowledged, silent and smothered.

As he wrapped her arm around her waist, pressing it tightly to him, something tumbled from his palm. But he did not notice. It was not important. Only this had any meaning...only this was precious.

To have Tara in his arms again. Tara whom he'd thrown away, let go, lost.

He had let fear possess him. Destroy his only chance of happiness in life.

He soothed her now, murmuring soft words, until her weeping eased and ebbed and she took a trembling step back from him. He gazed down at her. Her eyes were red from crying, tear runnels stained her cheeks, her mouth was wobbly and uneven, her features contorted still...

The most beautiful woman in the world.

'I once took it upon myself to announce that you were my fiancée,' he said, his voice wry and his eyes with a dark glint in them. 'But now...' His voice changed again, and with a little rush of emotion she heard uncertainty in his voice, saw a questioning doubt in his eyes about her answer to what he was saying. 'Now I take nothing upon myself at all.' He paused, searching her eyes. 'So tell me—I beg you…implore you—if I proposed to you now, properly, as a suitor should, would you say yes?'

She burst into tears once more. He drew her to him again, muffled her cries in his shoulder, and then he was soothing her yet again, murmuring more words to her, until once again she eased her tears and drew tremblingly back.

'Dare I keep talking?' he put to her.

She gave another choke, but it was of laughter as well as tears. Her gaze was misty, but in it he saw all that he had hoped beyond hope to see.

He bent to kiss her mouth—a soft, tender kiss, that calmed all the violent emotion that had been shaken from her, leaving her a peace inside her that was vast and won-drous. Could this be true and real? Or only the figment of her longings?

But it *was* real! Oh, so real. And he was here, and kiss-ing her…kissing her for ever and ever…

And then he was drawing back, frowning, looking around him.

'What is it?' Tara asked, her voice still trembling, her whole body swaying with the emotion consuming her.

He frowned. 'I had a ring here somewhere,' he said. 'I need it—'

She glanced down, past where the emerald necklace lay on the garden table in its box, into the grass beneath. Something glinted greener than the grass. She gave a little cry of discovery and he swooped to pick it up from where it had fallen.

He possessed himself of her hand, which trembled like the rest of her. Slid the ring over her finger. Then he raised her hand to his lips, turned it over in his palm. Lowered his mouth to kiss the tender skin over the veins in her wrist. A kiss of tenderness, of homage.

Then he folded her hand within his own. 'I knew that I had gone way past mere desire for you,' he said, his voice low, intense, his eyes holding hers with a gaze that made her heart turn over, 'when on the evening of the bank's autumn client party—which Hans always comes to—I realised that for all the blackness in my heart over what I thought you had done, there was only one emotion in me.'

He paused, and she felt his hands clench over hers.

'It was an unbearable longing for you,' he said, and there was a catch in his voice that made Tara press his hands with hers, placing her free hand over his. 'As unbearable as my longing to see my parents again after their deaths—'

He broke off and she slipped her hands from his, slid them around him, drawing her to him. She held him close and tight and for ever. Moved beyond all things by what he had said.

Then, suddenly, he was pulling away from her.

'Tara…' His voice was hollow. Hollow with shock.

Her expression changed as she realised what he had discovered. And she knew she must tell him why she had made the agonising decision that she had.

'You didn't want me, Marc,' she said quietly. Sadly. 'So I would never, *never* have forced this on you.'

He let his hands drop, stepped back a moment. His face was troubled.

'Are you angry?'

He heard the note of fear in her voice. 'Only at myself,' he said. 'My fears nearly cost me my life's happiness,' he said. His voice was sombre, grave. Self-accusing. 'And they nearly cost me even more.' His face worked, and then in the same sombre voice he spoke again. 'I tried to find proof—proof that you did not value my wealth above my-self.' He took a ragged breath. 'But if I wanted the great-est proof of all it is this. That you were prepared to raise my baby by yourself...never telling me, never claiming a single *sou* from me—'

Her voice was full as she answered him. 'I could not have borne it if you had felt any...any *obligation*. Of any kind.' She drew breath. 'But now...'

She smiled and took his hand in hers again. Slowly, carefully, she placed it across her gently swelling waist-line. She saw wonder fill his face, light in his eyes, and her heart lifted to soar.

French words broke from him, raw and heartfelt. She leant to kiss his mouth. There was a glint in her eye now. 'I'm going to lose my figure, you know... Turn into a barrage balloon. You won't desire me any more—not for months and months and months!'

The familiar look was in his eyes—that oh-so-familiar look that melted the bones of her body.

'I will *always* desire you!' he promised, and he laughed. Joy was soaring in him, like eagles taking flight. And de-sire too—heating him from within.

She gave a laugh of pure happiness that lifted her from her feet—or was it Marc, sweeping her up into his arms?

She gave a choke, felt emotion wringing her. 'Marc, is this real? *Is* it? Tell me it is! Because I can't be this happy—how *can* I?'

The future that had loomed before her—empty of all but the most precious memento of her brief time with him—now flowed and merged with the past she had lost...be-coming an endless present that she knew she would never lose!

His arms tightened around her, his eyes pouring into hers. 'As real as it is for me,' he said.

Happiness such as he had never known since the carefree days of his youth overflowed in him. Tara was his for ever, and she was bringing to him a gift that was a wonder and a joy to him: the baby that was to be born.

He was striding with her now, towards the cottage. He glanced around, as if seeing it for the first time. 'Is this the new life you said you were making for yourself?'

She smiled, tightening her grip around his neck with the hook of her arm. 'A new life—and an old one,' she said. 'The cottage belonged to my grandparents, and they left it to me. It's always been my haven...'

'And it will be ours, too, if you will permit me to share it with you,' he said, his voice warm. 'In fact it seems to me that it would be the ideal place for a honeymoon...'

The glint in his eyes was melting her bones as he negotiated the narrow doorway, sweeping her indoors and ducking his tall frame beneath the beamed lintel. Purposefully, he headed for the stairs. There must be bedrooms upstairs, and beds...

He dropped a kiss on her mouth as he carried her aloft, following her hurried directions to her bedroom, lowering her down upon the old-fashioned brass bed which creaked under their combined weight, sinking them deep into the feather mattress.

'Starting right now.'

'Now, that...' Tara sighed blissfully '...is a *wonderful* idea!'

Marc gave a growl of satisfaction at her answer and began to remove their entirely unnecessary clothing, covering her face in kisses that would last their lifetimes—and beyond.

EPILOGUE

MARC STOOD ON the terrace of the Villa Derenz, his infant son cradled in his arms. Out on the manicured lawn, under the shade of a huge parasol beside the pool, Tara dozed on a lounger.

His eyes went to her, soft with love-light. Here she had first beguiled him and entranced him, lighting a flame within him that his own fears had so nearly extinguished but which now burnt with everlasting fire.

He walked up to her, feeling the warmth of late summer lapping him. At his approach she roused herself and smiled, holding out her arms expectantly.

'Afternoon tea is served, young Master Derenz!' she said, and laughed, busying herself settling him to feed.

Marc dropped a lingering kiss on her forehead, then turned as two figures of military bearing emerged from the villa, coming towards him and Tara.

'Feeding him up? Good, good...' Major Mackenzie nodded approvingly at his grandson's nursing.

'Latched on properly?' the other Major Mackenzie asked her daughter.

'Mum, I'm not one of your subalterns,' Tara remonstrated good-humouredly, with a laugh, patting the lounger for her mother to sit down beside her.

Her parents had welcomed the news of their daughter's

marriage with open delight, and her mother had organised the wedding at the little parish church near the cottage with military precision. Her father had even summoned a guard of honour for the bride and groom, formed by the men of his regiment.

And if a tear had moistened her mother's eyes, only Tara had seen it, and only she had heard her mother say, with more emotion in her voice than her daughter was used to hearing, 'He can't take his eyes off you, that utterly gorgeous man of yours! And he is lucky—*so lucky*—to have you!' Then she had hugged her daughter closely.

The arrival of their grandson had also persuaded her parents to return to Civvy Street, and they would soon buy a house on the Dorset coast, near enough to for them to keep an eye on the cottage. Tara was glad for them and glad for herself—she would be seeing more of them, and they were safe from future military deployment.

She was also glad that Marc's son would have grandparents on her side to grow up with. But there would be happy memories in the making here, too, at the villa on Cap Pierre, just as Marc had from his own boyhood with his parents and their friends.

The Neubergers, with Hans's new grandchild on the way, would soon be here to spend a fortnight, after her parents had returned to the UK. Hans had not been slow to express his gladness that Marc and she were so happy together.

She looked up lovingly at her husband and he met her gaze, his dark eyes softening, his heart catching.

How can I love her so much? How is it possible?

All he knew was that he did, and that theirs was a love that would never end. And to have found it made him the most fortunate man in the world.

There was the sound of a throat clearing and he glanced across at his father-in-law.

'If it's all right with you, old chap,' said Major Mackenzie, 'we'd like to take out that very neat little boat of yours! Wind's rising, and we're keen to try out the spinnaker.'

Marc smiled broadly. 'An excellent idea,' he said warmly, and Tara added her own encouragement.

Her mother rose briskly to her feet and she and Marc watched them stride across the lawn to the path leading to the jetty, where the boat was moored.

'You could go out with them too, you know,' she said to Marc.

He shook his head. 'I was thinking, actually, of a quite different activity. When, that is, young Master Derenz requires his afternoon nap...'

Tara's eyes glinted knowingly. 'And what might that be, Monsieur Derenz?' she enquired limpidly.

He gave a low laugh. 'Well, Madame Derenz, I was thinking,' he said, returning the glint in her eye with a deeper one of his own, 'that perhaps it is time to consider the addition of a Mademoiselle Derenz to the family...'

She caught his hand and kissed it. 'An *excellent* idea,' she agreed. 'Happy families...' She sighed. 'It just doesn't get better.'

And Marc could not help but agree—with all his heart.

* * * * *

MILLS & BOON

Coming next month

UNTOUCHED UNTIL HER ULTRA-RICH HUSBAND
Dani Collins

You told me what you were worth, Luli. Act like you believe it.

She *had* been acting. The whole time. Still was, especially as a handful of designers whose names she knew from Mae's glossy magazines behaved with deference as they welcomed her to a private showroom complete with catwalk.

She had to fight back laughing with incredulity as they offered her champagne, caviar, even a pedicure.

"I—" She glanced at Gabriel, expecting him to tell them she aspired to model and should be treated like a clothes horse, not royalty.

"A full wardrobe," he said. "Top to bottom, morning to night, office to evening. Do what you can overnight, send the rest to my address in New York."

"*Mais bien sûr, monsieur,*" the couturier said without a hint of falter in her smile. "Our pleasure."

"Gabriel—" Luli started to protest as the women scattered.

"You remember what I said about this?" he tapped the wallet that held her phone. "I need you to stay on-brand."

"Reflect who you are?"

"Yes."

"Who are you?" she asked ruefully. "I only met you ten minutes ago."

"I'm a man who doesn't settle for anything less than the best." He touched her chin. "The world is going to have a lot of questions about why we married. Give them an answer."

His words roused the competitor who still lurked inside her. She wanted to prove to the world she was *worthy* to be his wife. Maybe she wanted to prove her worth to him, too. Definitely she longed to prove something to herself.

Either way, she made sure those long-ago years of preparation paid off. She had always been ruthless in evaluating her own shortcomings and knew how to play to her strengths. She might not be trying to win a crown today, but she hadn't been then, either. She'd been trying to win the approval of a woman who hadn't deserved her idolatry.

She pushed aside those dark memories and clung instead to the education she had gained in those difficult years.

"That neckline will make my shoulders look narrow," she said, making quick up-down choices. "The sweetheart style is better, but no ruffles at my hips. Don't show me yellow. Tangerine is better. A more verdant green. That one is too pale." In her head, she was sectioning out the building blocks of a cohesive stage presence. Youthful, but not too trendy. Sensual, but not overtly sexual. Charismatic without being showy.

"Something tells me I'm not needed," Gabriel said twenty minutes in and rose to leave. "We'll go for dinner in three hours." He glanced to the couturier. "And return in the morning for another fitting."

"*Parfait. Merci, monsieur.*" Her smile was calm, but the way people were bustling told Luli how big a deal this was. How big a deal *Gabriel* was.

The women took her measurements while showing her unfinished pieces that only needed hemming or minimal tailoring so she could take them immediately.

"You'll be up all night," Luli murmured to one of the seamstresses.

The young woman moved quickly, but not fast enough for her boss who kept crying, *"Vite! Vite!"*

"I'm sorry to put you through this," Luli added.

"*Pas de problème.* Monsieur Dean is a treasured client. It's our honor to provide your trousseau." She clamped her teeth on a pin between words. "Do you know where he's taking you for dinner? We should choose that dress next, so I can work on the alterations while you have your hair and makeup done. It must be fabulous. The world will be watching."

She would be presented publicly as his wife, Luli realized with a hard thump in her heart.

Continue reading
UNTOUCHED UNTIL HER ULTRA-RICH HUSBAND
Dani Collins

Available next month
www.millsandboon.co.uk

Copyright ©2019 by Dani Collins

COMING SOON!

We really hope you enjoyed reading this book. If you're looking for more romance, be sure to head to the shops when new books are available on

Thursday 16th May

To see which titles are coming soon, please visit

millsandboon.co.uk/nextmonth

MILLS & BOON

LET'S TALK
Romance

For exclusive extracts, competitions
and special offers, find us online:

f facebook.com/millsandboon

🐦 @MillsandBoon

📷 @MillsandBoonUK

Get in touch on 01413 063232

For all the latest titles coming soon, visit
millsandboon.co.uk/nextmonth